PUR

"*Pure Blood* pounds al
Life, and is every bit a
ries. With a gutsy, likable protagonist and a well-made
fantasy world, *Pure Blood* is real enough to make you
think twice about locking your doors at night. A swiftly
paced plot, a growing cast of solid supporting characters, and a lead character you can actually care about—
Kittredge is a winner."
                                        —Jim Butcher

NIGHT LIFE

"Dark and cutting-edge."
                        —*Romantic Times BOOKreviews*

"I loved the mystery and the smart, gutsy heroine."
                                        —Karen Chance,
                            New York Times bestselling author of
                                        Claimed by Shadow

"Don't go to bed with this book—it will keep you up
all night. It's that good."   —Lilith Saintcrow,
                            national bestselling author of
                                        Working for the Devil

"Luna is tough, smart, and fierce, hiding a conflicted
and insecure nature behind her drive for justice and
independence, without falling into cliché. It's also just
a lot of fun to read."   —Kat Richardson,
                    national bestselling author of *Greywalker*

MORE...

SECOND SKIN

A Nocturne City Novel

CAITLIN KITTREDGE

St. Martin's Paperbacks

This is a work of fiction. All of the characters, organizations, and events portrayed in this novel are either products of the author's imagination or are used fictitiously.

SECOND SKIN

For information address St. Martin's Press, 175 Fifth Avenue, New York, NY 10010.

ISBN: 0-312-94831-X
EAN: 978-0-312-94831-3

Printed in the United States of America

St. Martin's Paperbacks edition / March 2009

St. Martin's Paperbacks are published by St. Martin's Press, 175 Fifth Avenue, New York, NY 10010.

10 9 8 7 6 5 4 3 2 1

For Mom and Hal,
who always gave me love, support,
and a place to do my laundry

ACKNOWLEDGMENTS

Thanks as always to Rose Hilliard and Rachel Vater, editor and agent supreme. To the team at St. Martin's who worked tirelessly to make this the best book possible.

Team Seattle, for friendship, trips to the gun range, and zombie-themed parties.

All of my blog readers, who provide endless procrastination on slow days.

Jackie, Sara, and Stacia, who never once rolled their eyes when I complained about my deadlines.

Thanks as always to Agent Heidi Wallace of the ATF for her endless patience and infinite knowledge of firearms and law enforcement procedure.

Most of all, to every single reader of the Nocturne City series, those of you who make Luna and her world much bigger than me.

Thank you all.

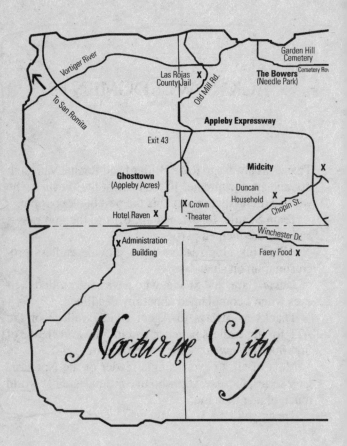

Garden Hill
Cemetery
Cemetery Row
The Bowers
(Needle Park)

Vortiger River

Las Rojas X
County Jail

Old Mill Rd.

To San Romita

Appleby Expressway

Exit 43

Midcity

Ghosttown
(Appleby Acres)

Duncan
Household

X

X Crown
Theater

Chopin St.

X

Hotel Raven X

Winchester Dr.

X Administration
Building

Faery Food X

Nocturne City

CHAPTER 1

No one could help the jumper on the ledge. You get a sense for these things, after a few months of listening to people scream, "I'm gonna do it, man—I mean it!"

Most of the time, they don't mean it. The man on the ledge did. Lucky me.

Sergeant Fitzpatrick tapped me on the shoulder. "Wilder, you good?" I flipped up the visor of my tactical helmet and pantomimed gagging.

"This negotiator would give a daytime TV host hives." The negotiator was a lieutenant from the Robbery Division named Brady. He was in way over his head, and had resorted to yelling into a PA.

"Think about what you're doing! I'm sure you have something to live for."

"Jesus Christ, I've got a parent–teacher meeting at eight," Fitzpatrick muttered. "Can we get on with this?"

I looked through the scope of my M4, centering the crosshairs on the man's face. He was halfway up an apartment building across the street from the Garden Hill Cemetery. A spotlight pinned him against the crumbling granite, his tennis shoes scrabbling for purchase against the ledge. Overhead, an almost swollen moon cast a harsher light.

The jumper had a blocky face and body, shorn black hair, and absolutely nothing remarkable about him, except for the fact that he was about to drop a hundred feet onto an ambulance crew, an engine from the Cedar Hill fire company, and Tac-3, Nocturne City's third SWAT unit, which included me.

"Just come on down and we can work it out!" the negotiator bellowed, his voice rolling from the hill of tombstones at our back.

"He's not coming down," I murmured, still looking at the man's face through my scope.

"No shit," muttered Fitzpatrick. "I don't want to be cleaning up sidewalk pizza. That's a grunt job. Our shift was over an hour ago." Fitzpatrick could go to a reception at the Playboy Mansion and bitch about the champagne being cold. Normally he was sort of an endearing curmudgeon, but now I punched him in the shoulder of his body armor.

"Fitzy, shut the Hex up. Do you really want to see some poor guy splatter himself over a one-block radius?"

"He ain't gonna jump," Fitzpatrick muttered. "They never goddamn jump. Just want the goddamn attention."

The jumper's eyes were calm as he flicked from the Nocturne PD prowl cars and their rotating red-and-white lights to the spot on the back of the ladder truck to the negotiator crouched behind his unmarked vehicle. He wasn't crying. He didn't even look upset. His jaw rippled as he clenched his teeth, but that was all the expression he allowed himself.

"I wouldn't be so sure about that . . . ," I muttered.

"You have a lot to live for!" the negotiator shouted. "It's a beautiful world!"

The man's eyes locked with mine, or seemed to, through the narrow crosshairs. I froze. He raised a hand, a sort of weak and half-regretted good-bye.

Then he jumped.

All the sound in the universe got sucked away from me for the few seconds it took his body to fall, small and dark against the white granite of the Garden Vista building.

Everything slammed into me again when Fitzpatrick grabbed my shoulder. "Move!"

He jerked me behind his riot shield as the man's body hit. I glared up at Fitzpatrick through my visor. "Were you expecting an explosion? Perhaps a couple of falling anvils?"

I shoved him off and joined Eckstrom and Batista, two of the remaining three members of Tac-3 at the body. Eckstrom, the squad medic, felt perfunctorily for a pulse in the man's twisted neck and shook his head. "He's roadkill."

Batista jerked his thumb at the small crowd gathered behind the cordon. "Wilder. Go help the uniforms with crowd control."

"Help yourself," I said, crouching next to Eckstrom and examining the man. His face was pulpy and bruised where it had hit. His internals would be liquid. He was staring up at me.

"Hey," Eckstrom said. "You ain't a homicide dick no more. Back off the body until the suits get here, all right? I'm not getting another reaming because we poked the deceased when poking wasn't allowed."

"Sorry," I muttered. Fitzpatrick finally managed to stir himself and made it to our little sewing circle.

"Hex me. Never thought the crazy bastard'd actually do it. Why?"

"You just said it: because he was loco," Batista said. "What other reason do you need?"

My radio crackled. "Looks like it's all over, cowboys. And girl. Lady. Whatever."

I clicked my set. " 'Wilder' would be fine, Allen." Greg Allen was our sniper unit, a military vet with no neck and no idea how to handle a female teammate. Otherwise, I had landed pretty lucky with Tac-3. Fitzpatrick was an equal-opportunity insensitive prick but Batista and Eckstrom actually sort of got along with me.

Considering I was an ex-detective, a werewolf, *and* had girly parts, that was a minor miracle.

"Ten-four," Greg said. "Let's pack it in."

"I'll clear us with the scene commander," I offered. Batista held out his hand for my rifle and gear belt and I handed it off to him, stripping my helmet as I ducked under the cordon to the negotiator, who was sitting in the passenger's side of his car.

"Excuse me, sir," I said. "Is SWAT clear to leave the scene?"

"I don't know why he did it," he said softly. His hairline was pulling back and he would have been ugly and hook-nosed even with a full head. Probably took the negotiation class in hopes of a promotion that never came around and got stuck talking to people like the man on the ledge.

He had looked at me so calmly. He *waved good-bye*.

"Stop it," I muttered out loud. The suicide had no more singled me out of the crowd than I'd chosen to be in it. "Sir," I said again, more firmly. "We're all tired. It's been a long shift and overtime pay doesn't really take the place of sleep. Well, except for Allen, and we have this sort of bet going that he doesn't actually *need* sleep."

"That sound it made . . . ," Brady muttered, and I knew he was talking about the body.

"Do you know his name? The jumper?" Not too long ago, more of my job involved talking to victims than running around in full body armor with a gun. Instincts are hard to kick.

"Jason," he said. "He told me, before you got here. He said his name was Jason."

"Well, sir, what Jason needs now is for someone to take care of his remains and for you to go home and try to put this behind you. We'd all like that. Could you make it happen?"

He rubbed a hand over his face and looked at me, really seeing, for the first time. "You're that detective."

Oh, fantastic. Another celebrity spotter. "I'm not with the Detective Bureau any more, sir. I'm a response officer with Tac-3."

"Good move. Not a lot of room for advancement once you've closed down a company that employs half the voting base in this city."

"Sir, don't take this the wrong way, but if you don't release us from the scene someone—and I'm not saying who—but someone is going to lose their temper and might punch you. Perhaps even in the face."

He turned his head away from me. "Get the fuck out of here. You're useless."

I had a feeling that the last was meant specifically for me as opposed to Tac-3, but I kept my temper in check. It had already gotten me into enough trouble over the last half a year. Being short-tempered is one problem, but being short-tempered and a were is a bigger one. Not so very long ago, my first impulse when someone pissed me off was to break their fingers . . . and that was on a good day.

Batista was leaning against the van, the rest of the team already inside, when I came back. "Everything cool?" he asked me.

"Other than Lieutenant Brady being a mean old bastard, yeah. We can go."

"About fucking time," Fitzpatrick muttered. "I'm gonna have to show up to this meeting in my tac gear, we keep going at this pace."

"I had a date two hours ago," Eckstrom said. "You whining about domestic issues don't even compare."

"Hex you," said Fitzpatrick.

"Funny, your sister said that after I turned down a blow job." Eckstrom grinned widely.

"Lady present," Batista reminded them.

"Go right ahead," I said. "Blow jobs and parent–teacher meetings are the spice of life."

"What about that boyfriend you got?" Batista asked me as Allen moved the van slowly out onto Garden. "He and you got any plans this weekend? Marisol thinks she's gonna do a barbecue."

I made a noncommittal noise, because really, that's much more polite than saying *Sorry, Javier, my boyfriend would rather take a plastic spork to his eyeballs than socialize with plain humans.*

"Well, lemme know," he said. We drove for a while, Eckstrom and Fitzy still going back and forth with their jovial bullshit, and got dropped in the motor pool at the bottom of the Justice Plaza, the area behind the courthouse that used to hold condemned prisoners just before they were hanged. Now it's a big warren of administration and one little nest of cubicles dedicated to SWAT.

"Sweet dreams, princess," Allen said when the team and I parted outside the women's locker room.

"They'll all be of you, Greg," I assured him. It was about 9 PM, long after most of the workers in the plaza had gone away for the day. I used to work night shift as a detective in Homicide, and my internal clock still thought it had six or seven more hours of good fun ahead.

I didn't bother showering, just stripped out of my body armor, black jersey, black canvas pants, and combat boots. They weren't as comfortable as the old steel-toed Corcorans I usually wore on the job, but they were made out of space-age material and assured me that if I really needed to I could stop a bullet with my toes.

Sweats and an old CHCC T-shirt would see me home. I whipped my hair into a bun, the pink streak I'd put in when I transferred twisting through it like a vein, and checked myself out in the wobbly mirror for blood on my face. One speck rested dead center on my cheek, and I scrubbed it off violently with a paper towel.

I got my sidearm, badge, wallet, keys, makeup bag, and then screamed. A male figure had appeared between the rows of lockers and was staring at me with the vacant and slightly bug-eyed expression I usually associated with pickled frogs.

"Seven hells!" The figure threw up its hands. "Wilder, keep it down! You want the whole building to hear?"

My heart jackhammered for another split second, and the were screamed *Attack* until I recognized the person in front of me. It wasn't a locker room peeping pervert. He was much worse. "David Bryson. Give me one good reason I shouldn't rip your trachea out through your nose."

He started to smile. "How you been, Wilder? You look . . . good. Love the hair."

I cut him off by thrusting my finger into his face.

"What the *hell* are you doing in the women's locker room?" I let him see my teeth, which had fanged out when he startled me. "Death wish? Please say it's a death wish."

Bryson hadn't spoken to me since I'd shown him my were on one memorably bad night when we'd both been detectives at the Twenty-fourth Precinct, but now he was looking at his feet and seemed almost desperate. "Wilder, I need your help."

"Very funny. The other one has bells on it."

"I'm serious!"

That made me snarl. "So am I: if you don't get out of here in the next five seconds you're going to be in a world of hurt."

Bryson tried to say something else, but I grabbed him by the shoulder of his Bisquick-colored polyester suit and shoved him out the door of the changing room, locking it. "Hex off," I muttered, collecting my gym bag and making my escape through the service entrance.

CHAPTER 2

When I banged open the door to employee parking, a scent of too much cologne and male sweat tickled my nose.

Bryson was standing next to my '69 Fairlane. At least he knew better than to touch it.

I sighed. "David, for the last time . . . no, I won't go to the prom with you."

"I meant what I said." He looked more earnest than I knew Bryson was capable of being, not a sneer in sight. He wasn't even staring at my chest.

"Are you in some kind of twelve-step program? Asshats Anonymous? Because I gotta tell you, David . . . I'm really not looking to make amends."

"Hex it, you're still such a bitch!" Bryson yelled, finally sounding less like a pod person and more like the testosterone case I'd known and loathed.

"I'm tired, is what I am. Is there a reason you chose me out of all the people in the gods-damn city to harass, Bryson?"

He clenched his fist, unclenched it, eyes roaming anywhere but my face. Finally he gritted, "I already told you. I need your help."

"David, I told *you* . . . waxing is the only way to get *all* the hair off your back."

"Gods above and daemons below . . . ," he started.

I cut him off with a gesture and dug my car keys out of my gym bag. "The answer is no, David. Whatever it is, no."

"It's a murder case," he said. "Wilder, you gotta give me an assist here . . . I am in over my goddamn head."

Strange as it was to hear Bryson on the verge of begging for something, especially from me, I held firm. "I don't investigate murders anymore. Now can I go home?"

My cell phone buzzed against my hip. The caller ID blinked DMITRI. "Hold on," I instructed Bryson, who stood obstinately in front of my car with a hangdog look.

"This bed is awfully big without you in it." Dmitri's voice sounds like dark red wine spilled on pale skin, Eastern Europe blended up with clove smoke.

"Hi, honey," I said flatly. Bryson gave me the eye, like I'd just started speaking in Esperanto.

"Do you know what I wanna do to you right now? I'd start right between your thighs . . ."

"Sure, no problem. Gotta go." I slapped the phone shut and jerked open my door. "The answer is still no, Bryson." I turned the Fairlane's engine over with a roar. "Either get out of my way or be my speed bump."

"It's weres!" Bryson yelled at me. "Dead weres! Four of them so far!"

I hit the gas and squealed out of the motor pool lot before he could finish, leaving him in a trail of exhaust.

At home, I unlocked the front door of the cottage softly. The sky was still light at the very edges, over the water, pink and frayed like glimpsing silk through a torn skirt. "Dmitri, you awake?" I called. It was a courtesy. Dmitri could scent me as soon as I stepped out of the car in the little circular driveway that pushed up against my broken-down rental cottage on the edge of the dune.

"Up here." He didn't sound husky and pleasant anymore. I kicked off my flip-flops and climbed up the stairs to the bedroom rather more slowly than a woman coming home to her sexier-than-anything were boyfriend who had given up his pack and his entire life to warm her bed should climb.

"Hey," I said, sticking my head around the door. "Thanks for waiting up for me."

The lights were off but I didn't have a problem seeing Dmitri wrapped in nothing at all atop my sheets. It was stuffy in the room, stale and unpleasant, and I sneezed.

"If you're sick, do me a favor and don't spread it around."

"Oh gee. Hex you, too." I sat down on the edge of the bed and slipped out of my sweats, rolling over to lie next to Dmitri. He shoved me away. "Get off. It's too hot."

"Oh *gods*," I hissed at him. "Look, I'm sorry. I was tied up when you called and I came straight home to apologize. I didn't realize that tonight was the night we both acted like twelve-year-olds."

There was silence for a long time, and I listened to Dmitri breathe and smelled his sweat mixed in with beer and a little bit of soap. "I'm sorry, too," he said finally. "Just . . . I heard someone else's voice, and I assumed . . ."

"Sweetie." I took his hand in the dark. "My captain is a man. I work with four guys. Hell, even my manicurist has a penis."

He stiffened again. "Was that your manicurist I heard on the call?"

"No," I said, moving my free hand over his stomach, fingers scrubbing in small circles. I stopped, thinking about the desperate way Bryson had followed me.

"Who was it, Luna?" Dmitri sucked in his breath.

"It doesn't matter. It was nobody I want to keep thinking about."

He jerked away from me and sat up with a snarl. "Tell me who was fucking there with you! I can smell him all over your skin!"

I sat up too, rod-straight, and we quivered silently with our backs turned to each other. "It was David Bryson," I said. "He accosted me in the locker room after I was washing the blood spatter from a suicide jumper off me, and he followed me out to my car and I have had a really *shitty* gods-damn night, by the way, so thanks for asking and you have sweet dreams."

I snatched my pillow and the blanket from the bed and started to storm out, but noticed just before I reached the door that my pillowcase was decorated with blood droplets.

Those hadn't been there when I'd left for work. "Dmitri?" I said.

He rolled over with a snarl. "Oh no," I exclaimed, grabbing him by the shoulder and rolling him back toward me. "What on earth . . ."

His face was puffy at the jaw and his left eye blackened. The orbital bone was scraped. The cuts had already healed over, but the old blood remained. I reached over Dmitri and turned on the bedside lamp, bumping his side as I did so. He hissed in pain when I brushed his ribs.

"Okay," I said, as I surveyed the cut lip, the array of

bruises on his torso and fresh scars on his knuckles. "Don't tell me. You went down to the slaughterhouse and beat up some meat, and the meat won."

"Funny," he muttered. "Real funny."

Guilt sucker-punched me. "I'm sorry. I didn't see . . . what happened? I'm sorry we fought." My words tumbled like gangly things, not sure of their legs. "I'm sorry," I mumbled again.

"No big deal," Dmitri said, throwing a hand over his eyes. "Just a misunderstanding."

I got off the bed and walked around to his side, and stood over him with my hands on my hips, glaring, until he rolled his eyes. "Bleeding all over the house?" I said. "That pretty much defines 'Big Deal.' Who did this to you?"

Dmitri sighed. "I walked down a street I thought was safe, and it wasn't. Territory had shifted. I got jumped."

"By what, a Transformer?" I said. The bruising was bad. Dmitri was tough, and big, and had daemon-powered blood running in him, a bite that turned him from were to something else whenever he got too angry or too . . . anything. The bite made him black out and a host of other unpleasantries, but it also made him damn near invulnerable. This shouldn't have happened.

"Six or seven weres from some pack running things on Cannery Street now," he said. "They came up on me fast, had baseball bats, mostly. And one of those police batons. Anyway. I knew you'd freak out so I thought we could discuss it after I healed."

"This shouldn't have happened," I said, out loud. "You weren't doing anything wrong. You don't even have pack status anymore. What would they gain from beating you?" I bit my lip. "*How* did they beat you?"

I was babbling like a cop, trying to work through the

permutations and find the conclusion, close the case. Dmitri showed his teeth. "I disrespected them." His fists worked. "They were within their rights, fucked up as it is. You wouldn't understand."

"*I* wouldn't understand?" I demanded, my old anger coming back.

"You never had to deal with pack law," said Dmitri. "You get off easy whenever you run into territorial borders because you're so damn willful. I just hope you never hit on a pack with a better hand at dominating other weres than you."

"Gee, thanks for the thought," I snapped. Silence again for a minute while we both tried to stay calm. Finally I tamped down my frustration and got myself under control. I was getting good at that lately. "Do you need an ice pack?"

"No."

"I still don't understand why you got into a fight in the first place," I said. "Can't you just back off, accept that they're dominant?" I knew that you could, from experience. That sometimes you had no choice.

"I could," Dmitri said, his eyes swimming with black. "But I didn't."

Oh, Hex it. My skin was full of thorn-pricks in that moment, as the air around me grew cold. "Dmitri. What did you do to those weres?"

His eyes were full black now, the daemon blood coming even as we sat there, calm. "Nothing they didn't deserve."

My own were instincts snarled *Get away* but Dmitri lunged across the bed and grabbed me before I could move. He was so much faster with the daemon bite . . .

One hand held the side of my face. The other traced

down my body, rough palm on my bare skin. Over my hips, past the V of my thighs. My body responded to him, but my brain was busy thinking *Oh shit* as I stared into his black eyes.

"Dmitri," I said softly. "Tell me what you did."

His hand stopped moving, just shy of its goal. "I didn't want to," he said, in a voice so small and wounded I wasn't even sure it was his. "I was gonna walk away but one of them said something, about my mate . . . about you. They knew who I was, who you were, and I . . ."

I shut my eyes, all of the fear and tension running out, leaving me rubbery.

"I have no standing in the Redbacks," said Dmitri. "If they got through me to you, I could do nothing. So when I felt it, the darkness coming on . . . I let it take me."

He'd let go of me, and I caught him this time, wrapped my arms around him. "I'm sorry," I whispered. "I'm sorry."

"You shouldn't be around me now," Dmitri said roughly. He put us at arm's length. "I just . . . I need to just forget."

"No," I said. "You need to not be alone. And this city needs not to have were packs running loose. Godsdamn animals."

"Luna, the packs . . . it's just the way things are." Dmitri sighed. "Times change. The packs have been jumpier than ever since that O'Halloran thing, and your department choking out the drugs and brothels downtown hasn't helped, either. You want to do something, tell Vice to ease off." He found a pair of shorts and put them on, and crawled under the sheet. "Please. Just go and let me heal."

"Don't do this," I gritted. "After what you just told me . . . *please* don't shut down on me."

Dmitri didn't answer, just gave a long shuddering sigh as his body tried to work through the daemon inside it and the injuries without.

After another long quiet minute, I went downstairs before I said something bitchy and insensitive.

On the sofa, I lay in high dudgeon for a long time, making myself be as still as possible except for breathing until the urge to tear and hurt had died down to a level where I wouldn't rip the neck out of the first person to cross my path.

The were had a lot of trouble staying at bay in me sometimes, but I had a lot of experience keeping it in.

One thing was clear as the bruises and the blood on Dmitri's body—whatever was in him was getting stronger, and the man I'd met was slipping away. Something cold and black as Dmitri's eyes uncoiled in my gut at the thought, the whisper that one day I'd wake up next to a stranger, who killed without a thought and didn't know the difference between me and prey.

Also clear was the fact that I wasn't going anywhere, even though the thought of seeing Dmitri change made me sick.

"Shouldn't this be easier by now?" I asked the darkness. Dmitri had tossed away his future with the Redbacks to be here with me, when his pack elders had forbidden us from being together. He'd chosen *me*. That should be enough. Should be, but that awful black thing was still there, laughing at me.

The dark didn't have any nugget of wisdom for me. It was more of a constant companion than an adviser, anyway.

The little digital clock on the wall of the kitchen told me it was nearly morning. I picked up the phone and dialed anyway. Dmitri would hear me upstairs if I spoke normally, and it spoke to the depth of my discomfort that I didn't particularly care.

"Mmhello?" Bryson muttered into the receiver. "Whossat?"

"David, it's Luna."

"Seven hells, Wilder, it's goddamn four AM"

"Five AM," I said. "You need to set your clock ahead."

"You call me up to be Mr. Science or is there a good reason for waking me out of a dead sleep?"

I worried the antenna of the cordless set and thought very, very hard about what I was going to say. Bryson was the person I probably came closest to hating during my time at the Twenty-fourth. He was rude, obnoxious, and mentally still living in a frat house somewhere. Plus he was a lousy cop, and his need for "help" might mean he couldn't figure out how to organize his case reports in the little colored folders.

"Wilder! Yo! Stop curling your hair and talk to me, babe!"

"Gods give me strength," I muttered. "Look, David, I . . . I've reconsidered."

His breath wuffed out on the other end of the line. "You mean it?" he said softly. "Hex it, Wilder, you just saved my ass."

"Hey," I said. "I'm just agreeing to take a look at the case file. *Nothing else.* Got that?"

"Whatever. I'll meet you at Sam's Donut Bungalow at seven."

"Bryson, seven is early."

"Well, sweetie-pie, that's when I come on duty so

that's when we're gonna meet up. Slap on some cold cream and get to work on your beauty sleep."

"Did anyone ever tell you you're a real asshole, Bryson?"

"My ex-wife, two girlfriends, my mother, and my aunt Louise. She was never really right in the head, though."

"Good night," I said, hoping he could feel me rolling my eyes through the phone lines, and hung up.

I growled in my throat at the drive downtown through rush-hour traffic, which did absolutely nothing to improve my mood. I contemplated putting the revolving light on my dash, but there was nowhere to go on the Siren Bay Bridge. The BMW in front of me lurched ahead and then laid on its horn.

My head started to pound, the light off Siren Bay dazzling my eyes. I flicked on the Fairlane's scratchy radio and put my forehead on the steering wheel. The last time I'd been on the bridge was months ago, and that time I'd taken the direct route down by jumping two hundred feet to the bay. It figured that the first time I came back I got trapped on the damn thing.

Over Pearl Jam wondering where oh where could their baby be? I almost didn't hear the rumble underneath my feet, down deep in the bones of the bridge. It wasn't the sound of rocks rubbing together that you hear in films, more of a great hum, and then a groan as the tarmac under the Fairlane started to ripple.

The most frightening thing was that it wasn't magick. Magick pinpricks my skin and makes my head ache and my stomach flip over. There was none of that here. Something in the earth was tossing and turning and taking me with it.

was spared from having to comfort someone who'd
once routinely tried to slap me on the ass.

"Why exactly am I the only person who can help
you with this, David?"

The waitress put down our food and I polished off the
cream-filled donuts while Bryson rooted in his scuffed
case for a file folder, dog-eared on all the edges, the tab
filled out in his crooked grade school printing.

"Look," Bryson instructed me. I shuffled past the
scene reports and pulled out the eight-by-ten glossy photos that the crime scene photographer had included.
Three men and one woman, all prone and naked, each
with a single large-caliber bullet hole to the head.

"I told you this was about weres," Bryson muttered,
leaning close. "*These* weres. They were all found at the
edge of the Sierra Fuego Preserve, starting about eight
weeks ago. All shot in the head. The vics lived in Nocturne City so the state police kicked it back to us."

I shoved the photos back at him. "Sad, David, but
I'm on SWAT now. I couldn't look into this even if I
wanted to, and that Internal Affairs investigation pretty
much cemented my desire to break down doors, not
chase down bad guys. Homicide doesn't need me and I
don't need them, alrighty?"

"It's been a *month*," he hissed at me. "No leads. I got
no way to get into their packs and figure out who had a
beef with these . . . people . . . and why. Then, two days
ago, I got off shift and went home and found this."

He rooted for another photo in his case and thrust it at
me. The shot was the door of a pricey Mainline condo. A
dead chicken was tacked to the center of the door, and
the words SOME PIG dripped blood down the wood.

I only partially stifled my snort of laughter.

"This isn't fuckin' funny!" Bryson shouted, crumpling the photo. "The packs think that the police don't give a shit and if I don't figure these murders out I'm going to end up as the rabbit in a dogfight! I don't wanna be the fucking rabbit, Wilder."

I composed myself and said, "You're right. The packs will deal with this in their own way and the last thing they want is interference. The dead bird was just a case of someone being polite." I leaned forward and took off Bryson's sunglasses, staring into his watery blue eyes. "I *strongly* suggest you let the case go cold and back the Hex off before you end up with your skin decorating the walls of this nice condo you've got."

The donuts were crumbs by now and I licked the frosting off my fingers and stood up. "Keep your head down, David. And stop buying your suits off the rack. You'll be fine."

I threw down a few dollars to cover my donuts and started to walk away. "You're a lot of things, Wilder," Bryson said. He was practically whispering, but the bastard knew I could hear him loud and clear. "But I never thought a lazy cop was one of them."

My glare could have cut sheet metal as I turned on him. "Excuse me?"

"Ain't you the one who always got on my ass? Dirty Harry-ette, telling me all the time how to do my job better and be perfect, like you? Now you're just gonna walk away from this?"

I came back and stood over him, crossing my arms so I wouldn't punch him in the nose. "Are you telling me you actually want to *solve* this case? David, the first time we met you told me you thought we should pen up weres in a national park and 'let nature take its course.' "

He looked at his hands. "So I don't like freaks.

Doesn't mean I'm going to let a quadruple homicide go
cold. Committees look at that stuff when they promote
you, Wilder . . . but I guess you wouldn't care about
that. Now that you're riding with SWAT you've got
lofty ideals and all that shit to keep you nice and warm."

"At least I have a few left," I snapped, snatching the
photos of the four victims back. Of course I was curious. I'd been a homicide detective for two and a half
years and the instincts don't curl up and die just because you spend your days in body armor, breathing in
smoke grenades instead of in business casual, swilling
bad coffee.

"Forget it," Bryson muttered. "You made yourself
clear." He tried to take the photos back but I pulled
them out of his reach.

"No, now that I know your interest is purely merce-
nary, I may actually be interested. If you had some sort
of altruistic motive, I'd have to look for wires coming
out the back of your head."

I slid back into the booth and looked over the sheaf
of photos again, not seeing the faces of the dead weres
this time but trying to find the print of the killer.
"You're sure it's the same perp in all four cases?"

"Same gun," said Bryson. "S&W .44 automatic, no
trace evidence on the bodies."

"Someone with firearms training who has access to
a vehicle," I mused, setting the four victims out in a
quadrant. Two of the men were skinny to average, one
white and one Asian, and the woman was pretty and almost delicate, unusual for weres. We tend to be big-
boned and tall, not that I'm really complaining

The third man was markedly different, heavy jaw
and brows that jutted, almost Cro-Magnon. "This one."
I tapped him.

"Ugly bastard," Bryson offered around a mouthful of bear claw. "Name's Bertrand Lautrec. His prints were in the system for assault." He rolled his eyes. "Imagine that."

"He's Loup," I said. "He must have gotten the bite . . . they only change bone structure like this when they get the bite rather than be born were."

"Thanks for the biology lesson, Professor X," Bryson said. "This means what, exactly?"

"The Loup are violent, drug-pushing sons of bitches," I said. "If anyone would nail a chicken to your front door, it'd be them." I tucked the photo into my bag. "I'll check him out for you, David, but my involvement ends there. I'm not bailing your ass out of this mess . . . I have my own job to do. Got it?"

"Fine, whatever," said Bryson. His face lit up like he'd just had a death sentence commuted. "You and the Loup go sniff each other's privates or whatever and get back to me. Here's my cell." He offered me a card and I reached out for it, then grabbed his index finger and bent it backward.

"*Shit!* Not again!" Bryson howled.

"Let's get something straight," I murmured in his ear. "I am helping you out of the goodness of my gods-damn heart, so use that thick head of yours for something other than squishing beer cans and show me a little respect." I applied a little more pressure to make sure I got the point across. "This time, I won't bother breaking it, David . . . I'll just rip it off at the root if you keep pissing me off."

"All right all right all right!" he yelped. "Hormonal bitch! Jesus!"

"Glad we got that straightened out," I said. "Now if

you'll excuse me, I'm going to try to go home and see if I still have a cottage after the quake, and if I do, I'm going to spend the rest of the day off with my boyfriend, *not* thinking about your case." I tucked Bryson's card away. "I'll call you."

"Wilder?" he said. "Sometimes you're not a total estrogen case. Thanks. For the help, not for almost breaking off my finger."

"Aw gee, David. Any more sentimentality and I'm gonna start crying." I dropped him a wink and left the Bungalow.

CHAPTER 3

At home I saw Dmitri's molten-copper hair first, backlit by the sun as he paced the driveway, motorcycle boots wearing a circle in the crushed seashells. I parked the Fairlane and collected the bags from Lemon Thai, the hole-in-the-wall restaurant up the beach that was Dmitri's favorite.

He stopped pacing and whipped his head toward me when I shut the car door. "Where the Hex have you been?"

I held out the bag of pad Thai and fried rice like a white flag. "I had to do a work thing. I'm sorry. Here's lunch on me."

"It's your day off," Dmitri stated flatly. He took the bag, stomped over to the front step of the cottage, set the bag down, and came back, taking me by the shoulders.

"I feel bad about last night," I said, even though the small part of me wanted to add, *I feel bad that you were such a self-centered ass.* I leaned up to give him a kiss hello, but Dmitri turned his head, his nostrils flaring and flattening. His black eye was already practically a shadow.

It took me a few seconds to realize he was scenting

me, and the only reason he'd be doing that was to seek out the scent of someone else.

I shoved him away, hard. "What is your damn problem, Dmitri?"

"It's the same man," he said. His grip on my arms tightened. "You're my *mate,* Luna . . . I don't want to smell other men on you. Ever. Do we understand each other?"

In, out. I breathed and then met his eyes. The black was starting to spill out of his pupils and across the dirty emerald of the iris. The daemon magick that fueled Dmitri's phase to full was roused by passion, but even more so by rage. Asmodeus, the daemon who'd given it to him, had anger in him like a living thing had blood. The daemon fed on Dmitri, on his emotions, the black eating his eyes.

Ignore it. This isn't about the Hexed daemon. "I understand that this is getting old, Dmitri." I slipped his grip with an angry jerk and went to get my food. "Either you trust me or you don't," I said simply. "Come inside when you've figured it out."

I turned my back on him and he growled. I was disrespecting his status as a pack member, however fallen, versus mine as an outcast.

"Don't flatter yourself," I sighed. "We both know you're not going to do anything about it." I looked back over my shoulder. Dmitri had that twisted-up confusion on his face, the kind that he wore too often around me. When he'd met me, and he was a murder suspect with a dead girlfriend. When he'd been called home to Ukraine by his pack and saddled with a mate who wasn't me. When he'd left them, and come to live with me.

It shouldn't be like this. "Shut up," I said. "Just shut up."

I went inside, and left Dmitri in the driveway staring at the water.

He came in after I'd eaten half of the pad Thai and sat beside me. After a few seconds he wrapped my shoulders with his heavy veined arms and muttered "I'm sorry" into my hair.

I rotated my head to nuzzle into his shoulder. "Yeah, well. You should be."

"I know I can be a real ass," he said, reaching across me to pick a prawn out of the nest of rice noodles.

"That's an understatement," I muttered.

"It's just that when I think about you leaving me, being with somebody else, and then to smell that man . . ."

"Bryson," I supplied.

"To *smell* him on your skin . . ." Dmitri growled softly. "The daemon doesn't always give me the best control."

"Here's a wacky way-out idea," I said. "How about trusting me a little?"

Dmitri's lips twitched a little bit, which was the closest he usually got to smiling. "Probably should, huh?"

"It might be prudent if you don't want to wake up with your eyebrows shaved off." I touched the tip of his nose and then kissed him quickly.

He turned it into something longer, and before long I'd forgotten all about the food even though I was still so hungry I could feel my stomach trying to chew through my spine.

We made love on the carpet in front of the sofa and he hissed in pain when I rolled him over and took the top. I saw more bruises, lower down near his gut, and I slowed even though it killed me. Sweat went into my eyes and stung. "They really got you."

Dmitri grabbed my hips and resumed our motion. "I told you I don't want to talk about it."

"Fair enough," I whispered, and returned to the business at hand, although I put my arms on either side of his face and supported my own weight without making a big deal of it. We all had our pride.

"Sweetheart?" I said, after I was nestled into his chest, listening to his heart beat.

"Mmm?" Dmitri's growl was more felt than heard, rumbling through me in vibrations that went to all the right zones.

"Do you know who's pack leader of the Loup these days?"

Dmitri stiffened. "Why would you want to know that? Why would *I* know that?"

"I dunno, maybe because you used to be the most feared pack leader in the entire city?"

"I think it's Gerard Duvivier nowadays, but you didn't answer my question."

Damn it all. I was hoping he'd let that one slide on by. But Dmitri was a lot smarter than his scraggly ex-biker outsides suggested. He'd been smart enough to survive a Soviet prison, become a pack leader in a tough city—and hell, he put up with me most days.

"I'm looking into some murders for David. It's just a consulting thing!" I added when Dmitri's face grew a sudden stormcloud of a frown.

"You told me that you were on SWAT. No more murders, no more people who commit them. No more of putting yourself in these situations where you can get killed!"

"I'm sorry," I said. "I was in my bra, Bryson was very insistent, and I just wanted to get rid of him. I think he might actually be on to something. I'm just going to go talk to the packs because he's not getting anywhere, and someone has started to send him presents in the form of dead birds. No one really deserves that."

"No," said Dmitri.

"Yeah, I mean Bryson's a complete ass, but he is a cop and someone is offing these weres . . . might even be another serial killer like Alistair Duncan."

"No," Dmitri said again. "You're not looking into this any longer, Luna."

I lifted my chin off his chest and looked into his eyes. They glittered, like the edge of a knife too close to the skin. "Excuse me?"

"You're Insoli," said Dmitri. "You're not even a detective any longer. I'm saying no, Luna. I won't let my mate put herself in danger just because she can."

"Oh," I said. "I see what you're saying."

"I know what you're thinking . . . ," he started. "Luna, I'm doing this because I care about you. Somebody has to."

"You're a jerkoff." I got up, pulled on my T-shirt, and walked upstairs, my footsteps heavy enough to rattle the few pictures of me and Dmitri that graced the walls of the cottage.

"I'm not doing this to . . . to dominate you. I just think . . ." He stood up, pulling on his jeans.

"No, Dmitri." I turned on him. "You didn't think. You never think that maybe I'm not some meek little pack wife now, that I still want to do things for myself, and that I miss being a detective more than anything!"

Wait, I did? That was news to me.

Dmitri chuffed out a laugh. "You know what? This is never gonna work as long as you assume that you can stay exactly the same and I'm just gonna take it. I expect things from my mate, Luna. If you'd been inducted into a pack, you'd know that."

"Oh, Hex you," I snarled. "Don't you dare bring that up."

"You go investigate the Loup and I can't guarantee that I'm gonna be around when you come back. I can't deal with you just thinking about you, Luna. I've tried, and it fucking doesn't work."

I fetched my worst glare against his impassive stare. "Threaten someone who hasn't faced down a serial killer or been thrown off a bridge by a blood witch, because next to them you just come off as sort of pathetic."

Torn between crying and screaming, I ran and locked myself in the bathroom. The tough-girl lines only went so far before Dmitri realized he had the most power to wound me, and that whenever he reminded me that I'd never be a member of his pack, he had.

It was after five when I parked at the Justice Plaza and took the creaky elevator to our floor. Cleolinda, our secretary, was still at her desk, punching the keyboard like it had done something to personally impinge her honor.

"Hey there, Cleo." I leaned on her desk and proffered an iced macchiato from the coffee stand at the curb.

"Girl, where you been all my life?" she asked, taking the coffee without breaking her stride at the keyboard. "What do you want?"

"Not much gets past you, huh?"

"That's why they pay me the big bucks. I'm busy, Wilder . . . what do you need?"

"I need a sheet on one Gerard Duvivier," I said.

"A sheet." Cleolinda whistled between her teeth. "Now, the last I knew, badass SWAT officers did not need to pull the history of the bad men they kick the door in on."

"I bought you a freaking macchiato, woman. What do you want, my firstborn?"

Cleolinda looked me up and down, one eyebrow ranging above her purple cat's-eye glasses. "Uh-huh. Duvivier, you said? Sounds froggy."

"French Canadian," I said. "Just print off the sheet, would you?"

"Bet you didn't give your desk man back at the precinct this crap," Cleo muttered as she pulled the file and hit the PRINT key. "There it is. Now get out of here before I kick your skinny werewolf ass."

"Love you, too, Cleo." I saluted her with the sheaf of papers from Duviver's file and beat a retreat.

The Loup ran the Bowers, a section of the city that had been nice for about five minutes eighty years ago, before the junkies coming off the boats moved in and turned the neighborhood into what everyone in a uniform called Needle Park. Keep the junkies all penned up in one atrophied limb of Nocturne City and leave the rest to the were packs, and the witches.

Usually, it kept everyone happy. Usually.

The Loup's pack house wasn't hard to find. It was a big, sprawling Victorian like everything else in the Park, converted into some kind of private club. The Loup made a lot more money than the average were pack in Nocturne, dealing drugs and keeping their little corner of paradise in a stranglehold so tight it was starting to turn blue.

I parked the Fairlane in an alley behind the mansion-

cum-club and didn't lock it. These days, with one head-light dangling and the chrome on the bumper smashed to hell, the Fairlane was looking about as dented as my love life. If someone was dumb enough to steal it, more power to them.

I sighed. There was a time when I loved that car like a baby. Suddenly, with the ground under my Hexed feet moving and Dmitri turning into someone I didn't know, it mattered less than gum on my shoe.

The kitchen door yielded to me and I pushed into a space that was too small and smoky and greasy for my nose and eyes to handle.

"Hey, you! Out! No dancers in kitchen!"

I flashed my badge into the smoke in the direction of the voice. It shut up and I spilled out into a back hallway that a heavy bass beat was doing its level best to shake the house apart. Black lights painted every-thing in corpse colors.

A couple pushed up against the wall, going at it in time with the music, blocked my way.

"Excuse me," I said. "Excuse me!" a bit louder. Noth-ing broke their rhythm.

"Gods," I muttered, shoving the girl into the guy. She squealed and fell off her platform shoes.

"The hell is your problem, bitch?" she screamed at me over the techno.

"I had a fight with my boyfriend," I said. "I was trapped in an earthquake. I had donuts for breakfast and now I'm just in a crappy mood." I surveyed her red sequined mini dress and teased platinum hair. "Now, it's safe to assume you work here?"

She nodded, warily. I realized I hadn't combed my hair or bothered to put on anything other than ratty jeans and a Smiths T-shirt when I left the house. She probably thought I wanted to lock her in my basement and put the lotion in the basket.

"Okay. Pull your wig on straight and go tell Duvivier that I want to speak with him."

"Hex you, lady. I'm not a fucking answering machine and even if I was, Gerard wouldn't talk to you." She looked me up and down. "He talks to girls who are polite. And pretty."

Under the black light, I opened my mouth and let my fangs grow to their full length. My eyes pricked at the corners, and I felt them flicker to animal gold from human gray.

The man finally spoke up: "Hey, leave her alone." He stood away from the wall, craggy and uneven like a little mountain of bad-tempered were. I snarled at him and turned back on the girl.

"Go find Duvivier. And while you're at it, find a new man to swap spit with. That one has chlamydia."

He lunged for me. "Insoli whore!"

I hit him in the throat as he came toward me, just under his blocky Adam's apple. I didn't hit hard enough to kill him, or even put him down for very long. Just enough to make my point.

"Duvivier," I told the girl. "I'll be at the bar waiting."

She glared at me from under false lashes crouched on her lids like glittering spiders. "Who should I say you are?"

I gave her a wide, fangy grin. "Tell him I'm with Dmitri Sandovsky."

After that, it didn't take long. I was halfway through some sort of pinky-red drink with a cherry at the bottom and sugar on the rim when two Loup appeared at my shoulders.

"You. Gerard wants to talk to you, Insoli."

I grinned up at the taller of the Loup, meeting a solid line of brow and a face that would give a troll pause. "I figured that would get your attention."

His lip curled unpleasantly. "Don't think that being Sandovsky's whore cuts any ice with us, princess."

"Yeah, I guess you'd know about that, being Duvivier's bitches yourselves."

The shorter Loup snarled at me and reached out a meaty, rock-like hand, presumably to twist my head off. I ducked him, since he had all the grace of a two-ton truck.

"The place is looking thin tonight," I said, pointing to the dance floor. It was virtually empty despite the DJ bouncing behind his turntables. "That because of your packmate getting a bullet in his frontal lobe? I understand that doesn't put people in the mood to dance the night away."

"Who the fuck are you?" said the coolheaded Loup.

"Oh, how careless of me." I held out my badge inside its gleaming new pleather case. It was silver, an officer's badge instead of a detective's gold shield. It didn't have the same effect, but the Loup grunted. "I'm looking into Bertrand Lautrec's death. Can I speak with Gerard now?"

"We had a detective in here," said the short one. "A dumbass in a cheap suit. We sent him out on his ass." They shared a chuckle like a tank tread driving over gravel.

Bryson hadn't told me that part. I'd be sure to mock him mercilessly for it later.

"Good thing for everyone that I'm not a detective then," I said.

The tall Loup put a hand on my shoulder. "This way. Don't get cute with me."

"Wouldn't dream of it." I smiled sweetly at him. Yes, I can be sweet when the need strikes. Shocking, I know.

Gerard Duvivier had turned the master bedroom of the mansion into a VIP suite. Lots of velvet on the walls, leather furniture that sat too low to the ground, and some kind of stereo system that could probably bring down satellites blaring house music from the corner cabinet.

A round bed with a blue satin coverlet and zebra-skin sheets dominated the space. Gerard sprawled in the center of it, black Armani crinkling around a too-lanky frame. Some girls that looked to be mutant clones of the one I'd cornered by the kitchen were on either side, feeding him champagne and smiles that would have blinded anyone meeting them head-on.

"Nice place," I said, waving to him when he rotated lazy, bloodshot eyes to me. "Very 1980s Miami coke dealer. Although, I must say, for the full effect you really need a few alligators doing laps in the hot tub."

"She was downstairs shooting off her mouth," said the short Loup.

"Was she, now?" Gerard looked me up and down. He was younger than I would have pegged a pack leader for, with a too-wide nose and mismatched cheekbones. A born were, with a stink to match.

Lank, greasy hair shielded his forehead and slid down into his eyes. He was bare-chested under his jacket except for a gold crucifix. One of the girls knotted her fingers in the curls of his chest hair. "Baby, you said no business after hours."

"Shut up," he said congenially, then turned his gaze back to me. It was a hot, intelligent gaze—at least twice the wattage of any of the other Loup. "What'd you say that's got Louis and Marius so fired up, Insoli?"

"I have a name," I said. "I think we'll use that from now on."

He spread his hands. "Okay. What is it, sweetheart?"

"Luna Wilder," I said. "I came here to ask about Bertrand Lautrec."

Louis and Marius moved in from behind me, and Duvivier sat up, shoving the girls off when they tried to follow him. "Did you, now? What do you want to know?"

I shot a glance back at Marius, who stared at me with all the reactivity of a slag heap. "I'm doing a favor for Detective Bryson, the loudmouth you ejected from your club? I need to know about Bertrand . . . is there a reason a killer might have targeted him?"

The press of male were stink was starting to make me a little dizzy, but I swallowed and kept smiling.

"I don't know," Gerard purred. "Boys? You think of any reason that Bertrand might have got himself shot through the brains?"

Louis grunted. "Nossir."

"He was on vacation," said Marius. "Not bothering a soul." Marius also lied about as well as a slag heap.

"Three strikes, missy," said Gerard. "We don't have anything that can help you."

"I'm out like Bryson?" I guessed. Louis and Marius pressed so closed to me I could feel their bodies all up and down my back. My skin started to crawl under my clothes, and sweat worked down my ribs with damp, ticklish fingers.

"Oh," said Gerard. "No, I don't think we'll get rid of you just yet, Miss Wilder." He reached over to an intercom box on the wall and hit the buzzer. A few seconds later the were from the back hall came in. Under good light he was even uglier, and he homed in on me like a pit bull on a man in steak underwear.

I've been a cop for a while, and you learn to recognize bad situations fast, if you don't want to end up dumped in a gutter somewhere. This was one of them. "About the whole throat thing," I said. "Wasn't personal. You'll be right as rain in a few days."

"Miss Wilder," said Gerard. "I'd like to introduce Pierre Maison. A time ago, he lost his mate to one Dmitri Sandovsky. Point of fact, Pierre lost all standing with the pack, just when he was poised to become a major player in the city's trade, because of his humiliation." He looked between me and Pierre, and I swore he was grinning. "Tell her what you do now, Pierre." A dominate shimmered the air between the two men, and Pierre grunted.

"Wash dishes in the club kitchen."

Gerard laughed indulgently. "How the mighty have fallen, eh? Pierre also appears to have taken exception to your inexpert medical diagnosis downstairs."

Yeah. This was about as bad as it could get without the Rapture taking place. Dmitri's stealing a girlfriend of Pierre's was something I couldn't even contemplate at the moment, if it had even happened. Pressed close to pack members on their own territory, all of them itching to turn me into pulp, I was more worried about keeping all of my limbs attached.

"You can't touch me," I spat. "Dmitri is my mate. He'll tear your fucking head off if you even smear my lip gloss."

Pierre and the other Loup began to chuckle, smiling like I was a particularly amusing pet. "Who said anything about touching?" said Pierre, stroking my cheek with the back of his hand. I turned and snapped my teeth at him.

"She's got fight," Gerard said. "Good luck. Don't mess up the carpet." He strolled away into the dancers, lighting up a thin cigarillo.

"Hold her," said Pierre, reaching into his jacket pocket. "I've got about ten grand worth of payback to take out of her skin."

"Oh, Hex you," I said. "You think you scare me?"

Pierre smiled, and there was no life behind it. "I think, a little."

He was right, a little. Nobody likes to be on the wrong side of a three-man team.

Fortunately, fear also makes me mean. I didn't give Pierre the chance to hurt me. I swung my foot up and square into his groin. It did all the good of kicking a brick wall, because Gerard's two goons were still holding on to me with hands like clamps.

"Hex!" Pierre screamed, on his side, both hands clapped over his privates. "Take this crazy bitch out back!"

"Move," Louis grunted at me. We plowed through the dancers and out a plain fire door to a set of metal stairs leading into the alley. I could see the Fairlane, patiently waiting under a street lamp below us.

"Sweet ride," said Marius.

"Would you focus for two seconds, you mongrel idiot?" said Louis. "Get her down the stairs."

"I'm doing my job," I snarled. "I don't play in pack politics."

"We're doing our job, too, lady," said Marius. "You and Sandovsky hadn't showed up on our doorstep,

Pierre wouldn't be a dishwasher, and this pack wouldn't be on the way down."

"Fine," I muttered. "I tried being nice." I stomped down hard on Marius's foot. He lost his balance on the slick steps and took me with him. Louis fell on top and shoved me hard against the railing as he tumbled after Marius ass-over-tail.

My legs got kicked out from under me, and I tipped over the railing.

Falling two stories isn't a big bag of fun under the best of circumstances. It's even worse when your fall is broken by the hood of a 1969 Ford Fairlane.

The Fairlane's car alarm began a warped shrieking, echoing off the alley walls. I started to move and felt windshield glass crunching under my motocross jacket. My right wrist was tucked under my hip, bent at an angle that sent thin hot blades up and down my arm.

"Stop her!" Louis yelled. "Get back here!"

"I think I threw out my back!" Marius moaned. "Hex it, I'm gonna need the chiropractor again."

When I rolled off the Fairlane and tried to stand, I was unsteady. The alley was blurring, the vibrations from my fall echoing in my bones. I managed to shove the key into the Fairlane's door and start the car one-handed. I laid on the horn and then revved the engine, steering with my forearm and using my good hand to pop the emergency brake and put the Fairlane in gear.

Louis and Marius got the message. I gunned it out of the alley, past their outraged faces, clipped a garbage can with my fender, and managed to drive myself to the hospital in Highland Park one-handed.

Even for me, this was shaping up to be one hell of a bad night.

CHAPTER 4

The doctor at Sharpshin Memorial took one look at my bruises and scrapes, and asked, "What happened here, Miss Wilder? Do you need to file a police report?"

"Would you believe I actually fell down some stairs? Well, off. Sort of off the landing and down, and then I hit a car."

He stopped writing on my chart and looked at me over the black rims of his glasses. "Any particular kind of car?"

"A sixty-nine Ford."

"It'd be very easy for me to get the cops in here, Miss Wilder . . ."

I sighed, fidgeting with my elastic wrist bandage and sling. "Check my jacket."

He went in and found my badge and ID. "Oh."

"Yeah." I sighed. "Could I get some painkillers? Or all the painkillers? Either way."

"I'll write you a prescription to fill. Your wrist is just sprained, not broken, so you should be right as rain in a few weeks."

Or a few days, with the way weres healed, but I didn't clue him in. "Thanks, Doc."

"Don't mention it. Do you have someone who can drive you home?'

From outside the curtains, I heard shouting with a Ukrainian accent, smelled cloves and leather. "Yeah," I said, sighing. "That's him."

"Sir, you can't go in there . . ." The nurse didn't sound particularly stern. Angry weres are pretty damn intimidating even when they're human.

"Hex you!" Dmitri snarled. The curtain thrashed and he appeared a moment later, grabbing me by the shoulders. "Luna! What the hell are you playing at?"

"Ow," I said through gritted teeth. "Sweetie, d'you think you could not squeeze the parts I used to break my fall with?"

He loosened his grip and stepped back. "Will you please tell me what is going on?"

"Excuse me, who are you?" my doctor asked. "I'm still treating Miss Wilder."

"I'm the guy who's going to twist your head backward if you don't give us a minute, buddy," Dmitri said without looking away from me. He spoke pleasantly, his eyes bleeding to black. My hand twitched reflexively to where my sidearm usually rested on my hip, except now it was all the way across the room with my coat.

The doctor reached for the phone on the wall, but I held up a hand. "Just give us a minute, please?"

"I'll be right outside," he said, giving Dmitri a look that clearly telegraphed he thought Dmitri was a psychotic wife-beater.

"Luna," Dmitri said when he stepped away. "What happened?"

"If I tell you, will you calm down?"

Dmitri rotated and looked at himself in the mirror.

"You know, I think I can be forgiven for getting a little upset when I have to get my mate out of the hospital." Still, he took a deep breath and the black retreated, only the faintest corona around his pupils.

"I fell and sprained my wrist," I said, flashing the sling. "No biggie."

He turned away from me, tugging on his messy copper hair. "I told you this would happen. I *told* you."

"You did," I agreed, getting up and collecting my things with my good hand. "And yet, strangely, I still decided to go out and do my job."

"It's not *your* job!" Dmitri growled. "You didn't have to do any of this. You're just being contrary."

"Darling, if you didn't know I was contrary until we started cohabiting, you're a lot less observant than I gave you credit for."

His face twisted up, but he didn't say anything. I didn't, either. I knew this wasn't my job. I knew I was being selfish. But I was also on to something, damn it. Four weres dead, Bryson was in a panic, and I was trying to unravel it all and keep Dmitri and me together at the same time.

I wondered how long the painkillers took to kick in.

Dmitri interpreted my silence as stubborn refusal to admit I was wrong, which was accurate. "Let's just go home," he said finally. "I could spend a lifetime without going to pick you up from some sawbones every time you get in over your head."

"The next time I do, I'll make sure you're off my emergency contact list."

His shoulders twitched like I'd stabbed him.

"Dmitri . . ."

"I just want to get out of here," he said hoarsely.

"Okay," I said. "Okay. Me too."

Outside in the car park, Dmitri held out his hand for my keys. "What about your bike?" I asked, passing them over. The little pentacle charm dangling from the chain jingled.

"I'll get it tomorrow, take it up the ass for parking," he said. "Get in."

I stayed where I was. "Why does this always happen to us, Dmitri?"

"Because you don't listen to me."

I shook my head. "You're just as stubborn as I am and I don't chew your head off about it." I sighed. "I'm just used to being on my own. I'm sorry, but this . . . our whole thing . . . is taking a long time to get used to."

Bracing myself to hear Dmitri say, *Too long for me,* wish me a good life, and walk away, I felt the roil in my stomach, the nervous twitch that came when the were realized its mate was about to leave it. It had happened with the man who turned me, and when Dmitri had left the time before. And the time before that.

"This wouldn't be a problem if I could induct you as a Redback," Dmitri said simply. "My stubbornness or lack of it has nothing to do with what's happening here. This is all you, Luna."

Quickly as I'd yearned for him to stay, the anger snapped back into place. "Me becoming a member of your pack is not a magic bullet, so leave off that before I get really pissy."

Dmitri cursed in Ukrainian, then jerked open the passenger's door of the Fairlane and motioned me inside. "We'll continue this later."

"No!" I shouted, my voice echoing through the empty cavern of the garage. "You've got a bug up your ass about this and I want to know why! Does it bother you that I'm Insoli? Are you *ashamed* of me?"

Dmitri pushed his hair out of his eyes, which were green and angry, but not bleeding into that cold outer-space black that signaled the daemon was riding shot-gun. It could be worse.

"You fucking know that's not what I meant. Did it ever occur to you that if you were Redback, we'd be home in bed instead of outside the Hexed emergency room? That the Loup never would have touched you? I just don't get why you do this to yourself when it would be so easy to fix. You'd understand me, you'd be safe. What's *wrong* with any of that?"

Then again, it could be a lot better.

"I don't want to be something I'm not," I said sim-ply. "You're a Redback, Dmitri, and I'm me." My head throbbed and the were snarled and paced inside my consciousness, scenting my anger and begging me to let it out, just for a second, just a sniff of blood . . .

"So you've made clear," Dmitri said. "And let me make myself clear: these problems? Are yours. You re-fuse to give even an inch to anyone. So we fight. I don't like it, but I stick around hoping you'll learn how to work with me."

"Stop patronizing me," I muttered. "You suck at it."

"And you refuse to see what's right in front of your face!" Dmitri bellowed, hitting the roof of my car with the flat of his hand. I narrowed my eyes.

"Which is what, exactly? You and your weird, ob-sessive need to have me in your little club? The fact that you're so hung up on controlling me you can't let this go even when it's ripping us to shreds?"

"The fact that *I can't protect you!*"

I froze. Dmitri pressed his hands over his face, his cheeks crimson and his heart thudding so loudly I could hear it clear across the car. "It's not going away,

Luna," he said from behind his hands. "And I have no one. I'm a Redback in name only, and if something happens . . . I *can't*. Do you understand me? I can't *do* anything to keep you safe, and even if I could, I don't know that *it* would let me."

I hobbled over to him and pulled his hands away from his face. "I've seen what it is to be in a pack, Dmitri," I told him. "I've felt it—that ugly, nasty dominate that anyone, *anyone* in a pack who's above you can give. I've seen the beatings and the rapes and the fear in those women's eyes."

Crap. Now I was starting to get emotional. My eyes stung, not from the phase but from tears. "I almost *was* one of those women, and I still wake up shaking, thinking about what would have happened to me if I'd stayed with the man who gave me the bite."

"It wouldn't be like that," Dmitri insisted. "The Redbacks are honorable. And they could keep you safe."

"You don't know that," I said. "All it would take is one time with a dominate stronger than mine—one dealer who didn't want a bust, one drunk loser who wanted some tail—and my job and my life would be over. I couldn't do my job. I'd have nothing except fear."

Dmitri grunted. "You'd have me."

"I already have you," I said, pulling him down and kissing him on the forehead. "Why can't you let me live my own life?"

"Because sooner or later you're going to find someone tougher than you," Dmitri said. He got into the Fairlane and started the engine. It made a clatter, and a little smoke curled from under the hood. "And I can't think about what will happen then. But I want you to think about this. That's all I ask, Luna: if you love me, consider that I might be right."

I did love Dmitri. And I did consider. But years of keeping myself out of a pack, from being someone's property and responsibility, wouldn't let me say it out loud. I wanted to keep Dmitri close, but every time we ran up against this wall of Redback/Insoli, I reacted badly, and I wasn't entirely sure I could ever change that. And it scared me.

But I would never say any of that out loud.

When most people are mad and confused, they sit around and brood, or take out their frustration on their loved ones. They drink or eat or go out and get into bar fights.

I'd done all of those back in my other life, when the were ruled me, and I'd found that none of these compared to a day at the firing range.

Fitzpatrick tapped me on the shoulder when I'd expended all the rounds in my Glock. "You okay, Wilder? You're shooting like you got something against life in general."

"Fine," I muttered. Batista and the rest of Tac-3 were arrayed down the alleys. SWAT officers had to requalify every three months and we tried to do it together, then go out afterward for beers. Bastista called his target back from the end of the range. The ten shots clumped neatly together in the center mass.

"Shit," Fitzpatrick muttered. He crumpled up his target and stalked off.

"Seriously . . . you all right?" Batista ejected his clip, cleared the chamber, and started to reload.

"Fine!" I said again. "Gods, I'm just fine. Everybody can just stop asking, all right?"

"You're pulling to the right there, a little," said Batista. "Something happen to your hand? You didn't get hit too bad by the quake out at the beach?"

I flexed my wrist, which was healed but still smarting like a hamster was chewing on my nerve endings. Weres heal up fast, but we're not invincible. "No," I said. "Just smashed some crockery at my place." To deflect Batista's bright black gaze I said, "How about you?"

"Don't ask." He rolled his eyes. "Smashed up the picture window, and Marisol's flower beds got torn apart. I haven't heard the end of that for two days. Where she thinks I get the cash to make everything better on a police salary, only her and God know."

I put a fresh clip into the Glock. "They can do marvelous things with credit cards these days, Javier."

"Hex me," he muttered. "My *abuela* told me Marisol was gonna put me in the poorhouse, but did I listen? No."

The intercom on the wall squawked. "Wilder, someone here to see you."

I looked over my shoulder at the range commander in his little glassed-in office. He mimed picked up the phone, but I gestured for whoever-it-was to come in.

Bryson appeared a moment later, goggles and ear protection mussing his greasy pompadour. "I've been looking all over for you!" he yelled at top volume.

Batista gave him the eye. "Wilder, you know this clown?"

"Unfortunately," I said. "What is it, Bryson?"

"What did you find out!" he bellowed. I yanked off his ear protection and bent my mouth close.

"I can hear you!"

Bryson winced and gave me a reproachful look. "What did you find out about the Loup?" he asked in a normal tone.

I sighted down the Glock, exhaled, and pulled the trigger. I put half the clip into the paper target, the recoil beating against my wrist, before I answered. "Nothing about your case."

"Nothing!" Bryson yelped. "What are you doin' to me, Wilder? Jesus!"

"Oh, settle down. You're gonna have a heart attack going on like this, you know. I *did* hear some mildly interesting chatter about how the Loup have been knocked off the top five list for scumbag drug dealers in the city, and they're hurting. Might be why they're so cranky about the Lautrec thing."

Bryson put a protective hand over his chest. "Did you at least get 'em to lay off nailing crap to my door?"

"Gee, David, between them threatening to kill me and falling off a fire escape, it sort of slipped my mind." I fired again, and a cluster of papery black flowers appeared on the target's head mass. I ejected the Glock's clip, cleared the chamber, and called the target back.

Bryson whistled appreciatively when the half-shredded human outline came close. "Nice work. Almost as good as my stuff. You know I had the highest score in my class when I went to the academy?"

"David, you shot yourself in the foot last year. With a flare gun."

He turned red. "There was a lot going on in my life back then. My concentration slipped."

"Whatever." I holstered the Glock and waved goodbye to Batista and Eckstrom before pulling David out of the alleys and into the antechamber. "Did you have some reason to come down here other than to interrupt my work with stupid bragging?"

"Actually"—he flourished a file at me—"I did. But the bragging was definitely a fringe benefit."

I pushed my protective gear over the counter to a

uniform and signed myself out. "Get on with it, then. Since you slithered back onto my radar I've been having a really shitty time, and this isn't helping."

"Boyfriend got one of those personal problems? They make pills for that."

"Too bad they don't make pills to cure rampant stupidity," I said. "Focus, David. What do you want?"

He opened the file and showed me a picture of a pretty girl, brunette, a short bob framing a round moon face and a turned-up nose. "Bertrand Lautrec had a girlfriend."

I took the photo and examined the sheet cursorily. Laurel Hicks. She was a nurse, her prints on file with the DEA. She lived in the unfashionable section of downtown and she was twenty-four years old. "She's not Loup. Not even the born ones look this good. Another pack?"

Bryson grinned salaciously. "Human."

That stopped me. Weres from different packs isn't unheard of—it's how alliances are made and broken. Alliances between pack weres and Insoli weres aren't accepted, but it's not impossible. Dmitri and I were proof of that. Sort of. I pushed away thoughts of the silence and towering black cloud of anger waiting for me at home.

Weres and plain humans, though? It doesn't happen. No human would be crazy enough to risk exposing herself to that without comparative were strength and quick healing. Plus, there's the off chance your beloved might tear you to shreds if you walk in during a phase. Some plain humans get off on magick, and witches intermingle freely, but I've yet to meet a plain human who would willingly go with a were.

"Okay, you got my attention," I told Bryson.

He grinned. "Thought that might do it. I'm going over to interview her. Wanna come along?"

I did. I did so badly that my stomach did a little flip at the thought of working through a case again. But if things with Dmitri were bad now . . .

"Sure," I said. "Let me get my stuff."

Laurel Hicks's apartment building would make a clown want to kill himself. One of those boxy gray numbers from the 1960s, exactly like every other boxy gray tenement in the surrounding street. Dust and oppressive summer heat pressed down over the street like water and made me sweat just by virtue of exiting Bryson's car.

A homeless man dozed in the building's doorway, mumbling about smoke and shadows. The lobby smelled like bleach and the arthritic elevator smelled like vomit.

"Cheerful goddamn place," Bryson muttered, punching the button for the third floor.

"I'll let you do the talking," I said as we rode. "Until you start fucking up, of course, at which point I'll step in."

"You're too kind," Bryson said, favoring me with a toothy grin. We knocked on Laurel's door and heard a cat meowing within. Bryson fidgeted.

"Don't like cats?" I asked.

"I'm allergic," he said shortly. I hid a grin by pretending to cough.

"Who is it?" A voice as colorless as the cardboard-colored walls and carpet around us barely penetrated the scuffed apartment door.

"It's the police, Miss Hicks," said Bryson. "Could you open up, please?"

"I'm afraid this is a bad time," said Laurel Hicks, suddenly sounding alert and panicky. "Could you please come back?"

"Can't do that, ma'am," said Bryson. "This is an urgent police matter."

"No . . . no, I really think it would be better if you came back later," she said. "I . . . I just can't . . ."

"Laurel," I said, stepping close to the door. "We want to talk to you about Bertrand. Just talk. I promise that the Loup will never know we were here."

A long silence reigned. Bryson glared at me. "Nice work."

"Just wait," I muttered. Laurel snuffled on the other side of the door.

"I don't know what you're talking about."

"Yes, you do," I said. "And I don't blame you. Now please open the door."

Another small eternity later, the deadbolt clicked back and Laurel's pale face appeared in the crack of the door. "You can't stay long. I have to get to my shift at the hospital."

She was still in her pajamas, eyes puffy and hair ratty, but I smiled politely and pretended to believe her lie. "After you," I told David.

He showed Laurel his shield, and she gestured us inside with a tired, boneless motion. As we passed the threshold magick prickled over my skin, and I looked up to see a twisted black root nailed over the door frame with a steel roofing nail.

A little bit gothic for someone who seemed strictly pastel.

"I can't tell you anything about Bertrand," Laurel said immediately. Her apartment was a tiny affair, low popcorn ceilings and a vinyl floor made to look like wood. A sad chintz sofa and ratty hooked rug hunched in the corner.

I scented another body in the place and a calico cat leapt to the back of the sofa, puffed up to twice its size, hissed at me, and took off into the bedroom.

"I'm sorry," said Laurel. "I don't know what's wrong with her."

"Don't worry about it," I said. Bryson cleared his throat at me and frowned so hard his eyebrows merged.

"Well, speak up then, boy," I said, stepping back and letting him close in on Laurel.

"Thanks," he hissed at me. "Miss Hicks, I just need to clear a few things up."

"You might as well sit down," she said in the same tone you'd use to talk about knee surgery. She flopped back on the sofa and dabbed at her eyes with a well-used tissue.

Bryson awkwardly took a seat in the threadbare velvet armchair across the way and I stood at his shoulder, trying to look laid-back. Also, standing behind Bryson gave me a dandy vantage into the rest of the apartment, which consisted of a pocket-size kitchen and bedroom, with a bathroom done in Pepto pink off it. All cops are inveterate snoops. Never leave them alone while you pop into the washroom.

"Miss Hicks, why didn't you contact the police when Bertrand . . . passed away?" Poor Bryson had slept through sensitivity training, that much was obvious.

Laurel stared at the wall and sniffed heavily. "Never thought you'd need anything from me."

"Miss Hicks, when someone dies it's customary to be a little more broken up about it than you are right now. You getting me, sweetheart?" Bryson leaned forward like a pit bull smelling hamburger meat.

My eyes roved over the countertops, which were covered in empty pizza boxes and Lean Cuisine containers, a dish of cat food, and a pair of orange prescription bottles.

I whacked Bryson on the shoulder and he winced. "The hell, Wilder!"

"Laurel . . . may I call you Laurel?"

She lifted one shoulder. "Whatever you want."

"Laurel, is it true that you didn't get in touch with the police because of Bertrand's involvement with the Loup?"

She looked me over, her eyes swimming up from their sedated depths to really examine me. Finally she asked, "Bitten or born?"

"It doesn't matter," I said. Rule One was keep the focus on the victim. Get your subject to empathize with him, and with you. "But I know how hard it can be to be an outsider with a pack, put it that way. Why are you afraid of Bertrand's pack?"

Bryson gaped at me and I snarled under my breath, letting my eyes flash gold, which he wisely interpreted as the signal to shut the Hex up.

"Gerard Duvivier is a nasty little worm," Laurel said, feeling making its way into her voice for the first time, "but I'm not scared of him. I'm a psychiatric nurse. He can't rattle me."

"Good for you," I said. "Now explain to us why you didn't come forward. You cared about Bertrand, didn't you?"

She shook once, like a plucked string, and started crying again. Bryson whipped out a monogrammed handkerchief, bright white against the stained tones of the apartment, and handed it over. Laurel took it and buried her face in it while she sobbed.

"I . . . only knew him . . . a couple of months," she managed. "But he . . . I think we would have fallen in love, if he'd . . . he hadn't . . ."

"I understand," I said. "And it's shattering when someone dies suddenly, I know. How did you hear about it? Did the pack threaten you?"

"No," said Laurel, gulping in air. "I was there."

Bryson sat bolt-upright in his seat, and I felt my own heartbeat pick up.

"What?" Bryson managed. "What?"

"I was there," said Laurel impassively. "We were camping in the Sierra Fuego Preserve."

"Why did you run?" I asked Laurel softly. She met my eyes.

"You'd run, too, Detective. Believe me. A human and a were, with his pack already in upheaval? How would that have looked? I'd be in a cell and I have patients who need me. It was too dangerous to stay."

"Oh?" I sat on the arm of Bryson's chair, ignoring his grunt, and didn't correct her on the "Detective" assessment. "What's happening in the Loup?"

"Bertrand was about to challenge Gerard for dominance," Laurel said. "To be pack leader. Bertrand had more right to it or something, he said. The Lautrecs have been in Nocturne for a long time."

"Fascinating as that history lesson is," Bryson said, "I'm gonna need you to come down to the Twenty-fourth Precinct and make a formal statement. Can you handle that, Miss Hicks?"

She looked to me. "Only if she comes along."

"Hex me," Bryson muttered under his breath. "All right, fine. You game to pay a visit home, Wilder?"

"Not my home anymore," I said. Going back to the Twenty-fourth ranked just above sitting on a bed of nails watching a snuff movie marathon.

"Wilder, for the love of the gods in the pantheon, will you please just go along with me so the skirt will come make a statement?"

I rolled my eyes. "Fine. This better not take long, though. I'm on call."

"If a Eurotrash terrorist tries to rob the O'Halloran Tower, you're free to leave," Bryson said. "Miss Hicks, why don't we get you ready to go and we'll take my car."

He followed her into her bedroom, standard procedure to make sure witnesses and suspects don't grab a gun and shoot themselves, or us. He left the door open, but his back blocked me from Laurel Hicks.

I grabbed the armchair and scooted it over to the door, yanking at the root charm until it came free of the drywall with a slimy grasping at my skin. I hate how magick feels. I wrapped the thing in the edge of my T-shirt before transferring it to a pocket, where it couldn't rub against my skin and cause me to accidentally Path its ambient power, which would result in unpleasant side effects like phasing and for all I know, shooting lasers out of my eyes.

I hadn't tested my Path abilities to draw in magick and use it to exacerbate my were side except for once, when a caster witch had me in his grasp and was squeezing for all he was worth. I didn't want to do it again. Too much bad happened when I dipped into the pack magick that my bite had given me.

Laurel came out of the bedroom with a coat and purse over her pajamas, Bryson trailing after her. He shot me a look and I gave him an innocent smile.

"What the hell are you up to?" he whispered when he passed me, guiding Laurel out the door by the elbow.

"Tell you when she's not around," I muttered back.

"Crazy gods-damn woman," Bryson muttered. Coming from him, it was almost starting to sound like an endearment.

CHAPTER 5

The Twenty-fourth Precinct appeared as it always had, a slightly dusty red-brick firehouse with patrol cars parked out front and dirty windows hiding what went on inside.

Today, though, the tenor of the place had changed and when I walked inside, trailing Bryson and Laurel Hicks, my insides jerked like I'd just gone over the first drop of a roller coaster.

Even the burnt-coffee smell mixed in with dirt and the accumulated stench of thirty years of felons passing through the place was wrong, and so very different from the bland, filtered air of the Justice Plaza.

"This sucks," I said, soft enough so only I heard.

"Interrogation Three," Bryson told the uniform, who gave Laurel Hicks a visitor badge and spirited her away. It was daytime, so Rick the night sergeant wasn't working. Thank the gods for small things. Rick would want to talk. Catch up.

Shelley, the day sergeant, barely looked at me. She and I had never really gotten along, due to her thinking weres were a menace and me thinking she was a bitch who wore tacky press-on nails, and I never thought I'd be so happy about that fact.

"Hey, so what the hell is up?" Bryson asked me when we stopped at his desk in the bullpen. My old desk was still vacant. I didn't know whether to be flattered or disappointed.

I pulled the root out of my pocket and showed it to him.

"That thing stinks," said Bryson, his nose crinkling. "Like old-man deodorant." He was right, but I pressed on to the important bits.

"It's a charm," I said. "A protection charm. Against what, I don't know."

"I see. And you stole it from the poor grief-stricken girl's apartment why, exactly?"

"Because it's not for protection against weres or blood witch curses or anything in the standard rulebook," I said. "I want to know why she has it."

Bryson rubbed between his eyes. "Wilder, I can't go in there and ask her that. What will McAllister say?"

Lieutenant McAllister's door was shut and the light in his office off. "Nothing," I said in relief. "He's not here."

"Regardless," said Bryson. "I'm gonna get her statement. You want to look over the other three vics' files, be my guest. Just don't eat my pastry snacks." He swept a packet of Little Debbie protectively into the center drawer of his desk.

"Happy to help," I said to his back, absently opening the drawer up again and unwrapping one of the cupcakes. Cream-filled. Divine. I pretended to read the case files until Bryson had gone into Interrogation Three and locked the door, and then slipped between the desks, down the hall, and into the narrow, nicotine-stained observation space behind the interrogation room's mirror.

I clicked on the speaker box in time to hear Bryson say, "Tell me exactly what happened that night. Start from the beginning. Don't leave anything out."

Laurel was starting to perk up from whatever she'd taken and she shivered when Bryson spoke. "I don't know how much help I'll be. I didn't really *see* anything . . ."

"Just talk, miss," said Bryson. "I'm begging you . . . you're my first break in this case."

"Why, Bryson," I murmured, smiling as I licked chocolate frosting off my thumb. "Who knew there was a sensitive man underneath all that hair product?"

"Gerard had sent Bertrand to pay some guy off, out at some rest stop on Highway Twenty-one. I waited in the car for that. Bertrand never wanted me close to the business . . . he took a gun. He never took a gun because, well . . ."

"He was an intimidating son of a bitch," Bryson supplied. "I got that much. So he pays the guy off and . . ."

"Um. Afterward, he wasn't happy. He said Gerard was an idiot to close off the deal they had going with the guy, but that was pretty standard talk for him, and he calmed down when we got to the preserve. We were camping . . . Bertrand loved to camp . . . he did it once a month in the summer," said Laurel.

"You get followed?" Bryson asked, twirling a paper clip in his fingers. "This payee have a beef?"

Laurel shook her head. "The fire went out . . ." A pause to tear up, sniffle, take a tissue and compose herself. The most animated thing in the interrogation room was the blinking light on Bryson's digital recorder.

"The fire went out," Bryson prompted. "And?"

"Bertrand went out," Laurel said. She left it at that until Bryson made a spinning-wheel motion with his hand. "He went outside the firelight to get more wood. He left the gun, and the light."

Bertrand Lautrec wouldn't have needed to take a flashlight. Most weres can see well enough in the dark not to stub their toes on things. Most weres would also be able to scent an attacker a mile away.

Unless they were city weres in the unfamiliar wild, with unfamiliar scents, disoriented in the dark . . .

"The wind picked up," said Laurel quietly. "It kicked leaves and dirt against the tent and I got scared so I took the light and went to find Bertrand. There was mist . . . blowing in from the coast. Droplets on my face."

I stood up straighter, examined her through the glass. Her recitation was earnest and inflected, and she was leaning forward, staring into Bryson's face as she twisted the tissue between her fingers.

Laurel Hicks was not lying. Never mind that we hadn't had any rain all up and down the coast, from valley to mountains, for weeks. There wasn't enough moisture in the air to wet my tongue to spit. The Sierra Fuego range was patchy with wildfires.

If there was rain the night Bertrand Lautrec died, something other than the weather had caused it.

"I walked for a long time, following Bertrand's trail," Laurel whispered. "Broken branches kept scratching my arms and legs. Then I heard a gunshot."

Bryson tapped his fingers against the edge of the table, eyes bright. "Yeah. Great. What'd you see?"

"Nothing," said Laurel.

Bryson slumped. "What? You're jerking me. You're out there alone in the middle of the gods-damn woods and you don't see *anything*?"

"I saw Bertrand," said Laurel, softly and sadly. "He was on his back, and his eyes were open. I saw the bullet hole. The air smelled bad."

"Gunpowder," I murmured.

Bryson's fingers stopped their rat-tat-tat cadence abruptly. "You didn't get anything about the shooter? Nothing?"

"I didn't see anyone," said Laurel. "Just Bertrand. Lying on the ground." She tucked her head to her chest. "I'd like to go home now, Detective Bryson."

"Okay, okay," he muttered. "Interview terminated at thirteen twenty," he said into the recorder and clicked it off. "Hang on here for a minute, sweetheart, and I'll see about getting you a ride."

I caught him when he came out of the interview and he jumped a mile. "Christ on a bike, Wilder! Were you spying on me?"

"I don't think it really counts as 'spying' when we're members of the same department. What do you make of her statement?"

"She's a damn creepy gal, is what I make of it," said Bryson. "And useless. She let the guy that plugged her boyfriend get away clean."

"She's a Hexed nurse," I said, "not John Rambo. Anyway, I think we may be dealing with something bad here, David."

"Don't say that," he moaned, pacing to the coffeemaker and pouring himself a tall travel mug, black, and dumping in three packets of sugar. "Don't start me on the Freak Squad. I'll never get promoted out of this sinkhole."

"Bertrand Lautrec—and all the victims—were shot at close range with a handgun," I said. "No silencer. And we were wrong about Lautrec's body being dumped. Something stalked him and hunted him down and got away before anyone could see them."

Bryson swigged his coffee down in four gulps. "I don't believe in ghosts, Wilder. Werewolves, fine. Blood witches and spooky-ass daemons, whatever. But I ain't buying that some invisible bogeyman got Lautrec."

"I don't think this was a ghost," I said. "I think Gerard Duvivier hired someone to hit Lautrec, so Gerard wouldn't lose his status with the Loup. That payoff was the setup. Murders on Loup territory have to be justified to the pack elders in Montreal, but outside the city . . ."

I was doing Bryson a big favor. By making it an internal war in the were packs, I was telling him it was okay to wrap it up neatly and not dig too deep. I was letting the victims lie quietly in their graves rather than trying to voice their last words for everyone to hear.

You are not a detective anymore, Wilder. Let them be.

"Okay, but I still got these other three bastards cold and dead with nothing to show for it," Bryson said, swiping his hand over the case files on his desk.

"Give me a few hours and I'll do what I can," I said. A uniform led Laurel Hicks past Bryson's desk. She gave me a long, mournful look before she turned her head deliberately away.

"Go nuts," said Bryson. "Can't fuck this thing up more than it already is."

"Get me some coffee and a bagel and I'm yours unless I get paged away to go fight crime," I said. Sitting in the Twenty-fourth in close proximity to Bryson was preferable to going home, and I tried not to think about how dysfunctional that was.

Bryson shuffled off to do my bidding, which, I won't lie, gave me a thrill, and I started puzzling out which dead were belonged to which pack and what connection they might have to Gerard Duvivier.

I'd missed this work. I'd missed sitting and letting the gears of my mind churn on to wherever they might go, until I finally honed the point of a theory out of the rocky crags of my case.

"Getting sentimental, are we?" I muttered as I paged through the scene reports from the state police. All four of the victims were found in the same fifty-mile stretch of the preserve, off access roads or illegal dump sites. Bertrand Lautrec had been the first to die, followed by pretty blond Priscilla Macleod and then the two other men, spaced randomly apart over the last month and a half.

Bryson set a coffee mug at my elbow, the liquid inside mocha-colored, and a sesame bagel loaded with spread. I looked up at him, slightly shocked. "You remember how I take my coffee?"

"You sat your cute ass across the aisle from me for two years, Wilder. I'm not totally unobservant over here."

"Touching. The dead girl, Priscilla, is from the Warwolves." I tapped the green Celtic knot inked on her neck. "I recognize the tat. Scottish. I think some of their pack members run numbers over in Mainline at the underground betting places. The other two will be more difficult." Especially since asking Dmitri for his help was right out.

"And their connection to this Lautrec guy is . . . ?"

"That's your job, David," I said. I picked up the root charm and slipped it into a spare evidence bag so I wouldn't have to hold it with my bare hands, and then secreted it in my pocket. "I'll dig into the other two vics' backgrounds a bit, try to get a shot at IDing their packs."

"I'll check out the Macleod girl's priors," said Bryson. "Text me or something when that long doggy nose of yours digs something up, okay, Wilder?"

I opened my mouth to shout at him, but a ruckus from the lobby beat me to it.

"Hey!" Shelley was yelling. "Hey! Hey! Settle down, people!"

"We demand to be seen!" a basso voice with an accent snarled at her. "Don't give me the runaround, missy."

Oh, gods. Was that a *Scottish* accent?

The scent of weres—nervous, angry weres—rolled slowly through the squad room and I tugged on Bryson's sleeve. "I think we'd better get out there, David."

"What the Hex is goin' on now?" he said, starting for the lobby. I followed him through the security gate and metal detector and smacked into his back when he stopped short. "Oh. Hex me."

Six or seven weres clustered together, some in suits and business casual, the three Asian males in bright satin jackets and tight black jeans, their hair spiked within an inch of being a deadly weapon.

The owner of the impressive, Connery-esque brogue was pounding his fist down on Shelley's high desk, in the full light of a television camera and reporter from *NC-1*, the trashiest and loudest of the city's cable news shows. They'd done a piece on me after the Duncan case titled "Were Bites Man."

"I want satisfaction!" the Warwolf bellowed. "I want Detective David Bryson to come out here and account for what's being done about my niece's murder!"

Priscilla's uncle was graying, and he sported an impressive network of scars on his hands and neck, one running from the corner of his mouth back to his ear. He looked like he chewed on beer cans for fun. Even the impassive Shelley was beginning to show panic in the corners of her eyes.

The Warwolf thumped the desk again. "Detective Bryson! Now!"

"He's right here," said Bryson, and I could have throttled him. Six pairs of eyes rotated to face David, and six sets of lips pulled back to show fangs.

"You know how you said you didn't want to be the rabbit?" I murmured. "Hate to say it, but your nightmare has come true."

"Shit," muttered Bryson. Louder, "People, I'm doing everything I can! Your cases are being handled with the utmost sensitivity!"

"Sensitivity?" spat one of the Asian men, stepping forward and crossing his arms. He moved fast, like liquid from one spot to another, and I shot a glance at the other two. They stayed flanked, eyes on their leader. "Is six weeks with no leads and no suspects your idea of sensitivity, Detective?"

"Y'all are gonna have to leave before I get you thrown out!" Shelley added, unhelpfully. "You can't come in here and cause a scene."

"We're taxpayers the same as you!" the Warwolf bellowed. "Don't you dare try to bar us from a public office, woman!"

"Sir, you're nothing like me," Shelley snipped. "Now go back to scratching behind your ears before I get you more involved with the police than you have any desire to be." She reached for her phone and the Warwolf snarled, moving for her.

"Don't," I said to him, my body blocking Shelley. Not that she didn't deserve whatever the old man had being going to give her. "Please. Can't we settle this?"

The Warwolf looked me over, scented me, met my

eyes. The rest of the weres stared at him to see what he would do.

Great. If he decided I smelled funny I'd be hamburger before Bryson or Shelley could flick an eyelash.

"Who are you?" he said finally. "Insoli. But who are you?"

"Luna Wilder," I said. "I used to be a detective here."

"You're trespassing!" Shelley shrilled, brave now that I was in the line of fire.

"Shelley." I turned on her. "I know it's hard with that weave weighing your head down, but *shut the fuck up.*"

"Yeah, Shelley," said Bryson. "Jesus."

Backup from Bryson. Wonders never cease in Nocturne City. "I apologize on behalf of us all," I told the Warwolf. "You can talk to me."

"Luna Wilder?" said the *NC-1* reporter. I recognized her as Janet Bledsoe, a perky bottle brunette who normally showed up doing cheesy shaky-cam exposés of crooked day care centers and elder homes. She must have thought she'd hit the jackpot with this story.

"That's right," I said.

"Luna Wilder who was *not only* involved in the death of Alistair Duncan, the district attorney, but also present when Seamus O'Halloran was shot?"

Before I could respond the camera's eye and Janet's mike were in my face. "What's your involvement in this case, Miss Wilder?"

I smiled right into the camera. "That's *Officer* Wilder. Just helping out a fellow member of the force."

"Miss Wilder, with your record of unprovoked violence on civilians and repeated suspensions, do you really think you're the best liaison for this highly sensitive case? Some might suggest that you're in over your head!"

I leaned past the lens and the light and grabbed Janet Bledsoe by one of her twenty-four-carat diamond stud earrings, pulling enough to make her squeal. "If you don't get that camera out of my face, I am going to break it in half and use the pieces to shoot home movies straight down your throat." I grinned at her, my fangs stretching out delicately to just brush her ear. Janet Bledsoe whimpered. "Are we clear?"

"Let . . . go . . . ," she squeaked, trembling all over. Elder-abusers and irresponsible nannies must not have prepared her for being threatened by a cranky were.

I released her and stepped back. "David, if you please?" I pointed at the cameraman.

"No unauthorized footage inside a police precinct," said Bryson. "Security risk. Give me the tape."

The cameraman attempted to argue, but Bryson closed on him and, I can only presume, stunned him with a whiff of cologne.

"Don't think this is the end," Janet Bledsoe yelled as a uniform ejected her from the precinct. "You can't silence the truth! Fascists!"

"I've never been called a fascist before," I muttered as the doors swung shut on her screeching.

"There's a first time for everything, miss," said the Warwolf. "You going to give me a straight answer?"

"That depends." I pointed at the rest of the weres. "Who exactly are you people?"

"I'm Donal Bruce Macleod, Priscilla's uncle and legal counsel to the Nocturne City Warwolves," he said.

The Asian man who'd yelled at Bryson gave me a curt head nod. "Ryushin Takehiko. I am pack leader of the Ookami."

I'd never even heard of the Ookami, but Ryushin

bore enough resemblance to the dead Asian were that they could have been related.

"Brother?" I asked. He gave me another single nod, his face tight. His eyes burned, though, and I realized he was a lot younger than he presented himself. The victim was his *older* brother, then. I was guessing Ryushin's promotion to pack leader had been sudden and unwanted.

A silent, black-haired male and female pair so tall and slim they would have made a scarecrow feel fat stood at the back of the group, regarding me with eerily pale eyes. Their irises might have been a really dark shade of snow white, but no deeper.

"Those are Aivars and Aija Kļaviņš, of the Viskalcis," said Donal. "They don't speak much. English, or at all."

The Viskalcis smelled of some manner of were, but I'd never met one face-to-face. Aivars and Aija didn't look like they saw daylight very often. Maybe it burned.

"Their pack leader was also murdered in this manner," said Ryushin. "Now you will tell us what you are doing about it."

Have I mentioned I hate being ordered around, especially by men? Comes from another lifetime as a waitress and a girl who always picked out the boyfriend guaranteed to have control-freak tendencies. Not that my track record lately was any better.

"I can't discuss the details of an open case," I said. "I'm truly sorry for your losses . . ."

Donal laid a hand on my shoulder. It felt like an iron vise. "We don't expect an Insoli to understand. Or a plain human, for that matter." He let his eyes drift to Bryson. "But we've come here for answers, missy, and answers we are going to have."

"Look," said Bryson. "I am busting my goddamn ass over this case, and it might be a little bit easier to close if you people would give up some information about the vics."

The Ookami weres snarled at that, and Aija's bloodless lips, nearly the same color as her teeth, pulled back. Only Donal stayed calm.

"Laddie, don't be pretending like you care about what happens to a bunch of animals. If you walked like you talk, we wouldn't be here. To you, my niece dying is the same as someone shooting a dog."

"It's not like that." I spoke up loud and sharp, to pitch myself over the rumble of agreement from the wolves.

"Then what is it like?" Ryushin said. He glared at me, and I stared him down. If he wanted a dominate, I'd give him one. Insoli can be dominant or submissive as they choose, and I was willing to bank a kid like Ryushin had never had his life depend on how strong-willed he could be.

"We *don't* know who killed your friends, and your family, it's true," I said. "But we have leads and suspects. David is doing the best work that he can to solve a crime he doesn't really understand. We think now that this might be an internal fight between the Loup and an unidentified party." I was defending Bryson. Somewhere in Hell, Satan was strapping on his ice skates.

"That sounds like codswallow to me, missy," said Donal.

"Well, tough, because it's my best theory," I said. "And if anyone wants your case solved, it's me. I'm an Insoli were and everyone in this city who's picked up a newspaper in the last year knows my face. Now someone is knocking *off* weres, and if you think I don't feel the big target painted on my back, you're wrong."

Donal and Ryushin chewed over my words for a moment, casting glances at the Viskalcis weres. Aivars grunted and then dipped his chin. I got the idea that for him, he was being hideously expressive.

"Mark my words," Ryushin said. "The weres and witches of this city are moving, Detective Bryson. We know we are not safe and we are taking measures to protect ourselves. With or without the police."

"Do your job," said Donal, "and we won't be back. Keep wanking us about, and you'll wish you'd run when you had the chance."

"You don't have to threaten us," I said. "We'll figure out who did this. We'll lay your pack's spirits to rest."

"Brave words!" Janet Bledsoe shrilled from the doorway. "But can you deliver, Miss Wilder?"

"Get the Hex out of here!" Bryson yelled. Janet, her cameraman, and his fresh tape fled.

"Perfect. Five bucks says she runs that verbatim on the six o'clock news," I said.

"We'll be in touch, miss," said Donal. "Count on that." He turned and walked out, Ryushin and his posse dogging Donal's heels. The Viskalcis in their long overcoats glided after them, feet never seeming to touch the ground.

Bryson slumped against Shelley's desk. "Shit, man. *Shit*."

"Notice anything?" I asked.

"I'm fucking dead if I don't solve this thing fast?"

I sighed. "Anything *else*?"

"Yeah, those creepy Goths. Long coats in the summer. Weird."

I gave him a crooked eyebrow. "You see the strangest things, David. I'd almost think your too-stupid-to-live act was an elaborate master plan to drive me insane if it wasn't quite so annoying. What I meant was—" I gestured after the weres disappearing down the steps. "—nowhere in that little group of concerned citizens was anyone from the Loup."

Bryson blinked at me. "Well, holy crap. I knew there was a reason to keep you around, Wilder. Other than the obvious, I mean." He stared pointedly at my chest.

"Just when I think it's safe to talk to you," I said, shaking my head. "Listen, I've got somewhere to go. Can you take me over to Battery Beach?"

He pouted. "I've got a case to work! What's so damn important?"

I fingered the root in my jacket pocket. "Bertrand Lautrec started all this. Whoever Laurel Hicks is afraid of . . . someone I know out there might be able to tell me who and what it is."

"You're putting in a mileage report for this," Bryson warned as we walked to the car. "My expenses are over budget as it is."

"I told you to stop buying hookers with the department credit card, Bryson."

"Hex you, Wilder. I get 'em for free."

I sighed. "Just drive. This'll be worth it."

CHAPTER 6

We drove to Battery Beach, Bryson complaining the entire way, except for when "Keep On Lovin' You" came on the radio. About halfway there, I noticed a green sedan manned by a grumpy-looking were keeping pace with us, always one or two cars back.

"Bryson," I said, looking into my mirror to fix my hair into a braid. Casual as anything, I memorized the plate and the face behind the wheel.

"Huh?" he grunted.

"You might be interested to know that somebody's following us."

"Hex me," he muttered, looking around. I slapped the back of his head.

"Relax. Nothing we can do about it, and he's probably just seeing what we're up to. He's not making a real effort to stay hidden." The sedan almost sideswiped an SUV to keep us in view, and the driver shook his fist.

Bryson hit the steering wheel. "It's those damn weres."

"Good guess," I said. Donal must not have as much faith in me as he'd let on. How hurtful.

I guided Bryson to my grandmother's cottage, parked

on an unfashionable bit of the cliff near the old fort that looked out into the Pacific and gave the beach its name.

"What is this?" Bryson demanded. "Bridge club and crumpets?"

"My cousin lives here," I said. I didn't add that she lived with my crotchety grandmother, who alternated between Not Speaking and Pure Hatred when it came to me and her.

"So, what?" Bryson said.

"She's a witch. She'll be able to tell me what the charm is supposed to fend off," I told him, and then added when his eyes bugged out, "You may want to just wait in the car."

"That's one weird fuckin' family you got, Wilder," he said, and then leaned back in the driver's seat, flicking his sunglasses down over his eyes.

"No argument from me," I said, heading for the house. Sunny's little convertible was parked in the open garage, and I knocked, not too hard.

She opened the door with a squeal. "Luna!"

"Hi, Sunny." I smiled. "Is Rhoda home?"

"No." She drew the syllable out. "She's in Cabo for some kind of brujeria gathering. I didn't ask. Not really my thing." She looked past me to the car. "Who's *that*? He looks like a Jehovah's Witness."

Bryson belched and adjusted himself. I pressed my fingers to my temples. "It's David Bryson. I'll be sure to pass on the compliment."

Sunny blinked once, twice. "I'm not even going to *ask* what you're doing riding with the man you once described as 'my smelly, obnoxious kryptonite.'"

"Probably a good plan," I said. "I have something I need you to look at, Sunny. It's important."

"Well then come *in*," she said, her face lighting up.

"And I'll pretend not to notice you only visit me when you need something."

"That is patently not true," I said. "I sat through four hours of Jane Austen movies with you not two weeks ago. This is only a *fraction* of the payback I'm owed for that experience."

"Luna, every woman loves Mr. Darcy."

"Mr. Darcy is a construct designed to make women feel bad about the partners that they're capable of attracting versus the fantasized image he presents."

Sunny gave me a look as she shut the door. "You scare me sometimes, Luna."

"What? I didn't spend *all* of high school sleeping off beach parties."

She led me into the kitchen, her preferred environment, and I drew the root out of my pocket. "It's this charm. I need to know what mojo it's supposed to work."

Sunny put cookies—homemade, of course—on a plate and served me a glass of iced tea with a twist of lemon. Only then did she pick up the charm. She dropped it again immediately. "Gods! It feels like dipping your hand in boiling water. Where did you get this?"

"From the girlfriend of a murdered man," I said. "Is it evil?"

"No," said Sunny, regarding the twisted thing balefully. "Just *strong*. Very raw, focused magick. Not a caster witch, or a blood."

"Then what? What other kind of magick *is* there?"

Sunny went over to my grandmother's sewing basket, shaped like a puffy pink satin heart, and took out a metal tin of pins. "You'd be surprised where it came from, at the beginning. Hold out your hand."

"Why?" I demanded suspiciously.

She took out a hat pin and grabbed my fist, uncurling my fingers. "Don't be such a baby." The point pierced my finger with a fuzzy stab of pain.

I yelped as a pearl of blood welled up on my fingertip. "Hex me, Sunny!"

"Hold still!" she demanded, turning my finger and squeezing blood droplets down onto the root.

Nothing happened for a few long seconds, my blood gleaming against the dark fibers of the charm. Then it began to shriek, thrashing on the table like it was alive.

Hell, maybe it *was* alive. What did I know?

Sunny leapt away from the charm as it lashed out, the pitch rising high enough that my ears gave me nothing but a feedback hiss.

"Do something!" I yelled. "Make it stop!"

She dashed into the kitchen, filled a deep iron skillet with cold water from the tap, spilled half of it on her way back to me, and shouted, "Throw it in!"

I picked up the root, feeling its magick bite into my skin as my body tried to Path it, and flung it into the water. The shrieking stopped immediately, revealing that someone was pounding energetically on the door. "What the fuck is going on in there?" Bryson bellowed.

"We're fine!" I hollered back, even though I felt like a particularly sadistic old lady had jammed her knitting needles into my ears.

"Let me in!" Bryson demanded. "I heard a bunch of screaming!"

"Sunny, watch that thing. Make sure it doesn't move again," I said. She nodded, biting her lip and prodding the charm a few times with her finger.

I opened the door on Bryson's sweating face, his tie

askew and his cheeks red. "Aw, David. You were afraid I was in peril."

He flushed even redder, bordering on maroon. "Was not."

"Come on in." I stepped aside and gestured for him to hurry up. Bryson stepped over the threshold, shoulders hunched as if he expected Sunny to swoop down on a broom, shrieking about him and his little dog, too.

"Luna?" she called. "I think I figured it out."

"Good, because if you stabbed and deafened me for kicks I'd be a little upset."

Bryson followed me back to the sitting room, eyes roving warily in every direction. "Stop that," I hissed.

"I . . . just . . ." He swallowed and gave Sunny what might have been a smile, on Bryson. "Nice place, er . . . Luna's cousin."

"It's so nice to see you again, David," she said, beaming at him. She was full of crap. Bryson grated her nerves into little pieces as much as he did mine, but my cousin is a lot politer about life's little aggravations than I am. People try to kill her a lot less often, so she might be on to something.

"Yeah," David said, looking anywhere but Sunny's face. "Say, what the Hex are you doin' to that thing? That's evidence."

"I stole it," I said. "It's not evidence of anything."

"Well," Sunny said, giving me the eye at the "stole it" comment. "It's a charm, a powerful one, but not elegant. Caster witches bespell charms against specific maladies or entities. This is like slamming down a steel grate over your front door and hooking up a shotgun to the latch."

"How come it didn't zap Wilder, then?" Bryson demanded. "She ain't normal."

"Blood witches didn't make it, either," Sunny continued as if Bryson hadn't spoken. "It reacted to blood as if it were a threat, so . . ." She shrugged. "It's a ward against evil. That's the plainest way I can say it."

"Really? You couldn't be just a hair more vague?" Bryson threw up his hands. I stepped on his foot, hard.

"Be polite," I murmured when he started to complain. "Sunny, that really doesn't help us much. If we knew what this woman was afraid of . . ."

"I just told you," said Sunny. "Evil. This is some sort of tribal magick, using totem spirits or power pulled out of crystals or feathers or animal forms. It predates casting and blood rites. It predates everything. That's why it packs such a punch, despite being simplistic. Whatever she was afraid of, it was nasty enough to warrant a serious working in a magick that's pretty much a dead art. I'd be worried, if I were you."

"Sunny, always the optimist," I said. "Um . . . you can keep the screamy charm o' evil . . . it kind of gives me a headache."

"You're not going to tell me what this is about?" Her forehead crinkled. I always told her what it was about, whether it was strictly legal to or not.

"The boyfriend of the woman this belonged to was killed," I said before Bryson could feed Sunny the party line. She'd helped me enough times to be trusted with case details, at the least. I owed Sunny a lot, more than I could ever repay. "He was killed by an attacker who shot him and then managed to vanish into a fog that just sort of magically appeared out in the forest preserve. We think it was a hit man. Hit thing. Nasty, either way."

"How awful," said Sunny. "I wish I could tell you more, but this type of magick doesn't require any sort of formal training . . . just a talent, and a willingness to use it. And there are so many sects and subsects of old Romany paths, native religions . . ."

"I get it," I said. "We'll just have to use what we've got. Thanks, Sunny." I hated just using what I had. It gave me the distinct feeling of walking around an unfamiliar room in the dark, banging my shins on the furniture.

"Luna, may I speak with you for a moment?" she said when we turned to leave. Bryson took a hint for once in his life and went out, and I faced my cousin.

"What is it?"

"I thought you transferred to the SWAT team?"

I shifted back and forth from the balls of my feet to my heels, trying to smile in an innocuous, carefree manner. "I did."

"Then why are you working on a homicide with David Bryson, of all people?"

Crap, I sucked at this.

"I'm just helping him out because the case involves some dead weres and Bryson is not exactly equipped," I said, crossing my arms. "Strictly extracurricular stuff."

"What does Dmitri have to say about all this?" Sunny asked, picking up the charm and putting it into the freezer. "Ice and iron," she explained. "Preserves the magick."

"Dmitri doesn't have anything repeatable to say," I told her shortly. "He's just all up in arms because I won't become his Redback Barbie doll."

"I'm sure he doesn't mean that," Sunny said. "That's not Dmitri."

"Yeah, well, you haven't lived with him for the past six months," I muttered. "Things change."

Bryson's car horn sounded from outside, and Sunny ran over to give me a quick, tight hug. "Promise you'll call me sooner than next decade."

"Sure," I said, disentangling myself. "I gotta go, Sunny."

In the car, I turned off Bryson's classic rock. "Okay," I said. "Laurel Hicks had a reason to be afraid of big nasty evil. She may not have seen what killed Bertrand, but she was damn sure scared of it."

"This case was supposed to get simpler, not weirder," Bryson muttered.

I leaned my head on the passenger's window. The sun glared down at me and I put a hand over my eyes. "I think that we have to accept that fact that Lautrec's killer may not have been a were."

Bryson hit the steering wheel. "Hex me. What, then? The Invisible Man snuck up and put a round in his head?"

"It could have been a blood witch," I said, thinking of some of the things I'd seen Alistair Duncan do. "Or a familiar, or a daemon, or even just a very, very skilled plain human." I rubbed my forehead. "What matters is that Laurel believed she was being stalked by something, which means she knows more than she told you."

"You believe she was?" Bryson said.

"No," I said. "I don't believe in nameless evil. There's enough of it that has a face. We'll find the perp."

Bryson swore again, but before he could get up a good head of steam his cell phone shrilled. He jabbed the SPEAKER button. "Yeah?"

"Detective Bryson?"

"Speaking."

"This is Laurel Hicks, Detective." Her voice was cloudy with tears and hysteria.

"Ah," said Bryson, rolling his eyes at me. "What can I do for you, Miss Hicks?"

"I want you to give back what you took," she whispered. "Give it back. It's mine!"

I shook my head at Bryson, mouthing *no*.

"I don't know what you're talking about, Miss Hicks," said Bryson. "We haven't taken anything from you. You feeling okay?"

"It's *mine*!" Laurel Hicks shrieked. "Now I don't have anything . . . to keep me safe . . ."

Bryson stabbed the END button on the phone and cut Laurel off mid-sob. "Crazy broad."

I didn't say anything to the contrary as he peeled out of Sunny's driveway.

"You owe me," Bryson stated after we were back on the highway to the city.

"For what? Would you bitch if I took a rabbit's foot off some guy's key chain?"

"If that guy was batcrap crazy and he called me about it, yeah!"

"You asked for my help, David," I reminded him. "Drop me at home."

He had to take the long way along surface roads since the Siren Bay Bridge remained closed from earthquake damage, but I still got a pang when Bryson screeched to a stop in front of my cottage. "My lady. Your palace awaits."

"You're welcome, by the way," I said as I got out of the car. "Feel free to send a fruit basket for all the help I gave you."

"Hey!" Bryson protested. "What about those damn weres? I'm no closer to solving this!"

"No," I said, "but you're being a jerk and pissing me off. Call me if you dig anything up."

"Wilder . . ." Bryson started to say something and then snorted, rolling his eyes. "Forget it. I can break this thing without you and your freaky damn magickal sidekicks."

I smiled indulgently. "Sure, David. You let me know when you get yourself stuck in the tar pits again."

He gunned the engine and roared away, looking as mightily irritated as a guy wearing a forest-green suit and driving a dirty Ford Taurus can look. I flipped a hand after him, and then walked down to the beach rather than toward the house. Handy as Bryson was for taking out my frustration, it didn't change what was waiting for me at home. I didn't want to be a Redback, and that should predicate a conversation that started *Hey, Dmitri, sweetie, I don't want to be a Redback.*

But if I said it, he might leave, and a surly Dmitri at home was better than the months and months when he'd been away from me, when I'd drifted on the currents, weightless and depressed.

"Fuck," I groaned, putting my head on my knees. Used to be, the guy cheated on me, and I kicked him out, or I threw a vase at his head and he kicked me out. When had it gotten so goddamn complicated?

It had gotten dark and I went in, and felt like an idiot when I realized Dmitri wasn't even there for me to avoid him.

Sure, a part of me would have liked to find wine and candles and a contrite apology in the form of a few hours of athletic sex, but an empty house was a relief. I showered and decided to take a nap, curled up in my big queen bed alone, like I'd been doing for quite some time before Dmitri came along.

Now I stretched out my arms and legs to cover the spot where he usually lay, but it was still a long time before I fell asleep.

CHAPTER 7

I woke from a dream about being chased through a 7-Eleven by cowboy-suited versions of Bryson, Dmitri, and Ricardo Montalban—go figure—to a small, insistent chirping.

My pager vibrated on the nightstand, ready to throw itself off the edge. I grabbed it up and saw the code for an urgent scramble of Tac-3 at the plaza. "Crap," I said, fumbling for my shoes and some real clothing. The clock on my nightstand read 11:30 PM. Another half an hour and Tac-3 would have been off their twenty-four-hour on-call rotation and I could have slept the night away in peace. But that would be lucky, and lately I was the black cat and broken mirror of luck.

Dmitri still hadn't come home.

Was he lying in some alley, beaten beyond recognition by a pack like the Loup? Or was he avoiding me like I'd been avoiding him?

The second option seemed way more likely, considering how our last conversation had gone. I got dressed and headed downtown.

The streets of Nocturne weren't deserted at night, not by any stretch. Things crept away from my headlights on two or four legs, and plain humans stumbled drunkenly down Devere Street near Nocturne University. It was Saturday night, it was summer, they were in high spirits. Beer and pheromones drifted past my nose.

A clutch of drunks lurched in front of the Fairlane and I hit the brakes, depressing the horn. They glared at me with bleary eyes and moved out of the way as I turned into the plaza. The lot was deserted except for Fitzpatrick's SUV with the #1 DAD bumper sticker, Batista's sporty silver bullet, a plain van from the cleaning company, and Eckstrom's Japanese bike. Allen was late, as usual.

"You oughta watch where yer goin', lady!" one of the drunks shouted at me from the entrance to the lot.

"Hex off!" I shouted back. "Keep your drunk ass out of traffic and it won't be a problem!"

He started toward me, his two friends attempting to hold him back. He was small and stocky, a ponytail and a plaid cowboy shirt with silver buttons that shone under streetlights undoubtedly designed to make him look like a badass loner, but he didn't scare me.

"You want to punch a police officer outside her work?" I asked him, squaring my shoulders. "Be my gods-damn guest."

He lunged again and his friends lost their grip. I shifted my weight into a stance and turned my body to present the smallest target. Getting punched in the gut is no fun for anyone, especially when I get up and hit them back. I didn't need an excessive-force complaint, which with the typical were strength is almost a given.

Just before he came in swinging range, I caught a whiff of his scent. He smelled like cigarettes and dust and burnt brush on a dry wind.

He didn't smell like booze.

"Shit," I said out loud.

Peripherally, I heard the door of the cleaner's van roll back and I whipped around to see two more men with the same dark hair and eyes and leather-colored skin egress the vehicle and come for me.

I went for my gun in its waist rig, but the drunk grabbed my wrist and twisted it behind me.

"Hold still!" he hissed. "Don't fight with us, bitch."

Kicking out and back, aiming for his knee, I connected instead with Ponytail's crotch. He was a lot shorter than me, and he went down to one knee, sweat popping along his jaw and hairline, nostrils flared out. But he didn't fall, and he didn't scream. Tough little bastard.

One of the false cleaning crew wrapped his arms around my torso, crushing my rib cage and lifting me off the ground as I thrashed and screamed. Fitzy and Eckstrom and Javier had to hear me, inside their bunker of stone. *Someone* had to notice a lone woman accosted by five men.

"Fuck off!" I shrieked, struggles degenerating into panicked twitching as I lost air. My attacker didn't seem overly perturbed. He wasn't built but he was very, very strong.

Stronger than me. Maybe even stronger than Dmitri. And that, boys and girls, is Bad News for Our Heroine.

"Let . . . go!"

"Shhh!" my attacker said. *"Mauthka!* She's fucking strong! Get the injection ready!"

The other cleaner grabbed a black nylon kit bag, like you'd carry deodorant and nail files and toothpaste in, and pulled out a disposable syringe. He primed it like battle medics in old movies do and grabbed me by the hair, jerking my neck to one side. I felt the bird's-wing beat of my carotid against my taut skin.

I caught the eye of the man with the needle. "Please don't."

He looked back at me with no flicker of remorse or hesitation. "It's the way things are, Officer Wilder," he said in a pleasantly soft voice that, in another time and place, I would have been glad to have at my hospital bedside.

The needle pricked as it went in and I saw gold halos in front of my eyes. I felt my limbs deaden, and my struggles stopped. My heart beat in a slow-motion *thub-thub*.

I wondered how the men had known my name. I wondered why they had chosen me to take. I wondered if I'd be lucky enough to die quickly.

The cotton haze of unconsciousness slipped over me before I could think of any answers to my questions.

Sunlight, a bar across my eyelids that burned them to dazzling whorls, woke me.

"Ungh," I mumbled. My jaw and all my joints were stiff as if they'd been tarred, and my tongue was glued to the roof of my mouth.

"Hey, hey," said a voice. "She's awake."

"*Mauthka,* that was fast," said another. "Doc, how much did you give her?"

"Enough," he said. "She won't be doing cartwheels for another couple of hours."

"We're here," said a third participant and my rolling, creaking world gently rippled to a stop.

Smell is usually the first thing to come back after I've been drugged, and I got whiffs of gasoline, frying oil from fast food, old carpet. Iron and sweat.

The sun was still in my eyes when the door of the van rolled back and bathed my whole body in light. Sunrise. I'd been out for a few hours, but nothing too serious. Now it would be on with the mutilation and the sewing of skinsuits, I guessed. Testing how well my legs and feet reacted, I determined I couldn't run just yet.

"Get her out," said a fourth. Ponytail's harsh voice from before everything had gone totally FUBAR. I attempted to snarl, snapping my teeth in the direction of the sound.

"Watch it!" Ponytail snapped. "Get rid of her, man. You don't want to be around when she wakes all the way up . . . trust me."

Someone shoved what felt like a steel-toed boot into my side, which my brain noted dimly and then I hit ground, soft and foliage-covered, and rolled down an incline, the flashes of green and orange from the trees and the sky painting themselves into an ugly smear across my vision.

I came to a stop against what I assumed was one of the huge evergreens converging around me to give shade. Every part of me hurt, in that detached, feverish way that only happens when you are well and truly flying.

Also, I was naked.

"Hex this," I whispered, through my sandy lips. I was trying to yell, but all that came out was a wheeze.

Inch by inch, I pushed feeling and motion back into my joints. I'd gotten the crap beat out of me by a were before—drugs had nothing on Joshua Mackelroy's fists and feet. I was better than this. Stronger. Even if my clothes had disappeared.

Get up, Wilder. Get your naked ass moving.

I managed to lean up against the tree and curl into a ball. The sun would be all the way up soon and I just had to find some sort of temporary clothing and then get to a road. My abductors had driven in. There would be a way out.

This theory calmed me until I realized it was getting darker, not brighter. I squinted through the tops of the evergreens, then levered myself up and, scraping my hips and butt on the bark, managed to look around. Shadows were long through the tree limbs and dozens of small skittering sounds started up as rabbits and squirrels and gods-knew-what-else came out to feed.

"Crap," I hissed. "Crap, crap, crap."

I was outside, with no clothes and no light, in the gathering darkness. In a few hours it would be dark, and I had no idea where I was.

And a few hours after that, the full moon would rise.

After I cried, and screamed, and yelled for help with no answers, I started to walk. Back up the hill I found tire tracks pressed into the soft needle covering of the forest floor. "Gotcha, you fuckers," I muttered. I followed the tracks, wincing at the stabs on the soles of my bare feet and the branches and needles lashing everything else, but otherwise feeling pretty good until I fetched up on the bank of a rocky, rushing stream. The tire tracks disappeared on the other side.

"Gods-*damn* it!" I shouted to the forest at large. A flock of small birds took flight at my yelling.

I'm a suburban girl and a city woman. I never liked camping and all that back-to-nature shit. Weres feeling some *connection* to the natural world never held sway with me. I like pavement. I like the smell of mist from Siren Bay mingled with steam from the utility tunnels below Nocturne City's streets. I liked Laundromats, all-night diners, movie theaters, and indoor plumbing.

Clothes and shoes and hair care products, too.

"GI Jane, you are not," I muttered, trying to follow the stream, planting my sore feet in soft moss along the bank without falling into the shallow water. The bastards who attacked me must have driven down the riverbed. Therefore, if I followed it I would find them and subsequently kick their asses hard enough to cause their ancestors discomfort.

Just as long as I did it before moonrise. If I found them afterward, there would be precious little left over for anyone to prosecute.

It was starting to get really dark now, blue-velvet light my only guide between the trees and rocks that hugged close to the bank. This forest was primeval, away from any sort of influence, and it was closer and darker and *bigger* than I had any conception of.

I decided that, should I come through this with my life and dignity intact, I was never leaving the Nocturne City limits again.

The stream wound and dipped through the low places, and I started to hear rushing ahead, the low roar of constant motion after I'd been walking long enough to cause my thighs and calves to glow with pain. "Oh, thank the bright lady," I muttered. I'd lost track of time, but it was full dark, and a silver paleness was starting to creep across the sky.

A highway wasn't ideal, but I'd trade some trucker seeing me naked for a lift back to the city before I phased here, in the open. I had to be close to the mountains, at least two hours from Nocturne. It would be a close call.

The sound grew louder, and then abruptly the land dropped away, and I groaned. A waterfall tipped off the rocky cliff and down to the pool below, creating the bubbling hush that I'd mistaken for traffic.

Sometimes, having were senses really sucks.

I went to my knees on the edge of the cliff and felt the first prickle of honest-to-gods panic crawl its insidious little path up my spine. I let out a snarl, more to reassure myself than anything. Panic kills, in the line of duty or anywhere else. I wasn't going to be one of those documentaries about girls who went into the woods, Little Red Riding Hoods who only turned up when hikers unearthed their skeletons years down the line.

The clouds peeled back to send a shaft of moonlight down on the little crevasse where the waterfall ended and I hissed, scuttling under an evergreen's outstretched branches. If it touched me, I was Hexed to the seven hells.

And then, soundlessly, the moonlight showed me something else. It appeared in the tree line at the edge of the pool, a flicker in the corner of the eye. No more substantial than smoke, it whisked from trunk to trunk and hesitated, all the trailing parts of it flowing back into a cohesive whole at the edge of the water.

Great. I was lost in the woods and it had only taken a few hours for the hallucinations to set in.

I shivered as the temperature dropped. Fog licked around my ankles and spilled out from the stream, thickening fast enough that it couldn't be anything natural.

My heart started to thump faster against my ribs, the thudding of blood all that came to my ears. The night noises had stopped.

I pressed myself against the tree trunk, knowing that I stood a better chance of hiding than making a break for it without being able to see anything in the thick, moisture-laden mist that had grown up through the trees. I could be cool and calm. I could be sensible.

Behind me and far off, a branch cracked, then, after a long pause, another. Closer. The mist swirled, leaving streamers of moisture along my cheeks and shoulders and breasts, and my own breath puffed out against the cold.

Then my ears pricked to a body breathing in concert with my own. Every hair on my body stood on end, and it had nothing to do with the temperature.

"Hex you," I whispered. I would never, ever show whoever was out there how helpless and bare I felt at that moment.

Closer still now, a low meaty chuckle, born from a throat that wasn't human, responded. The laughter deepened and ran together and ended as a low, spine-twisting snarl.

Fuck sensible. I gathered my legs under me, sprang to my feet, and ran like beasts from all seven hells were chasing me.

Trees loomed and sped past through the fog and the weak moonlight, and more than once I felt a rock or a broken branch slice at my feet and legs, but I kept running.

Whatever was behind me made barely more than a whisper of air and fog against my back, but I could feel it, hear it panting as I ran flat-out.

Hours passed, or seemed to, and my side began to cramp as my breaths got shorter and shorter. Even with my extra lung capacity and my dense muscles I was fading fast, and the thing behind me didn't seem to be tiring at all.

I chanced a look over my shoulder and saw nothing but shadow play on light. The branches of the fir trees began to ripple as something passed between them, faster than the eye could see. I saw eyes, silver and pupil-less, and a maw open wide with teeth that gleamed like they were made of mercury. The body was nothing but smoke.

Pain streaked across my cheek and my left arm followed by blood and I fell through a tangle of blackberry brambles and rolled to a stop in a clearing full of some kind of tiny, fragrant white flowers.

From behind me, the thing let out a howl. It wasn't a wolf's howl, or a sound of pain. It sounded like a human scream wrapped up in something ancient, the kind of sound you'd hear in nightmares that you mercifully didn't remember upon waking.

I wiped the blood off my face and out of my eyes from the dozens of tiny scrapes. They would heal, but I had put my blood into the wind and by the crashing of undergrowth the thing had abandoned stealth. It knew it had me.

"Shit," I muttered. "Shit, shit, shit." What erudite last words I was turning out to have.

The mist swirled and parted and a dark shape, at least as high as a horse, began to fade in. All my attempts to breathe and stay calm evaporated. It wasn't a were or a witch, or any daemon I had ever seen.

"Leave me alone!" I screamed, picking up a rock and hurling it at the shape from my prone position. It passed harmlessly through the great outline and thudded away into the darkness.

The fog rolled away as the thing came closer and I caught a flash of a face, of milky silver eyes in the indistinct shadow.

Eyes, and teeth. Too many teeth for one mouth. Too many teeth to be anything but a nightmare-thing . . .

Feeling my body throb and my lungs saw with pain after my sprint, I knew that there was no way I was going anywhere but to my death under the toothy shadow's fangs. It was a monster and I was one were. What could I do?

The clear sky sent a spasm through my lower back, and without even consciously making the decision I rolled to my left, landing on my back, exposed, directly in the shaft of moonlight.

The phase gripped me, sending clear bell tones of pain and pleasure through my skin and nerves and bone. I smiled up at the thing, my teeth already fangs and my eyes turning molten. "Hex you," I snarled.

And then I changed.

I've only given myself over willingly to the phase once before, and that ended with me ripping out a man's throat. This time I felt my limbs give a violent twitch, then another. My back arched as if the most powerful orgasm of my life hand gripped me, and I flipped over onto all fours.

When I didn't try to hold the phase back, it came fast, and hard, like an express train coming around a curve when your car stalls on the tracks.

My fingers and toes curled, sprouted claws, and I felt my jaw dislocate and my spine lengthen and ripple as my body settled into its form of a black wolf.

The pain passed and I had the momentary sensory overload that always comes with a phase, the smells and sounds magnified to levels excruciating for the small scrap of human consciousness that rode on the back of the were.

I could smell the earth, the dampness of the fog, the evergreens winding through everything, and underneath all that something cold and wet like rusted iron, something that didn't belong in the cacophony of the forest.

Whatever time I'd bought myself phasing had run out, and I took off again, now fully able to navigate with the eyes of a wolf. I didn't look back again, just ran and ran. My body still hurt, but my feet were tougher now and I slowly began not to care as the were came to the forefront and my human side subsumed. I would run, escape, hunt, feed . . .

The Thing gave chase and I snarled at it but did not slow my pace. It wanted to take my territory, to hunt me like I was something less than dominant, and while I could not let myself be caught, I couldn't show I was afraid.

Thinking of what it would do to me, how I would deal with prey were our situations reversed, made me taste metal on my tongue from fear and a desire to hunt my own kill. It would rake at my flanks, tear my neck, feast on the meat of my ribs, and break my bones between teeth the size of my snout.

I ran faster, still scenting the metal smell of the Thing, its complete Other-ness to my were senses.

The animal terror of the pursuit dogged me until I burst from the forest onto a plain of scrub brush and high desert rock, my tongue lolling as I scraped up the last reserves of energy, most of it gone to my weak human form before I had become my strong self, my real self that could run and run for hours. The timer had run down.

I crawled under a scrub sagebrush bush to hide, knowing that in the shadows I could watch, be the hunter and not hunted, conceal myself from the Thing and the Terror that wanted to challenge my dominance.

At the edge of the forest I saw the shape, just a

blotty outline even to my eyes. It flowed along the tree line, snarling and prowling as it searched for me.

A howl of rage and frustration floated toward me and then with a flash of silver from its eyes and its open, hungry mouth the Thing turned and disappeared back into the forest.

I panted, head on my front paws, listening and alert as I could be after the chase, until the moon had gone down and dawn began to burn away the smoky blue-gray darkness of the night sky along the horizon. Exhausted, I curled into a ball and fell asleep.

I woke up at dawn, when the sun crested the skyline and I was human again, rocks and twigs poking me in the back and . . . sort of everywhere.

Covered in healing scratches and scrapes, I found deeper cuts on my arms and a painful gash on the sole of my right foot that was still bleeding. I felt as if I'd been dragged behind a stagecoach for maybe four or five days and then gotten really drunk and hit my head repeatedly against a rock.

"Bright lady," I muttered when I tried to sit up and was treated to a display of vertigo and lights spinning in front of my eyes. I made it to my feet and took stock of my sad situation. I was still sans clothes, utterly and completely lost—who knew how far I'd run phased?

On the bright side, I was conscious, most of my minor injuries had healed when I was a were, and Hex it, I was alive.

I started to walk across the open plain, away from the sun. Nocturne City was west—eventually I'd hit ocean, or civilization. Preferably a civilization with some clothes.

As things got hotter and I started to realize just how banged up I was, and how thirsty and hungry and exhausted, I wondered if I'd even seen the thing that had chased me. I was drugged—I remembered that, if nothing else. Had I hallucinated, running blindly through some wild place, and ended up here?

"Does it matter?" I demanded. The sun was almost overhead now, and I could feel a burn starting on my shoulders and back. I crested a hill and almost cried when I saw a small silver Airstream trailer below me, nestled into the desert ravine. A road led away across the rocks, and far away, just visible to my eyes I could see the ink ribbon of a freeway.

I half slid down the hill to the trailer, and crept up on the side with no windows. There was no vehicle outside and no sounds or smells from within, but some laundry hung limply on the line, a man's black work shirt and dungarees.

They were far too big for me, and still damp, and smelled like cheap detergent, but I put them on like they were fine vintage Valentino and began the painful, barefoot walk to the road.

CHAPTER 8

The third truck I tried to flag down pulled over for me. The driver looked me over and shook his head, chewing reflectively on the end of a jerky stick. "Hex me, lady. You sure got put through a wringer."

"That's the nicest possible way of saying it," I muttered. "You going to Nocturne City?"

"Close to it," he said. "Doing a long haul from the other side of the mountains. DVD players. Thought you might be lookin' to hijack me at first."

"If I was planning to jack you I would have put on shoes." I sighed. Once I'd collapsed back into the sweaty, weed-scented seat it was hard to keep my eyes open. The sun heated up the cab and made me sweat a little, and I felt all the cuts and scrapes of the night before sting.

"Guess you would have at that," said the truck driver. "Where you from?"

"The city."

He paused to mumble something into his CB radio. "Got any family?"

"Look, sir, much as I appreciate the lift I'm not in much of a talking mood."

"Hey, now," he said. "I'm just tryin' to make sure that whoever worked you over ain't gonna find you again."

"If they do," I said, "they'll also find the business end of my service weapon." Right now, tired and sore and still shaky from being abducted and drugged, I knew for a certain fact that if I ever saw any of the men who kidnapped me again, I'd kill them. There wouldn't be any discussion or internal debate. One shot, right between the eyes, like the person who killed Bertrand and the other weres.

Justice.

"You in the army or something?" said the truck driver. "Doesn't look like you've got a gun under there."

"I used to have one," I said. "Before I was kidnapped from my parking lot, drugged, stripped naked, and thrown into the nature preserve to die. Is that enough information for us to ride the rest of the way in silence?"

The trucker blinked once, long and slow. "Yeah. Sure. So you're not some kind of assassin?"

"I'm a SWAT officer," I said. "And I'm very tired."

He shut up and let me be, and I fell asleep, only waking up when we pulled into a gas station on Highway 21.

"Far as I go before my turnoff," said the trucker. He fished in the ashtray amid the roach butts and pressed two dollars in quarters into my palm. "You got someone you can call for a ride?"

"Yes, yes," I said impatiently. "Thanks for the lift. You can call the SWAT Division of the Nocturne City PD if you need to be reimbursed for your mileage."

"Shit, don't mention it," he said as I dismounted the cab. "Always happy to help a lady in distress."

"All men should be like you," I muttered, and picked my way across the blacktop to the bank of pay phones. My foot had stopped bleeding at least.

I hesitated after I fed the phone my quarters. I could call the cottage, where Dmitri would surely have worked himself into high dudgeon over my being gone with no explanation. Did I have enough change to convince him that I'd been abducted by crazies rather than out having a torrid affair?

That would only end in screaming with the mood I was in. I dialed Sunny's number instead.

"Luna!" she shrieked when I identified myself. I held the phone away from my head, shaking it to dispel the feedback.

"Sunny, what's wrong?"

"You're what's wrong!" she shouted. "Are you okay? Your team said you didn't show up and Dmitri came home and didn't know where you were . . . everyone's in an uproar. But you're all right!"

"Well I was, right up until you ruptured my eardrum," I said. "Sunny, I need you to do me a favor and tell Bryson to come pick me up."

"Not me?" She sounded confused. "Not Dmitri?"

"Definitely not Dmitri," I said.

"Luna, he's been going crazy."

Great, now I felt like a world-class bitch in addition to crap. "Sunny, I was kidnapped."

That started another litany of shrieking and rapid chatter. "Calm down!" I finally yelled. "I'm okay!" How close I had come to not being okay, my cousin would never know.

"I'm . . . I just . . ." She breathed in and out a few times. "There have been so many times when I thought it'd be the last time I saw you, Luna."

"Not this time," I said, trying to be conciliatory. Normally I'm not very good at it, and right then I flat-out sucked. "But the fact remains that I'm a kidnap victim and Bryson needs to take my statement as soon as possible and collect any evidence that might be on me."

."Okay," said Sunny. "I'll call the Twenty-fourth. What's the number there?"

I gave it to her and hung up, watching the traffic swoop past on the highway and trying not to think about the previous hours.

Bryson showed up in an hour or so and said, "Jesus juggling flaming swords, Wilder. You look like a hermit."

"Thanks, David. That suit you've got on makes you look dead."

He touched the lapels of his powder-blue number protectively. "Don't gotta get all pissy."

"I just spent a night naked in the woods," I said. "Trust me, now is not the time for rebuking."

He opened the car door for me, at least, and made sure I was buckled in before heading back to the city.

"So what happened?" said Bryson.

"I . . ." I saw the men's faces, blurred under the street lamps, and felt the needle prick my neck. After that, until I'd woken up under the bush, there was so little I remembered that wasn't blurred with fear . . . "I don't wanna talk about it until I have to."

"One thing," said Bryson. "D'you think it's the same people that offed the other four?"

The men had let me see their faces, unconcerned. Methodical. They hadn't expected me to still be alive.

"Yeah," I said. "I think so."

"Shit," Bryson muttered, gripping the steering wheel hard. "Why does my life get so gods-damn complicated every time you show up, Wilder?"

"Sorry," I yawned. "Next time I'll try harder not to get drugged and thrown in the back of a van."

We made it to the hospital and Bryson made me wait in the car while he went and got a pair of flip-flops for me to wear in. "David, you're being nice and it's really freaking me out," I told him.

"Don't take it personal," he said. "You're a witness now. I need you in good shape to make a statement."

In the ER, people stared. Patients, doctors, and everyone gave me at least a startled glance. I felt my face heat. "Can I get a curtain, please?" I hissed at Bryson.

"Yeah," he said. "I called ahead. The CSU tech should be here any second."

The doors to Emergency hissed back and Pete Anderson appeared, carrying a steel case and looking harried.

"Hey, Detective," he called when he spotted us. Bryson and I both started to reply, then Pete really took a look at me and his eyes widened.

"Officer Wilder, are you . . . ? I mean, what happened?"

"I need you to do a collection on her clothes and anything else you might find," said Bryson. Pete nodded, still looking at me. We'd met on the Duncan case, when he was an AV geek and I was suspended from the force. He'd gotten field-certified and shaved his head, and contact lenses made him almost look like an action hero.

"Okay, Officer. I'm following you."

"She ain't PD today, son," said Bryson. "She's a vic. Do your job."

"I'm showing respect," said Pete. "If the situation were reversed, I doubt you'd take kindly to me ordering you to strip down." Pete and Bryson had never gotten along, but I jabbed Bryson in the arm before he could say something that made Pete punch him. A nurse in pink scrubs decorated with flying hearts came and led me to an examination area, where she handed me a paper gown. I stripped behind the curtain and put my clothes into the paper bags that Pete had provided. He taped them up and initialed them, then combed the dirt and sticks in my hair into a bindle.

He looked me over. "You had it rough, Luna."

"Pete, you have no idea."

"You catch the creeps that did this, I will be happy to personally put a foot up their ass," he said.

"You're gonna have to stand in line behind me and my cousin and my very large boyfriend," I said.

The nurse returned with a plastic box about the size of a Tupperware sandwich carrier. "Mr. Anderson, could I get you to step outside? I need to perform a rape kit on Miss Wilder."

"No," I said, before Pete could react. "I wasn't raped."

"Standard procedure," she said, putting on gloves and beginning to arrange the swabs. "It won't take long and it doesn't hurt. Please lie back on the table."

Pete touched my shoulder and then made a hasty exit. "I wasn't raped," I said again, louder.

"Miss Wilder, with all due respect," said the nurse. "You were drugged for nearly a day. You don't know what might have happened. We'll give you the morning-after pill to be safe."

Inside me, down where the butterflies in your stomach usually live, everything went cold. My vision spun away from the sterile beige-and-blue examination room just for a second and I was fifteen again, scratchy carpet under my naked back, a heavy arm across my chest, and thick, drunken fingers tugging at the waistband of my cutoff shorts. Pain in my neck as he sank his teeth in . . .

"Miss Wilder?" said the nurse. "Should I page Dr. Bradshaw?"

"Just make this fast," I said. I was here. Not in Joshua's van. Not getting the bite. Here, thirty years old, in the hospital, in control. Joshua hadn't gotten his chance to rape me. I wasn't a victim.

"If you'd feel more comfortable with a sedative . . ."

"Look, lady, what part of 'fast' isn't sinking in?" I snapped. "Can we do this without platitudes? I don't need the post-trauma speech. I know it by heart already."

She did the rape kit and I kept my eyes on the fluorescent light above my head, staring until I saw stars in front of my vision.

The nurse gave me extra scrubs to put on along with the flip-flops, and I swallowed the pill before I went back to Bryson, clenching and unclenching my fists to contain the claws that threatened to sprout inside.

"You ready to go make your statement?" he asked, following me out the door. I stood and breathed the outside air for a few minutes to calm myself down, and dispel the stink of Joshua Mackelroy, my progenitor and would-be rapist, from my memory.

He'd made me a were, but he didn't own me, not then and not ever.

"Yeah," I said to Bryson finally. "I'm ready."

Nobody at the Twenty-fourth looked at me when Bryson led me through the back entrance. Detectives and uniforms studiously averted their eyes as we walked through the squad room to the interview closet. It really had been a closet, and now it was a slightly more friendly version of the interrogation rooms.

Matilda Morgan, the Twenty-fourth's captain, came out of her office as we passed and stopped me. "Officer Wilder. I was so sorry to hear about your attack."

Morgan and I had a rocky relationship when I

worked under her, and I wasn't exactly sure that we'd parted on good terms. She'd signed my transfer without so much as a flicker of emotion in her icy eyes or a hint of disapproval around her prim mouth. "Thanks, Captain," I said. I was too tired to even attempt to spar.

"Lieutenant McAllister is waiting for you in the interview room. He was quite perturbed as well," she said. She patted me awkwardly on the shoulder, reaching up from her short, round height to do it. I hissed as she hit one of the spots that I'd pulled running and phasing, and she whipped her hand back to her side. "Detective Bryson, please see me after your interview is over."

"Yes, ma'am," he said meekly. I couldn't resist a half smile after Morgan walked away.

"She trained you good, David," I said.

"If you weren't an invalid right now I'd smack you," he muttered.

"Kinky," I commented. Troy McAllister leapt to his feet as soon as we opened the door to the interview closet, long limbs going everywhere.

"Luna!" He offered me a chair and whispered, "What the Hex happened to you?"

"I wish I knew, Mac," I said. Unlike Morgan, I *had* regretted leaving Mac behind. He was a good cop, a good friend, and a genuinely decent guy who had accepted me being were without so much as a raised eyebrow above his slate-blue, unflappable gaze. If it didn't impact my case work, it didn't bother Mac. If I was into that touchy-feely crap, I'd say he was almost brotherly.

Bryson turned on his digital recorder and said, "You wanna stay and observe, LT?"

"If it's all right with you," said Mac. "Get going, David. Let's not keep Luna here any longer than she has to be."

"Thanks, Mac," I murmured. Honestly, I didn't mind being at the Twenty-fourth nearly as much after what had happened. It was familiar and secure, and even if Bryson's cologne was stinking up the tiny room, it was seven long hells better than being stranded in the wilderness.

"Okay," said Bryson. "This is Detective David Bryson interviewing Luna Wilder in connection with her kidnapping and also a series of four homicides, case numbers 33457, 33420, 33458, and 33409. Luna, can you state your full name for the record?"

I swallowed, my throat feeling very dry and closed. "Luna Joanne Wilder."

"And what is your occupation?" Bryson used a clipped tone that was almost professional, and totally foreign to me. I looked into his pinched face and saw that he was as uncomfortable as I was.

"I'm a SWAT officer with the Nocturne City Police Department."

"Uh-huh, and can you describe what happened in the course of your kidnapping?"

"I was paged to a scene with Tac-3," I said. "I arrived at the Justice Plaza and was accosted by three men who were apparently drunk . . ."

Thinking about how fast they'd come up on me, how easily I'd been subdued, made me squirm. I was supposed to be better, stronger than that.

"And?" said Bryson. McAllister glared at him.

"They distracted me, and two more men got out of a van from the cleaning service the city uses. They subdued me and gave me an injection of something and then drove me out of the city." I licked my lips. "After that the next thing I remember is waking up in the woods."

"Can you describe the men?" said Bryson.

"Darker skin. Black hair. One of them had a pony-tail and silver buttons on his shirt."

"Anything distinctive you got a look at?" said Bryson.

"No," I said. The interview closet was starting to get very warm, or that may have been my abject humiliation.

"Did you get a license number off the van?"

"No."

"Did you see *anything* that could be useful in getting these guys?" Bryson demanded.

"I was *drugged,* David," I snarled at him. "You try playing Sherlock Holmes when you're stoned out of your gourd."

"Sherlock Holmes *was* stoned out of his—" he started.

"Ease up, Bryson," said McAllister shortly. "Move on."

I gave him a grateful half smile, but I was doubly sorry he had to be around to hear about how badly I'd let things go FUBAR this time.

"Fine, fine," Bryson muttered. "After you woke up in the woods, what then?"

"Then," I said, "then, it was a really long fucking night and I finally managed to find the highway and get back to the city."

"C'mon, Wilder," said Bryson. "I'm not stupid. What else?"

"That's debatable," I muttered. It seemed like the thing behind me, the noises, the certainty that if I didn't run I would die were years ago, not last night.

"Luna, help him out," said Mac. "Gods know he needs it."

"There was . . . something, in those woods," I said. "I don't know what it was, but it wasn't a human or a were. I'm sure I got left there for it to hunt. Those people didn't expect me to get away."

"How did you?" Bryson asked. I looked him straight in the eye.

"I ran like hell, David."

"Okay." He reached over and flicked off the recorder. "Off the record. You got any enemies, besides the ones I know about? You been poking people that don't want to be poked? I know you, Luna. You could piss off a nun."

"Considering that the O'Halloran case tanked my career and I have no personal life, David, no." I crossed my arms and dared him to pry harder. I'd already gone over a list of anyone who could want me dead. Mostly, they were dead themselves. I didn't plan it that way, but it was fact. I had no idea why I'd been chosen.

It infuriated me.

Mac cleared his throat at Bryson after he stared at me with the fish-eyed expression for a few seconds too long. Bryson smoothed his tie and recovered. "All right. Thanks, Luna. You want me to take you home? We've already got uniforms on the place in case they try again."

"No," I said. "I want to stay and go over case files. The guy who snatched me might be in there."

Mac and Bryson exchanged a look. "What?" I demanded.

"Luna," said Mac, "you're part of this case now. I couldn't let you assist Bryson any longer even if I wanted to."

"So I'm supposed to just go *home*?" I hissed. "They tried to kill me! I can't just sit on my ass and do nothing about that, and you shouldn't ask me to!"

"It's what I'd ask of any victim," said Mac. "Not just

you. Go home, Luna. Sit tight, let Dmitri pamper you, and we'll call as soon as we have any news."

"Yeah, there's a huge Hexed chance of that," I snapped, then got up and stomped out of the interview room, slamming the door hard enough to rip the handle out of the frame.

Sunny picked me up without asking any questions. She was quiet most of the way to the cottage except to make sure I wasn't grievously injured and left me off in the driveway. I knew she was working herself into a royal snit about me getting myself hurt—again—so I didn't push for conversation.

"Wait," I said when she put the car in gear to drive away. "Can you . . . come in?"

Sunny's eyebrows crinkled. "Everything okay between you and Dmitri?"

"Have things ever been 'okay' between me and Dmitri?"

She shut off the ignition and walked with me to the cottage, where Dmitri jerked the door open with a wild, black-eyed expression on his face.

"Where the Hex have you been?"

"The police station," I said wearily. "Giving a statement."

I expected more yelling, but I didn't expect Dmitri to grab me and crush me to him, kissing my forehead and my eyelids and finally my lips, long and slow enough that my wire-strung body finally relaxed a bit.

"I came back and you weren't here," he murmured against my lips. "I thought you . . . well . . . I don't know what I thought. Luna, I can't lose you."

"I'll just go make some chocolate milk for Luna,"

said Sunny, slipping past us. "She used to like that after a hard day . . ."

"Sweetheart, I'm okay," I whispered into Dmitri's neck. "I'm here."

"Come on," he said, wrapping his arm around my shoulder. "Let's get you upstairs."

I let myself lean on Dmitri as he guided me to lie back on the bed and got me clean pajamas and a washcloth. He dabbed the dirt off my face, his breathing next to my ear going rough and hot.

"Something the matter?" I asked.

He stopped washing my face, and looked up at me, and then crushed one of my hands in his. "Luna, I'm sorry."

I blinked. "Sorry for what?"

"This . . . what happened . . . this is all my fault."

"Oh, Dmitri." I squeezed his hand. "Don't be silly. None of this was anyone's fault, except maybe the bastards who kidnapped me."

"No!" he growled, hitting the headboard. "If I had been there, I could have protected you! If I had just made you listen . . ."

I removed my hand from his grasp. "Hey."

He stopped mid-tirade. "What's wrong? Are you hurt? Do you need your pain medication?"

"Do I *look* like I need my damn pain medication?" I put my hands over my face and pushed the tangled black mass that on good days was my hair away from it. "Dmitri, the only thing that would have happened if you'd been there is that you'd be as banged up as I am, or worse. These people knew what they were doing. Nothing you *or* I could have done differently would change what happened."

Before my internal censor could suggest that the

next words were maybe not the best idea, they were out. "Believe it or not, Sandovsky, not everything that happens *around* you is *about* you. If you were really concerned, you'd be asking what you could do to find the sons of bitches that did this."

"Oh, they're dead," said Dmitri. "That's a given. Luna, I understand that you're upset . . ."

"No," I said softly. "You don't. I want someone to stand next to me, not in front of me. I'm going to deal with the people who did this to me in my own way. What I'd really like is to know that you'll help me, not chastise me."

He paced away to all the corners of our bedroom, the cords in his arms standing out as he looked for something to hurt . . .

"When you went missing," he said finally, looking out the window at the gentle whitecaps rolling under the afternoon sun outside, "my first thought wasn't that you were cheating, or stolen. I thought *Well, man, that's it. She finally got sick of your ass and she left.* I promised that if you came back I'd try to do better. But you make it so goddamn hard, Luna."

"You don't make it easy, either," I told him.

"I'll back off this thing," said Dmitri, and his jaw twitched even speaking the promise. I knew it went against every instinct he had as a pack were. Pack weres avenged wrongs done to their mates. They protected them. But I didn't want that, and I knew it wounded him.

"Thank you," I said. I stood up, even though it hurt, and went to him, leaning my cheek against his back. I slid my arms around his waist and swayed as he swayed, listening to his heartbeat echo itself. "I love you, Dmitri," I murmured. "I like it when things are like this. Let's try it more often."

He purred as my fingers stroked over his stomach and then sighed. "Luna," he said. "I'll back off here, but you have to promise me something."

I went stiff before I could stop myself. "What?"

"If I leave you to dispense justice on this, you let me make you a Redback. Once and for all, you and me. Together."

I jerked away from him and crossed my arms, breath coming in furious little pants. "Not *this*. Not *again*."

Dmitri threw up his hands. "What? What's so un-fucking-reasonable about wanting my mate to be committed?"

"You don't get to attach some kind of gods-damn *conditions* to any of this!" I shouted. "This happened to *me* and *I* am gonna be the one to see it through. I want your help, Dmitri, but I don't want this!"

"Well, tough shit, princess, because this is what you signed on for!" He jabbed his finger over the place where his heart beat. "I look after my women, and I don't let them run off and get hurt!"

"I'm not your *property*," I shrieked, "and maybe if you'd done a little bit better job of looking after *your women*, Lilia would still be alive and I wouldn't feel second-class whenever you bring up your fucking pack!"

Dmitri stopped, just froze in mid-shout like I'd zapped him with a stun gun. "Shit," I said, the words slipping out and tumbling over one another like water as I tried to make right what I had just done. "Dmitri, I'm sorry. That was so uncalled-for. Lilia and you is none of my business."

"It's like that?" he asked me, and I could tell that he was close to losing control, that the daemon was cleaving his conscious mind with a desire for my blood.

Lilia was Dmitri's former mate, before he and I even met. She died at the hand of a serial killer, and Dmitri still moaned her name in the night, when he tossed and sweated in his sleep.

"No," I said. "No, it's *not* like that. I love you, Dmitri. I'm just not sure how to make this work. You don't want me Insoli, I don't want to be . . . committed. I just haven't figured it out yet, but I *will*. I will." I was begging and I pressed my fingers over my gritty eyes, disgusted with the whole situation.

"I'm leaving before I do and say something I regret," Dmitri almost whispered.

"I'm sorry . . . ," I started again.

"You should be," he snarled. That got my hackles up again.

"Fine, if you're gonna be a child, then Hex you!" I yelled.

Dmitri spun to leave and almost walked into Sunny, who entered the room carefully balancing three mugs on a tray. She looked at me, at Dmitri's rage-clouded face, and gave a game smile.

"Who's for chocolate milk?"

CHAPTER 9

"He's not coming back," I said after Sunny had gone to the window for the fiftieth time. It was dark, but not much cooler. "Hex him. I'm so sick of his *Join me or die* bullshit."

"You might try being a little more understanding," Sunny said severely. "To him, it looks like you don't care enough to even consider it."

I held up my hand. "I do not need to be getting this in stereo. I'm me. I'm not a Redback. Why does he have to change me? I'm not a DVD player he can take back to the store and trade up. I'm not here to be a silent partner for his rage issues."

"Tell him that," said Sunny, and I heard the rumble of the bike. I groaned and put my hands over my eyes.

"You want my advice?" Sunny said as the bike's headlamp swept the living room.

"No."

"You accuse Dmitri of being selfish, but you're being self-righteous. Every time he brings up the pack thing, it's an excuse to fight. You like fighting. Stop it. Say no and let that be the end."

And of course, being Sunny, she made perfect sense. I growled. "Maybe if I hadn't been chased through the woods by a hellbeast made of fog and teeth, I'd be more inclined to listen, Dr. Phil."

"Hellbeast?" said Dmitri from the doorway.

Sunny spread her hands. "News to me. What happened, Luna?"

I told them about the thing. Thinking about how it had moved, how rocks passed through it, how it moved so inhumanly fast . . .

"I probably just hallucinated it," I said. "I mean, it sounds like Dracula, and vampires are firmly in the Don't Exist column."

"Yes . . . ," Sunny replied slowly. "But there *are* things that drink blood. Or were . . . they're extinct now."

"Tell that to the thing in the woods," I muttered. I tried to stand, and my foot spasmed. Dmitri caught me. "Easy."

"There are texts that I studied when I was training with our grandmother that mentioned shapeshifters other than weres," Sunny said. "Skinwalkers, kitsune, Wendigo. But they've all died out in territorial wars, hundreds or thousands of years ago."

"Wendigo," I said, seizing on the only name that sounded familiar. "What are they?"

"Fucking savages," Dmitri rumbled from where he held me, one arm lightly around my waist.

I twisted to look at him in surprise. "You know about this?"

He set his jaw and didn't meet my eyes. "All pack weres around here do."

I pushed away and faced him. "And you were just going to keep that to yourself, then?"

Dmitri sighed and rubbed his forehead. "Luna, the Wendigo are nothing you want to get involved with. Trust me on this."

"You say that about a lot of things, Dmitri, and in case you haven't noticed that hasn't stopped me yet," I snapped. "Spill it."

"Yes, do," said Sunny, coming to my shoulder. I felt the uncomfortable prickle of her power on the back of my neck. Sunny might not show it nearly as often, but she got angry as easily as me.

Dmitri looked between us, nostrils flaring. "I hate it when you two gang up on me. You know that."

"Tell me," I growled.

"Fine!" Dmitri said. "Wendigo are barbarians, monsters who have no decency and no humanity. It's no wonder that one attacked you. They hate weres. They hate humans. All they know how to do is consume."

"You're using the present tense," I told Dmitri quietly.

"Yeah, I am," he said. "They're still out there, but nowhere in our city, you can be sure of that."

"Why would a Wendigo attack Luna?" said Sunny.

"Better question," I said. "Why did a bunch of psychopaths kidnap me and leave me for a Wendigo to hunt?"

"I can't help you with that one," Dmitri said. "I don't get involved with that. Redbacks don't deal with Wendigo and we like it that way. Packs that do always end up fucked over because that's what happens when you deal with monsters."

"Your delicate sensibilities aside, where could I find these things?" I asked.

Dmitri crossed his arms. "I put my foot down there, Luna. A Wendigo almost killed you, and you're not going to rush in like you always do and make things worse."

"Hey," said Sunny. "Don't talk to her like that. I didn't see you showing up to save the day when she got kidnapped."

"You stay out of this!" Dmitri rumbled. "You couldn't understand all the politics at play. If a were confronted the Wendigo, the repercussions would be disastrous for all of us. Luna just doesn't understand what consequences her recklessness might have."

"Oh, I know you didn't just tell me to sit in the corner like a good little woman while the men keep me safe from the big bad monsters," Sunny said. "I think you're forgetting who stepped in when Alistair Duncan was about to arrest you, and who looked out for Luna for all that time when you just *left* . . ."

"Okay, *enough*!" I bellowed. "Both of you. Sunny, you're being rude. Dmitri, stop telling me what to do."

"Luna, I *can't* let you go looking for the Wendigo," said Dmitri. "If you contact them, every pack in this city will be out for your blood. Packs that use them as underground hitters guard their assets jealously, and everyone else will see you as a traitor to weres."

"Somebody already is," I snapped. "Gerard Duvivier. I just have to find evidence."

Dmitri stopped pacing and frowned. "No. That doesn't follow. The Loup are small-time and they mostly deal with plain humans. No way would they go after weres in other packs. They'd get their entrails strung out over a ten-block radius."

"But . . . ," I started, and then realized he was right. The murderer was the same four times over, and Duvivier didn't fit. Something about the deaths was hidden, like the thing in the nighttime forest.

"Okay," I said. "Then I have to go to the source. I have to meet the Wendigo."

Dmitri came to me and wrapped his arms around my shoulder. My head clunked against his collarbone and I left my arms at my sides. "Why does it always have to be you?" he whispered into my hair. "Why can't you leave this one?"

"Because it's my job," I said, putting my hands on either side of his face and looking into his eyes. "And if I live with this, I'll have to be afraid for the rest of my life."

Dmitri's eyes went hard as jewels, not black and not passionate. Not the eyes I knew at all. "I guess you'll do what you'll do," he said finally. "Like always. I'm going to go make us some dinner. Sunny, you staying?"

She nodded mutely.

"Well, that could have gone better," I said to Sunny after Dmitri had disappeared into the kitchen.

"He's just worried about you," Sunny said. "It'll blow over." She was a terrible liar.

"Forget it," I muttered. "How are we going to find these Wendigo? I mean, are they always so . . . hungry? And misty?"

"Texts say that most of the time, they're human," said Sunny. "The Wendigo change can only be passed by blood, and they only change when they hunt. But . . . they hunt a lot. Almost every recorded sighting of a Wendigo has been in, um, creature form. And that's just the witches who lived to tell about it later."

I went into the kitchen, where Dmitri was chopping carrots like they'd insulted his mother. "Where are they?"

"Who?" he grunted.

"The Wendigo. You *have* to know, even if the Redbacks didn't deal with them. A community of people doesn't just disappear into the landscape." No matter how romantic it seems for gangs of outlaws to roam a state forest, a group of any size needs food and shelter and bathrooms, and people notice that sort of thing.

"I haven't changed my mind," Dmitri said. "I'm not helping you do something this foolish. Wendigo and weres stay apart for a reason, Luna. Trust me."

"Fine," I said. "If you won't do it for me, then think about the four people they've killed so far. Three of them were good people, at least."

Dmitri stopped chopping and jammed the knife into the cutting board. "Damn it."

"Please, Dmitri."

"The abandoned Paiute reservation," he said. "Out past the fireworks stand on the interstate. That's the last I heard of them."

I touched his shoulder and then went to the front entry and got my gun, badge, and a map of Las Rojas County.

"Hey!" Sunny said. "You're not going out there alone?"

"Unless you want to get turned into jerky snacks," I said, "then yes. I'm on my own."

"Far be in from me to stand in the way of the charge of the Luna brigade, but you're bleeding," Sunny said. I looked at the floor where I was standing barefoot, and saw a crimson print. I hit the wall.

"Hex me." I couldn't very well go wandering into a Wendigo nest with a bloody cut. I'd seen what blood did to weres—I could only imagine the reaction something like the thing in the forest would have. Even though the cottage was stuffy, I shivered. "I hate this," I said aloud to Sunny. "I can't access any of the case files and

David isn't sharing information with me anymore, not with Mac and Morgan staring at the back of his head."

"What would you advise me to do?" Sunny asked, folding her arms. I pressed an old sock over the re-opened cut on my foot and glared at nothing. "Well?" she demanded. Even though she was smaller than me, with a cherubic face and angelic farm-girl falls of wavy brown hair, Sunny had a grit to her that I lacked. She got what she wanted, one way or another, and kept smiling politely the whole time.

"I don't think you'll ever investigate a murder, dear cousin, much as I have supreme faith in your witchy powers."

"It must get awfully dark inside your box, Luna. Step outside it for two seconds."

"Gods, you're bitchy," I said. "All right. I'd try to find a link between the four victims and myself. Dig into their backgrounds. Find out what they didn't tell us. Rattle their closet skeletons until something breaks."

She grinned at me. "What are we waiting for? The library's open late."

The downtown branch of the Nocturne City Library looks the way a library should look: gray granite on the outside, somber wood and hushed voices and the smell of a million dusty pages on the inside. A bronze statue of Jeremiah Chopin regarded Sunny and me with blank, gleaming eyes as we mounted the steps and passed through the iron-bound front doors.

We went down the marble steps to the cool, slightly misty-feeling basement that housed the newspaper morgue, the genealogical society's records, and the computer lab.

"This would be so much easier with a police computer," I muttered, sitting down at one of the battered gray terminals.

"Even cops use Google," said Sunny. She had a point there. "Give me two of the names and I'll see what I can find." I gave her Priscilla Macleod and Jin Takehiko, keeping Aleksandr Belodis and Bertrand Lautrec for myself.

We surfed in silence for a few moments before Sunny said, "The Macleods have a history in Nocturne City. The historical society has a bunch of pages on them." She typed for a moment. "The Takehikos, too. Mariko Takehiko was the first woman *and* the first immigrant to own her own business in the city limits. They still own a textile import business. Lots of charity work."

"Sweet," I muttered. "Legit, charitable weres. What about the Macleods?" Similar pithy, congratulatory statements were turning up on my screen concerning the Lautrec family—financiers who rivaled the big downtown firms, at least until Bertrand took a left turn into drug pushing—and alarming clips about the Belodises, who escaped Latvia ahead of some horrific political regime and went from a single tavern on the waterfront to the sort of verbiage that newspapers use to dance around organized crime.

Well, the Viskalcis looked the part.

"Macleod . . . lawyers, until the early 1950s," said Sunny. "Theodore Macleod was disbarred for jury tampering in a corruption trial. After that, the family sort of fades away . . ." Her breath hitched. "Get this: the police detective on trial for taking bribes? His name was Jim McAllister."

I rolled my ergonomic stool over to Sunny's terminal

and looked at the photo. Aside from a comb-over so shiny with Brylcreem it could deflect a laser and a slightly more sullen set to his face, the man in the picture could have been Mac, down to the half-smoked Lucky Strike clamped between his lips.

"I didn't know Lieutenant McAllister's father was involved in the scandals," said Sunny.

"Everyone was in deep to the were packs back then," I said. "Cops, crooks . . . they ran this city." The Macleod trail dried up after the trial and their money and name went the same way so many weres did as the twentieth century wore on—straight down.

"So," said Sunny, tapping her teeth with her index finger. "All old families. All strong packs. What's it mean, Luna?"

Something tickled me, in the part of my brain that's the first to see the caravan of hunches coming around the bend, and I stood up. "Let's take a look at some papers, Sunny."

She followed me to the newspaper morgue and with the help of a mostly mute reference librarian we located the first five years of the *Nocturne City Inquirer,* the paper Jeremiah Chopin had founded when he built his city on top of timber and tide flats.

The papers were sparse for the first year, four or five pages each, most of the stories written by one Emmaline Stout, with a chatty style and questionable grammar. Most of the photos were Jeremiah Chopin felling a tree for the new city hall, Nocturne City's chief engineer driving the spike into the end of the Northern Pacific Railway line to connect Nocturne and Seattle, the skeletal frame of the Blackburn mansion going up on the site that in thirty years would be Nocturne University.

In year three, a column by a Spiritualist called Mortimer Edgars appeared. Sunny shook her head as we read the tiny, crooked type. "This guy was on the far side of nutty-nuts, let me tell you."

Edgars talked mostly about his "companion spirits," who prophesized that there would be reliable train transportation to Mars in the next fifty years, but occasionally he delved into witches, weres, and daemons, and got most of the facts wrong every time. Angry letters to the editor from families whom Edgars had smeared became prevalent.

Edgar's last column was titled "On Foreigners" and it began, *Do not mistake my usage of the word 'foreigners' to mean those denizens of Nocturne from the dark continent or the shores of Araby . . .*

"This is going to make me lose my lunch," said Sunny. "The purple prose alone would be enough to stun an elephant."

"Patience," I said. Edgars continued, *No, dear readers, I speak of a far more insidious menace: those that bear a friendly face of comparable color and composure to your own but who underneath hide the most dastardly and blasphemous of secrets . . . the secret of the Non-Human . . .*

"Hex me," I muttered, skipping ahead. If Edgars had attempted to out the witches and weres of Nocturne, he was suicidal as well as a terrible writer.

These so-called wear-wolves don human guises, and their families and clans are numerous and far-flung. The primary clans that I have investigated (and indeed, who claim to be the original five in our fair city, with pride!) include the Warwolves, the Loup, the Oriental Ookami, and the strange and reclusive Viskalcis.

"Holy shit," I muttered, already reaching for the PRINT key on the document scanner's terminal. "It's them," I explained to Sunny. "It's all the packs of the dead weres."

"Luna," said Sunny in a tight voice, "read the last bit."

But the most prideful and ostentatious and indeed hateful of these Wear-wolf clans, and the one who has the unmitigated nerve to claim that they are the city's protectors, are the Serpent Eye. A rough and unrefined lot . . .

I felt like someone had injected ice water directly into my heart. "No," I said.

If you want to get technical about it, I *chose* to be Insoli. Joshua, the were who gave me the bite, was a Serpent Eye. If I'd stayed with Joshua instead of running like heaven and hell were after me, I'd be one of them now. Prideful and ostentatious and hateful, just like him.

"Why me?" I asked Sunny, loudly and desperately. The librarian shushed us. "I'm not a Hexed Serpent Eye," I hissed at her. The printer whirred and spit out my selections and I grabbed them in a fist, practically running from the room. Sunny followed me, lugging my shoulder bag.

"Luna, there's got to be an explanation."

"The explanation is that Joshua couldn't screw me that first night so now he's gonna screw me any way he can!" I said. "It's his fault those sons of bitches came after me!"

"Joshua disappeared six months ago," said Sunny. "Really, Luna, he's probably on some Mexican beach. How could he have engineered four murders when he's in hiding from the feds and the SEC?"

"Okay," I said, forcing myself to breathe normally. "Assuming Joshua is incidental in all this, then what's the link beyond pack?"

"Family," said Sunny simply, pushing open the door to the genealogy room. "All of the dead weres are descendants of the first families of the first packs in the city."

"Makes sense," I agreed, a little bugged that I hadn't seen the connection first, "but they'd have no reason to go after me. I'm nobody in the scheme of the Serpent Eye. Hex it, I'm *not* Serpent Eye." I kicked the nearest file cabinet with a growl.

"Joshua is," said Sunny. "Maybe they wanted to get to him and so went to you?"

"That doesn't make any sense—we fucking hate each other's guts," I said, "and anyway, Serpent Eyes increase their pack with the bite, not by birth, so . . ." I trailed off as I saw where my logic had led me. "Oh, crap."

Sunny looked up from the census record she was scanning. "What?"

"Serpent Eyes make mates and pack members by the bite and always have," I said. "Crap. Crap. *Crap.*"

"Stop with the 'crap' and tell me what's wrong!" Sunny snapped. I put my face in my hands and groaned.

"I have to find Joshua Mackelroy."

I left Sunny and drove myself to Batista's subdivision. The same three house patterns repeated over and over again, Day-Glo lawns, the whole bit. Out of all the men in Tac-3, Batista was the one I trusted. Mostly because he was the only one who'd never made a comment, intended kindly or not, about me being un-human. It just didn't seem to register. He reminded me of Mac, if Mac was a gun-toting Puerto Rican.

Batista looked just this side of stunned when I turned up on his doorstep. "Javier, I need a favor and I need you not to ask any questions," I said when he answered the bell.

"Luna," he said, sounding nonplussed. "You holding up okay? Heard you got slapped all to hell when those *putos* snatched you. Shouldn't you be resting or something?"

"I'm fine, fine," I said. "But I really need this, Javier. Help me out?"

"You know I'd do anything for anyone on the team," Javier said. He cast a look over his shoulder. A late-night talk show blared from farther inside the house. "Marisol's in the kitchen," he said. "But we can talk." He stood aside and let me in, taking us into a small study. Marisol's hand was obvious in here, too—pictures of kittens decorated the wall, and the carpet was pale green. "What's up, Wilder?"

"I need you to log on to the FBI database and look up the last known whereabouts of a subject. Name's Mackelroy, Joshua." I paced, the memories I had of Joshua making it impossible to sit.

Batista paused in his typing on his sleek computer. "Why do you need me to do that?"

I bit my lip before I told him. "This is my case, Javier. My . . . my kidnapping. If anyone at the Twenty-fourth finds out I'm digging . . ."

"Okay, okay," Batista said. "I get it. But if anyone in the department finds out about this I am *not* losing my pension. *¿Comprende?*"

"Crystal," I said. Batista typed and I looked out the window at his spotless yard, trying not to think about the last time I'd seen Joshua. I'd let him go so easily after he'd almost beaten me to death, and then done worse. Trying to be the bigger person, to hold the moral fucking high ground. Tried to let it go for Dmitri's sake.

"You're in luck," Javier said. "The Feebs picked up

Mackelroy two days ago trying to fly from LAX to Guam and from there to God-knows-where. They're holding him at the field office."

"He's in custody?" I said. I shouldn't have been surprised—Joshua was brutal and efficient but intelligence wasn't an attribute he rolled high on.

"Probably married to his cellmate by now," said Batista. "That what you needed, Wilder?"

"Yeah," I said. "Thanks, Javier."

"You bet," he said. He took me back to the door, alert for Marisol. "Wilder, you be careful, hey?"

"I always try, Batista, but the bad guys usually have other ideas."

"Mackelroy has warrants," said Batista. "One of 'em is for assaulting a police officer. That wouldn't be you, now, would it?"

"It would," I said. "But believe me, I'm after him for something bigger now."

"If you're gonna beat the shit out of the guy, try not to leave any marks," said Batista. "Marisol will skin me alive if I lose my job. Not to mention the guys holding her gold card."

"I've got my phone book and toilet seat all warmed up," I said with a tiny smile. "*Muchas gracias,* Javier."

He raised a hand to me as I walked to the Fairlane. "Watch your back, Wilder."

CHAPTER 10

I drove straight through to Los Angeles, nine hours and change, getting me to the FBI field office at 8 AM, just as their day was starting.

At the front desk, I flashed my badge and asked for the agent in charge of the Mackelroy case.

"I'm sorry, but Agent Capra isn't available," said the secretary, who was blond and sleek as any wannabe movie star.

"This is important," I said. "It's about a quadruple homicide."

She sighed and rolled her eyes around the lobby looking for help. The somber suits filing past us didn't pay their secretary and one skinny dark-haired woman jittery from too much caffeine any mind.

"Is Mr. Mackelroy directly involved?" she finally asked. I had a brief moral dilemma about whether or not to lie my ass off and then told her yes.

"I *suppose*," the secretary said, "you can go ask Agent Capra directly and *maybe* he'll let you speak with Mackelroy, but this in no way constitutes a promise, all right?"

"Sure, fine, whatever," I said. "Which way is Capra?"

"Fraud Division," said the secretary. She pointed a desultory red fingertip over her shoulder at the elevators beyond the metal detectors.

I got scrutinized, patted, and wanded by a security guard with the federally requisite surly attitude in place, and when I had the temerity to ask "Which way is the Fraud room?" he grunted like I was terminally stupid.

"Elevator," he muttered.

"You're so helpful I may go into shock," I said with a wide smile, and stepped into the elevator with a crop of tall, white, well-dressed agents, not one of whom was wearing jeans, combat boots, or a rumpled David Bowie T-shirt.

The Fraud Division was quiet, and more somber than I'd expected an FBI office to be. Everyone had nicely arranged cubicles and indirect lighting. The ASAC had a big glassed-in office. Occasionally a phone rang or a besuited agent got up and walked to the fax machine/photocopier combo that gleamed next to a watercooler and a plate of pastries, but otherwise everyone kept their heads down. It was all very corporate and sterile, and it made my skin crawl up and down my spine, much like I imagined the eponymous village from *Village of the Damned* would.

"Help you?" said a voice from one side, and I faced a very handsome suit in blue pinstripes, a blue tie, and shoulders that nicely set off a mocha-caramel face and a smile that would have blinded anyone within ten feet.

"I'm looking for Agent Capra," I said, returning the smile.

The suit whistled. "You sure? You look way too alive and engaged with the human race to be in need of Capra. Wait, don't tell me." He held up a finger. "Undercover. Busting some hard-core DVD pirates?"

"I'm not with the bureau," I said, smiling in spite of myself. "I take it Capra's not popular among the rank and file?"

"Let me put it this way," said the suit. "Capra's ideal fantasy is ten minutes alone in a room with Kenneth Lay and a lead pipe. Guy's sort of a freak. I'm Mike, by the way. Special Agent Mike Hardy."

"Luna Wilder, from Nocturne City," I said, shaking the proffered hand. "I actually need to see about speaking to one of Capra's prisoners."

"I pity the inside trader who brought you down on them," said Agent Hardy. "If you're not an agent, you should be. I could turn you loose at a neo-Nazi meeting and those boys would be giving you their mama's cookie recipes."

"Um, thanks?"

"I used to work organized crime," said Hardy. "Put in for a transfer. Must have been out of my goddamn mind. Anyway, Capra won't let you see any of his suspects in custody. He screeches even if you bring a warrant."

"How do you know I don't have one?" I asked. Hardy strode over to the coffee-and-pastry array, and I followed. He offered me a cheese Danish and I took it, plus a jelly donut.

"Trust me," said Hardy. "Cops like you never come with warrants. Just hopes and dreams."

"I *need* to talk to Joshua Mackelroy," I said. "It's important."

Hardy swallowed a swig of coffee and made a face like it was drain cleaner. "How important?"

"Lives-at-stake important."

He whistled. "Serious, no doubt. And you did drive all the way down here. But Capra won't let you talk to his prisoner. The marshals are coming to take Mackelroy over to Pelican Bay later this morning. He's got an arraignment for the conspiracy charges attached to the O'Halloran securities fraud next week."

I kicked the watercooler. Hardy jumped. "Godsdamn it!" I shouted by way of illustration.

"Whoa, whoa," said Hardy. "What's this about, anyway?"

"Joshua Mackelroy is directly linked to four people who've been murdered in my city and a fifth who almost was," I said, shivering despite my best efforts to appear badass and unflappable, "He has information that I can't get any other way."

Hardy put his hands on my shoulders. "You okay? You seem awful involved with Mackelroy."

I pushed his hands away, grabbed my collar, and pulled it aside to expose the four silvery scars where my neck and my shoulder met. "He did this to me. Hell yes, I'm involved."

"Everything Hexed and holy," Hardy whispered, examining my bite scars. Four teeth instead of two. The thing that marked me as Serpent Eye whether I wanted it or not.

"You said it," I muttered.

"Look," said Hardy, "Capra went to get coffee and that always takes him at least thirty minutes, especially if he stops to kiss the ASAC's ass. I'll let you in with Mackelroy if you're gone in twenty."

I goggled at him. "You could lose your job."

"Yeah, but Capra's an asshole and you're a damsel in distress." Hardy winked at me. "Make it fast, Detective Wilder."

He led me down a gray corridor beyond the cubicles to the holding cells, and I didn't bother to correct him before he opened Joshua's cell door.

Joshua had his head tipped back against the cement wall, eyes closed. A three-day rash of stubble ranged over his crooked jaw, and his dishwater-blond hair was longer and stringier than when I'd last seen him. He looked thin, and hungry. Dangerous as a captured carnivore.

He inhaled deeply, his nostrils flaring until they turned almost white, and then his head snapped up and his eyes fixated on me. "You need a bath, Luna."

"You need to time-travel to 1985 and give Bret Michaels his hair back. But let's not get hung up on details."

He snorted, one side of his mouth twitching upward. Joshua wasn't what you'd call handsome, if you were sober and old enough to know better, but not many fifteen-year-old girls are, especially the ones who are trying to say *Fuck you* to their parents as loudly as possible.

"Knew you'd eventually come back to me," he said. "Has that pretty-boy Redback used you up and spit you out yet? Funny how you have no problem being a whore to someone who can sweet-talk you. Discriminating against me because I'm not a fucking hypocrite. You're something else, Luna."

I sat down on the single chair in the cell, which was bolted to the floor across from the cot where Joshua . . . lounged, was the best word for what he was doing. "You seem to be under the impression that you're dominant and I'm afraid of you," I said. "Hate to break it to you, Mackelroy, but you haven't scared me for a long, long time. Also, I'm not a member of your pack, so save the posturing for some high school freshman who'll give a rat's ass."

"Then how come you're sweating, Luna?" He smirked

and folded his arms behind his head. "Is it that I get you hot?"

He brought it on himself, he really did. I got up, very slowly, and walked over to Joshua until I was mere inches away. His scent roiled my stomach but I stared him down, never blinking, letting my anger ride roughshod over anything else I might be feeling.

"If you open your filthy mouth about me again," I whispered, feeling the pull on my were side from his dominate, "I will force you down on the ground to lick my feet like the crying bitch you are. And after that, I'll kick your goddamn teeth in."

Joshua growled and started for me, and I pulled out my sidearm, pressing the barrel of the Glock between his eyes.

"Make no mistake," I said, still hissing. "There's many a day when my deepest, fondest desire has been to put a bullet in your brain, Joshua. Someone like you, I'd shed no tears over killing." He was absolutely still, teeth drawn back over his lips. I snarled in return, showing my fangs. "But you know something? I realized after I met you again, after you tried to take me back into the pack and failed, that I don't *need* this gun to deal with you."

Part of me had fully intended to put a slug in Joshua if he tried anything, and that part of me screamed in disappointment when I holstered the weapon. But the were was riding me now, and my voice wasn't entirely my own when I growled, *"Weak."*

I locked eyes with Joshua and I pushed his will back, and down. A hot iron wand slipped through my midsection, where the phase spread from. This wasn't like dominating another Insoli, or a pack that I happened to encounter. This was my *maker,* my rightful mate, the man who had turned me from Luna Wilder, screwup human, to Luna Wilder, werewolf.

Joshua's blood was my blood. Fighting him was like fighting my own darker impulses.

Still, I pushed him away and he howled. *"No! Stop!"*

"Yes," I gritted, or maybe I merely growled, I don't really know. "You are *weak*. You are *mine*."

"Bitch . . . ," Joshua gasped. "You can't . . ."

He was so strong, and the pain was incredible when I tried to subsume his will, but in that instant I felt him slip, just a little, no more than an inch.

"Joshua," I hissed. *"You* do *not* tell *me* what to *do*."

And like a crack in a dam, I felt his dominate break. Joshua's will splintered and disappeared under the force of my rage and he slumped back to the mattress, sweat running down either side of his face like misplaced tears.

"Stop it!" he whined, and if he'd had a tail he would have stuck it between his legs. "Gods damn it, haven't you done enough to me?"

"You did start it," I reminded him, sitting back down.

Joshua's thin chest rose and fell rapidly under his jumpsuit, and I could hear the faintest *thud-thud* of his heartbeat. "Why'd you come back here?" he demanded plaintively. "I washed my hands of you when you ran out on me the first time. Why are you torturing me?"

"Jesus on a bike," I said, borrowing an expression from Bryson, "were you always this whiny?" I crossed my ankles primly. "Joshua, I know Serpent Eyes only pass on their change through the bite. I know that you passed pack magick to me whether I like it or not."

"So?" he muttered.

"Sooo," I trilled, leaning forward. "A vanful of psychopaths who seem to be targeting the first families of Nocturne's weres dragged me out into the woods and tried to kill me. I started thinking, why would they do that? And then it hit me: your progenitor must've had a link back to the granddaddy of all Serpent Eyes!"

"Well, yeah," said Joshua. "Why do you think it went so bad for me when you split?"

I paused, a little shocked he'd given the information up so easily. I had expected that pseudo-clever caginess Joshua was an expert at. Maybe I'd kicked him a little harder with my dominate than I thought.

"Thanks, jerk," I said. "Now that I know to look out for crazies obsessed with bloodlines, I can rest easier."

I stood up and made for the door to signal Agent Hardy that I was ready to go.

"Oh," said Joshua with a soft exhalation that may have been a spiteful laugh, "I don't think they'll be bothering you again."

Feeling ten degrees colder all over my exposed skin, I turned back to him. "What the Hex does that mean?"

He lay back on his cot, and damn it all if he didn't look as indolent and in control again as the leader of a pack, beset by his harem and without a care in the world.

"Joshua," I said again, pushing on him with the dominate. "What are you talking about?"

"You really think you were the only piece of ass I gave the bite to, Wilder?" he said with a grin. "My, my. That's awfully narrow-minded of you, Miss I've-Got-It-All-Figured-Out."

"You're lying," I said instantly, to beat back what my brain recognized as the truth. "Weres have mates. They give the bite once and that's it."

"I'm a Serpent Eye," said Joshua. "What makes you think I give a fuck about any pack law but my own?"

Cold, and with all the deadly force I could muster into my voice, I asked, "Who is she?"

"You're the great detective, Wilder," said Joshua, lips peeling back into a smile that showed his fangs. "You figure it out."

He squealed when I grabbed him off the cot and held his head over the steel toilet in the corner of the cell. "You have five seconds and then I'm giving you a shampoo, you piece of crap."

Joshua laughed, his bony shoulders quivering. "Oh, don't bad-cop me, Luna. You don't have it in you."

I bounced his head once off the rim of the toilet, and he yelled. "Don't pretend like you know me, Joshua," I warned. Crouching so that I was at his level, my fingers knotted in the collar of his jumpsuit, I met his eyes. "Who is she?"

I'd dominated pack weres before, at a cursory level so that they wouldn't tear my throat out, but this was different. I felt like I had put my hand inside Joshua's head and scraped it clean. I caught his pain and scented his fear.

It was horrible, violation in the extreme, and I knew exactly why weres like Joshua enjoyed it so much.

"Who?" I demanded. Joshua began to tremble, and then the stink of piss filled the cell. I saw the stain on his jumpsuit and my already jumpy stomach bucked against my rib cage. "All things Hexed and holy . . ." I made a quick few steps away from Joshua as he shook uncontrollably.

"C-carla," he whispered. "Carla Runyon. Back in Nocturne."

I buzzed for Hardy without another word, more desperate to be out of that cell than I'd ever been, for anything.

Hardy followed me all the way to the lobby, which was how far I paced before I realized he was still with me. "The thing with Mackelroy didn't go well?"

"He's a daemon spawn," I spat. "He deserves to have his testicles chewed off by ferrets."

"Bastard, no lie," said Hardy. "He got a good deal to turn state's against O'Halloran. Posthumously and all . . . guess there's not much to lose."

I could feel tears starting so I smiled at Hardy and said, "I have to go back to Nocturne City now."

"Okay," he said, kindly averting his eyes so he didn't see the sheen in mine. "Hey, if you're ever down in LA give me a call. I'd love to take you out, try and lure you into the bureau."

He passed me his card and I took it, and walked back to the Fairlane with the midmorning sun dazzling my eyes. I felt scarred, and shaken, but most of all, at my core, I felt nothing. Joshua's hold on me was broken. Yet somewhere in Nocturne there was another girl, someone who wasn't lucky enough to be able to confront her devil. My kidnappers had been well organized and well informed, and now it was a race between me, them, and the ticking clock to see who found the poor girl first.

At the Twenty-fourth I ducked Shelley by using the prisoner entrance and sat at Bryson's desk, spinning his chair until I got dizzy, and then getting coffee, and then finally throwing the stir-stick across the room. Where the Hex was the man?

His phone shrilled just as I'd decided to leave him a sticky note and drive out to find the Wendigo. I wasn't bleeding anymore, and thanks to Joshua I was also spoiling for a fight.

"Bryson's desk."

"Why, Luna Wilder. I thought I'd never hear your dulcet voice again," said Bart Kronen.

"Dr. Kronen, my favorite medical examiner," I said. "The same. What's up?"

"I'm trying to reach David," he said. "Something unusual with the victims in his four homicides that I needed to discuss."

"You know," I said in my brightest tone, reaching for a pen. "Bryson and I are working the case side by side . . . me being were and all. Sort of a consulting deal."

"Ah," said Bart.

"So I could come by and look at your findings." Gods, this was so wrong. I would be so fired. Forget fired, I'd probably end up at Los Altos with my former homicide captain and a passel of angry mercenaries who had worked for Seamus O'Halloran.

"I'm working my usual shift at the morgue," said Bart. "I'll look forward to your visit."

"Thanks, I . . ." Sweet orchid perfume blanketed my nose just before Matilda Morgan came to my shoulder, and I managed to slam the phone down in the nick of time. "Ma'am."

"Officer Wilder. To what do I owe the pleasure?

I plastered a smile on. "Just waiting on Detective Bryson, ma'am."

Her eyebrow arched delicately. "I see. Officer, I'm sure I don't need to tell you that the city's ability to prosecute your case and all cases attached to it goes down exponentially every time you—the victim—interfere with the investigation?"

"You don't, ma'am," I agreed. "But really, I just

came here to share some information with David. So he might clear the other cases a little faster."

"Your altruism never ceases to astound me," said Morgan in a voice so dry you could set it on fire. "However, the next time I catch you in my precinct sticking your nose into an investigation you might directly compromise, I'll have your badge, Luna. You are not the only competent law officer in this city." She jerked her chin at Bryson, who had appeared from the hall carrying a bag from Big Darn Heroes, the sub shop one block over. "Give Bryson your information and get out."

"But ma'am . . . ," I started. She had to understand that Carla Runyon was most likely a were now, and that Bryson wouldn't be able to get to her alone.

"I think I've made my position clear, Luna," said Morgan. Her tone was still even but her expression was fierce. "Don't make me repeat myself."

"What's up, Wilder?" said Bryson, plopping his lunch down on top of a stack of paper. Meatballs and sauce and delicately melted mozzarella cheese tickled my nostrils.

"A were named Carla Runyon, from the Serpent Eye pack," I said. "That's who they'll be after next."

"Hey, thanks," Bryson exclaimed. "I'll get a couple of uniforms on her pronto."

"No," I started. "Her pack won't allow—"

"Bryson will investigate the lead in due time," said Morgan, glaring at Bryson. "Good day, Officer Wilder."

"No," I said. "No, it's probably going to happen tonight. David, you have to get to her now, and make her pack understand what's happening—"

"*Leave,* Officer," said Morgan, squeezing my elbow.

"Do not make me call Captain Delahunt at the SWAT office," she hissed in my ear as she propelled me toward the front entrance.

"Find her, David!" I yelled over my shoulder. "Tomorrow will be too late!"

CHAPTER 11

Nocturne City's morgue is straight out of a horror movie from the 1970s: down in a basement, past a set of barred metal doors, dimly lit with flickering fluorescents. Tailor-made for zombies, slashers, and Dr. Kronen, the only ME who never seemed to leave.

"Hey, Doc," I said, rapping gently on the open door of his office.

"Officer Wilder." He tilted down his glasses and gave me a small smile. "Glad you could make it."

"Anything for you, Doc," I said. "What do you have for me?"

Dr. Kronen pushed his chair away from his desk and stood up, fixing his tie so that it hung crookedly on the left instead of the right. "You know, Luna, I heard about what happened to you. If the DA gets wind that I allowed you access to the investigation of a crime you were a victim of . . ."

Damn it. Damn it and double damn it and damn it again once more just for good measure.

"Kronen, these guys threw me naked into a forest to get killed, and even though the methodology is different, I think they did the same thing to four other people," I said. "I'm just helping Bryson out. Cut me a little slack here."

Kronen tapped his teeth. "Perhaps not so different as you think."

"What the hell does that mean?"

Kronen gave me a small smile. "Let me show you something."

He led me down the hall and through a set of swinging doors. The cold room within was silent, linoleum floor and steel walls giving off a soft glow as the overhead vents kept the room at Corpsicle. The cadavers here were John Does, overdoses, natural causes who died in state-funded nursing homes. Anyone the morgue couldn't fit in the freezers down the hall went to the cold room.

At least in here, the smell was bearable.

"Full house tonight, huh, Bart?" I said when he hit the row of hanging lights dangling lopsidedly from the ceiling.

The rows of bodies zipped into their bags were identical except for the white tags tucked into the windows on the front panel. Kronen led me down the center row and stopped at a form midway, slipping on gloves and zipping down the bag.

The silent face of Bertrand Lautrec stared up at me and I flinched. "Jesus, Kronen. Don't you even close their eyes?"

He shrugged. "Doesn't bother me."

Bertrand's face was pristine except for the wide, dark bullet hole with the ring of powder burns in the center of his forehead.

"Upon examining him, I thought the same thing you're thinking now," said Kronen. "Gunshot wound, yes?"

"Close range," I agreed. "Poor bastard."

"Notice anything?" said Kronen. When I examined the wound again and shrugged, he reached out and stuck his finger into the hole the bullet had carved.

I jerked back. "That's just creepy, Bart."

"Keep calm, Officer Wilder," Kronen said. He pulled his finger out. "Now. Do you notice anything odd about this wound?"

The skin around the bullet's entry wound was still as pale and bloodless as ever. Pristine, almost, like someone had put out a cigarette on Lautrec's forehead.

"There's no blood," I said. "Not even clotted blood."

Kronen smiled at me and stripped off the gloves. "Which is logical, considering that Mr. Lautrec had lost nearly two-thirds of the blood in his body. The exsanguination is what killed him. The gunshot was an afterthought, or purely symbolic."

"Uh, we may have reason to believe that the killer, um, drinks blood," I admitted, remembering what Sunny had told me about the Wendigo. Was my pale, drained body next in line for a skull shot? "Seems like overkill," I agreed aloud. "Not even a were is getting up from that kind of blood loss."

"Or perhaps not passion but precision," Bart said. "Someone who cared to keep the true cause of death concealed."

"That could be anyone at this point," I said, rubbing at my nose to expel the stench of old, dead flesh.

"At any rate, I examined the bodies more closely," said Bart, unzipping the bag next to Bertrand Lautrec. Jin Takehiko lay within. Fortunately, his eyes were closed. His chest was smooth and hard except for a stitched Y-incision, muscle ridges stark where the blood had pooled. The rough stitches bisected his tattoos of wolves racing through clouds, dragons wrapped around cherry trees. The meager—and magick—tattoo at the base of my spine was a shadow by comparison.

Kronen took out a penlight and shone it down on a spot in the middle of Jin's left pectoral. "All four of them are marked," said Kronen. "I haven't been able to discern the cause."

I leaned close and saw four oval bruises on Jin's skin, so light that you'd have to almost be not looking to pick out the imperfections on his blue-white inked clouds. Death had paled him and brought them into sharper relief, which was the only reason I spotted them at all.

"Kronen," I said, spreading out my hand. My reach was smaller than whatever had made the mark, but the pattern was the same. Five fingers, pressed down over the dead man's heart.

"How extraordinary," Kronen murmured. "Almost as if something compelled the life-force from the body . . ." He flicked off his light. "All four victims' hearts are missing. That's why I'm inclined to believe there is more to this than Captain Morgan is willing to admit."

"Yeah, I think you made a good call on that one, Bart," I murmured. *Missing?* Sunny admitted the Wendigo drank blood, but nowhere was there a story about stealing hearts. "Their chests don't seem . . . disturbed," I said, my hand still overlaying the eerie marks.

"Therein lies the mystery," said Kronen, reaching out to zip up Jin Takehiko's body bag.

The next bag over rustled. I yelped and even Kronen jerked his hand away faster than I'd ever seen him move.

"What in the . . . ," he started.

"Who's bag is that?" I demanded. Louder, "Is someone playing a Hexed joke?"

"That is Aleksandr Belodis," said Kronen softly. "I know it. He has not moved from that spot since I completed his post."

"Call me crazy," I said, "but aren't dead bodies— especially dead bodies *sans* heart—supposed to, you know, *stop moving*?"

The bag jerked again, more violently this time, and a hiss issued from within.

"Dear gods," said Kronen. I didn't bother with gods, but I did jerk my sidearm out of my waistband and shove Kronen back with my free hand.

"Get behind me."

A moan issued forth from the bag, a hungry, haunted sound that rattled up and down the length of the metal-lined cold room. The body of Aleksandr Belodis sat straight up inside its confinement, and inside the stiff black plastic I saw the outline of a head rotate to stare at Kronen and I.

"New plan," I told Kronen. "Run your ass off."

Bart, never one to ask a lot of questions when the dead were rising, turned around and made tracks for the swinging doors. I backed up slowly, keeping my gun trained on the writhing body on the steel table.

There was a dry crackle like leaves underfoot, and a set of long claws, way too long to belong to anything were, tore quadruple slits down the front of the body bag. Aleksandr poked his head out and hissed at me. Most of his hair was gone, the rest falling off in patchy clumps, and his eyes were pure silver, gleaming under the lights with an oily life that sent a sharp icicle straight to where my fear lived.

"Crap," I whispered. All right, I squeaked. Perhaps even whimpered a little.

Aleksandr slid off the table, the body bag falling

around his feet. As I watched he took a step toward me, then another. His body began to change, smoothing and losing features, the stitches from his autopsy popping out and falling away. His nose flattened out and his teeth grew, fangs where none had been before appearing along his gums. He walked jerkily, but with a purpose, and the small slits he had left for nostrils flared when I felt sweat start all over my body. Cold, just like the rest of me.

"Wolf . . . ," he hissed.

Aleksandr's skin began to ripple and slough away, like he was phasing before my eyes, and I realized that the moisture on my exposed skin wasn't sweat but a heavy, clinging sort of fog that felt as if I were standing next to a glacier.

"Wolf," Aleksandr hissed again, his foggy shape pulsing and re-forming every time he took another step. He paused and gathered himself in, his lips peeling away to reveal more silver teeth. Too many teeth. Way too many teeth.

Then, terrifying as Aleksandr was in that moment, I saw something even worse. On his gurney, Jin Takehiko gave a great shuddering gasp and then sat bolt-upright.

"Oh, *fuck,*" I snarled.

Aleksandr returned my snarl, and I saw him crouch to spring. I turned and beat a retreat, slipping on the floor and going down hard. My gun spun away into a shadowed corner. The things behind me screamed, and I tried to pull myself up, but panic and the pain of falling made it a clumsy attempt at best.

"Luna!" Kronen shouted from outside the swinging doors. I looked back, saw Aleksandr about to latch his teeth into some vital part of me, and then a shrieking sound started, so loud in the echoing cold room I swear my skull split in half.

A moment later it began to rain from the ceiling sprinklers and an automated voice told me to proceed to the nearest emergency exit, this was not a drill. Kronen stared through the glass at me, his hand on the fire alarm.

I got up and got my ass moving, skidding along the slick floor with Aleksandr snapping at my heels. He was fast, faster than me by a long shot, but the noise wasn't doing him any favors, either.

Falling again, I slid along on my side and hit the swinging doors, rolling out into the hallway. Kronen pushed the doors shut and twisted the latches behind me.

"You all right?" he shouted over the Klaxons.

I pulled myself to my feet. "I'll probably live!"

Behind me, Alexsandr hit the door, his claws leaving long flay marks on the security glass in the windows. "Holy gods!" Kronen yelped. "What is going on, Luna?"

"I wish I knew, Bart, believe me," I said. We were both pressed against the opposite wall, watching the four silvery shapes inside the cold room snarl and hurl themselves at the door.

"How long do you think those locks will hold?" Kronen asked me conversationally.

What used to be Jin Takehiko, and was now another walking-talking death masque with teeth, rammed into the door at full speed. A screw popped out of the hinges and rolled away into the stream from the sprinklers.

"Not long enough," I said. "We have to get out of here."

"Follow me," said Bart. He hurried down the hall, and I backed away from the door after him. Before we'd gotten five steps, the door burst off its hinges and the two males fell into the hallway, followed by Priscilla's shape and then slowly, as if he was in pain even in this gut-churning new form, Bertrand Lautrec.

"Bart, move!" I shouted, grabbing him by the tie and pulling him into the nearest open door. I slammed and locked it after us. "Where are we?" The place was dark and I flinched as a body hit the other side of the door.

"The autopsy bays." Bart turned on the lights and the green tile floor and steel tables gleamed serenely at me.

"Shit," I said. "Is there another way out of here?"

"No," said Bart sadly. "Just the big freezer, there. That's the only door."

Outside, the scrabbling and snarling abruptly stopped. Everything was so quiet I could hear the blood beating too hard through my veins, and Bart's heart thudding underneath his soaked buttondown. At least in here there were no sprinklers and the shrieking alarms were muffled.

"We can wait until the police and fire departments respond," said Bart. "The door is very secure."

I started to answer him, but I was drowned out. From outside came a howl, a scream that cut through the metal, through my ears, and sent a cold, cold hand down my throat.

The same sound I heard in the woods that night. But now it was closer, and I had seen its face.

"Bart," I said, as everything went quiet except for the echoes and our panicked breathing, "Is there any other way *into* this room?"

"I can't think of any offhand," he said, but his lips compressed and the spots of color in his cheeks dimmed. "Are you suggesting we may have been flushed into our abattoir?"

"I think that these things are smart," I said, turning in a slow circle. "And that makes things pretty bleak for us."

From beyond a tiled archway, in a tiny room off the main bay, I heard hissing breath and the scrabbling of claws behind the wall. The only thing inside the small room was a plain metal door with a window in the center. I grabbed Bart's shoulder.

"That another freezer?"

"No," said Bart. "No, that is the incinerator."

"Where does the chimney vent to?" I demanded.

"The main ventilation system, one floor up, but . . ."

I saw a black shape drop into view inside the tiny window of the crematory furnace and my stomach dropped with it.

"This night couldn't just stop getting worse, could it?"

Kronen was backed up against the wall near the banks of equipment used in routine autopsies, and I gestured at him to get down. The thing scraped at the inside of the door, fighting the latch with brute strength.

"Where's the switch?" I hissed. "For the furnace?"

"On the wall next to it," Kronen whispered back. Shit. There went my master plan.

I cast around for anything I could use to defend us. Inside a tile-lined room one story below the earth, I couldn't pull the trick of phasing like last time.

The tray nearest to me was set up with a sterilized set of scalpels and surgical tools, but if the thing in the furnace could get up after a gunshot wound and massive blood loss I didn't think sticking it with a knife was going to do much except piss it off.

With a *chank* the glass in the window of the furnace shattered and the thing snaked out a long-clawed paw and slipped the latch on the door.

It *spilled* into the room, re-forming into a cohesive shape with each movement, and stood upright, walking shakily, taking its time. Like the bastard child of the smoke creature in the woods and the corpse of a were that had been underground for a few months. Priscilla's wiry frame and scraps of blond hair were all that the thing had left to recognize the former person by.

Not-Priscilla took one tentative step, then another. It could afford to. Not like we were going anywhere.

The drawers to my left were all closed and labeled, and I ripped open the one that seemed most likely to be helpful. I'd never used the machine within but I grabbed it in a defensive position. "Plug me in!"

Kronen obeyed, staying low, and the thing rotated its blank silver eyes to face him. Its nose-slits rippled as it scented the air and then with a hungry, guttural moan it started for Kronen, picking up speed. Its toenails clacked, digging chunks out of the tile.

"Hey!" I shouted. "Priscilla! You deal with me, you mutant bitch!" I let out the loudest, most territorial growl I could muster. Borne on my fear and my pain and rage, the were leapt to the forefront and I felt my eyes and teeth sting with the phase.

The thing swiveled back toward me and screamed a challenge, crossing the space between us in two leaps, faster than I could process. Just smoke and shadow and hunger, coming straight for my throat.

As the thing's bony hands reached out for me, I lifted the bone saw and depressed the power button, driving the circular blade in and up along the thing's sternum.

Priscilla screeched, reeling away from me with her arms akimbo. One set of claws caught me across the cheek but I swiped back with the saw and caught her on the shoulder, hacking her collarbone in two.

She retreated, mewling, one arm hanging useless from the socket and silver-black blood, like oil mixed dirty gray water, oozing from her wounds.

I let out a long breath that I hadn't really meant to hold, still brandishing the screaming bone saw between myself and the hunched thing that had been Priscilla Macleod.

"Luna," said Kronen, tugging at my pant leg. A booming started up outside the autopsy bay doors.

"Not now, Bart!" I snapped.

"Hey, anyone in there?" a voice bellowed from outside. I let my finger release the power switch on the saw.

"Don't come in!"

"Fire department!" the voice shouted. "Can you open the door, miss?"

"Meat . . . ," Priscilla whined from her corner. I may have been imagining things, but her wounds were starting to close.

"There's a dangerous . . . er . . . person in here with me!" I shouted. "I'm a police officer! Stay away from the door!"

"Miss, if you don't open up we're going to have to break the door down!" the firefighter shouted.

Where were the other three bodies? Had they gotten out of the morgue and into the labs above? I thought of the technicians working second shift and my stomach fluttered.

"Stay back!" I yelled at the firefighters, but even as I did, I heard the whine of another saw, one of the portable metal shredders that they use on car wrecks.

"Meat . . . ," Priscilla moaned again.

"Bart," I said, "we gotta get rid of her."

He nodded slightly, his eyes wide and all pupil behind

his glasses. Bart may get scared, but he'd never go into shock over something as trivial as a dead body coming back to life and trying to gnaw the flesh off his bones. I liked that about him.

"When I start moving," I said, "open the big freezer. And be ready."

I dropped the saw and stepped toward Priscilla. She showed her fangs and I bared mine in return, moving in a crouch so that I looked like I was going to fight with her.

She smelled chill, over the stink of the autopsy bay, like frozen iron and smoke on a cold morning. Also dead, with the necrotic stench of a corpse.

"Come on," I taunted her. "You afraid of me now? Don't tell me that you're gonna tap out after losing an arm. An arm's nothing." I circled her, forcing her out of her corner, away from the streaks of her black blood on the tile.

"You couldn't take me even with two good arms," I snarled. "You're a pathetic little bitch. You understand what 'pathetic' means, right, Ugly? It means *weak*. It means *prey*."

She hissed at me and I spread out my arms, letting my eyes go to gold. "Are you gonna stand there bleeding or are you going to make a move? *Come on!*" I screamed the last, a battle cry, and Priscilla sprang for me.

Clumsy as she was from her wounds, she still hit me and dug her claws in before I could react. I felt the bite in both of my shoulder blades and smelled my own blood over her stink as we fell back and I hit the floor.

I dug one leg into her gut, foot-first, and extended it straight, using her weight and momentum to push her over my head and crashing to the tiles behind me. Spinning, I got into a crouch.

She was still faster. She swiped at me and her claws rent flesh along my shoulder and my forearm as I threw it up to block her. I felt her claws dance along my bones and the jet of hot blood that hit her face made her pupils dilate and strings of drool grow at the corners of her mouth.

"Wolf . . . ," she moaned, in a tone rife with desire of the most perverse order.

"Bite me," I said, and kicked her in the gut with all of my were strength. On a good day I can dent a brick wall and right then it was a *bad* day, and I was pissed off and cut up and tired of this shit.

Priscilla went back, falling and rolling like she'd been hit by a truck, into the mouth of the freezer. I screamed, "Bart, now!" and he slammed the door shut after her. The automatic bolts clicked into place and a green light came on above the door.

Bart slumped, breathing heavily. I tried to go over and make sure he was all right, but everything went soft at the edges and I sat down hard in a pool of blood. Mine or Priscilla's, I couldn't be sure.

"Oh dear," said Kronen. "You're injured very badly."

"I'm . . . fine . . . ," I gritted, but it sounded like crap even to me. The were could heal up from small things, but Priscilla had cut me to the bone, literally. I could hear her screaming from inside the freezer as my blood pumped and soaked my shirtfront and my jeans. Kronen grabbed my arm and made a tourniquet out of the sheets used to cover up the cadavers. He fussed and made me hold my arm above my head. Slowly, things started to heel back over toward consciousness.

"She's not . . . gonna get out, right?" I whispered to Bart.

He shook his head. "I jammed the lock. You're all right, Officer. Just keep still."

The door to the bays crashed open and a two-man fire team came through, almost falling over each other as they drew up short. "Hex me," said the taller one. I recognized him as the voice from outside. "What happened here?"

"One of the patients got lively," I muttered. "Listen, we need to get out of here right now . . ."

"Control," said the firefighter, "I need paramedics and police down here right away . . ."

He got cut off as I stood, walked over, and ripped his microphone cord out of the base of his mouthpiece.

"You can't do that!" he yelled.

"Listen, tall, dark, and dumb," I hissed. "There's something down here that's got a taste for humans, and if we don't haul ass back to the surface right now—"

A scream echoed down the hallway, and my head dropped to my chest. "No . . ."

"Check it out," TD&D ordered his partner.

"Dude, you do not want to check that out, believe me!" I said. "One of that thing's friends did all this to my arm!"

He hesitated, but the first firefighter yelled at him. "Get moving, Orris! Somebody could be hurt!"

"Please," I said to Orris. "Just come with Dr. Kronen and me and let's get the Hex out of here."

"Who's out there?" Orris called nervously, casting glances back to his commander and me before he stepped out into the hall.

I saw the shadows unfold behind his head, and then Orris was jerked backward off his feet, Aleksandr's mouth opening wide enough to wrap around the back of the firefighter's skull. The crunch and spatter were all that followed, and then Orris dropped, just a sack.

Kronen turned away, putting a hand over his mouth. The firefighter ran forward before I could grab him with my good arm, screaming and brandishing his hand ax.

Jin came from the other direction under the erratically flickering hallway lights and leapt on the man's back, taking him to ground and digging in his claws, wrapping his jaws around the firefighter's throat and biting down.

Aleksandr, not satisfied with Orris, dropped from the ceiling, looked up at us, and snarled.

"Observation room," I said to Kronen, pulling us into the small space that had a window on the autopsy bay and locking the door. It was flimsy compared with the metal bulkhead that the firefighters had chopped through, but it was something. I braced myself against the wobbling barrier as Aleksandr howled on the other side. My blood had started to go cold against my skin in the proximity of the monsters. My heart felt like it would break my breastbone.

We were so Hexed.

Kronen tugged his key chain out of his pocket and unlocked a metal cabinet replete with hazard signs and stickers. He pulled a heavy jar off the top shelf and hefted it. "Open the door, Detective."

I jolted against Aleksandr's assault. "I don't know if that's such a good idea, Doc!"

"If we stay here, we'll die," said Kronen. "Give me a moment to prepare, then open the door." He slipped on a rubber apron and gloves, then picked up the jar again.

Aleksandr's malformed, taloned hand snaked through

the crack in the door, and I felt a slow hot pain in my back where the doorknob cracked against it. "Go, Bart!" I said, and stopped trying to hold Aleksandr back.

Bart brought the jar over his bald head and smashed it down on Aleksandr's shoulders. Foul-smelling liquid gushed over his skull, the shards of glass embedded in his skin making blood spout. The stuff Bart had hit him with made Aleksandr's skin peel back from his wounds, shrivel, and turn necrotic before my eyes.

He collapsed to the ground, twitching and groaning. "Formaldehyde," said Bart. "Best to move out of here before the fumes get too bad."

My eyes watered and my nose stung like I'd shoved a lit match into it, but I still managed to stumble over Aleksandr's body. I stopped at the door to the autopsy bays, keeping Bart behind me. "Where's the other one?"

I couldn't smell Jin over the chemicals, but I knew he was out there, waiting. "Listen," I told Bart. "I want you to run. Get out and make sure no one else comes down here."

He nodded. "I won't pretend I wish to be noble, Officer. Do be careful."

"Don't worry," I muttered, stepping out into the hallway. "I'm always careful."

Kronen slipped away toward the emergency exit lights and I went the other way, being sure to make enough noise to draw Jin away from the doc.

"Hey you!" I shouted, banging open each door. Gods, my arm hurt. It wasn't healing at all, just quietly bleeding. "Jin Takehiko! I'm talking to you! Show your lumpy face!"

The last door at the end of the hallway was the pathology lab. I'd been in there exactly once, during my first year in Homicide. My training officer, Detective Burke, and I were here regarding a dismembered woman dragged out of Siren Bay in the propellers of a garbage barge. I remember the smell, the mouth in her severed head frozen open in a scream. Her teeth were pulled, and the killer had chewed off the first digit of each finger to prevent identification.

Detective Burke retired not long after that case. Myself, I developed a healthy dislike of the pathology lab. Seeing dead bodies whole is one thing, but seeing them in all their bits and parts, organs and slides, was too close to mortality for me.

Still, I kicked open the door and bellowed "Jin!" to the blackness inside.

He emerged from the shadows, the bones and stringy embalmed flesh of someone's dead hand in his mouth.

"You're disgusting," I sneered, making sure to keep a lab table between us. Mark enough time for Kronen to get clear, and then run like hell. Simple plan. Of course it wouldn't work out that way, but plans give me a nice sense of security.

Jin dropped the dismembered limb and stood up from his hunched position, the mist clinging to him like a coat of dewy fur. I picked up the nearest jar, which was labeled ALCOHOL, and unscrewed the lid. It wasn't toxic, but under the circumstances I'd settle for stinging like hell.

"Back off," I warned Jin. He purred at me, and I swear he smiled around his awful teeth, a long blood-red tongue snaking out to wash his jaws and chin with spittle.

"Fine," I gritted. "Be that way." I tossed the alcohol, splashing Jin square in the face, then I grabbed the

Bunsen burner sitting on the lab table and spun the valve all the way open.

A jet of flame leapt the space between Jin and me and set him ablaze, his skin puckering like a sausage under a broiler. He screamed and staggered backward into another table, sliding down to the floor as he bucked and convulsed underneath the sheet of fire.

I just stood and watched, and as I did Jin began to ash, his limbs blackening and sloughing away. He made feeble sounds of pain.

I just held my injured arm against my stomach and closed my nostrils against the scent of smoke and overcooked meat that filled the lab. Jin stopped moving, slowly but surely the ashy rot creeping up his body until he was nothing but a skeleton, and then not even that.

It wasn't until I got outside to Kronen and the fleet of police and fire vehicles that I realized Bertrand Lautrec had gotten away.

CHAPTER 12

Bryson shoved his way through a knot of emergency personnel and spread his hands in disbelief. "What the Hex happened?"

"Hold still!" the EMT bandaging my arm ordered as I swung to face David.

"We've got a major problem."

Bryson craned to look into the morgue. "Like what?"

"Bertrand Lautrec," I said. The EMT jabbed me with a hypo of painkillers and released me with a glare.

"Christ, check out those two on the stretchers . . . they look chewed." Bryson turned back to me as Orris and his commander were wheeled by. "Lautrec's dead."

"Yeah . . . not so much," I murmured. Bryson shut his eyes and pressed his hands over his face.

"Tell me the painkillers are making you loopy, Wilder. *Please.*"

"He got up, along with the three other vics, and they did all of this," I said. "Except Lautrec. He took off."

"Assuming that a gunshot victim has any sort of brains left," Bryson said, yanking on his tie in a defeated fashion, "where would he go?"

I turned and walked away from the cordon, just to be

going somewhere. Then an iron fist wrapped my gut, and I stopped. "Laurel."

Bryson paled. "Oh, Hex me."

I beat him to his Taurus, even with the sling and the painkillers slowing me down. Bryson slapped the flasher on his dashboard and violated a dozen traffic laws to make it to Laurel's apartment.

"What's the move?" he asked as we crossed the lobby. "Shoot 'im in the head? Holy water?"

"Guns don't do crap from what I've seen," I said. If a bone saw didn't dent Priscilla, I didn't think bullets would have any luck. "Fire's the only way."

"Great. Let me pull out my handy napalm tank," Bryson muttered. We rode the elevator, feeling the air vibrate around us. "What the hell is taking backup so long?" he said.

"Most of them are still cleaning up after the quake," I said. "Tac-3's been on forty-eight straight hours of calls." I was chattering to fill the silence, so my thoughts wouldn't run to *You're willingly going to confront a guy who already died once and was no prize in life.*

The elevator stopped, and I indicated that Bryson should get out first. I held my pistol one-handed and slid along the wall, covering him as we approached Laurel's door. My heart began to thud as I caught that cold metal stench.

"He's here," I hissed at Bryson. He didn't respond, just swallowed and tightened his grip on his Sig Sauer. I could hear Bryson's heartbeat, too fast, and smell his sweat—pure fear. I gotta say, he hid it like a trooper.

"Laurel?" I called as Bryson kicked open her door. The latch was broken, and it creaked feebly as the door hit the wall.

Something hissed from within the dark apartment.

Bryson raised his sidearm, then yelped as Laurel's cat shot past us and disappeared down the hall.

"Jesus," Bryson said, leaning against the wall. I tried the light, and a floor lamp responded, tilted on its side. It sent up a red glow from the blood pool it was lying in.

Laurel Hicks was on her back, her eyes open and her face bloodless. She wasn't marked except for a row of punctures across her cheeks, as if someone had held her head in place. Tried to make her look at them, understand what was happening. The blood from her body was across her sitting room, like someone had spilled it out of a jug. Her heart, I could only assume, was with Lautrec.

"We're too late," I said softly. Bryson slumped, holstering his weapon.

"No—" I started and then Lautrec sprang from out of the darkness. He hit Bryson in the chest and knocked him back, the stocky detective denting the thin wall of Laurel's apartment.

Lautrec landed on the linoleum and hissed at me, scraping his claws together in a hellish screech.

I darted around him, slapping at the knobs on Laurel's old stove. The hiss and stench were welcome, considering the night I was having.

"Feed . . . me . . . ," Lautrec groaned, scrabbling at his own stomach as he bared his fangs and snapped at me. I grabbed a box of kitchen matches and dropped under his swipe, sliding on my butt across the linoleum, as far from the stove as I could get.

"Bryson, cover!" I yelled, and I struck a handful of matches.

The explosion wasn't big, as far as explosions go, but it took out all the windows in the apartment and fried Lautrec where he stood. He screamed and disintegrated, still trying to claw at me.

Bryson helped me up, grunting when I bled on him from my freshly opened arm. "Crap. I hate this shit, Wilder. I loathe it." His tie and cuffs were singed—and a little bit melted—but he looked none the worse for wear. Even his hair was still in place.

While Bryson wielded a fire extinguisher over the blackened kitchen, I bent down and closed Laurel's eyes with my good hand. Her skin was ice to my touch, like she'd been dead for days. "I hope it was fast," I whispered.

In the hallway, backup units had started to arrive and uniforms crowded in the doorway. I pushed through them and kept walking until a wall cropped up, and then I leaned my forehead against it. The world spun slowly beneath my feet.

A charm against evil. If what I'd seen tonight wasn't evil, then my perception of the world was hopeless. And I'd stolen it, because I didn't believe real evil could be fended off . . .

"Hey, Wilder?" Bryson said as the elevator opened to reveal a CSU team.

I swiped at my eyes with my thumb before I looked at him. "Yeah, David?"

He was holding Laurel's cat, and she growled at me. "Shh," Bryson told her, and sneezed. "Look, I'm sorry about what I said before."

"Oh?" I muttered.

"Yeah. You are *far* from the biggest freak in this city."

I looked back at the sad, dim little apartment that had contained Laurel's life, and now her ghost. "This was my fault."

"What?" Bryson started shaking his head. "That's crazy, Wilder. Your blood loss is talkin' for you."

"I took her charm," I said. "I took away what was keeping her safe. She knew, David. She knew something bad had happened to Lautrec and I got too wrapped up in figuring out how."

"Okay," said Bryson. "Number one, I don't believe in that hoodoo crap, and number two, I think you need to go to the hospital."

"I'm fine," I said, shutting my eyes on the tableau of Laurel's body. Bryson could say whatever he wanted— the dead woman in the apartment was my fault, my shame.

"You're pumping red stuff pretty good," said Bryson, in a tone approaching gentle. I looked down and saw a scatter of droplets on the linoleum at my feet. My arm, I realized, felt like hell.

"Go," said Bryson. "I'll mop up here and let you know what the move is."

"The move is we catch these sons of bitches," I said. "Before they do this to anyone else."

Bryson sighed. "Yeah, Wilder. I'm working on it."

That night in the hospital, I slept better than I had in over a year. Before Alistair Duncan started killing girls in my precinct, before Joshua and Dmitri had both wandered into my life.

But my nightmares were the worst they'd ever been. Laurel dead, Laurel alive, Wendigo tearing me apart, every murder victim I'd ever worked asking me why, why, why I didn't save them. And I knew all the time that their deaths were on my hands.

Finally, I dreamed that I smelled Dmitri's distinctive

mix of cloves and were and himself, spicy and heady like some open-air bazaar in another part of the world, and I knew he was gone, and that the scent of him was all that remained.

When my eyes flicked open under the persistent sunlight, I saw I wasn't dreaming, at least not wholly.

"Hey, darlin'," Dmitri said from the chair across the room. "You've looked better."

"Felt better," I said.

"Thought you were going to go kick down the Wendigo's door."

"I got sidetracked," I muttered, reaching for a pitcher of water left by the bed and not managing it.

Dmitri got up and poured me a glass, then sat on the edge of the bed. "Sidetracked, you? By what?"

"The gnawing dead," I said, sinking back into the stiff pillows. I tried to growl but it came out more like a frustrated cough. I hurt in places I hadn't imagined existed the night before, and the painkillers had lost the battle against my were physiology and worn off.

"What are you doing here?" I asked Dmitri when he pushed my hair off my forehead.

"That Bryson guy," he said. "Called and told me that you had some serious trouble at the morgue and you were hurt."

"Did you come down to say *I told you so*?" I said. "If so, consider it said and let me suffer in peace, okay?"

"I came to say I'm sorry," Dmitri said. Of course, I couldn't just be beat up and have bad breath from hospital food. I had to seem like the world's bitchiest girlfriend on top of it.

"Oh" was what I said out loud. "Well. Um. Thanks."

"I shouldn't have pushed you," Dmitri said simply.

"I want to give this another try. I didn't leave the Red-backs just to wander around this goddamn city, getting drunk by myself because I can't stop thinking about you, because I'm afraid of what the fucking daemon bite might do. I'm not gonna be afraid to stand by you."

I poked him on the arm, to cover the twist my stomach gave at his words. "Are you sure you're Dmitri? Switch bodies with a hopeless romantic lately?"

He grabbed my hand and pressed the fingers to his lips, then pulled me close and kissed me. I squealed when he pulled against what felt like a needlepoint design stitched into my arm and shoulder. Dmitri winced. "Sorry!" He held up my forearm and examined the bloody swath of bandages and the many neat stitches that decorated me like a map of railroad tracks. "Hex me, Luna. What got you?"

"I wish I knew, I really do," I growled. "Because I would find them and shove their heads up their mutant asses." I flopped back against the stiff stack of hospital pillows. "I got them, though. Even Lautrec. But I was . . ." I pressed my lips together. *Responsible for an innocent woman's death.*

Dmitri cocked his left eyebrow. "Thought Lautrec was dead."

"Yeah, so did I."

He fluffed my pillow to prop me up. "The doctor said you could go home when you were ready. Need a lift?"

I bit my lip. I wanted Dmitri back. I was lonely, and life was hard and occasionally fraught with the walking dead. But how long before we got back on the merry-go-round of fighting over every gods-damn thing?

Hell. I wasn't famous for making good decisions and I wasn't about to tarnish my reputation. "I'd love to go home," I said. Dmitri pulled me close and kissed the top of my head.

"No more fighting."

"Not for at least a good hour and a half," I said. "I think that's how long it will take for my stitches to start itching. After that, all bets are off. Ask Sunny about the time I sliced my finger open with a pedicure file."

I got up and found my clothes on the small table under the window. I had just started to slip out of my backless hospital robe when the door banged open and Bryson appeared, in a seersucker jacket and white pants, clutching a bouquet of daisies like a nightmarish, unshaven candy striper.

"Oh man!" he said when he saw me. "Sorry, Wilder! I'm averting my eyes!"

"I'm naked here, David!" I yelled at him.

"Yeah, I can see that."

"*Get out,*" Dmitri snarled, showing his fangs. Bryson yelped and ducked back into the hall.

"You decent?" he said.

"I am now," I said, pulling on my mostly shredded T-shirt and zipping my jacket over it.

Bryson came back in. "Sorry. I just wanted to come by and make sure you were still in mostly one piece." He stuck out his hand. "Yuri, right? I'm Dave Bryson."

"Dmitri," said Dmitri, not taking the proffered hand. "Luna's told me about you."

Bryson paled slightly. "Uh, listen. That stuff . . . uh . . . what she said I may have done . . . I'm very, very sorry."

Dmitri's eyes went to full black. "You better be. You caused her a lot of pain. I don't like you."

"Oh *gods,*" I said, putting myself between the two. "Lay off the testosterone, okay? David doesn't need any more body hair." I took the daisies out of Bryson's fist. "Thank you, Bryson. These were very thoughtful."

He gave me a weak smile. "Not the only reason I came down here."

"Oh?"

"Yeah," he said. "We found Carla. Morgan thinks I'm going to bring her in on my own, but fuck me if I walk into another den of werewolves solo."

"Bryson, you could get axed from the force if I go with you," I said.

He lifted one shoulder. "Better unemployed than dead to my way of thinking, Wilder."

Dmitri put his arm around my shoulder. "The only place Luna is going is home with me."

I ducked out from under Dmitri's embrace and took his hands. "Sweetheart, I gotta go. This is my job." I begged him, silently, not to put up the same old fight.

Dmitri's jaw tightened. "I'll come with you. You're in no condition to be running around in the field."

"No you won't," I said. I put my hand out and pressed it against his chest. What I was about to do hurt far worse than anything yet today, but Dmitri had brought it on himself. The daemon bite could get us both into trouble.

"What do you mean, 'No'?" Dmitri's face twisted. Bryson watched us both like we were caged animals at a circus.

"I mean . . ." I took a breath so my voice wouldn't tremble. "I don't want your help, Dmitri, and I don't *need* your help so just leave me alone and let me do my job without pulling your stupid macho crap!"

"Luna, stop it," he said in a low voice.

"Me?" I threw out my arms. "What am *I* doing, Dmitri? You're the one with a monster inside, the one

who scares me, and the one that I *can't have around on this case*. You got that, or should I send you a text message?"

"Damn," Bryson muttered. "That's cold."

"Oh, shut up," I said. "Dmitri won't accept that I can't do this anymore. I can't let him be beside me while the daemon is in him." That part was true, and I blinked hard to dispel tears.

Dmitri stood there, nonplussed, while I turned my back and jerked my head at Bryson to move along. I didn't let myself look back at Dmitri. It was for his own good. If I looked back, he might see I didn't mean it.

In the hallway, Bryson let out a whistle. "Damn, Wilder. Your boyfriend is some piece of work. He got any priors?"

"If you don't want to live life with a straw to breathe through, Bryson, I suggest you keep your opinions to yourself."

"No kidding," he muttered. "Carla's living down by the water, some squatter's place on the old piers."

"I know it," I said. Were packs congregated in Waterfront. Too many people, too few police, easy to blend in with human junkies and criminals and fade right out from view.

"Can't wait to get this over with," said Bryson. In the parking lot he threw a hand over his eyes and cursed. "It just keeps getting gods-damn hotter. It's like I'm in my own little circle of hell."

"I can't accept that," I said, shucking my jacket. Torn shirt be damned. In hundred-degree heat, I could work the grunge look. "Because if this is your hell, that means you and I share a hell, and that's something I'm just not ready to deal with."

That quieted Bryson down enough to drive us down

the hill to the Waterfront. There was a sheet on Carla on the dash, a missing persons report from six years back. She was a heavyset teenager, lots of black eye-liner, hair spiked and purple. Disappeared from behind a club on Magnolia Boulevard. Survived by a mother, who had made up several iterations of a HAVE YOU SEEN ME? poster that were appended to the report.

Whatever torments federal prison visited on Joshua, they would never be enough.

Bryson started sweating again as we pulled up out-side the Serpent Eye pack house. He made me get out of the car first. I left Carla on my seat, glaring out from her yearbook photo. I hoped she was tough, a survivor, but I wasn't counting on it. Joshua liked them vulnerable.

"David, I never thought I'd say this," I said when Bryson pounded on the mental bulkhead, "but I think you should do the talking."

"What? Why?" Bryson demanded. "I can't talk to these gods-damn people. They hate me!"

"They're gonna hate me more," I said. "Trust me."

"Why, Wilder? Just tell me!" Bryson hissed.

I jerked my collar down and exposed the four round marks on my shoulder. "This scar means that the were who bit me was a Serpent Eye. I took off. That's insult-ing. They'll probably try to beat me up."

Bryson blinked at me for a second. "Well, damn. Why didn't you just say so? Don't gotta do the show-and-tell."

The door rolled back and we were faced with a man who could have been a roadie for Whitesnake, or just really reluctant to wash his hair. "What?" he de-manded.

"Police," said Bryson, flashing his shield. I offered up my silver badge, smiling and praying that he wouldn't scent us. The tangy stench of Waterfront did a pretty good job of covering, but Serpent Eyes weren't dumb, just mean.

"Get a warrant and come back," said the roadie, starting to shut the door.

"Whoa whoa whoa, my friend," said Bryson, shoving his white loafer into the gap. "We don't need any search warrant to speak with a material witness."

"Huh?" said the roadie, scratching behind his ear. Bryson rolled his eyes.

"Son, move your ass out of our way and go buy some conditioner. We're here on business."

The roadie stepped aside when Bryson shoved him, and I slipped past. His nostrils flared when I brushed against him. "Hey . . ."

"One word," I told him, "and I will rip off your manly parts and turn them into a Wiener schnitzel."

He paled and backed away from us.

The warehouse on the pier was rotted, many panels in the glass roof open to the sky, the walls like the rib cage of an ancient metal juggernaut. Rough-hewn boards creaked under our feet, and everything was damp and filmed with salt.

The Serpent Eyes had set up tents and boxes on the main floor of the pier, plus a few shanties made from scrap metal. Electrical wires spat as droplets of water splashed into their transformers, crisscrossing the open space above our heads and giving the air a harsh, burnt taste. Smoke from camp stoves mingled with the pungent scent of seaweed and bay water.

If this was what I had missed out on with Joshua, I can't say I was shedding any tears.

"We're looking for Carla Runyon!" Bryson caterwauled, stopping at the center of the open space. I'd never thought his obnoxious bellow would be of any use, except as a repellent to rodents and small children, but I've been wrong before. "Carla!" Bryson yelled again. "We just want to talk to you!"

"I'm Carla," said a voice from among the tents and smoke. "Quit yelling, okay? Some of us are trying to sleep."

Carla was a lot older than her last picture, still weighted with poseur-goth makeup, cigarette wrinkles puckering the corners of her mouth. Her hair had grown out at the roots to mop-water blond. She was thinner now, too, and her shredded fishnet stockings and black velvet dress barely clung to her frame.

"Could you come here please, miss?" Bryson said, beckoning.

"No," said Carla. She pulled a cigarette from her garter belt and lit it. "You can talk to me from right there."

I was starting to like Carla.

"Miss, we have reason to believe your life may be in danger," said Bryson.

Carla snorted. "Buddy, you looked around? I'm in danger from sons of bitches like you every Hexed day of my life. You're not telling me anything new."

"Look, lady, just get your ass over here!" Bryson yelled.

"Hey, leave her alone," said someone from the crowd.

"Yeah," another agreed.

"Fuckin' cops, always coming down here and hassling us . . ."

"*She* ain't just a cop," said the roadie from the door. "She's one of us. She's a disrespectful fucking rogue."

Having thirty-five hostile sets of eyes suddenly fixate on you is a little bit like having your hand shoved against a hot grill. It's uncomfortable as hell and there's not a whole lot you can do about it except twitch.

A few of the Serpent Eyes growled and showed their teeth in displays of dominance. I kept still, arms at my sides, and didn't let any of the phase show on my face. If it had been just me, I might have tried to growl back, but I wasn't going to present a threat with a plain human around.

"She's Insoli now," said the roadie. "Somebody oughta teach her to respect territory."

"Aw, Christ," Bryson muttered. I would have told him that once weres catch the scent of an outsider, the deities pretty much agree that you're on your own, but before I could speak the second earthquake hit.

It started in the soles of my feet, as before, but this time the noise and the thunder were all around me.

The camp stoves tumbled over, spilling coals and fuel across the wood, and a tent caught fire with a *whoosh*. The Serpent Eyes screamed, running and falling, trampling over one another. Bryson grabbed on to me as the floor bucked under our feet. "Gods damn it! We gotta get out of here!"

"Wait!" I shouted at him. Carla was still standing there. Her cigarette fell out of her slack lips, and a larger Serpent Eye slammed into her, sending her to the ground.

I shoved my way through the throng of people milling around in panic, trying to get to her. "Carla! Stand up!"

She had curled herself into a ball, making her body small, the way women who are used to taking a beating do it. A passing were caught me just under the ribs and all my air went out, stars spinning in front of my eyes.

I dropped to one knee, and then howled as something small and jagged lanced my back.

With a sound like a glacier breaking, the hundreds of glass panes in the roof of the pier began to splinter, the smaller shards raining downward like a shower of frozen droplets.

"*Shit.*" I grabbed Carla by the back of her dress and rolled us both under the outcropping of one of the metal shanties. "Bryson, get under cover!"

He pressed himself back against one wall, cursing and covering his eyes. The screams of the Serpent Eyes were louder than anything.

"Get off me!" Carla yelled. "Let me go!" She was almost as stubborn as I was. I could understand why Joshua had picked her out.

Pieces of the shanty fell around our ears, and with a great moan, like a legendary beast surfacing from the deep, the walls of the pier expanded and then bowed inward, the metal supports bending like cheap coat hangers.

The quake stopped, and there was the kind of silence that only people who survive bombs and tornadoes and trauma ever get to hear. A dead space, so quiet that even breathing seemed impossible.

"Man! Look at this shit! This was a brand-new jacket!" Bryson yelled, brushing glass chips off his shoulders and out of his hair. "Jesus line-dancing Christ, what the Hex is going on in this city?"

Sound came back to me, sobbing and screams from trapped weres, and the crash of debris dropping into the bay. I rolled Carla over and checked her pulse. Strong and fast, like an animal's heart under my fingers. Thank the bright lady.

"Wilder!" Bryson shouted at me. "We gotta get moving! This whole place could go under!"

Human-size chunks of the floor had been ripped off their iron nails by the quake, but I got Carla up and we half stumbled through the glass and debris to Bryson, who took her other arm.

The floor groaned and tilted under our feet, one end of the pier beginning to collapse now that the walls and pilings could no longer sustain its weight.

"Sometime this year, Wilder," Bryson panted as we dragged Carla free. The Serpent Eye's pack house gave one final outcry and then settled at a distinctly downhill angle, seawater boiling around the end where the pilings had collapsed.

"I can't swim," Bryson told me. We made it back to the doors among the crush of Serpent Eyes, none of whom stopped to help us. The door was half crushed, stuck fast in its frame. I put my shoulder against the collapsed bulkhead and heaved with all of my were strength. The hinges groaned and the bolts rotated out of their holes, far too slowly.

"Come on, Luna!" Bryson shouted. "Harder!"

"You think it's so easy . . . ," I gasped. "Get your . . . fat ass . . . up here . . . then." I hit the bulkhead again, and with a shriek both from the metal and my injured shoulder the door gave way, crashing outward to let in dusty sunlight.

Outside, it was how I imagine the Hex Riots must have smelled and sounded. Dust and smoke filled the air, making it so thick and stale I could barely see up the hill to Highland Park. The skyscrapers down the waterfront rose out of the turmoil like fingers with all their flesh stripped, and sirens and car alarms droned, mingling to make one constant whine of chaos.

Bryson pulled out his cell phone, leaving me to lay Carla out on the pavement and check her vitals. "This is David Bryson at Pier Twenty-nine. I need fire and rescue, stat. I *know* the city's gone crazy but we got civilian casualties down here." He listened for a minute, his mouth going tight. "Listen, lady, I'm a Nocturne City detective, so quit fuckin' arguing with me and get some goddamn ambulances down to the piers!" He slapped the phone shut and paced in a circle. "You believe this, Wilder? It's like the end of the world."

I coughed on the dust, and nodded. The earthquakes weren't normal, even for a city that felt shakes every now and then from the fault line that ran through the mountains. I thought about the sort of things that could make the ground under my feet shake, and wished I hadn't.

Bryson jerked his head at the were pack. "What about them?"

The Serpent Eyes were gathered in a tight knot a few hundred feet away from us, checking one another over for injuries and shouting the names of the missing. No one made a move to go back into the sinking pier. When you live in a were pack, some of your friends survive and some don't. You start to be grateful for every day with food and shelter and accept the rest as a will beyond your own.

At least, that's what Dmitri had told me. Personally, it seemed like conciliatory bullshit, Reason Number 242 why I stayed an Insoli.

Nobody seemed to care that Carla was under the auspices of a human and a packless inferior. Without Joshua around to give her status, she probably ranked as low as I did among the Serpent Eyes. "Forget them," I said to Bryson. "We've got to take Carla with us."

Her eyelids fluttered after a minute and she opened her eyes, a hand going to touch the back of her head. "Something clocked me."

"You'll be all right," I said. "Blurred vision? Funny smells? How many fingers?" I held up two.

"Eleven," she said, rolling her eyes. She sat up fast, trying not to show that it made her wobble and hiss in pain. "I gotta get out of here . . ."

"Easy," I said. "You got whacked pretty good in the quake. Let Bryson and me take you to a hospital."

"Hex you, gutterwolf. I'm not going anywhere."

"It's not like you have a choice in the matter," I said, putting a hand on her shoulder and pushing her back to the pavement. She snarled and snapped at my hand, but I was faster.

"You don't understand," she said. "I gotta get back to Josh. I was just here to get some cash the pack owed me for my share of . . ." She looked at the badge clipped to my belt and reconsidered finishing her thought.

"Josh is Joshua Mackelroy, right?" I said.

"Not that it's any of your business," she muttered, trying to sit up again. She managed it, but made a little coo of pain when she tried to hold her head up.

"Hate to break it to you, Carla," I said. "But you're gonna have to try and smooch your boyfriend through bulletproof Plexiglas. That is, if the FBI agents will let you past the front desk."

She frowned at me. "What're you talking about?"

"Joshua is a slimy son of a bitch and he's going to prison," I said. She winced, but I kept on. "So instead of letting him drag you around like you're on a Hexed leash, how about you go with Detective Bryson and let him put you in protective custody?"

"I don't need protecting!" she snarled. "And you shut up about Josh! You don't know him at all! You're a liar. All Insoli lie."

"Did that nugget of wisdom come from the man himself?" I said. I reached for my collar and then put my hand on my knee instead. She didn't need to know who I was, or hear about my time with Joshua in the O'Halloran Tower or any of the rest. It wouldn't change her mind. I knew from my own string of boyfriends with bitter exes that if anything, it would send her running away from me, far and fast.

"Carla, a kidnapper and a killer is targeting weres in this city and you're next on the list," I said. "Other girls have been taken. *I* was taken. It's a miracle I got away, but he'll come after you this time because you're weak. Josh isn't here to protect you. You've got no one."

I wasn't, however, above shameless manipulation. Call it a means to an end that didn't involve a bullet in anyone's skull or Carla rising from the dead to feast on my flesh.

"I ain't heard of anything like that," Carla muttered.

You didn't hear about the first girl Joshua gave the bite to, either, but that's a whole other session of therapy, I thought. I said, "It's a different were pack every time. The Serpent Eyes—and you—are next."

"But you're Insoli," said Carla.

I shrugged, arranging my face in a kind, sisterly smile that sort of hurt. "I guess they wanted a complete set."

"Luna!" Bryson bellowed. "The Taurus made it through the quake! Let's get moving! This damn place smells like wet dog," he muttered, but only loud enough for Carla and me to hear. Bryson wasn't as dumb as he looked, some days.

"Please," I said to Carla. "You don't know what's out there, but I've seen it, and there's no way you could survive."

She whimpered, and curled in on herself and I fought the urge to get in Bryson's car, drive back to LA, and beat the snot out of Joshua all over again. He'd done everything I had escaped from to this girl. He knew I'd see it, and he was probably laughing about it in his cell right now.

Bastard.

"O-okay," Carla sniffed. "I'll come. But if I don't like it I'm walking out!"

"That's fine," I said, sighing. I inhaled smoke and it made me cough. "Let's just go, please."

Carla followed me obediently to Bryson's unmarked, like a trained spaniel. "She's all yours," I told David. "Keep her safe, and don't tell any more people than you have to where she's stashed. Not even me," I added, when he started to talk.

"You need a ride?" he said instead. "Most of the roads are probably closed, but . . ."

"Just back to the morgue," I said. "I left my car there, before the scene last night."

"Yeah," said Bryson. "What happened there?"

I got into the passenger's seat of the Taurus, once Carla was safely strapped into the back. "That's what I'm gonna find out."

CHAPTER 13

Before I could make good on my quest for knowledge, my beeper began buzzing angrily. I saw the scramble code on the screen. "Can you drop me at the plaza instead, Bryson?"

"Thought you were on leave," he said.

My arm still felt like something large and starving was chewing on it, but I wasn't bleeding anymore. That was a victory. "I still have to report in if I get a call." That wasn't true at all, but I was making a habit out of lying to everyone, so I figured Bryson was feeling left out. If Tac-3 ran into more of those things . . . well, that wasn't worth thinking about.

"No one else," I muttered as Bryson made an illegal left turn into the plaza parking lot.

"Say what, Wilder?"

No one else dies when I could have stopped it.

"Nothing. Get going, David. Keep her safe."

He dropped me a salute and gunned the Taurus out of the lot. I went inside, trying to ignore the various hot points of pain all over me.

Cleolinda raised her eyebrows at me as I ran past. "It's hitting in there, girl. Whole damn city's gone crazy."

Captain Delahunt was pacing back and forth while Eckstrom, Batista, Allen, and Fitzy traded looks. I tapped Javier on the shoulder. "What's up?"

"Hostage situation," he said. "Over by River Road. Something damn weird is going on, lemme tell you."

Delahunt finally spotted me. "Didn't I send you home for a few weeks, Wilder?"

"I got the code, sir," I said. "I showed up."

"Good, because we're shorthanded," he said. "Naturally, I assume any injuries that might result from active duty won't be claimed as workers' comp?"

Delahunt was one of those bullnecked ex-military types who thought health insurance and personal days were for weaker specimens. He was one of Mac's poker buddies, though, and I'd never seen him be anything but decent.

"No, sir. Absolutely not."

"Good." He flicked the remote on the display set up at the far end of our situation room, and a sound file began to play.

"Nine-one-one emergency, how may I assist you?"

"Oh gods, they're coming in!" The scream overloaded the speakers and feedback hissed.

"Sir," the operator's voice hitched. "What is your location?"

"It's inside . . . it's *eating me* . . ." The screaming became wordless, and Delahunt cut off the file.

"That was an hour ago. Seventy-one River Road, on the far side of Garden Hill. Officers on the scene report at least two subjects inside the house, plus the hostage." He clapped his hands. "Let's go to work."

"That tape was some freaky shit," Fitzpatrick said after we'd loaded into the van. The reassuring press of my tactical gear was somewhat mitigated by the slow swirling nausea my arm was causing, but I held it together.

"PCP," said Allen. "You know all the hopheads go back into the old part of the cemetery and shoot up. Serves those assholes on River Road right for building their mansions so damn close to a boneyard."

I thought about the things in the morgue. PCP-addled junkies seemed like a treat by comparison, but I wasn't convinced that was what we were getting into.

The scene was small, two patrol cars and a negotiator arrayed behind a cordon. The house itself was a big Tudor pile that backed up to the greenbelt hiding the cemetery from view. There were no screams any longer—no birds, no traffic. It was so quiet it made my skin crawl.

"About time," said the negotiator, who was thankfully not Lieutenant Brady.

"We just had our second quake in a week," said Batista. "Sorry we couldn't skip right over here."

"Whatever. I've been trying to get through on the house line. No answer. No visuals from inside for almost thirty minutes. Owner's name is Donovan Hess. Good luck."

Batista stared through his binoculars. "Okay, I see a side patio door that looks likely. Big sunroom inside, no hidey-holes for surprises."

Allen pointed to a small gazebo up the lawn from the side of the house. "I'll set up there. Give me five."

He sprinted away with his rifle case slung over his back. I checked my M4, loaded it. Fitzpatrick clapped me on the back and I staggered.

"You ready to rock-and-roll, Wilder?"

I had probably never been *less* ready, but I nodded and flipped my face shield down. I felt green—could only assume I looked it, too.

Eckstrom used his portable battering ram to bash through the patio door, and I followed him in, painting the far wall of the room with my laser crosshairs.

Nothing happened. No one yelled, no one shot at us. It was sort of a letdown. "See anything?" Batista panted in my ear.

"Not a damn thing," I said. "I'll check the kitchen."

We all moved off, each covering a room. "Clear!" Fitzpatrick bellowed almost instantly from the front room.

Batista and Eckstrom both cleared their rooms, and I was about to when I heard giggling.

I stepped into the kitchen, broken glass from a picture window over the sink crunching under my boots.

A man who must have been Donovan Hess lay faceup on the stone flags, hundreds of bite marks covering his exposed skin. The smell of fresh blood and recent death made my stomach do unpleasant sideways movements, but I breathed in through my mouth and swung around slowly, trying to find the source of the giggles, which were sliding up the scale into insane rather more quickly than I was comfortable with.

A cabinet door banged behind me and I spun, rifle jumping up. Something small and black crawled up the wall, little talons digging pits out of the plaster and laughing away. It reached the ceiling and rotated its head toward me, hissing.

"Hex me," I muttered.

Batista appeared in the door. "Wilder, what's up? You didn't clear your room . . ." He saw Donovan Hess. "Ah *dios mio.*"

"Javier, move!" I shouted as the thing let go of the ceiling and landed on his back, talons finding purchase in the Kevlar.

Batista let out a bellow and spun around, trying to swat the thing off. I grabbed a frying pan from the rack by the stove. "Hold still!"

He stopped, groaning as the thing's talons cut clean through his body armor and into his skin. It bared silver teeth at me, a square ugly little face in a body like a rat's. Its scaly tail lashed. I caught a whiff of its scent. It was the cold-metal, ice-water smell of the Wendigo, and that made my heart sink.

But I still hit the thing right in its ugly face with the frying pan. It squealed and flew off Batista, grabbing on to the wall again.

"Christ!" Batista shouted, taking aim. "What the Hex is it?"

"Your guess is as good as mine," I said. Batista let off a two-round burst and the bullets passed right through the thing, its slick black hide re-forming over the holes.

I dug under the sink and came up with industrial cleaning fluid. "Get back, Batista," I said. I faced the thing, which could have been the pet of what Priscilla had turned into. "Come on, Ugly. You know you want to sink your teeth into this."

I unscrewed the cap on the bottle and when the thing leapt for me, I tossed the contents over it. It cried out, shaking all over, and I turned on Batista.

"Give me your flare gun."

He tossed it, and I drew down on the quivering creature and fired. The flare took it through the window and out into the yard, where it exploded in a puff of ichor, squealing.

It would be nice to say I had a pithy sentiment as I watched it burn, but I just shuddered with relief as it started to ash.

"Good gods above," said Batista. Eckstrom and Fitzpatrick piled into the kitchen as the thing finally disintegrated. "Wilder, what the hell?"

I looked out the broken window, seeing gravestones between the gap in the trees. "Came from the cemetery," I said. "Guess it was hungry."

Sunny's car was in front of my cottage when I got there, along with Dmitri's bike. A big section of the driveway had fallen down the hill to the beach, but the cottage seemed intact and only heavy surf gave away that anything had even happened.

"Is this some kind of intervention?" I said when I came in and found both my cousin and my boyfriend sitting on the sofa. "Because I already know owning a hundred and sixty-seven pairs of shoes is a problem, trust me. I don't even have closet space for those old Christmas decorations of yours anymore, Sunny."

"I just came by to make sure you were okay, and Dmitri told me you took off," she said.

"And then, you know . . . earthquake," said Dmitri.

"Everything okay?" I asked him.

"Yeah, just a couple of plates got broken like the last time."

"Thank God my parents don't have heirloom china and Grandma Rhoda disowned me," I said. "No harm done."

"Your arm is bleeding," Sunny pointed out.

I saw red teardrops leaking through the gauze and cursed. "This damn thing just won't heal up."

"Dmitri told me the doctors gave you about forty stitches," said Sunny. "Be reasonable—even your body won't heal from that."

"When zombies get up and try to eat you," I said,

"and freakish voodoo makes critters crawl out of the cemetery and attack the living, 'reasonable' becomes moot."

"*Vaudun* witches can't actually reanimate the dead," said Sunny. "It's a discipline of blood magick with a very strong compulsion over a person's will. A *bokor* can stop the heart, but he can't make it beat again."

I rubbed my face. It was cold and wet with sweat. "I have no idea what those things in the morgue were. They started as weres, but they acted like Wendigo. Eating hearts, drinking blood . . . I wish I knew what the Hex was going on, I really do."

I worked a nail under the bandage and pulled the gauze away. The four slash marks on my forearm were inflamed, blood leaking from between the sutures. Sunny hissed when she saw it.

"That doesn't look normal, Luna. Can you tell me any more about what attacked you? Maybe I have a working that will help you heal."

"These things were like . . ." I sighed, thinking of their flat silver eyes, their teeth. The sounds they made as they stalked their prey. "The closest thing to what they were is Stephen Duncan, when he was bespelled into a were," I said. "But . . . *not,* at the same time. Stephen was a puppet . . . and these things were intelligent. They hunted Bart and me like we were rabbits in a hole."

And turned to ash in fire, and healed from wounds faster than any were. "Strong, too," I said. "Stronger than me."

Sunny and Dmitri traded a look. "Wendigo don't transform other species," she said. "This sounds like something a summoning would call."

"Well, isn't that help—" I started. My arm throbbed, and I hissed, tucking it into my abdomen reflexively. I could feel dull, hot pain spreading from all of my claw cuts, persistent as if Priscilla still had her hooks in my shoulder. I was about to say that maybe I should lie down for a while when everything spun gently sideways and I found myself on the floor, with Dmitri standing over me, shaking me and slapping my face.

"Ow," I said. The back of my head had joined the pain chorus. "What was that?"

"You blacked out," said Dmitri. "Just fell over like a tree."

"I don't . . . feel so good," I managed, my tongue feeling thick. Pain overtook everything. The only time I'd felt this bad was my first phase, one month after Joshua had given me the bite, when I'd almost forgotten about him except for the wounds that refused to heal.

He'd given me a lot more than the STD I'd been worrying about. Being a Serpent Eye meant rolling the cosmic dice, having no pack magick of your own. He'd turned me into a Path along with a were, made sure that I could never get close to magick without nasty side effects.

"Luna," Dmitri said and my eyes fluttered open again. "Hex it. Sunny, she checked out again. You better call an ambulance." He growled. "What were you *thinking,* running off to work after you'd been hurt?"

I tried to tell him this wasn't right, that my wounds were *doing* something to me, making me feel like I was fading away. I thought about the barely visible fingerprints on Bertrand Lautrec's chest. Had whatever killed him and the others infected them? Would I die only to get up again with a taste for living flesh?

"Hurry!" Dmitri yelled at Sunny, and I felt him shake me. "Come on, Luna. Come on . . ."

I tried to tell him to stop, but I didn't have the breath. Priorities, Luna. "Sunny . . . ," I croaked.

She dropped the phone and came to me, grabbing my hand. "I'm right here, Luna. Tell me what's wrong."

I squeezed in return, feeling the prickle of my Path magick between our palms. "Sorry . . . ," I breathed, and then let the magick in.

Everything exploded into a cacophony of senses. My ears picked up the sound of triplet heartbeats, the waves outside, even far-off sirens in the aftermath of the earthquake. I could smell and taste everything, and my vision cleared and almost blinded me as I stared up into the lamp hanging in the center of the ceiling.

I fought and pushed against the thing the monsters had put inside me, feeling it in my blood like threads of black oil on clear water, and with a fierce ripping sound, my stitches broke free as my wounds finally began to close.

Dmitri tore my palm from Sunny's, and she sat back hard, shivering and pale.

"Gods!" Dmitri said. "Luna, are you all right?"

"Sunny?" I said in return. The magick I'd Pathed from her started to fade and I could hear and see again without overloading myself.

"I'm okay," she said faintly. "You?"

"Yeah." I sat up and shook my head, pushing my hair out of my eyes. "Yeah, I think I'm all right now."

"That's really interesting," Sunny said, pulling herself to her feet using the wall. She trembled when she stood up, and I looked at the floor, guilty.

"How's that?" Dmitri demanded. "She blacks out and then almost kills you."

"I did not," I protested. "I only Pathed a little bit. And I said I was sorry first."

"No, your wounds," said Sunny. "It's like you were infected. Like a were." She pressed her hands over her eyes. "Look, truth be told, I *don't* know that the Wendigo can't infect you, Luna. I only have the texts to go on, and the most recent is still two hundred years old." She looked at Dmitri. "You have more information than I do."

"I already told you, I never dealt with them," Dmitri snarled. "And I have even less reason to now."

Sunny put her hands on her hips, the spots in her white cheeks like flames. "Dmitri Sandovsky, I am not a police officer and I have no desire to be, but even I can spot a liar. Luna almost died, so you better give up what you know before I do something *really* medieval to you."

I grinned, despite feeling like I was falling off the edge of the world.

"Bright lady, save me from your women," Dmitri muttered. "Look, all I know is the guy's name. Lucas Kennuka. He runs the clan that lives out on the interstate. They stay out of the city, we stay off their land, and I fucking like it that way." He snarled at Sunny. "That good enough?"

"Perfectly adequate," she said with a sincere smile. I patted Dmitri on the knee.

"Thanks, sweetie." I stood, and my dizziness receded. I felt good—strong, even. It was as good a time as any to go see the monsters.

CHAPTER 14

I drove toward the Sierra Fuego range as the sun set behind me, making long shadows along the road like the teeth of a giant. The turnoff for the fireworks stand was obscured by blackberry vines and scrub, and the wooden sign had faded and fallen on its side.

The track that led up to the settlement was rutted as a broken rib cage and I winced each time the Fairlane's undercarriage scraped on the earth.

The road—if you could call it that, even charitably—ended at a collection of trailers that looked like they'd been thrown down in no particular order by Dorothy's tornado, and a few log houses with broken windows and moss-covered roofs.

Nobody was in evidence, but I parked the Fairlane next to a '57 Chevy pickup that was so shiny and new looking I felt ashamed to stand next to my own car, with its cracked windshield and layer of earthquake dust.

"Hello?" I called. A few birds shrieked from the forest, old and much larger than anything the humans, or Wendigo, had managed to put up.

I sniffed deeply and got smoke, both wood and tobacco. The scent of an outhouse or a leaky septic tank.

Something meaty and spicy that made my nose twitch. I realized I was almost unbearably hungry.

"Hello!" I shouted again. "Anyone here? I'd like to speak to you!"

Silence, as crystal as the small stream that tripped down the hill beyond the trailers. I unsnapped my holster, just in case, and walked a few yards past the tumbledown cabins, looking for life signs. It was spooky around there, in a Camp Crystal Lake sort of way, but it hardly looked like the lair of a zombie-making, mass-murdering crazy.

I walked on, finding small trails cut through the brush, and let the case facts turn over in my mind. Someone who was not Gerard Duvivier was killing weres, for no apparent reason except their bloodlines. And whoever had killed the weres also had the power to turn them into . . . what?

There were no answers, but I stopped caring when I came to a clearing and saw what was scribed in the bare earth.

Pine needles had been swept aside and three working circles were drawn, unevenly, in the baked dirt. They weren't pretty, but they were powerful. I thought about the charm with its raw, crude magick. I unfolded the small pocketknife attachment from my key chain and pricked my finger, squeezing a droplet of blood into the closest circle.

Nothing happened. My heart started to beat again. "I'm getting crazy," I muttered. Just because someone in the Wendigo was having a half-assed go at magick did not make this in any way connected to what was happening in the city.

Right. If only I could believe myself.

From beyond the trees, I heard a steady *thunk-*

thunk-thunk, and the tinny screech of music filtered through crackling speakers. I touched my gun, and started up the small footpath.

The music got louder, as did the sound, and I remembered the movie where the policewoman finds the guy in the wood chipper.

"Hello?" I said once more, rather more softly than I would have liked.

I rounded a bend in the trail, my heart hammering, and came upon a lone man, his back turned. He was wearing a dusty white T-shirt and torn jeans, long black hair clipped back with a leather thong. Thankfully, he at least *looked* human.

He was also wielding an ax and listening to Golden Earring at an earsplitting volume. I reached out and turned the dial down. "Excuse me."

He spun, the ax coming up in a defensive stance, and his nostrils flared when he saw me.

"Hi," I said, holding up my hands. "I come in peace."

He snorted, not lowering the ax. "You're trespassing."

"Considering that this land belongs to the federal government, so are you."

That made him stop for a second. I kept my eyes on the ax blade, trying to focus on the silver cutting edge and not the guy's face, which wasn't hard to look at by any stretch. He had an action-hero jaw, but full lips and a narrow nose that gave him a fey, liquid quality in his features. His hazel eyes were cold as they flicked over me and back to my face in the most clinical of ways. I'd seen that look before, from suspects deciding whether or not they could beat the crap out of me and escape.

"You from the government?" he said finally.

"No," I said cautiously. "Nocturne City."

His jaw twitched, but he turned around and went back to chopping. "What did you want to talk about?"

"I was hoping to speak to Lucas Kennuka. I heard he was the person in charge of your . . . commune." The most inoffensive descriptor of the place, and I always went for courtesy over accuracy when speaking to a guy holding an ax.

"Well, lucky you." He threw the split logs into the massive pile that filled up most of the clearing and stuck the ax into the chopping block. "I'm Lucas."

"Luna Wilder," I said. I watched him closely in the eyes and gauged the grip of his hand when he shook the one I offered. His gaze warmed up, but never flinched, and his grip was firm and hot from the friction on the ax handle.

"I can't say it's good to meet you, since I don't know what you want," said Lucas. He picked up a red plaid buttondown and put it on over his T-shirt, concealing his slim, ropy torso under the baggy flannel.

"Aren't you hot?" I said, and then swallowed when he looked at me with his head cocked to one side. A little smile bent the corners of his mouth.

"No," he said finally. "I tend to be a little cold-blooded." He started back down the path toward the settlement. "So you know that we're squatting here. You after money? You a reporter, looking for a story?"

"I'm not either of those," I said, feeling the small nervous knot in my stomach grow to Gordian proportions. "I . . . I came here because I needed to talk to the Wendigo. About four murders in the city." Almost sheepishly, knowing it could be the last dumb thing I ever did, I drew out my badge. "I'm a police officer."

Lucas examined my credentials and grunted. "Fair enough. You look legit. I'm that double-wide with the geraniums. Go on in." He ushered me ahead in a gentlemanly manner, holding the screen door open.

The scent of cold metal warned me, but too late. I heard the sound of a shotgun racking and the barrel pressed a long, icy kiss against my temple.

"Now," said Lucas, shutting and locking the door behind me. "Why don't you go ahead and tell us why you're really here?"

"Us?" I asked, trying to stall him into some sort of expository monologue so I could kick the person holding the shotgun and wrestle it away.

Lucas struck a match and lit a kerosene lamp. Three other faces popped out of the darkness, holding weapons to a man.

None of them were the ones who had taken me. "Hey, look," I said. "Whatever it is you're thinking, it's not like that."

"You're a were who's trespassed on our territory. You're a fucking cop. You're out here to pin four murders on us," said Lucas from my shoulder. I felt his breath on my neck, and my stomach dropped. "What should I be thinking, Luna?"

I turned on him. He was still wearing that smug expression, grinning a little bit now, rocking back and forth on the balls of his feet.

"How long have you known I'm a were?"

"Since you were about a hundred feet away from me on the trail," he said. "We have a treaty. You broke it. That gives me the right to kill you and leave your body for the crows." He snapped his fingers and two revolvers joined the shotgun leveled at my head.

"You don't want to do this," I warned, pushing against the phase as the were boiled up out of my unconscious in the face of rival creatures. Pinpoints of blood sprouted from my palms as my clenched fingers grew claws.

Lucas growled as he stepped into me. "No, sweetheart. This is what I want to do more than anything right now."

"Well," I said, never breaking eye contact with him. "Then I'm very sorry to disappoint you."

I ducked left and went around his skinny frame. Lucas was my height and build, but he was solid muscle and looked like it would take a hurricane to knock him over. It also made him slower than me, and I had my Glock against his neck and my off hand clamped across his chest before he could react. "Back the fuck up," I snarled at the three men with guns.

Lucas tensed under me, then relaxed. "Do as she says."

"*Kennhuhke . . . ,*" one of them started.

"Now!" Lucas bellowed, with nearly enough force to shake me lose. The man ducked his head and the guns went down.

"What now?" Lucas asked me. "You're trapped in a ten-by-ten space with no way out and a hostage who outweighs you by eighty pounds. You're not going anywhere, sweetheart."

"Stop calling me sweetheart," I said. "It's very condescending. And I don't *want* to go anywhere. I *want* to talk to you like reasonable people. Wendigo. Whatever."

"We're way beyond that," said Lucas. "You violated the treaty. You have no rights."

"I don't know about any gods-damn treaty!" I yelled in his ear. He flinched, grunting. His sweat smelled like water condensed on the outside of a steam pipe. "I'm not from any pack. Not the Serpent Eye, not the Redbacks, *no one*. You guys are the ones who snatched me and tried to kill me!"

"What?" Lucas demanded. "Hex me, you do jabber on. None of that makes any sense."

"Talking crazy," agreed one of the other men.

"All right!" I shouted over the agreement. "I'm gonna let go. Are you gonna be polite?" I asked Lucas.

He snorted. "I'm never polite, *sweetheart*. Let go of me at your own risk."

I lowered the Glock and pushed Lucas away from me. He spun, fist cocking back, and hit me. My head snapped around, but I dropped my shoulder and punched him in return, a fast front jab directed at his face. More of a reflex action than anything. Blood fountained out of Lucas's nose.

The guns came up again. "No!" he said sharply, massaging an old bump on the bridge of his nose. I hadn't broken it—I'd pulled my punch. Just a polite rejoinder. We examined each other, our breath ragged. "Put 'em away." Lucas grinned at his buddies, and at me, looking happier than a man with a bleeding nose had any right to. "We understand each other."

I put the Glock back into holster, a pinch of trust that I hoped wasn't misplaced. "Are we cool?" I asked. My jaw throbbed a bit, but nothing had shaken loose.

Lucas looked me over, head-to-foot, and I felt heat all over my skin this time. He was sizing me up, now, for something other than a fight or a feeding. "You're Insoli?" he said, jabbing his finger at me. "Not here on behalf of any pack?"

"We've been over this," I said, the grip of the Glock damp and sticky under my hand. "No pack. Just me."

"Okay," said Lucas. "I'm willing to buy that you

don't know about the treaty. But what's this about us kidnapping you?"

"You sons of bitches threw me into the back of a van and released me for one of your buddies to feed on," I said. "And you've done it to four weres before me, who then got back up and tried to do me in all over again. Am I wrong?"

"Well, yeah," said Lucas, releasing his ponytail and retying it. "No one has hired me to kidnap you or kill anyone, and we don't freelance. The Kennuka clan edicts are strict in that respect." He looked at the biggest shotgun goon. "How does it go, Danny?"

"No Wendigo shall spill blood upon the pregnant earth without just cause and the seals of office, or payment in silver," Danny recited in a monotone. Lucas looked back to me, satisfied.

"No one breaks the rules. My great-great-grandpappy wrote them down and he was a scary son of a bitch. As am I. My men don't go rogue."

"Look, I know it was a Wendigo," I said. "I got the claw marks and hallucinations to prove it."

Lucas rubbed his chin. "I'm not saying it wasn't *a* Wendigo, but it wasn't one of mine. We stay out of the city limits without a pack contract, and you stay the fuck off our land, period."

"Outsourcing," I muttered. "How progressive."

"We aren't the only Wendigo in these parts," said Lucas. "The ones snatching weres are probably a wild clan. They don't obey our laws."

"Animals," put in one of the other men, in the same tone Dmitri had used.

"So these wild Wendigo . . . you wouldn't, say, *know* any of them . . . ," I started.

"Look," Lucas said. "This is not a topic that I can

cover in five minutes. Why don't you stay for dinner and I'll tell you anything you want to know?"

"Am I going to get another shotgun held to my head?" I asked.

Lucas laughed, cracking a real smile for the first time. It softened all the planes of his face and made him actually look human. "Only if you refuse to eat my world-famous chili."

Danny caught his shoulder. "Lucas. *Chektah mescht tah . . .* "

Lucas hissed, a sound that made my teeth grate sideways. The other Wendigo whimpered and backed away, heads down. "That's what I thought," Lucas said mildly. "My home, my rules. Luna, follow me."

We crossed the packed dirt to a small Airstream trailer wafting a scent that put my taste buds into orgasmic overdrive. Lucas went around to the rear of the trailer and fussed with the hoses on a small propane tank. "Nothing in this damn place works right for more than a day," he said by way of explanation, pulling out a small bone-handled knife and cutting a section of the propane line away.

"Sounds like my life," I muttered.

Lucas reattached the line and opened the valves. "Better," he said. "Come in and get washed up."

Lucas ushered me ahead of him again, and I tensed, growling. "Relax," he told me. "I was raised to be polite, whether or not I'm planning to hold someone at gunpoint."

"I thought you were never polite," I told him.

Lucas winked at me. "I can be persuaded."

"My knight in shining armor," I said, stepping into his trailer. A sense of overwhelming order greeted me. The place was tiny but immaculate, a threadbare sofa covered by a bright afghan. The walls were papered with a geometric '60s vintage print mostly covered with photographs. A record player and a nook with a tiny card table and chairs took up the rest of the space.

"Please sit down, Luna. Would you like some iced tea while we wait for the corn tortillas to bake?"

My stomach howled at me and I said, "Yes, please."

Lucas disappeared into the kitchen, beaded curtain clacking in his wake, and I heard ice cubes hitting glass and smelled the tang of lemon.

Even though he smelled like the things in the morgue, and what had chased me through the woods, it seemed very far removed from his serious, heart-shaped face and the easy comfort this tidy little home engendered in me. I wasn't used to feeling so at ease with people I'd just met, especially blood-drinking predators.

"Put the record on, if you want," Lucas hollered at me. I dropped the needle on the turntable, using the opportunity to look through the cracked door into Lucas's bedroom. REO Speedwagon issued from speakers that were half static with age.

The bedroom was as immaculate as the rest of the trailer, military corners on the bed and a few dress shirts hanging next to an army jacket in the tiny closet. Everything else was obscured from my vantage.

"This is one of my favorites. This song."

I jumped at least ten feet as Lucas spoke from directly behind me. "Gods above!"

He laughed, setting down two glasses with lemon circles floating on top. "You're wound pretty tight, even for a were. Don't you ever get any R and R in the city?"

"I . . . I do okay."

"Got a boyfriend?"

"As a matter of fact, I do."

"He's doing a piss-poor job, from the look of you." He took his glass and drained it in a gulp, and I followed suit so I didn't have to answer him. I hadn't realized that my mouth was dry as the dirt outside. Lucas sat next to me on the sofa and I choked on the dregs of my tea, an ice cube sliding down my throat.

Lucas reached over and hit me sharply between the shoulder blades. His hand was still very warm and I tried to smile gratefully as I coughed. "Thank . . . you . . . ," I gasped, finally able to breathe again. He grinned with one side of his mouth.

"Rescuing pretty women is one of my hobbies. Don't mention it."

I felt my cheeks warm up, and cleared my throat to cover. Lucas was disconcerting to the worst degree. He smelled wrong and he looked too good for me to reconcile what was hiding under the skin.

And damn it, I shouldn't even be noticing. Dmitri and I were making it work. He was, as he liked to state often, my mate.

Just remember that, Wilder, and a cute shapeshifting monster or two won't be a problem.

"So," said Lucas. "You wanted to know about wild Wendigo."

"I'm going to level with you," I said. "I know that Wendigo are responsible for the deaths I'm investigating. I know they're hunting weres and eating their hearts and turning them into whatever attacked and almost turned *me* in the city morgue—zombies, minions, whatever you want to call them. What I don't know is why. If you don't want me looking too hard at you squatting on this land, or incidents in Nocturne City

during times you and your . . . clan . . . were in town—
you're going to help me. Got it?"

Lucas put his twist of lemon into his mouth, sucking
the pulp off the rind and wincing at the sour. "The hard
sell usually work for you?"

"Don't avoid the subject," I snapped. "I can make
life really uncomfortable for you if you piss me off."

"All right," he said, and stretched languidly, one arm
traveling out of sight behind my head. I moved to a
stool by the record player. Pretty he may be, but pretty
was a far cry from trustworthy. "I'll tell you what I
know, but we need a free exchange of information
here," Lucas told me. "You say Wendigo attacked you
in the city morgue?"

"I hate repeating myself," I said. "They were dead
weres. Then they got up, and they were alive again. I
don't know *what* they were then."

"Well," said Lucas. "Wendigo have to be born. What
you've described is magick and I don't hold with that
hand-waving crap."

My eyebrows climbed. "I saw the working circles
behind the cabin."

"Some of my clan believes," said Lucas. "Me, I believe in what I can see. I'm a Wendigo, not one of the
faithful. Magick never did anything good for my ancestors, and it's a damn sight less useful than a bullet." He
got up and fiddled with the tuning knob on the record
player. "So whatever got you, it wasn't a Wendigo. It
was probably someone's idea of a sick joke."

"Well, I killed their sick joke, all four of them," I
said. "And I still say it was Wendigo-bred."

The silence stretched long and thin. Speedwagon
told me I was under the gun, so I took it on the run.

"You expecting me to flip out and eat you alive?" said Lucas finally, his eyebrows raised.

"Uh . . . I was expecting some form of anger management issue, yes," I said.

"My clan has nothing to do with this," said Lucas. "Maybe a wild clan messing with blood magick, but not mine." He sat again. "So, a werewolf detective. Against the packs and their criminal activity, against the plain humans and their blind eyes. They must hate you in the city."

I flinched, curling my mouth into a smile so Lucas wouldn't see my weak point. "Yeah, most of 'em. A few think I'm all right."

"Like your boyfriend? The werewolf smoker?"

"How do you do that?" It would be impressive by any standards, but considering that the most contact Dmitri and I'd had in days was a hug, it was miraculous.

"We don't get to curl up and sleep in our doggy beds at night," said Lucas. "We have to survive with absolutely nothing except our senses. So mine are good." He took the end of his ponytail and stroked it, an unconscious motion, and then looked back at me.

"Magick or not, I know that Wendigo killed the four vics in the first place," I said. "*That,* I think you know something about."

"It was a wild clan," said Lucas again. "I told you."

"And yet I'm asking again," I said. "I'm Insoli, and even I hear when a pack takes over territory or a leader gets courted out. You have to at least know who they are. I'll take a name, even a made-up one."

"Wendigo are a solitary people by nature," said Lucas. He stared out at the little encampment and his voice got far away, like he was retelling a legend he'd first heard when he was small and scared. "They band together only to hunt and feed, or to mate and form clans of their own. When the last scion of a clan dies, the clan breaks apart. That's how you get wild Wendigo. They meet in the wild and form bands, and they hunt. They feed. And that's all."

"Something else," I said. "My SWAT squad ran into some nasty little imp-like things that had your same smell. Know anything about that?"

"Hmm. *Brakichaks,* most likely," said Lucas. "The spirits of wild Wendigo summoned back by a shaman— a shaman with no scruples who doesn't mind someone getting eaten," he added when I gave him my best wide-eyed look. "Probably got one running with their band. That's your bet for the zombie act. I told you—the sane among us don't give magick the time it takes to piss on it."

"How do I find the band that kidnapped me?" I said. "And doesn't someone like you control your territory? I mean, you seem like you're strong."

"I am, and a mean son of a bitch," Lucas said. "But I'm not my father. He was the last of the old-blood Kennuka line. Once I decide to keep a mate, this clan will break up and re-form into something else. It's the way of things." He sighed. "I burn them when I find them, but I can't keep the wild bands out of these woods. They hunt where they please." He pulled up his shirt and revealed two broad, weeping wounds on his stomach that were only partially healed. "I met a wild one about six weeks ago. The result."

"If a shaman . . . changes someone into one of those things," I said, "is there any way to get them back?"

Lucas shook his head. "Wendigo are the wind and

the hunger forever. We exist to hunt, we're hard to kill, and if one of our shaman turns you into his construct, it's permanent."

"Sounds like a lonely life," I said.

"It is," said Lucas, looking me over in that penetrating way again. "But it's the only one I've got. Now I think we're done talking about this."

"I have more questions," I said.

He shrugged. "I don't have anything to hide, and you're just going to ask the same things different ways to entrap me. You think I'd fall for that chestnut? Working in the police has made you pretty damn arrogant."

After a long moment I said, "Hex you."

Lucas laughed, his face opening up again. "Don't take it personally. You're not too insufferable, for a fucking cop." He patted my knee and went into the kitchen. "Dinner's ready. We'll speak more after the meal. Then you should be getting home. The back roads aren't safe with the wild ones out."

"I can take care of myself," I said, bristling a little.

"I have no doubt," said Lucas. "Hell, you kicked my ass. But those things you fought were young and too hungry to think straight. These wild Wendigo fooling around with magick won't be. You're outgunned whether you like it or not."

"If this is reassurance, it's crappy," I said. "You could come back to the city with me to watch my back, and give this information to the department . . ."

"No," said Lucas, setting a plate of corn tortillas at my elbow. "The treaty forbids it. Don't ask me to do something I could be killed for."

"Sorry," I muttered. "Didn't realize the treaty was so scary."

"It's archaic and outdated," said Lucas with the old grit in his tone. "It hardly bears speaking about. Now eat. Then I'll see you to the edge of our land. You should be out of the forest before the moon comes up."

After I downed two bowls of chili so hot it could strip paint off my car, a pile of tortillas, and more iced tea, I put my hand over my bowl when Lucas offered me more.

"No, thank you. It was great, but I'm stuffed."

"You're all gristle," said Lucas, pinching my bicep. "What do you eat normally, salads and diet water? Maybe on special occasions the smoker lets you have a rice cracker?"

"I like the bacon cheeseburgers at the Devere Diner," I said, swatting his hand away. "I burn through a lot chasing down bad people and clapping handcuffs on them."

"I didn't mean anything by it," said Lucas. He pushed back his chair, seeming oversize in the tiny space as he stood up and shuffled our plates into his hands and up his arm. "You're not bad, for a were."

"My ego has just been engorged," I said drily. "Stop, before I lose all reason."

Lucas ran water into the sink. "And then, there's that mouth of yours. So Luna. What makes a good-looking girl like you decide on being a police officer?"

I decided to be honest. "I got tired of smelling like cooking oil and having drunks grab at my ass as a waitress, and the police academy was admitting." I drained my last glass of tea. "I'm sure I failed the written test, but I did fine on the physical." I'd done so well that the academy had given me a blood test and a stern interview, and only admitted me when they were sure I wasn't taking steroids. It had taken some work to find the balance of hiding my were strength versus using it to get ahead, but I'd managed to make it through the basic training, the classes, the gun training, and the forensic units, all without outing myself as a were. At least until a blood witch decided to turn my city into his own personal abattoir.

"At first it was money, and just something to do until something better came along," I told Lucas. "I'm not exactly sure what I thought *would* come along. I was a trainee doing a traffic stop with my senior officer when a passenger we stopped took off running."

Short and skinny, a black-haired, hollow-eyed junkie whose paranoia got the better of him. Fast and agile enough to get past Officer Dixon, he jumped the guardrail of the freeway and took off into one of the dark underparts of the city.

"Just for a minute," I said, "I forgot about hiding what I was. I forgot to be afraid of what would happen if I lost it and started to phase. I just knew the guy wasn't getting away from me."

I made the jump, fifteen feet down, the breath slammed out of me as I hit the concrete at the wrong angle, but I got up and I followed the reek of sweat and cooked meth. I followed the trail of the junkie's fear until I caught him and tackled him into a pile of rotted cardboard boxes.

"I arrested him, and I called for backup and I just felt . . . calm. Like when you know you're in the right place at the right time. I knew that right at that moment, handcuffing that guy was where I was supposed to be. Only time I'd ever felt like that."

Lucas dried off his hands and came over to me,

close enough to trade body heat. "You're lucky. My mother worked in a beauty parlor before she married my father. Not many Wendigo women make it to adulthood without a mate."

"Did your father . . . Did he have this crazy idea about protecting your mother all the time, by any chance?"

"He was a good man, but he was a hard man," said Lucas. "On the balance, my brother and I and our mother were better off when he died." His eyes clouded, but he took a breath and changed the subject. "You have any family?"

"Yeah, but they don't want much to do with me," I said. "My cousin is the only person who I can hold a conversation with without it devolving into a screaming match." Since my family wasn't a subject *I* wanted to be on, I stood up and looked at the photographs on the trailer wall. "Are these yours?"

"That's our father," he said, pointing to a formal portrait circa the 1970s. "That's me, when I was a baby." Baby Lucas was bald and had a bad-tempered cast to his brow even as an infant.

Lucas jabbed the center photo. "My brother, Jason, and me, just before Pop passed."

I paused, staring at Jason's face. He was taller and stockier than Lucas, more of a fighter than a runner. He was also very, very familiar. "Jason . . . doesn't live with you anymore," I said flatly. Lucas blinked.

"He left to find his own way a few years ago." Lucas lowered his voice. "I'm trusting you with this next part, you understand? Don't go gossiping."

"I don't gossip," I said.

Lucas's jaw worked. "Jason just went wild. Didn't even try to start his own clan. He just . . . gave up."

"Lucas," I said, lifting the photo off the hook. "Do you mind if I borrow this? I promise to bring it back."

"Why?" he said. "Will it help your investigation?"

"Very much so," I said, still staring at Jason's face. The whine of the bullhorn and the screams of the people behind the cordon came back to me from a long way off.

You must have something to live for . . .

"The sooner you find that wild clan and their shaman, the better," said Lucas. "I don't like to speak ill of my own people but some of them are just bad. Makes it hard for the rest of us to lead decent lives."

"Some weres, too," I agreed.

"We should go," said Lucas. He got the army jacket from his bedroom, even though I was still sweating through my top.

"All right. I'll follow you back to the road." I watched him walk ahead of me and felt guilt stab me between the shoulder blades. It's never easy telling someone the family member they haven't seen for a while won't ever been seen again. It flat-out sucks, actually. But Lucas didn't know, and he had to.

Outside the heat was still drifting out of the dirt and sending zephyrs across my face like spiderwebs, but the air had started to cool down. Lucas stopped me as I stuck the key into the Fairlane's door.

"I enjoyed our meal."

"Lucas," I said in a rush, at the same time. "I have to talk to you about your brother, Jason."

"You got some reason to think Jason's involved?" he shot back.

I shook my head, not breaking our eye contact. If he thought he was going to pick up on my tell for lying, he had a disappointment coming. Spend enough time talking to liars and you learn to be a pretty damn good one yourself, on or off the job.

Lucas startled me by putting a hand on the curve where my neck and shoulder met. His hand was bigger than Priscilla's, but my skin pricked at the memory of the claw wounds in my shoulders. "I have not seen, heard from, or talked to my brother since the night he blew up at my father and me and walked out. Not when Pop died. Not ever. I don't know what he's been doing, just that he's wild and I don't give one thin ass-hair about him since he turned his back on us. He's living his life." Venom had crept in, and Lucas's face twitched, ugly, even though he remained dispassionate, to a casual observer.

His hand was much cooler than my own skin, dry and slightly puckered from the dishwater. He smelled like lemons on top of the normal copper and steam. I fought the urge to turn into his grasp.

"You haven't heard from him? At all?"

"That's what I said. Not a phone call, a postcard, or a gods-damn Pony Express rider."

Oh gods. Telling someone their family member is dead should be some sort of torture in the hottest of the seven hells, not a bullet point on a job description. "Lucas, there's a reason you haven't heard from Jason."

Jason looked at me, unconcerned, and then simply leaned out and down off the ledge.

"I'm sorry," I whispered. "But your brother . . . we had him as a John Doe, but I recognized him from the family pictures. He's dead, Lucas. I'm very sorry."

Lucas stuck a hand straight out and caught it on the side of my car, letting it support his weight. He blinked twice, long and slow, shock painting broad strokes across his face. "Why . . . ?"

"I don't know," I said. "I was hoping maybe you would."

He shook his head, looking away from me. "Jason would never . . . who killed him?"

I blinked. "He wasn't murdered, Lucas. He jumped off his apartment building. His body is still in the morgue."

"Oh . . ." Lucas let all the air out of his lungs. "I have to go inside."

"Wait!" I caught his arm, and he hissed softly. "Do you think . . . when you're able . . . you'd mind talking to me a little bit about Jason? Coming into the city?"

"Can't," Lucas whispered. "The treaty. If I get caught by a were who still follows it, I'd be killed on sight for trespassing."

"I won't tell if you won't," I said. "And you have my personal word nothing will happen while you're with me. Just a few hours. Please?"

Lucas sighed and rubbed his hands over his cheeks. A few spots still gleamed when he took them away. "All right. I'll come get the body taken care of but that's all. I can't help you anymore. I have to see to my own people. They need me."

I nodded silently. "I can find my own way back to the highway. Thank you, Lucas. I'm sorry."

"He was my brother . . . ," he murmured as I got into the Fairlane and gunned the engine. "I can't believe it . . ."

I watched Lucas in the rearview mirror as I pulled away. He was angry, yes, and grieving, but he had not been surprised. He faked it well enough, but he'd known something before I opened my mouth. All the blinking and gasping is show—people who get slammed in the gut with death usually just shut down. That "unemotional" facade that juries hate so much. It's the only way to hold together, sometimes.

But Lucas had no need of it.

He was probably afraid, I reasoned, if his brother had indeed been palling around with the Wendigo who had made those things in the morgue. The "why" still eluded me, but I could taste it now, a solution. The wild Wendigo would give it to me.

Lucas was a good actor, but something else was going on during his impassioned speech about his people and how they needed him. Something that he thought I didn't need to know.

You spend enough time talking to liars, and you learn to recognize the bad ones, too.

CHAPTER 15

At home I found leftovers in the refrigerator and Sunny gone. Dmitri was sprawled on top of the covers in the bedroom, snoring softly, wearing boxers with flying toasters printed on them. I leaned down and kissed his forehead. "I'm home."

"Hey," he murmured, pulling me down next to him. "You're all right."

"Of course I am," I said, turning on my elbow. "What, did you think they'd drag me off and make me into jerky strips?"

"You never know with the gods-damn Wendigo," Dmitri muttered. "They hate weres."

"Not all weres," I said. "They were perfectly polite to me." Once they got through holding a shotgun to my head.

"You stink of them," said Dmitri. "Like rusty metal."

Figuring that was as close to an endearment as I was going to get, I kicked off my boots and headed toward the bathroom, shedding clothes. "I'll take a shower."

Dmitri got up and padded after me, leaning against the wall while I started an arthritic jet of water into the old tub. "Thought I fixed that thing."

"No," I said. "You talked about fixing it, before we had that huge fight."

"I should do it," Dmitri mused. I stepped into the water and let it beat down on me. I knew better than to pop my head out, bright-eyed, and chirp *So does this mean you're sticking around?* Were men were even more skittish than plain human men, and plus it would probably just come out bitchy in my current state.

I changed the subject instead. "Tell me about the treaty between the Wendigo and the were packs."

Dmitri snorted in surprise. "Who told you about that?"

"Lucas."

"That figures."

"He seemed pretty pissed over the treaty. What's the deal?"

"Let me guess," said Dmitri. "He gave you the speech about his 'men' and his 'clan' and batted those pretty-boy eyelashes at you."

I peered around the curtain at Dmitri. "You've been holding out on me."

"Hey, I met the guy once. Didn't say I knew him."

"Look," I said, squirting shampoo into my palms, "are you going to tell me about the treaty or not? Is it some big pack mystery? Will you lose your secret decoder ring if you tell the gutterwolf?"

He shot a glare at me before I ducked back under the water. "You're taking this way too personally. I can't tell you much because I don't *know* much. The treaty was laid down by the five founding packs of Nocturne City, and all weres who want to live within the limits abide by it."

"What does it say?" I asked. "What are the particulars?"

"That Wendigo are not to trespass within the city limits without some hoodoo bullshit going down, and weres stay the hell off the Wendigo's land, and everyone holds hands and fucking sings 'Kum Ba Yah,'" said Dmitri. "That's it. That's all the old pack leader ever told me when I took over."

"Towel?" I said, turning off the water. Dmitri held one out and then snatched it away playfully.

"Oh come on," I said. "I'm wet and naked over here."

His mouth lifted at the corners. "So I see."

"Dmitri . . ." I warned. "Better give me that towel."

"Or what?" he said, backing toward the bedroom.

"Or I'll come get it from you and get you all wet!" I threatened, jumping on him and using his Fram T-shirt to dry myself off.

"Quit it!" Dmitri yelped. "I had a bath today!"

"Shouldn't have taken my towel away, sucker!"

He pinned me down on the braided rug just inside the bedroom, both of us giggling like schoolkids on helium. He tickled me, and I shrieked, wriggling under him. "I give!" I finally cried. "Knock it off!"

Dmitri dropped his head to my neck and gently lapped the skin, making me wriggle in a new and different way. "I'm glad you don't smell like them anymore."

"Mm-hm," I said, undoing his belt. He put his hands on my hip bones.

"I'm glad you got out of there okay. It kills me that I couldn't be there to protect you."

"Please, for once, don't start with that and just be happy I'm here," I said, not unkindly, pressing myself into him. The wet fabric cooled and caused gooseflesh to blossom on my skin. "And be happy that I'm ready for my night to get very enjoyable."

"Luna," Dmitri whispered, and kissed me. His hands slid up to my shoulders, holding me fast to him, and for the first time in weeks I let myself relax and remember that this was how it should be.

"Luna," Dmitri said in my ear. "I don't want to lose you . . ."

I looked, and saw the tiniest hint of black ripple across his eyes. I tamped my unease down. It was fine. He was in the throes of it and I was, too, the phase curling under my skin. It always made for the best sex I'd ever had. I didn't fight it. "You haven't lost me," I said. "I'm here."

Dmitri kissed over to my ear, behind it, over my neck, his teeth fanging out and raking down the curve to my shoulder, his tongue on my bite scars.

His teeth pricked me, and I smelled my own blood. "Luna . . ."

Dmitri landed halfway across my bedroom before he had a chance to blink. He looked up at me, eyes black, from a pile of my clean laundry.

"What the *fuck*," I snarled, "was *that*?"

"I . . ." Dmitri passed a hand over his eyes and they went green again. "I'm . . . I'm sorry."

"You tried to give me the bite!" I had bypassed indignation and gone straight to yelling. "I don't believe this! You sneaky Hexed bastard!"

I grabbed a nightshirt and jerked it on, covering myself from Dmitri's eyes as he stared up at me.

"I couldn't help it . . . ," he said almost plaintively as I got into bed, throwing his pillows onto the floor with vicious *plops*. "I just thought about you being with the Wendigo, and not coming back to me, and you smelled so . . ."

"Do me and your nuts a favor," I said, "and don't

make this about me." I spitefully pulled the covers up to my chin.

Dmitri followed after a time, but he didn't say anything and I didn't try to make him. He curled up facing me, but I turned my back and turned out the light so I wouldn't have to feel his eyes on me as we lay silent.

"This isn't working, is it?" he said finally. "We want it to, but it isn't." I tried to ignore how crestfallen he sounded, but I rolled over and looked at him, finally. He was subdued and hollow-cheeked in the slim moonlight coming through my windows.

"It sucks," I said, crushing the pillow in my fist. "What were you *thinking*?"

Dmitri got up and put on his jeans. "I was thinking about you, being my mate. My real mate. I can't stay here."

Little bits and pieces of me wanted to yell at him, and beg him not to leave, but mostly I just felt a grim sense of anticlimax. It was a whimper, rather than a bang, that was for damn sure.

And I wouldn't admit that I was also relieved Dmitri had been the one to break it off. The black mark was in his column. "Where are you going?"

"None of your business at this point," Dmitri said. "I'll call. If you want me to. Later."

He's doing this, I whispered to myself. *You're not responsible. You're not the cause.* It was a cold little sliver of comfort as I listened to Dmitri leave.

I got up and out of the house before sunrise, and made the trip downtown in under an hour, which was a miracle with all the roadblocks and closures from the quake. I was waiting at Bryson's desk when he stumbled into the Twenty-fourth at 7:17 AM. "You're late," I said.

"Lord, what have I ever done to you?" Bryson asked the ceiling. "I pay alimony. I don't cheat on my taxes since the audit. I visit my Aunt Louise in the home even though she thinks I'm her brother Rupert who died in 1971. And yet, you curse me with my own personal harpy, who dogs my dreams."

"You dream about me, Bryson? That's sweet," I said. "Here, have a donut. Cops love donuts." He eyed the jelly-filled on the paper plate that I offered him.

"Is it a Sam's donut?"

"As if I'd ply you with anything less."

Bryson gulped the pastry down in two bites, frosting crumbs spilling down his shirt and tie. "Whaddaya want, Wilder?"

"I need you to look something up for me," I said. "I went out to the . . . Paiute reservation last night, and I found a lead on your killer. Perhaps even The killer. Can't be sure yet."

"Hot damn, are you serious?" Bryson demanded, turning on his computer. "You got no idea how happy you just made me, Wilder."

"Well, don't go giving me a gold star," I said. "You're never gonna be able to prove it in court."

Bryson licked jelly from the corners of his mouth. "Why the hell not?"

"He's a Wendigo," I said. "Look up a suicide for me . . . a John Doe that happened last week." It seemed like a lot more time had passed since Jason Kennuka took his plunge, but time can expand and compress easily as breathing when you work a case hard. Dmitri was the first boyfriend I'd had who didn't care about the odd hours and the long absences.

Thinking about him made me snarl a little, under

my breath. Bryson cocked his eyebrow at me, and I pretended to be clearing my throat. "Allergies."

"Whatever. What the fuck is a Wendigo?"

"A shapeshifting creature who stalks prey and drinks blood to survive," I said.

"Great. Fucking perfect," Bryson muttered. "Because I can absolutely stand up in front of a grand jury and say 'Yes, Your Honor, these four victims were shot in the head to conceal the fact that they were *actually* killed by a mythical creature that has a funny name and drinks blood.'" He banged on the keyboard. "You're killing me, Wilder."

"There's more to it," I assured him. "The vics were targeted for a reason beyond feeding, and the Wendigo I spoke to are hiding something. Things are in motion."

"Ain't that helpful," Bryson snorted. " 'Things.' You're a brilliant Hexed detective, Wilder, let me just say."

"Listen," I snapped, "I'm doing the best I can to save your ass here, so why don't you try shutting your trap and being grateful for once?"

Jason Kennuka's face flickered up on the screen along with the coroner's report on his death. "You want to do something useful?" I said. "That's the brother of the guy I talked to. He killed himself, and he was in deep with the group that made those walking were-dead things. You want to find the killer and try to get him in human form, there's your lead. Go fetch, Sherlock."

Bryson grunted. "Sorry. It's early. I ain't had my coffee."

"That and you're sort of an asshole," I muttered.

"You're no prize yourself, Wilder," Bryson said. "So, we going?"

I blinked. "What are you saying?"

"I'm not walking into the home of some freaky-deaky blood drinker on my own," said Bryson. "Something wanted this guy taken out, so you say, and if it's still around . . . better you than me."

"Gee, David," I said, "I'm almost touched." My blood beat faster at the thought of going out to a scene, and the were scented the air for prey. "Yeah, I'll come," I said out loud.

Jason Kennuka's apartment in the Garden Vista building was about as cheerful as the execution chamber at Los Altos. An army cot, the covers crumpled to one side, sat in a corner of the studio space, which had a high ceiling clothed in rusted stamped tin, a flickering light fixture, and fingers of mold creeping out of the crevices. To one side an ancient gas stove and a dripping sink took up most of the space. The only other furniture in the room was a dresser.

Bryson kicked a mildewed Persian carpet. "Smells like dead grandmothers in here. Lots of 'em."

I stood in the center of the room and surveyed the detritus of Jason Kennuka's last days. The man hadn't had much, and what there was, was on the floor. I narrowed my eyes at the mess, which included the rug crumpled in a corner and rifle marks on the one locked drawer in the dresser. It was so filthy anyway that it was hard to believe, but there was broken glass around the sink, and a suspicious lack of personal objects anywhere.

"Bryson, this place has already been tossed."

"Shit," he muttered. "Who even cares about some freak-job suicide?"

"Whoever wants the weres dead," I said. A pot sat next to the stove, a rucksack overflowing with dirty clothes and books, and a squat black manual camera with a long lens.

"That seems sort of pricey for a guy living in this craphole," I said, pointing.

Bryson nodded and slipped on gloves, picking the camera up. "Pawnshop sticker. No film. What'd he even need this thing for?"

"Beats me," I murmured. "Glove?" Not that we'd find anything in the wake of the Wendigo.

Bryson flipped one at me like a rubber bullet. I snatched it out of the air with a snap. "Don't throw things at the woman with animal reflexes," I said when he grunted.

"Wilder, I been thinking," he said as we started searching the mess.

"Oh no."

He stopped and crossed his arms. "I know you got some high horse you're ridin' on about me and my deductive skills . . ."

"Or lack thereof," I muttered.

". . . but even Your Highness has to admit this case is thin. What are we into here, some kind of werewolf/blood slurper vendetta match?"

"Maybe," I said. "People get shot for their cell phones and stabbed for their rims every day in this city, Bryson. Maybe revenge is all the Wendigo are after."

"Okay," said Bryson. "But why now? Things have been quiet for a damn long time if this is the first I'm hearing of some big blood feud."

"When you start making sense, I start worrying that maybe it's time to check into Cedar Hill Psych for a few days," I muttered. Bryson had a point. If revenge was the motive, *I* didn't fit as a victim. I had never wronged them. The only thing I had in common was blood, reaching back tenuously to a treaty that no one even obeyed any longer.

Thin, like Bryson said.

He began to rattle the locked dresser drawer, cursing when it wouldn't give. "Oh, move," I said, sighing. I wedged my fingers into the gap and popped the lock with a small exertion, sending it shooting across the room.

"You'd be real handy in a rugby match," said Bryson. "Anyone ever tell you that?"

"The shorts are unflattering," I said. A manila envelope caught my eye, one edge raised over the lip of the drawer like a tiny sail.

The envelope was shiny with dirt and use, and crumpled at the corners. It was stuffed full of prints, a street map of Nocturne City scrawled over with notations in some kind of private shorthand, and a few newspaper articles from the previous month, neatly clipped out and shoved to the bottom of the stack.

"Bryson," I said, turning over the first print. "You need to look at this."

He came to my shoulder and whistled when I showed him the photo of Priscilla Macleod, the grainy long-lensed framing marking it as a clandestine shot. "Well, Hex me. What is he, some sort of shapeshifting perv?"

"They're all here," I said. "All four victims plus Carla." And me, caught as I unlocked my car outside the Justice Plaza, as I ate at the Devere Diner . . . I pushed down a shudder and unfolded the map. Now that the photos were arrayed next to the map, the shorthand contextualized. P.M. for Priscilla, along with a green spider track of ink around a neighborhood in downtown that I recognized as Warwolf territory. J. T.

for Jin Takehiko, crawling among the pricey avenues of the Mainline district.

"Was he . . ." Bryson cocked his head and crouched to examine the map. "Was this motherfucker *stalking* them?"

"Hunting," I said softly. "This is way beyond a thrill. Jason was a pro." Everything in the apartment spun around my already formed thoughts like debris in the tracks of a tornado. Jason was involved. Did Lucas know? Was that the lie?

"Well, this is motive," said Bryson. "Far as I'm concerned, my number one suspect is now pancake boy. That would explain why no one's made a move on Carla yet."

"Why?" I muttered. I wasn't speaking to Bryson but to Jason, and by extension Lucas. "No reason to kill them . . ." I stood up and paced to the window, looking into the rows of tombstone teeth in the cemetery across the street. "This doesn't make sense, David."

"Told you so, Wilder," he said. He gathered up the map and the photos, separating out the ones of Carla. "Say one thing for this fruitcake, he knew his job. This is good, detailed surveillance. He'd been on to Carla for months. All of them, a four-month lead on the murder at least."

I half turned my head. "Really?" The disturbed stirring of illogical evidence turned to something colder and more pressing, like being suspended by a cable over a dark space with skittering, hungry sounds at the bottom. That feeling always engulfed me when there was more to a case than I realized.

"Yeah," said Bryson. "The weres never made him, either. So much for your sniffers, eh?"

"There's no sense in that," I said. "If Jason was

hunting prey, he wouldn't stalk them for four months. Wendigo are hungry, always, and they're good predators." Probably better than weres and definitely better than me, but I didn't articulate that part. "There's no *reason* to do it like this."

"Let's finish this search," said Bryson. "I can feel my clothes starting to grow fungus."

"Polyester doesn't mildew," I said halfheartedly. Bryson went over to the tiny kitchen and began rattling cabinets, and I examined the rest of Jason's space with a perfunctory eye. The wall over the bed was sunken just a bit, but what really caught my eye was the fact that the plaster was new and free of mold. I rapped my knuckles against the spot and got a hollow popping sound in return. "There's something back here," I said to Bryson.

"Hang on, I got a pocketknife," he said. I drew back my fist and punched through the plaster, digging away the chunks of joint compound from the hole and revealing a small square space set between the joists and the brick of the outside wall. "Never mind," Bryson said with a sigh.

A little shelf held a leather bag stuffed full of dried-out herbs and a small circle of flat stones surrounding a squat black statue with a distended belly and a huge mouth replete with roughly carved teeth.

"What the Hex is that?" said Bryson. "Some kinda shrine?"

I picked up the herbs and sniffed. They had a sharp tang that wasn't familiar to me. The stones seemed to be regular riverbed rocks like the type Sunny and I used to collect for Aunt Delia in the summer when drought dried up the streams. Together, nothing about the elements of the odd, secret altar suggested menace, but the hairs on my neck went stiff all the same as I examined all the pieces of ritual.

"I don't know," I murmured to Bryson. "It was hidden back here for a reason. I've never seen anything like it, really. Witches use casters to focus, not statues." Though who knew what Wendigo used. How had I not asked Lucas these questions?

Because he had nice eyes and a fantastic chest, that's why. Idiot.

"Maybe it's the statue," said Bryson. "It could be gold on the inside, like. Some kind of Maltese Falcon deal."

"Let's see," I said, and picked it up.

The magick hit me like stepping in front of an express train, and threw me off my feet and backward into the center of the damp, crumpled rug. I felt it in me like teeth in my flesh, magick so dark and dense that it stole air from my lungs.

I screamed, back twisting as the were clawed for the surface of my mind. The phase gripped me unawares as the thing fed me more and more power. I thrashed, unable to loosen my rigid fingers from the splintery grooves of the statue.

Through the black vortexes in front of my vision I saw Bryson pull his gun, change out the clip for another he carried in his inside pocket, and aim at me.

I howled, the were meeting his challenge and I knew, impossible as it was without a full moon to do it under, that I would change and kill him. The dark magick was forcing my phase, just as Alistair Duncan had once forced his plain human son to become a wolf . . .

"No," I choked, under a pain that was a thousand times worse than the phase. My muscles and bones rippled and bucked under my skin like the city in the throes of the earthquake. *"No,"* I snarled. There was a time when I could not hold back the phase, but it would not be now.

I pushed against the were, shaking like a plucked string and fighting with every bit of myself that was still *me* to keep the phase at bay. I was stronger than this. The days when I feared the phase were gone. "You are not me," I hissed at the were.

The pain peaked to an unbearable crescendo and then I felt it lessen, inch by inch, over my skin. My rigor-tight grip on the statue finally lessened and I threw it down. It rolled into a corner and thumped against the wall.

Bryson lowered his weapon, flipping the safety on with his thumb. "Wilder?"

"I'm okay," I gasped. I was soaked in sweat and my fingertips and gums started to bleed as my fangs and claws receded. "I'm okay . . ."

I got to my knees and Bryson extended a hand to help me up. "What the Hex was that?" he asked.

"Bad magick," I said. "Do me a favor and get that thing. I can't touch it."

"Yeah . . . okay," said Bryson, picking the thing up like the massive wooden jaws might close around his fingers. "You sure you're all right?"

I didn't feel all right, but I pulled my shoulders back and nodded, keeping my jaw tight and swallowing blood. "What's with you changing the clip of your gun? You do that every time you have to shoot? It's cramping your style."

"Nah," said Bryson. "I went to one of those basement stores down by the university when I caught this case and got some were-proof ammunition. For insurance."

I splashed rusty water on my face from Jason's sink. "Insurance?"

"Silver bullets," said Bryson. He threw up his hands when I glared at him. "Don't look at me like that! I gotta look out for myself!"

"You better hit whatever you're aiming at with a kill shot," I said. "Otherwise it just pisses us off. And I've seen you qualifying at the range. I think you'd be better off with some Mace and a good pair of running shoes." My bicep still bore a faint streak of scarring from where a silver slug had plowed through the flesh one night almost a year ago.

Bryson ejected the clip of silver and I snatched it from him, putting it in my back pocket. "Your insurance is canceled. I'm not going to explain to some enraged pack leader why you panicked and plugged one of their charges with a damn Van Helsing round."

"Those bullets cost a hundred and twenty bucks!" Bryson complained.

"Overpriced," I said, popping my back to ease out the last kinks of the abortive phase. "Let's get out of here."

Grumbling, Bryson picked up the statue and followed me.

I called Sunny after Bryson dropped me off on the corner of Devere across the street from Second Skin Tattoo. "How long will it take you to get downtown? I've got something you need to see."

The statue was dangling from my elbow, wrapped in a layer of plastic shopping bags and shoved inside a gym bag from the trunk of Bryson's car. The odor of socks and athelete's foot ointment wafted around me, and I tried to hold the bag farther away.

"Luna, I have a life," said Sunny. "I have to pick Grandma up at the airport and I have lunch plans."

"Look, Sunny, I don't ask unless it's life or death," I said. "Blow off Grandma this once."

"You ask a lot more than life or death," she said. "You ask every time you get yourself into something you can't handle because you have a big mouth and a short temper."

"Sunny," I said quietly. "This isn't about me. I need you. I don't know what I'm doing here."

"Hmph," she said. "For you to admit you have no clue is pretty rare, I will say. I'll come, but *only* until Grandma calls me to come get her."

"Thank you," I breathed. "Meet me in Perry's shop. I need a second opinion about something."

"Can you dial down the cryptic a bit?" Sunny said. "You sound shaky. What's happened?"

"Tell you when you get here," I said, feeling the statue's magick crawling across the air and over my skin. "Just get here fast."

CHAPTER 16

Perry's shop was as dim as the inside of a black cat, and blaring something post-industrial from the speakers mounted in the corners. The man himself was sitting on a rolling stool with his back to me, wispy salt-and-pepper ponytail trailing over his neck. He was working on a client who looked like an undead cheerleader—a violently blond girl with breasts that could have floated her across Siren Bay, strapped into a leather vest and shredded cutoff shorts. She'd topped the look off with boots, fishnets, and the grinning demon's head Perry was tattooing in the crevice of her cleavage.

"Perry," I said. "Perry!" to cut into the music. He stopped the needle and spun on his stool.

"Well, well, well," he purred. "Detective Wilder. I thought I smelled something sweet in the air."

"I'm talking to Perry," I said to his dead, cloudy gray eye and twisted lips. "Not to you."

The bad side of his face, bulging eye and burn-victim skin, hissed at me and he rotated all the way around. "Sorry about that," said Perry, scrutinizing me with his good eye. "The ink, you know . . . I get into it. Been a hell of a long time, Wilder. Thought you didn't love me no more."

"Now, you know that could never happen," I said.

"Excuse me," said the pep squad reject. "I'm not paying you to chitchat."

"Go back to waving your pom-poms or something," I said. I drew the statue out of the bag, careful to hold the evidence wrapper by the edges, and showed it to Perry. "Got any idea what this is?"

"Hot damn," said Perry. He got off his stool and limped over to me, his leg brace catching the low light. A long time ago, something had happened to Perry that trapped . . . well . . . not Perry in half of his body. You had to be careful which side you talked to, depending on the answer you wanted.

"This is some hard-core mojo," said Perry. "I was doing tats in Wyoming about ten years back and I ran across some medicine men working with fetishes. Nasty-ass for whoever they turned it on."

"This was used by Wendigo," I said. "It's for *what* that I don't know."

"Right, right," said Perry. "Looks like a hunger god. The shapeshifters got one they call Wiskachee. Supposed to crawl up from the ground and devour your enemies, or something."

I felt a little cold air on the back of my neck, just enough to ruffle the hairs. "Is that so."

"Bunch of bullcrap if you ask me," said Perry. He extended the fetish to me but I put my hands up.

"One touch of that thing is more than enough."

Sunny arrived then, jangling the bell on the door. "Hi, Perry."

"Sunflower." He nodded. "Anyway, the shapeshifters feed Wiskachee, honor him with his fetish worship while he sleeps, and he wakes up and makes them all motherfuckin' Superman." Perry snorted. "Or something like that. Not like I sat in on Mythology One-oh-One or nothin'."

"They . . . feed him?" said Sunny. Perry set the fetish on the counter, where it glared at me balefully. I stuck my tongue out at it when he turned his back.

"Wendigo drink blood, and from it they draw their power," said Perry. "The legends of Wiskachee speak of an unceasing, all-consuming hunger that will someday swallow the world unless the god is appeased regularly with the blood of the faithful."

I wondered if the little statue was the reason Jason Kennuka had plunged to his death. Had his wild Wendigo buddies convinced him to donate a little bit of his faithful blood? The dark magic that wrapped the fetish in layers dense as razor wire spoke to *something* pushing Jason to jump off that ledge.

"Like I said, crap," said Perry. "I ain't saying that Wiskachee and his magick aren't real, but that business about the end of the world—do you know how many bargain-basement necromancers spout the same shit?" He stumped over to the cash register to ring up the irate coed. "Wendigo are first-class freaks . . . you know their burial grounds are underneath the whole city? Shallow graves all over the damn place. Gave the caster witches a turn when they were building up back in the 1800s. At any rate, Luna . . . you find anything else like that fetish, bring it here. I'll add it to the collection."

"I won't *live* long enough if I ever brush up against something like that again," I said.

Perry gave a wet laugh that came out the twisted side of his mouth. "We all gotta go sometime, Wilder. Might as well make it with a bang."

In the hallway, as we walked to the stairwell, Sunny looked at my face. "You're thinking. That face always means you're thinking. What are you worried about?"

"I'm not worried," I said. "I'm frustrated and confused."

She worried her lip. "About what?"

I banged open the stairwell door, stamping harder than I had to on the narrow stone steps. "About how I'm going to explain all of this god-summoning, human-killing madness to someone who doesn't believe in any of it."

With most grief-stricken relatives, *By the way, your brother was a religious nut who threw himself off a building for Hungry Jesus* will get you outraged sobs at best and fisticuffs or restraining orders at worst.

But then again, Lucas hadn't been straight with me, either. I snarled as Sunny and I walked through the university gates. "What's so gods-damn hard about being honest, Sunny?"

"The truth hurts," she said.

"Me putting a foot in their ass is going to hurt the Wendigo a lot more," I grumbled.

Sunny pulled me back as I, in my righteous indignation, almost walked into traffic. She punched the button for the crosswalk light and shook her head. "Calm down, Luna."

"I've had a shitty-ass day," I said. "*You* go ahead and be calm. I'll stay over here in my rage bubble, thanks."

"What's really rare is for you not to be in a rage bubble," Sunny said. If it was anyone but her, I would have slapped the smug taste right out of her mouth, and I was considering it with Sunny when I caught the scent of wet dog over my shoulder. I whipped around and saw the green sedan parked directly across the street from Sunny's convertible.

"Wait here," I said to Sunny, starting to walk.

"Luna, what . . . ," she called, but I held up a hand, going to the passenger's-side window and looking in.

Donal Macleod's pet were was hunched over the steering wheel cursing and trying to fidget a digital camera's battery back into its slot. I walked around the car into the street, flashing my badge at a car that honked, and then put my elbow through his window.

He yelped and scrambled away from the shards as I reached in, grabbed him by the back of his collar, and hauled him, kicking and screaming, out the broken window and into the road.

"Why the fuck are the Warwolves following *me*?" I shouted.

"There's a truck coming!" he screamed. A few hundred feet up Devere Street, a semi barreled toward us, horn blatting.

"Then you'd better answer fast," I said.

"I'm just following orders!" he cried.

"In about five seconds you're going to be just a bunch of meat in the middle of the road. Good luck following them then."

"Donal told me to!" he said finally. "He said to follow you and make sure you were doing the job! We had to get justice for Priscilla! Pack justice!"

The semi was close enough for me to feel the heat from the engine. I jerked the Warwolf to the side and sent him sprawling on the hood of his car. He was gasping, sweat pouring down his face. "You crazy bitch . . ."

"None crazier," I said. I took my handcuffs off my belt. "How much did you hear?"

"Everything," he gasped. "Filthy, stinking monsters."

Pendantics are so unattractive. I thumped the Warwolf on the back of the head. "Roll over and put your hands behind you before I throw you into traffic again."

He did as he was told. I like that in a suspect. I got the handcuffs on one of his wrists and started to reel off his Miranda. "You have the right to remain . . . *oof.*"

His foot came up and back and got me in the gut, the tender section just above the belly button that makes all of your air vacate your body at once. I doubled over on my knees in the gutter between the sedan and a fire hydrant, making loud sucking sounds as I tried to breathe.

The Warwolf took off up the sidewalk, spinning Sunny around as she tried to catch him by the jacket, my handcuffs jangling merrily from his wrist.

That was the second time I'd lost my handcuffs to a recalcitrant were, and I vowed then and there it would be the last.

Sunny crouched next to me. "Luna, are you all right?"

"No . . . ," I wheezed, and then abruptly retched and vomited onto the pavement. "Better . . . now . . ."

"Come on, hon," said Sunny, maneuvering me gently to my feet. "Let's get you home."

"No . . . ," I insisted. "I gotta . . . get that guy . . . before he tells the other packs and screws the case."

"If you vomit in my car," said Sunny matter-of-factly, "I am going to kill you slowly. Buckle up."

I protested, but by the time Sunny supported me upstairs to bed, the combined events of the day had piled on my shoulders and all I wanted to do was sleep.

I rocketed out of a muddled dream about Lucas and

blood on naked skin and an ancient, aching hunger inside of me to the telephone shrieking next to the bed. Sunny had left a scrawled note on my pillow. *Gone to airprt., back after G-ma @ home.*

I jerked the old-style rotary phone out of its cradle. "Yeah?"

"Luna?" the voice said. I recognized it immediately, straight and biting as edged metal.

"Lucas."

"I hope you don't mind me calling," he said. "I need to know what the morgue hours are so I can identify Jason and . . . well . . . I thought it'd be better to call you."

Gods, why did he have to sound so lost? Maybe I was just turning into a paranoid gun-toting nut who saw everyone as a liar. It would be easier to believe if 90 percent of the people I came in contact with in daily life *weren't* liars, of one stripe or another.

"They open tomorrow at nine," I said, "but Lucas . . . one of the packs that the dead weres belonged to got wind that Wendigo were involved." I didn't go into how because I already felt bad enough without feeling like a dumbass on top of everything else.

"I'm coming," said Lucas, a snarl creeping into his voice. "Jason was my brother."

"I really think this is a bad idea," I said. "I know what I said, but pack justice is taken very seriously and as an Insoli, I can't protect you."

"I'm not worried," said Lucas. "You're going to be there with me. You're all I need."

Yup, I was definitely a paranoid nutcase.

"You really trust me? I gotta warn you, that hasn't worked out so hot for a few other people."

Lucas gave a short chuckle. "Luna, the only thing you could possibly do is make this a little easier. I'm not doing so hot, but I'll hold it together because that's what Jason would have wanted. Will you meet me there in the morning?"

"Of course," I said, feeling my core and other parts of me warm slightly at the tone of his voice. I felt a ridiculous surge of happiness at the thought of visiting the morgue. "Don't worry about anything, Lucas. This treaty bullshit won't cause any unpleasantness for you when you come to get Jason."

"I'll see you tomorrow, Luna."

"See you tomorrow," I agreed, and hung up the phone with a huge, irrational smile on my face.

Lucas finally showed up at the morgue an hour late, after I'd worn a groove in the stone steps, pacing and waiting. There was a hot, wet wind off the bay and I kept scenting the salt, thinking I'd catch another were.

He climbed out of the passenger's side of a rusty pickup, and waved the driver off when he saw me. "Let's get this over with," he said, shoving his hands into his pockets.

"All right," I said. "Have trouble finding the place?"

"Not as much as I would have liked." Lucas was stiff, and his eyes moved from face to face as we went through the glass doors and across the lobby. He also looked shredded—like he lost ten pounds since I'd seen him last. His face was covered with uneven stubble and his eyes were sunken and red. He coughed, and it rattled inside his rib cage with a wet sawing sound.

I put a hand on his shoulder. Lucas wasn't putting out any heat—he was the temperature of the air. "You okay?"

"Peachy," he coughed. "Just perfect."

The guard at the metal detector glared at Lucas. "Going to have to search your backpack."

"He's with me," I said, moving my T-shirt to show my badge. "Let us through."

Lucas breathed out and shook his shoulders. "This is going to be harder than I thought."

"You just have to look in through the viewing window," I said. "And tell the morgue attendant where to release the body to."

"We don't have any goddamn money for a funeral," Lucas muttered. I led him over to the elevator and punched the down arrow.

"The city has a few forms you can fill out for help with that."

Lucas hissed. "I don't want your help." His eyes silvered for a moment.

I held up my hands. "Look, Lucas, I know this is tough but nobody here is trying to give you a hard time. I'm trained to be sympathetic at times like this. If you think I'm being disingenuous, that's your problem."

As soon as I snapped at him I felt awful, and to see Lucas's eyes fill up with apologies made it ten times worse. "Lucas, I'm sorry . . . I open my mouth when I shouldn't a lot and . . ."

"No," he said. "You're right. Jason's dead. He's gone."

I touched his hand. "That doesn't mean that you have to pretend like it doesn't bother you," I said quietly.

A grim smile flickered across his face. "Wendigo once ate their dead. He's less than nothing to me."

"Okay then," I murmured, staring at the old elevator dial as we descended into the bowels of the building.

The car took us to the sterile, fluorescent hallways of the morgue, where an attendant sat at the battered metal reception desk playing a handheld game that buzzed and chirped. A stark sign behind his head proclaimed NOCTURNE CITY MORGUE — NO ADMITTANCE BEYOND THIS POINT. "We're here to identify the John Doe," I said.

"Room five," he replied, never breaking concentration from the screen.

"Come on," I said to Lucas, taking his elbow and leading him into the viewing room. The drab salmon-pink curtains were pulled across the small window, and I hit the intercom button on the wall. "Are you ready for us?"

"Ready," said the morgue attendant. I turned to Lucas. "I want to prepare you—falls don't leave the body in the best condition."

"Just open the curtains," Lucas snarled.

"Fine, fine," I said, and pulled back the curtains. Jason Kennuka had the blue paper sheet pulled up to his chin, covering the worst of the damage from his fall. One side of his face was misshapen and bruised, as if a sculptor had brushed up against his medium and thrown all the lines out of joint. Jason's hair was matted with blood where his scalp had caved in, but thankfully the attendant had arranged what remained over the fractures.

Lucas stared at the body, his eyes silvering and his nostrils opening, fluttering like wings as he drew in a long breath. He put one hand on the glass, his sprouted claws screeching down the divider between us and the body.

I took a step back, unconsciously, the were putting me at optimum striking distance. "Lucas?"

"That's him," said Lucas. His voice was flat, like a

long hot highway when you run out of gas alongside. "That's my brother Jason."

"Thank you," I said quietly into the intercom, and the attendant hurried in and covered up Jason's face with the sheet.

"We're done," I said to Lucas. "You holding up all right?"

"I need some air," he whispered. His teeth were all silver fang as he spun and ran from the room.

"Shit," I said to the empty space and the flapping door. "Lucas!" I shouted at his retreating back. "Lucas, wait!"

He made it to the wide entryway where ambulances and hearses backed up to deposit or receive their particular brand of cargo, and was bent over, hands on knees, shaking and coughing. "I could smell his blood . . . ," he ground out.

"No," I said. "You smelled a lot of blood. It's hard for people . . . like us . . . in there. You did well." I held out a hand to rub his back, and then hesitated. Dmitri would go ballistic if I suggested with actions or words that he wasn't tough enough to cope without any sort of support.

But this was Lucas. I gasped as a little bit of black blood hit the loading dock from his coughing fit. "You're not all right. I'd better take you somewhere." I touched him gingerly between the shoulder blades and he let out a cry, just a single dry sound that was all he allowed himself. Then his eyes were his own again, and his cough subsided.

"Do you know once, when I was a dumb kid, I was in a bar over the state line, and I got into it with this gang of neo-Nazi assholes. I figured no big deal, I'll shift if they get to be too much of a problem. But Jason came in and he stood next to me and he said, 'If you show yourself now, think of what will happen to the clan. Think what will come down if the secret gets out.' "

Lucas swiped at his eyes. "And then he turned to the biker sons of bitches and said, 'If you want to take him on, you take me on, too, and a pair of Kennuka brothers is something no pig's asshole wants ruining his day.' " He sighed. "Until he went off, there wasn't a day that went by that I didn't see him. He was my brother."

I crouched down next to Lucas and put my arms around him. "I know," I murmured. "And he was a good brother." Then, because I'm neither a coward or a completely heartless bitch, I said, "Lucas, there are some things that have come up about Jason. I need to talk to you."

"All right," he said.

I let go of his solid form and reached into my jean pocket for a tissue. "Here."

Lucas wiped the blood off his chin. "I'll be fine in a little while. Must have a bug."

"If you say so," I said. "Do you like Mexican food?"

"I'm hungry," he murmured, and his eyes flared silver again. "I mean, yes. I eat Mexican. What's wrong that you need to take me somewhere I won't cause a scene to hear it?"

I closed my eyes and sighed. "Just . . . some things I think you need to hear from me. From someone who understands your situation. You take my meaning?"

Lucas nodded silently. "Yeah, okay. I have to deal with the funeral arrangements . . . can we meet this evening?"

"I'll wait," I said. "Not letting you out of my sight, remember?" That got me a small smile.

The coroner gave Lucas a metric ton of forms for funeral assistance, and it was dusk by the time he finished. "Let's get out of here."

I offered him a hand, which turned into me keeping my arm around his shoulder. Lucas didn't say he was grateful or not, but from the way he leaned against me I think he was just glad to have someone prop him up. I know that if our situations were reversed, if it had been Sunny or Mac under the blue sheet, that my body would have been a useless bag, unable to contain my grief.

Lucas was handling it a lot better than I would have. I just tried not to think about how I was going to explain the scent of him on me to Dmitri. If he came back.

CHAPTER 17

I took Lucas to El Gato y Ratón, a Mexican burrito joint tucked away down an alley off Magnolia. The neighborhood mostly caters to winos buying Ripple from the liquor store that took up the front half of the building, neon beer signs pushing against the smudgy fog that had drifted in over the course of the day, and methheads using the sidewalk for a mattress.

"Spare change?" one of them bleated at me, flashing dirty fingers and a mouth with more gaps than teeth.

I showed my badge. "Get lost."

"Bitch," he spat.

Lucas turned on him. "Another word and I'll pick your bones clean."

The speed freak backed off, and I nudged Lucas. "The chivalry really isn't a big thing with me. I've been called a lot worse by guys that *weren't* out of their minds on meth."

"No excuse for human filth," said Lucas. "I was doing the world in general a favor."

"Fair enough," I said, pushing open the door of El Gato. The sensor over the jamb played an electronica version of the Mexican Hat Dance. The decor ran to light-up cacti, beer signs with coyotes and XX symbols on them, and chili-shaped Christmas lights dangling from the ceiling, but it smelled like pico de gallo and warm tortillas and caramel, the burritos served were as big as my forearm, and the beer was kept frosty cold.

Lucas slid into a sticky blue vinyl booth and I followed him, picking the side that let me see the door and the kitchen with relative ease.

"What did you want to tell me about Jason?" said Lucas, after he had waved off a beer and settled on plain iced water.

"Well," I hedged. Gods, how much did I *not* want to have this conversation with Lucas? About as much as I wanted a walk-in vault full of designer shoes and vintage purses. As much as I wanted to go back home and find Dmitri and an un-Hexed life waiting for me.

"Well . . . ?" Lucas prompted. "Luna, I'm not going to get violent. Jason dying is what it is. If you think I should know something, spit it out."

Luna. My name sounded so soft-edged, so dark when it rolled off his tongue.

Okay, Wilder. Focus.

"There's some indication that your brother had become involved with the wild Wendigo shaman," I said, letting it all out in a rush. Lucas carefully set his water glass down in the center of a coaster advertising a *telenovela* and met my eyes.

"So?"

Perspiration stippled my skin and matched the water droplets on my beer bottle. El Gato wasn't air-conditioned and the humidity outside was still making the temperature climb. Nearly dark, and still the city cooked at a slow boil.

"I went to his apartment with the lead detective in

the murder case," I said. "And we found certain . . . things . . . that made me believe Jason might not have been entirely forthcoming with you, Lucas."

His face shut down, into that planar shell I was beginning to recognize as Lucas's carefully neutral expression to hide some form of rage or hunger. "Things. Like objects?"

"Yes," I said, shredding my napkin and not realizing it until I dropped my eyes to see my upper thighs covered with paper snow. "A fetish statue, specifically, for some kind of Wendigo god?"

Lucas rubbed his forehead, his fingers creasing the wrinkles that hid there and releasing them. "Those fucking things aren't real. Jason couldn't have believed in any of our gods." He slapped his palm down on the table. "My gods are all dead."

"Even so, there was magick there," I told him, backing up a fraction in my seat. Lucas's moods were changeable as his eyes. "I felt it."

"Then what you felt was a fraud," said Lucas. "Blood magick, or even caster magick, worked by someone who thinks it's funny to prey on the guillible savages. Where's this fetish now?"

"I left it with a friend," I said. "Lucas . . . did it occur to you that the shaman might have caused Jason's death?"

"No. Jason wouldn't have been into all of that religious junk," said Lucas. "And you can't compel somebody who doesn't believe. Isn't that the principle of casters and *vaudun* and all the rest of the bullshit artists?"

"It's amazing what someone charismatic can influence a good man to do," I said, putting my hand over Lucas's. "I think you know it's possible. You must, or you wouldn't have let me speculate this far."

After a long, long silence when the only sound was an old Los Lonely Boys track on the restaurant's tinny PA, Lucas moved his hand out from under mine, folded them in his lap, and said, "I do know. Jason had been gone for a long time. I knew something had gone wrong—wronger than him running wild—but I didn't want to bring it up to the clan and have it get back to our mother."

"Any idea at all why Jason and these wild Wendigo might be ritualizing their kills?" I said. "It doesn't make sense from what you've told me about your people."

"That's just it," Lucas snarled. "The wild ones don't do what we do. They only obey hunger. I'm not like them, so don't ask me to get inside their head."

A waiter set down our steak burritos, giving Lucas a glance when he raised his voice. *"No te precoupes,"* I said to him with an apologetic smile. He rolled his eyes and went back to the kitchen.

"I'm sorry," I told Lucas. "But I've got a job to do here, and I'm trying to stop this before it gets bigger than either of us can handle."

Lucas stopped in mid-bite, sniffed, and his head rotated toward the door like he was a missile locked on to a target. "I think it already has."

Over the pleasant combination of scents from my beer and my burrito, something drifted to my nostrils that was too familiar and very, very unwanted. The distinctive wet-dog scent was different for every were pack, but it meant the same thing: Lucas and I were screwed.

I pulled a twenty out of my wallet and threw it down, standing up and unsnapping the strap on my holster. "Come on," I said to Lucas. "Stay behind me."

He flowed up from his chair, his speed displacing

my eye, but he refocused just behind me. "Is that what I think it is?"

"I'm afraid so," I said, pushing open the door of El Gato with my free hand. The other one was welded to the butt of my service weapon. Not that a regular bullet would do much good if the weres outside were good and pissed off.

The strains of the music cut off as the door swung shut behind Lucas and me.

Five figures stood in the alley, arms crossed, knowing that eventually we'd have to come outside. I recognized Donal, and the four with him all sported the green knot tattoo and the surly expression of were muscle.

"Evening," I said, trying hard not to let the shiver in my gut work its way into my voice. Five weres against the two of us, and not a full moon in sight.

That was it. We were freaking dead.

"You are in direct violation of the treaty, you Wendigo filth," Donal snarled.

"Hold on there," I held up a hand. "I know I didn't just hear you threaten someone's life right in front of a Nocturne City law officer."

The other four growled at me and Donal remained unamused, his face like a stone. "Stay out of our way, Insoli. You're interfering in pack business. Leave now, or I will put you down."

"Dude," I said, staring into his eyes, "threatening me is a really bad idea. Especially right after you've interrupted dinner at my second-favorite restaurant. By the time I deal with you, the whole thing is going to be cold. Do you have any idea how much a cold burrito upsets me?"

"Is she serious?" his tallest goon muttered to Donal.

"You have no idea how much," I told him, slipping

my gun out of holster and holding it down at my side. "*Dead serious* would be an accurate expression to use."

"Missy, you're involved in something that you can't possibly understand," said Donal. "I don't know what this filth has told you, but I guarantee he's a liar."

"*Mauthka ye,*" Lucas spat at Donal. "You're the filth, dog. Go scratch your fleas."

"Aye, I'll scratch my fleas here at home in my own bed while your people squat in the dirt and chew on the bones of what we weres decide to throw at you!" Donal bellowed.

"Let's peel his skin off," a goon giggled.

"There won't be a death, but there will be apology for what he did to my poor niece," Donal growled. "I'm in charge here. You made a bad mistake coming this close, you Wendigo coward."

The tall Warwolf made a move toward us, claws sprouting from his hands, long and deep red. That was new. Also sort of creepy. The were let out a roar, his lips pulling back.

I fired my gun straight up into the air, the report rolling away like a miniature thunderclap down the alley and back from the stone walls all around us. "Everybody settle the fuck down!"

Donal stepped closer, arms crossed. "Stand aside, girl. There's more to this than your little mind can handle. Last warning you're going to get."

"Just go, Luna," Lucas said, smiling at Donal the way a psychopath smiles at a pretty blond. "I can handle this. I *want* to." His tongue flicked out, rose-pink. "I'm still hungry."

"No," I said. "I won't. I'm not a member of your pack, Macleod. The treaty doesn't apply to me, and I offered Lucas my protection. Lucas is here to *help* me find the person who killed Priscilla, so if anyone has a problem with that, then you can go Hex yourselves."

Donal smiled and tilted his head. "So be it, Insoli." He grabbed me by the shoulders, lifted me off the ground, and tossed me in one smooth movement that I never would have seen coming from someone his age, were or not.

I spun, my vision turning into a blur of neon and grinning were faces, and then I hit the brick wall next to the door of El Gato, splitting my lip and bloodying my nose. My gun slid away underneath a Dumpster, and I was paralyzed for a few seconds as flashbulbs went off in my brain.

"Set yourselves on him!" Donal howled, and the Warwolves closed in on Lucas, the tall one catching him in the gut with a kick that doubled him over. I saw Donal pull out a short steel baton from his pocket and close in on the group. It may not have been the full moon, but that didn't mean five rage-fueled weres couldn't damage Lucas and me beyond recognition.

"Get up, Luna," I muttered, making it to my knees. My mouth tasted of hot iron, my blood and the scent of Lucas's fear mingling hotly on my tongue. I went for Donal, since he was the skinniest and totally involved in hitting Lucas's hunched back with a baton.

Donal had a mess of shaggy red hair hanging beyond his collar, and that was what I grabbed for, jerking his head backward and ruining his balance. I put my foot between his, exerting backward pressure on his knee while I used the reins of his hair to push his head forward. When my sweep had doubled Donal over, I brought my other knee up and into his face with enough force to make his nose crunch like someone had just stepped on a box of crackers.

Donal grunted and dropped the baton, holding his nose and hissing invective at me.

A blow caught me low in the back and I got spun around, going down on one knee and wheezing as flames spread up and down my left side. "Back off," said the tall goon. "I don't want to hurt you. You're a waste of my time."

He moved into a stance that was far more formal and trained than the Thai boxing I employed to beat on punching bags and thugs, watching me intently as I tried to think of something witty and biting to retort. *Ow* was all that sprang to mind, so I just got up and went for him, trying to duck his defenses.

I got a hit in the jaw and in the gut for my trouble. Goonie was faster than me, and I was willing to bet he actually worked at his arts instead of relying on punching harder than the other guy. I blocked one of his blows with my forearm but he dipped and got me in the midsection again, and down I went, on the ground eye level with Lucas. His eyes were wide and tinged with silver as two Warwolves hit him.

"Stop," I gritted. "Leave him alone . . ."

Donal landed on me, his legs on either side of my hips, pinning me down. "I should tear your throat out," he snarled, his voice thick from blood and his shattered nose. His face was a spatter painting of red and white, blood smeared to his cheekbones and down his chin, bringing his scars into relief.

"Get off me!" I cried, trying to throw him off, but he twisted a hand into my hair and in what I can only assume was the bright lady's sense of supreme irony held me down with it.

Lucas had gone still under the thug's fists, and I groaned. "Oh gods . . ."

"Keep quiet," said Donal. "The last thing we need is the ruddy police down on us." His fangs grew as he crouched over me. They were long and ocher, needles more than teeth. I imagined a vampire would have such teeth, that when Donal was finished murdering me he'd swallow my blood down.

"Luna." The voice was so low I doubted any of the squealing, snarling weres heard it, but I twisted my head around and met Lucas's eyes. They were slitted and silver, but he stared directly at me. I saw him work one hand free from the goon, and he sent Donal's steel baton rolling toward me.

I grabbed it up and snapped it open. Donal roared at me and I glared back. "Chew on this, you Dracula freak." I whipped the baton sideways across his face, heard a howl, and saw one of his red fangs fly free as blood spurted afresh from his mouth. Donal rolled off me, grasping his face and cursing.

"You may never be pretty again," I told him. "But on the bright side, there wasn't much there to work with before."

Goonie hit me from behind, throwing his entire weight into the blow, but I shifted and lowered my shoulder and he went spinning over it to land on his back, gasping. I lifted my foot and kicked him in the throat. The were beat in my blood and I honestly didn't care if I killed the Warwolf or not. He'd challenged me and I was answering in the most final way I knew how.

"Stop!" Donal's voice rang off the walls of the alley as my gunshot had a few moments before. He held a squirming Lucas by the neck, big hands on either side of the Wendigo's jaw. "Stop or I break his neck," Donal said. He twisted Lucas's head to the side for emphasis.

Lucas's face was swollen and his nose and mouth

were bleeding, but he didn't so much as grunt in pain, just glared steadily ahead at nothing.

"None of this had to happen," I said, feeling my breath rip in and out of my lungs with a hot, weightless tug. The Warwolf squirmed under my foot and I pressed down harder. "Hold still," I snarled. To Donal I said, "Both of us let go at the same time. Everybody walks away."

Donal shook his head. "That won't happen, missy. We're teaching this filth a lesson one way or another."

"He *didn't do anything!*" I bellowed. "He's not what you should be afraid of!"

Donal laughed once, short and dry and more like a cough. "Oh, you poor girl. How he has you fooled. You're loyal as a panting dog to that sweet smile and those melting eyes, aren't you?"

"Patronizing the person who decides whether your friend's windpipe stays in the same shape is not the brightest move," I warned. "Might wanna shut it."

"You never should have gotten in our way," Donal said, twisting Lucas's neck farther.

"You never should have made me," I said, lifting my foot in a threat.

"Donal," his thug croaked, "maybe we should reconsider this . . ."

"You keep your mouth shut, puppy!" Donal shouted. Under his grip, Lucas shivered. It was the slightest of movements, one almost any bystander would mistake for fear. But Lucas looked at me as he did it, and his lips spread in the barest smile. Underneath, his mouth filled, under my eyes, with silver-tipped fangs.

"Oh, Lucas . . . ," I said. "No . . ."

"That's the end. I warned you . . . ," Donal started, moving to snap Lucas's neck, but he cut off as Lucas heaved under him. "Bright lady!" Donal swore, struggling to hold Lucas.

Lucas's features melted together, his hair sloughing and his ears pointing and pinning themselves close to his head. His body lengthened and became little more than skeleton and sinew bound up in gray, mottled flesh. His teeth and tongue elongated and his eyes gleamed pure silver. Talons ripped free from his fingers, trailing threads of skin and dried blood.

With a cry, Lucas wrenched the bottom half of his body 180 degrees around, his spine popping out under his skin. His feet scrabbled for purchase against the brick and he opened his mouth impossibly wide and hissed at Donal.

Donal shrieked and grabbed his ears, scuttling away from Lucas on his rear end.

Goonie had gone dead-still under me. "What on the burnt, Hexed earth is going on?"

I took my foot off his throat and hauled him to his feet. The three other thugs had long since vanished. Smart bastards. "What's going on is that you better run like hell if you don't want to be next."

The Wendigo turned the upper half of its body around to match its hips and legs, bones and muscle sliding and rebuilding under its slick hide. Donal let out a whimper, his eyes blank and glassy with shock. "There's no moon . . . ," he muttered. "There has to be a moon . . ."

The Wendigo choked out that same fleshy laugh I remembered from the forest. "I don't need the moon," it rasped, a voice like a cut throat emanating from somewhere deep in its chest. "Just hunger."

Lucas moved like air, the lines of his body blurring into smoke. "Crap," I muttered. With Lucas changed into a six-and-a-half-foot-tall blood-drinking monster, I doubted human emotion had much of a place. But son of a bitch or not, Donal Macleod didn't deserve to die just yet.

I stepped forward. "I can't let you do this."

Lucas rotated his head toward me, his neck twisting far more than was natural. I watched tendons and veins expand in his trunk, and his tongue flicked the air in front of my face. "Let him die."

"No," I said, and my voice came out a squeak, high school scream-queen variety. Great. "Lucas, let's just walk away. He can't hurt you now." I gestured at Donal, who was staring up at us from my feet, his breath shallow as he waited to see who would come out on top of our dance. "You made your point. He's not going to hurt . . ."

My speech got chopped off with a sweaty blood-stained hand over my mouth as Donal leapt to his feet and grabbed me in a bar hold across the throat. He pressed his free hand over my nose and mouth. "One step farther and I damage her beyond repair."

Lucas hissed and took a step toward us. "I'm quite serious!" Donal shouted, shaking me like a rag doll. Pretty pink-and-black tunnels of light kaleidoscoped in front of my eyes as he slowly pressed all the air out of me.

"You picked the wrong damn day to take me as a hostage," I muttered under his hand. I drew back my foot to drive the heel of my boot right into Donal's undoubtedly inadequate balls. Before I could, though, Lucas *flowed* across the space between us.

He was translucent, like smoke pushed before a hot wind, blurring limbs and features. Standing in stark relief were his hungry, gleaming teeth and eyes filled up with rage as he bore down on us.

Claws latched on to the front of my shirt, ripping gashes through the fabric and digging into my skin, and the ground dropped away from me as Lucas tore me free from Donal's grip. My neck snapped back painfully against Donal's arm and then I was flying across open space, weightless for a few seconds.

Pain went everywhere as I hit what I assumed was the opposite wall of the alley, ricocheted off it, and landed at the bottom of an empty Dumpster with a clang that would shake the teeth out of a dead man's mouth. I thought I was deaf, and possibly dead until I heard screaming.

Pulling myself to my feet with one shaking hand, I managed to hook an arm over the top of the Dumpster and peer out. Lucas had Donal backed up against a wall, advancing on him in the drop-shouldered pose that Priscilla had used to stalk me. Donal was shaking his head, graying copper hair wild, his eyes wide. "Leave . . . leave me alone . . . I order you . . . !"

Lucas hissed. "You don't order shit, mutt." He stretched out one hand, tipped with talons nearly as long as his fingers, and plunged all five of them into Donal's chest.

Donal twitched as Lucas impaled him, still very much alive and screaming, hands scrabbling at the Wendigo's grip.

"You hurt me," Lucas hissed. "You are filth. Die and be consumed." There was no venom in his voice, just a chill that stippled as water droplets on my skin as the fog rolled around us.

The mist that clung to Lucas took on a glow that expanded and darkened as his belly distended, the blood beating under his skin beginning to pick up speed as he drank Donal Macleod's life away through those awful talons. It was what I had felt inside the charm that Laurel Hicks kept over her door—primal and blunt and so very strong that my knees gave out as my Path abilities frantically scrambled to translate the ambient magick into power and failed.

Goonie broke the spell, smashing into Lucas with a snarl and taking him to ground. They rolled over and over and Lucas was on top, and his talons were in the were's chest, and this time it happened so much faster.

The Warwolf went still, pale as a vampire's ghost. His cheeks were sunken and the veins in his neck stood out. Eyes open and looking ahead in the fear of his final seconds, he was dead as dead could be.

I sagged as the magick lifted a fraction, weaving spindly webs through the air around me as Lucas's chest heaved with the stolen life. I attempted to scramble out of the Dumpster and *do* something, stop him somehow, but Lucas flowed up and toward Donal again. The were had torn his shirt and was trying to stanch his wounds, but he was shaking and his eyes were black with shock.

"Help me—" he cried, but Lucas sank his talons in deep again and fed.

I hauled myself over the lip of the Dumpster, twisted my ankle, fell and got up again. I was limping but I had a clear goal in mind, the only thing that I thought might stop Lucas before he killed Donal.

"Your soul tried to run from me," Lucas hissed. "But you can't escape my hunger, dog. You never can." His words were barely more than high whines, and I felt like my ears were bleeding.

Donal gurgled, his face going purple-tinged in the cheeks, trying to speak.

"Lucas!" I shouted, scooping up my prize from where it lay in a puddle under an arthritic streetlight.

His eyes met mine and he grinned. "Do you like this, Insoli? Do the screams excite you?"

"Let him go," I said. "This is over now. And *no,* the screams don't excite me! What kind of gods-damn creepy thing is that to say? Hex me."

"No," said Lucas, twisting his talons in Donal's chest. The were screamed, a completely human sound of pain that sliced my ears. "No, I'm still hungry."

I got a look at his eyes, and my finger stiffened on the trigger. They were dead and silver, inhuman. Something Other stared out at me, like when the daemon overtook Dmitri, but this wasn't an involuntary reaction. Lucas knew exactly what he was, and he was enjoying it. That galvanized me, got my legs back under me after the cold shock of staring at something so alien.

"Have it your way," I said, and pulled the Glock's trigger twice. The bullets went into Lucas's shoulder and passed through his upper arm. I cursed my shaky stance. I'd meant to go wide, but not that wide.

Lucas jerked as the bullets hit him and then shuddered, his knees bowing and his limbs losing rigidity as he staggered back. His talons slid out of Donal's chest with a sucking *thock* and Lucas went to ground, blackish silver blood running from his wounds.

"You . . . shot me . . . ," he said in shock, his already thin gray skin going translucent.

"Don't take it personally," I said, stepping over him, one foot on either side of his neck. "Now change back or the next one goes into your brainpan."

"You . . . wouldn't . . . ," Lucas hissed. "You *like* Lucas . . . sweet Lucas . . ."

I racked the slide on the Glock. Not necessary, but a

hell of a dramatic effect. "I don't like you that much. You wanna test the cranky, armed werewolf's patience? Go ahead."

Lucas shuddered again and then sighed. "For now." He closed his eyes and the Wendigo skin started to peel away, revealing his human shape. Naked and bruised, he curled and shivered as red blood from his wounds slowly emerged. I grabbed up his discarded shirt and shoved it into his hands.

"Put pressure on the wound, and don't you dare fucking go anywhere." I turned and went to Donal, wheezing on his back, his pulse barely more than a flutter. I took Lucas's jeans and pressed down on his richly bleeding chest wound. "Macleod. Can you hear me?"

His eyeballs roamed under his lids like a dreamer in REM sleep, but he nodded weakly.

"Okay," I said. "Stay with me. Don't fall asleep, or you'll never get to see my gorgeous face again. You got that?"

"Y . . . yes . . . ," he managed. I could hear fluid in his chest every time he spoke or breathed. Still, I smiled at him. Never let victims know when it's bad. Smile. Think of puppies and unicorns and double-decker bacon cheeseburgers served twenty-four hours. Don't telegraph *Hex it, you have a sucking chest wound* with your face.

"Good man." I felt in my back pocket and came up with a crushed cluster of plastic and silicon chips, held to a dead LCD screen with wires. I have the worst luck with phones. "Crap," I hissed. "Donal, where's your cell?"

His jaw tightened with the effort. "In my jacket . . . pocket . . ."

I felt first in Donal's left pocket and then his right, and came up with a wallet, a pack of cinnamon gum, and a butterfly knife. Finally, in the inside pocket I touched a BlackBerry covered in blood. I swiped it on my jeans and dialed the EMTs' direct line. "This is Officer Wilder." I rattled off my badge number. "Shots fired on Magnolia Boulevard. I need a bus for a gunshot wound and a stabbing outside the El Gato restaurant in the alley behind Uncle Jack's liquor store." I looked at Donal, whose breathing got shallower on each inhale and added, "Hurry."

CHAPTER 18

As sirens pricked my ears, still far enough away to be inaudible to anyone but a shapeshifter, I went back to Lucas and grabbed him by his free arm. "Get up."

"I still can't believe you shot me," Lucas groaned. "You're crazier than those damn Warwolves."

"Oh, flex your muscles and man up," I said. "It's just a flesh wound. Someone who heals like you won't even have a scar for more than a few days."

"Let me guess," said Lucas. "You were aiming for my head?"

"How I wish that were true," I muttered, getting his good arm over my shoulder. My knees vibrated under his weight. Lucas was solid as he looked, every ounce of him sinew and bone. He was a good four inches shorter than Dmitri, but he staggered against me like a drunk twice his size.

"Call me crazy," Lucas muttered as the sirens slipped into range, red lights tracing off the alley walls as they raced up Magnolia. *Shots fired* always gets their blood pumping. "But shouldn't we wait for the EMTs?"

"Not if we want to stay out of trouble. And jail," I said. Lucas and I were performing an odd and blood-soaked hop-skip away from the scene, his pain-weighted body pressing against mine like a punishing weight had been lashed across my shoulders. Behind us, an ambulance screeched to a stop at the mouth of the alley and I breathed a silent breath of relief. If Donal died, it wouldn't be because of me.

"I'm with you on the staying-in-front-of-bars part," said Lucas, "but in case you forgot, *you shot me.*"

"Lucas?" I snarled, tugging us down one of the throughways that spilled out onto Brewster Street, the smaller, dirtier back side of the Magnolia strip.

"Yeah?" he grunted, air huffing out of him as I dragged us faster now that we were out in the open.

"Quit your whining and just be glad I dragged you out of there, you son of a bitch!" I snapped.

A drag queen coming out of the twenty-four-hour convenience store on the corner made an *ooo* noise. "You tell him what it is, girl."

Lucas made a defeated sound, his other hand going around my waist and snagging in my metal-studded belt. "Damn it, I'm going to pass out."

"Not on this sidewalk, you're not," I told him. "Not unless you want to catch the kind of disease that makes parts fall off." Brewster Street used to be called Pin Street, and in Jeremiah Chopin's day was replete with seamstress shops fronting for brothels. Now it was replete with sex shops and plain old sex workers, strolling the sidewalks and the streets. There were fewer girls and boys than usual posing at the slowly cruising cars—the heat was getting to everyone.

"This way," I said to Lucas, leading us toward a drugstore with soaped-over windows. "Not much farther." The side door of the druggist's was marked DE-LIVERIES, but I wasn't fooled. Waterfront had hosted me for the five years I was a beat cop, and I remembered Officer Dixon pointing out Pop's Drug Store and Soda Fountain. "For when some types don't wanna bother with the hospital" was all he said as we cruised slowly past, keeping time with the john cars and dealers who passed back and forth along Brewster like shadows on the X-ray of an artery.

I kicked the door, rusty and stark under the old globe light, since I was holding on to Lucas with both of my hands to keep him standing. "Hello!" I bellowed. "Open up, Pops!"

After a time, I heard a chain slide back and the door cracked open, revealing a face haloed by hair that would have done any mad scientist proud. "Password?" Pop's voice was far from tremulous, old and battered as his liver probably was, judging by the smell of bourbon that rolled through the crack. Thirty years of cigarettes carried on the phrase.

"Open this door or I'll break your nose?" I guessed.

Pop's eyes narrowed. "Who the hell are you? You ain't one of my reg'lars."

Lucas stumbled against me, leaning down to Pop's level through the crack. "Let us in, old man." His eyes flowed into silver and Pop yelped, springing back and taking the door with him.

"That's my trick," I muttered to Lucas.

The back room of the drugstore was a surgery, with the equipment straight out of a horror movie from another decade. Nothing was gleaming or even particularly sterile, but I dropped Lucas onto the white-sheeted operating table with a groan of relief. "Bright lady, you're heavy."

"Been meaning to lose weight . . ." Lucas murmured. "Eating my own cooking . . ."

"Look," said Pops nervously. "I don't truck with any non-humans in here. Gives the place a bad reputation, you understand? People get worried about contamination."

"If you want to make us leave, you're welcome to try." I said, grabbing a handful of gauze and pressing it over Lucas's bullet wound. Blood soaked through the white in a starburst and Lucas yelped.

"It's not that I don't appreciate you thinking of my establishment for your discreet medical needs," said the old man, shifting from foot to foot nervously. He wore print pajamas and a raveling brown sweater. Glasses pushed up high on his head were streaked in grime. He reminded me of a gnome, and not one of the cute ones you stick in among your begonias. "But, non-humans and all . . ."

"He's a gunshot victim," I said, pointing at Lucas. "Now, are you going to do your job or am I going to deck you and use the tools myself?"

Pop's face twitched. "Can you pay?"

"Not at the moment," I said. "Think of it as a public service."

We stared at each other, Lucas's soft moans the only sound except for car horns and the catcalls of street-walkers outside. "I need to get my surgical kit from the upstairs," said Pops finally. "And morphine. Gunshots are tricky. If he wriggles all around while I'm hauling a bullet out of him . . . could be nerve damage."

"Go," I said. "And if you call the cops on us, just remember . . . nonhumans don't need guns and blades to make your demise really fast and really, really painful."

Pops let out a squeak and ducked into the front of the store through swinging doors. I sat down on the edge of Lucas's bed. His hand slid over mine and I twitched involuntarily. The skin was cold like he'd been sitting in one of Bart's freezers for a few days, and I tried to pull away, but Lucas held on. "What's wrong?" he muttered thickly.

"You have some goddamn nerve asking me what's wrong after you killed a man back there," I hissed.

"No choice," Lucas said, with a surprisingly nonchalant shrug for a guy who'd had two bullets pass through him in the previous hour. "Besides . . . you don't seem like . . . you'd be bothered."

"*Of course* I'm bothered!" I shouted, and then wondered why I was. Donal Macleod, in my situation, would probably be dancing the Highland Fling or chowing down on a haggis. He wouldn't be weeping about the grisly death of one Insoli woman who had gotten in his way.

So why was I so bothered that Lucas had killed one Warwolf and almost Donal?

"Why?" he asked me, in echo.

"Because you didn't have to," I said. It came out soft and flat, the way the truth usually sounds—anticlimactic. "You had him, Lucas. You had him and we could have gotten away. But you were going to kill him."

"Yes," said Lucas. "I was." He sat up on his elbows, a little color in his face. "It's my nature. You thought you wouldn't see my monster?" He reached across me and came back with a fresh handful of gauze, pressing it to his own shoulder. "You thought I was just like you?"

I looked at the discarded bandages on the dirty mustard-colored linoleum of the surgery, their blood so red and bright it appeared almost like a flower petal rather than something that had come from a wound. "I made a mistake," I whispered. "I have to find out why the Wendigo are killing weres and I have to find out soon. Lucas, this is all going to come crashing down because I helped you."

The detached expression chased away from his face, replaced by the warm, understated smile that was familiar. "But you did, and I'm grateful."

"We'll get you fixed up," I said. "Then you can stay low at my house until the police are finished with Donal and that body." The were's screams were still with me, and I shivered, feeling the fog of magick on my exposed skin. Whatever his faults, I severely doubted anyone deserved death in the manner Goonie had met it.

"Then?" Lucas prompted as I went quiet again. I shoved all the fear and sickness that had rushed up at me when Lucas attacked Donal back where it belonged, down below the surface where all police and soldiers and trauma workers keep their natural, human reactions to horror.

"Then I'll take you home," I said. "And we should probably try to forget we ever met each other."

Lucas squeezed my hand harder. "That's going to be rough for me, Luna."

I met his eyes, saw something there that was familiar, to a degree. It was the same lust tinged with fascination I saw when Dmitri looked at me, but there was a hesitant, shy cast to Lucas's face.

And if I was any kind of woman, I would stand up, walk out of arm's length, and never get this close to him again.

But he was making it pretty damn hard.

I detached my hand from his. "I'm with someone, Lucas."

His gaze went blank. "The smoker's a lucky bastard."

My lips twitched. "Thanks for saying so." Realizing I hadn't heard any sound from the store for some time, I got up and poked my head through the door. "Hex it. Pops ran out on us."

"I guess you'll just have to do the job," said Lucas. "Don't worry," he added when I let my horrified expression surface. "I have faith in you."

"Great. That makes a whopping one of us." I went behind the counter and found a banged-up medical box, which contained a tray of instruments and a few vials of morphine. I took it, plus a bottle of alcohol and more gauze, back to the surgery. "I don't do this sort of thing a lot."

Lucas filled an old-style syringe and held out a piece of rubber to me. "Tie my arm off."

I did, and he slapped a vein and injected himself with morphine. "Do it fast enough and I'll still be dreaming of pink bunnies and happy leprechauns," he said.

"Bright lady," I cursed. I poured alcohol over a likely pair of tweezers and took the gauze off Lucas's wound. "Hold still. This is where the pain comes," I warned, and doused the bullet hole with alcohol.

Lucas jerked, his hands clenching on the sides of the table, and I nearly lost my tenuous grip on the bullet. "Hold still!" I use hollow-point rounds, so it was still inside his shoulder, and I drew out the crumpled slug and dropped it into the wastebasket.

"You okay?" Lucas giggled. "You're not okay. You're gonna faint. Girly-girl."

"You're high," I returned. "Lightweight."

He just laughed. After I patched Lucas up and dressed the wound, we went out into the street and hailed a cab. The cabs in this part of town always smell like stale beer and exhaust and have drivers whose faces you can't see in the glow of the dashboard light.

I gave the silent driver my cottage's address and he grunted. "Driving there's gonna be hard."

"Oh no," I assured him. "Grasp the wheel, apply your foot to the gas, and Newtonian physics will do the rest."

"No." He sighed. "Ain't you been watching the television? Freeway's closed. Overpass fell down. From the quake, and all."

"Take the surface streets," I said. "Charge me whatever. Just get us out of downtown."

"This is exciting," said Lucas as the taxi puttered away in a cloud of smoke. "Never been on the lam before." He shifted so our shoulders, mine sore from tossing the thug and his swathed in bandages, touched. "How about you?"

"Once," I murmured, watching light and shadow blur into one as the cab picked up speed down Watermark Street.

"What happened?" Lucas asked. Morphine made him positively chatty.

"People died," I said, and shifted away from him on the plastic-covered cab seat, looking out my window for the rest of the ride. Self-storage units and off-track betting was the order of the day as the city devolved to urban sprawl and then faded away altogether closer to the coastline. Dilapidated houses, looking more like beached shipwrecks than dwellings, flashed in and out of the cab's headlights. A skeletal rowboat marked the turnoff to my cottage.

"Nice place," said Lucas, stepping out while I paid the cabdriver. "Looks cozy. Nice view. You ever decide to move, I'll take it off your hands."

"Wouldn't your clan have something to say about that?" I asked. The cab briefly painted Lucas and me red with its taillights before it pulled away and turned the corner. I scented the breeze coming off the water, but there were no other weres in the vicinity, Dmitri or someone who might be even more unfriendly. Although if he saw Lucas leaning on me like he was now and hobbling toward the cottage, I didn't know if that would be possible.

"Those people on the state land aren't my clan," Lucas said, with vehemence that surprised me, considering he'd been shot and drugged. "Just my family."

"Same thing," I said with a shrug, turning my key in the lock.

"It's not the same thing at all," Lucas said. "Blood means nothing. Strength is all. Weres aren't capable of understanding that."

"Gee," I said, depositing him ungently on the sofa. "Thanks a bunch, Lucas."

His mouth crimped. "I'm sorry. Shouldn't have said that." He grinned mischievously at me. "I've had a hard day, after all."

"No, me too," I said. "I have this habit of spewing out conversation with no regard for who's hearing it. The doctors think that with a well-placed surgical zipper the problem should subside on its own."

Lucas didn't laugh, just grunted. He propped one foot up on the coffee table and rather than be irritated, as I was when Dmitri put his feet all over my things, I felt myself settle and stop shaking. Lucas seemed a right fit on my sofa.

This was bad.

"Thanks for everything you did today," he said after a bit, when I got the nerve to sit down beside him. This close, I was reminded of what lived under his skin, but I didn't want to move away.

Lucas's monster didn't frighten me. I wanted to be closer to it, to see what it would make him do if we touched.

"No one has ever gone out of their way for me before," he elaborated when I was silent.

"I can't imagine why," I said, making myself move back to Just Friends distance. "It's not like you're that difficult to get along with, when you're human."

Lucas instantly sobered. "I'm not human, Luna. Why do you say these things?"

"I . . . ," I started. Lucas sat up and faced me. His eyes were narrow and had deep lines at the corners I hadn't noticed. They made him look older and rougher than he was.

"Are you so ashamed of being were that you have to try and convince yourself that when you wear human skin, you *are* human? Because that's just plain fucked up, Luna." He touched my cheek. "You're so much more beautiful than any of them."

"Stop it," I warned, pushing his hand away. "I'm not ashamed of anything, Lucas, but in case you hadn't noticed, parading around as a nonhuman doesn't make you real popular in this city. I don't have the luxury of hiding under a tree every time someone takes exception to the fact that three days out of the month, I'm fuzzy."

Lucas dropped his gaze. "This has been the worst day of my life," he said. "Seeing Jason dead . . . getting jumped. I apologize."

"It's fine." I sighed. "I'm sorry I had to insinuate he might have helped to kill four people."

"Weres," said Lucas absently. "Not people."

"Whatever," I said. "I'm just glad we got to the fifth before they snatched her."

"She's under your protection?" Lucas drawled. "That's sweet."

"Not that she really wants to be," I said. "She hates me. I'm unworthy, you know, plus I'm sort of the evil ex-girlfriend of the man who bit her."

Lucas moved a ribbon of hair away from my eyes. "That I can see. I wouldn't want to make you mad."

"Lucas." I sighed for the third time, grasping his wrist. He rotated it and squeezed my fingers between his.

"Can I just be close to you for a bit? I need it . . ."

"Technically, Bryson's protecting Carla . . . ," I babbled. "He's this guy who wears stinky cologne and horrible polyblend suits and drives a . . ."

Lucas pressed his lips against mine, soft and fast as if he'd closed his hand over my mouth. "Shut up, Luna."

I did. And he kissed me again.

To be fair, I only let it last for about ten seconds before I started trying to push him away again, but that was enough. Lucas was very gentle, cool, and sweet, and he fired every one of the instincts that the were had, the ones that overrode my human sense a lot more often than I'd like.

"I *can't*," I whispered frantically against his mouth. "Please understand . . . I won't do this to Dmitri . . ."

Lucas breathed out, his free hand on my neck. "You're so goddamn good and pure, Luna. I'd think it was an act if you weren't so earnest." He closed his eyes for a second. "Still, all good things must come to an end."

"What?" I said with a dumb-blonde blink. Lucas smiled, showing just the tips of his teeth.

"I'm still hungry." His teeth struck at my neck, close to the spot where my scars rode, and I screamed, shoving him in earnest.

"Why fight?" Lucas said, pinning my arms to my sides. "You know that sooner or later someone is going to put it in you."

"Get *off* me, you fucking psychopath!" I snarled, and twisted one hand free. I dug my thumb into his bullet wound, hard.

Lucas howled, the sound from the forest. Somewhere in the cottage, glass shattered and I went momentarily deaf.

We split apart, panting, me with a scraped neck and Lucas with a newly bleeding shoulder. "Luna?" he said in confusion, backing away from me. Understandable, because I was heading for my gun in the desk drawer by the entry. "Luna, what happened . . ." He looked at his shoulder in surprise. "I'm sorry. I'm so sorry . . ."

I yanked open the drawer and got a clip, too angry to care.

"This is all wrong . . ." Lucas got his hand on the doorknob. "Luna, you have to believe me that I'm sorry. I'm leaving. I'll . . . we'll talk later." He ran out of the cottage, the screen door flapping.

I was still sitting on the sofa with my gun when Sunny pulled up. She stopped in the doorway, eyebrow sliding up. "Is this a bad time?"

"No." I sighed, sticking the Glock in my waistband. "Just wondering if I'll ever understand men. Or if they'll get less psycho."

"Not likely," said Sunny. "I came to see if you wanted to go to a late-late dinner. Grandma's playing poker at the Indian casino. Gods know when she'll be back."

"I already tried supper," I muttered. "Got attacked

by a bunch of pissy weres. No closer to finding out why the Wendigo are playing executioner. Made out with Lucas. Think I may have broken something when I got thrown into that trash can."

"Wait, wait, wait." Sunny came in and threw her purse down, sitting on the footstool across from me. "Go back to that third thing."

"Made out with Lucas? Believe me, that's the least of it right now."

"The Wendigo. The one who might have ties to the killings. The sworn enemy of all things werewolf. You were snogging him?"

I pressed my hands over my face, flopping over on the sofa. "I screwed up big-time, Sunny."

"Yeah, you did," she said. "And now you have to figure out how you're going to fix it."

"Get a fake passport and move to Turkmenistan?"

"You could close your case, for starters," she said, crossing her arms. "Did Lucas know anything?"

"Nothing useful," he said. "He doesn't believe in Wendigo magick, which is exactly the thing I need to find the shaman . . ." I stared at Sunny through my fingers. "I have to get downtown. I know how we can find the guy. Girl. Thing. Whatever."

Sunny gave me an approving nod. "Better already. My car's outside."

After we swung by the cottage and got the charm, we drove to the Twenty-fourth to find Bryson. His desk was empty.

"Damn it," I muttered. "Come on, Sunny. Let's get out of here before somebody yells at us."

"I think they might do worse than that," she said, pointing behind me. I turned my head, already knowing what I'd see. Captain Morgan appeared through the general come-and-go of detectives and uniforms, arms crossed over her periwinkle suit jacket and its Nocturne City Boosters pin. She had a look on her face that might lead to saying *We are not amused* in a prissy accent.

I secreted the charm in my pocket and spun around. "Hey there, Captain Morgan."

"Officer Wilder. I wish I could say I was surprised to see you again, so very soon after I ordered you out of my station."

I tried smiling, but that just made Morgan glare harder, so I gave up. "Same here, Captain."

"I'm totally not involved in this," Sunny said from over my shoulder. "I was just driving because somebody beat Luna up and she's a little woozy."

"What a completely unsurprising development," said Morgan. "Officer, may I ask what exactly you think you're doing in my precinct?" She tilted her head. "*What* have you been into?"

I shrugged in what I hoped was a devil-may-care manner. My shoulder twinged where I'd smacked the wall. I gasped. "Just hungry, I guess. Bryson's always good for a snack. Where is he?"

"He's with a witness," said Morgan. "As you well know. Now, I'm not stupid, Officer. What are you doing here?"

"I thought of something pressing I needed to share with Bryson about the case," I said. "But he's not here, as you so eloquently stated, so I'll just be on my merry and slightly lopsided way."

"You must think I'm just in this station to push paper and look good," said Morgan. "Well, I'm not, Luna, and you are in serious trouble."

"I can't do this with you right now, Matilda," I said,

turning. "I'm sorry, truly, but you wouldn't believe me even if I tried to explain what's really going on."

"Officer!" she shouted as I started to walk away. "You stop right there. I order you!"

Sunny squeezed my forearm. "Luna. Don't do anything stupid."

I turned around. "I don't give a good gods damn what you think, Captain Morgan. I understand that I can't be in this case officially, but unofficially, without me, you are all fucked. Every last one of you is going to be worse off for shutting me out, so how about you bite down hard on that sour little candy you call a heart and let me do my job? Unless you want to hold me for interrogation, I believe I'm still allowed to come and go as I please, as an officer in good standing?" I jerked my arm free of Sunny's grasp. "Let's go. We have work to do."

Once we were clear of the precinct house, Sunny threw up her hands. "You're impossible, Luna."

"What?" I said. "You told me not to *do* anything stupid. Nothing in there about *saying* anything stupid."

"Like I said," Sunny muttered.

I took the charm out of my pocket, holding it by the edge of the bag. "It doesn't matter, anyway. We have this."

Sunny took it from me. "And are we planning to cast a dark spell, make this thing sit up and talk, and reveal the villain's evil plot?"

"I was more thinking we'd take another crack at figuring out who made it. If the Loup were dealing with Wendigo, there's a good chance the witch knows the shaman we're after."

"That I can do," Sunny said. She opened the driver's

side of her convertible and started the engine. "Of course," she said, "finding the shaman is the easy part. Wendigo can't be killed, not the way weres and witches and humans can. I trust you factored that in."

"One of these days," I muttered. "You're going to forget something, and then I am going to point and laugh."

"Until that day, why don't you be quiet and rest your shoulder?" Sunny suggested.

"Not because you tell me to," I said. "Just because I'm too tired right now to think of a witty rejoinder."

She turned the car onto a closed off-ramp that led down past the Port of Nocturne, down a dock that was pitted and rotted, showing flashes of light from the bay underneath.

"Sunny," I said. "Are you sure this road is safe to be driving on?"

"Not much farther," she said. "We're going to have to walk."

We rolled to a stop under the belly of the Appleby Expressway, a girder dropping rusty water onto the hood with soft *plonks*.

"What is this place?" I wondered out loud. The smell of the bay hit me as soon as I opened the door, along with exhaust and something else, the charred scent I associated with magick. Not the good kind.

"This is Undertown," Sunny said. "Grandma took me here once when I was about fourteen, after you'd run away."

"What a field trip," I said sarcastically. "Did you buy matching shirts?"

"Actually," said Sunny, locking the convertible carefully, "we were looking for you."

She started down the rotten dock toward the collection of buildings at the end that could have been shops at the turn of the last century but were lit with neon now, and painted with murals of everything from the Virgin Mary to Duran Duran.

"Wait, what?" I called after her, exasperated. "Sunny, get back here!" I ran to catch up with her, regretting it when my injuries stabbed me all over again. "What do you mean, looking for me?" I demanded, matching her pace.

"Well, it's pretty simple, Luna," she said. "Grandma and I came to the city to look for you, about six months after you took off. A contact she had here in Undertown had heard something about a young female werewolf, but it turned into nothing. You're right, though. It was an education for me. Undertown was where I realized I would be a caster witch, no matter if Grandma kept teaching me or not."

"Personally, I would have gone for the 'or not' option," I said, to cover up the deep pit that had suddenly appeared in me. When five years went by with no contact from my mother and father, I wasn't surprised, not at all. My mother preferred to pretend the real world was a pleasant illusion, and my father was so far inside a bottle of Pabst most of the time he probably didn't even know I was gone. The surprise came when Sunny *did* eventually find me, and moved to the city. "You never mentioned this," I said out loud.

"Well, now I have," said Sunny. "Anyway, when they built the expressway in the fifties a whole parcel of Waterfront and the surface streets got shut down. Mostly Spanish families, Chinese, magick users all. They weren't going to abandon their homes just because the sky closed over, so they stayed. Can't say I blame them."

"How come I never heard of this place?" I asked. "I

know Ghosttown like I know that a kitten heel looks better on me than a stiletto. Like I know where to find the best burger in the best dive bar in Waterfront and the best knockoff jeans. How did I miss a colony of witches living under a freeway?"

Sunny gave me a conciliatory pat. "You don't know everything, Luna." She pointed at a bodega with a Chinese dragon scribed across the front, in blues and greens so vivid they glowed even in the half-light of this bottom-dwelling place. "This is the shop we went to last time. I think the woman who runs it might remember me."

"It's so nice to go places with someone who doesn't have an enemies list," I said. "Is this woman a witch?"

"No," said Sunny. "She was an herb healer . . . used hearth magick and Chinese astrology, as I recall. Elemental stuff."

"I never knew witches could do that," I said as we pushed open the door. A little bell jangled over my head, along with a soft feeling all over my skin, like I'd walked through a cloud of feathers. Magick, but not the usual unpleasant prickle that caster and blood workings evoked in me.

"I never knew werewolves had nasty blood-drinking cousins who lived in the woods," Sunny said. "Hello? Anybody here?"

A small woman in a purple sarong appeared, her face gleaming with sweat in the close spice-scented heat of the shop. "I can help you?"

Sunny stepped forward, into the light of the red lantern that hung from the center of the shop's bare rafters, along with herbs and jars in rope nets. Some of the jars had moving objects inside. Apothecary shelves lined the walls, labeled in English and Chinese. The entire place had the effect of making me feel like I was in the attic of a pleasant, cookie-baking grandmother.

"I hope so." She held out the charm. "I was in here about fourteen years ago. Looking for my cousin."

"Found the cousin, I see," the woman said, taking the bag. "And some trouble."

"Always, with that one," Sunny said. "Can you tell us who might have made this charm?"

The woman clucked between her teeth. "What does a nice white witch like you want to know a thing like that for, hm?"

"Blame it on me again," I volunteered.

"It's not one of mine," said the woman. "This is very dark magick, made to combat dark magick, requiring a sacrifice of blood and soul." She shoved it back at Sunny. "I don't want it in my shop."

"I respect that," I said, "but nasty as this is, it could help us catch something even nastier. Please, just tell us who around here could have put it together."

She sighed and then pointed behind her and to the left. "Behind the bodegas, in the alley where the transients sleep. He deals out of there. Gets way too many customers for a sack of mean old bones. Cuts into legitimate business."

"Yeah," I said, "bet the chamber of commerce down here in Fraggle Rock is real upset."

The clerk let loose with a stream of abuse in Mandarin, and Sunny grabbed me by the elbow. "Thanks. We'll be going now. Why do you always do that?" she hissed at me.

"What?"

"Antagonize people!"

"I do not," I argued as we pushed back out into the salty, fetid air.

"Oh, yes you do," Sunny said. "It's why you get shot at and stabbed so often. You go out of your way to make people dislike you."

"Much as I appreciate this exploration into my many failings," I said, "we've got a bit more pressing matters."

"Just saying," said Sunny. "You might be here with Bryson or Dmitri instead of me. But you've pushed everyone away, as usual, and now you're standing alone."

"Sunny, shut up," I warned. "We're not having this conversation."

"Fine," she replied. "But you know it's true."

I did, but I stormed ahead of her around the corner behind the bodegas so she wouldn't see it in my face.

The alley backed up to a brick retaining wall made to keep the old roads above the bay. It was marked with graffiti and fungus, and garbage from the expressway above made drifts on either side. Naked electric bulbs were strung from a wire that spit sparks every time water fell from the road.

I realized with a start that what I'd mistaken for garbage bags were human figures, hunched or sleeping, a few of the faces lit by cigarettes.

A semi truck went by on the expressway and the ground under my feet rattled in time with the pistons. "I'm Luna Wilder," I said above the rumbling. "I'm looking for the man who made this charm." I nudged Sunny and she extended the bag in front of her. In the low light the charm was blacker still, like it bounced light off it or simply sucked it in. I felt bad magick in the air, and breathed deep through my mouth, keeping calm like I did before a kickboxing bout. Just breathe and let everything else fall away.

I still started when someone reached out and

grabbed my ankle. Sunny screamed and jumped be-hind me. "Hex me!" I shouted. "Watch it, buddy!"

"Down there," he wheezed. "Under the last light be-fore they go out." A knobby finger directed us deeper into the humid darkness.

"Great, because the thing I wanted most today was to wander down the creepy alley and talk to a dark witch who probably wants to peel my skin off and use it to make a party hat." I sighed. "How did you guess?"

"Thank you for your help," said Sunny politely, try-ing to give the humped figure a dollar. He waved it off with a cough.

"I take my trade in something a bit more personal, darling. Got any blood for me?"

I pulled Sunny away before she could say anything that would end with our bodies floating up on some rich executive's private beach down at the mouth of Siren Bay, and started down the alley toward the flick-ering place underneath the last bulb before blackness.

A voice stopped us before we reached the shadows at the end of the alley. "Who are you?"

I swallowed and answered in my best Cop Voice. "Luna Wilder."

He started to laugh. "You're a long way from home, Luna Wilder."

"So what if I am?"

The shadows unfolded and a small, stooped man leaning on a broken cane came into view. He had a braid of smoke-gray hair well past his waist and a face that could have been made from a wrinkled leather jacket, but his eyes were very, very bright and in the dimness they flickered from black to silver and back, just like Lu-cas's. "So, you don't belong down here is what, wolf."

I felt Sunny draw closer at my shoulder and I reached for her hand. "I don't have anything against the Wendigo," I said quietly. "Just the one who tried to kill me. I'm Insoli. Can I talk to you and not have to worry that you're going to rip my heart out of my rib cage?"

The Wendigo looked me over, his teeth gleaming silver as his tongue passed over them, and then he doubled over in a coughing fit. "Fine, fine," he gasped. "What do you want?"

"This charm," I said. "You made it for Laurel Hicks. Why?"

The Wendigo grinned. "She had trouble. Boyfriend was dead, and she was troubled by our kind, so I made her a . . . repellent."

"You made a charm against *yourself*?" Sunny demanded. "Isn't that sort of counterproductive?"

"Cutie, look around you. The clans outside the city got no love for me. They were content to leave me to the were packs when the *treaty* was signed, so why the hell am I gonna help out some psycho pups with hardons for werewolves?"

"Wait a minute," I said. "The Wendigo left you here when they moved out of the city?"

"You deaf underneath all that shiny hair?" the Wendigo demanded. " 'S what I said."

"But . . . that was over a hundred and twenty years ago," I said.

The Wendigo dug into the pockets of his overcoat, which he shivered in despite the heat that was spreading sweat underneath my T-shirt, and pulled out a rusty flask. I smelled sour, rotted blood and saw a dark stain appear on the Wendigo's chin. "You read a history book. Good for you." He wiped his chin and sank back down on the pile of trash against the wall. "Now go away. I'm tired."

"Please, just a minute more," I begged, crouching to his level. "What can you tell me about Wiskachee? And a wild Wendigo shaman working bad magick?"

Sunny clapped a hand over her mouth as the Wendigo drew out a bone and began to chew reflectively on the end. "The hungry god. He who consumes and envelops. A clan deals with Wiskachee, they deal death to us all."

He grunted and folded his arms around himself. "Now, I'm tired and I ain't hunted and fed in a month, so unless a junkie comes along I gotta make my flask last. Don't have the energy to be telling ghost stories."

"Can your magick be dispelled?" I asked.

The Wendigo spat. "It thrives on disbelief. Wiskachee rides the backs of the unwary. He feeds on ignorance. So no, little wolf pup. No, there's no cure for what ails you now." His chewing turned into the hacking long-term cough that comes with tuberculosis. "Now take your were treaty and get gone. I ain't a library."

"I thought the treaty was a mutual agreement," I said. "That's what Lucas Kennuka made it sound like."

"Kennuka," the Wendigo said. "Good name. Means 'iron jaw.' No, the treaty ain't ours. They came on a night a lot like this." He shivered and ducked inside his coat. "Hot. Summertime, but dry. No rain for weeks, no fog. We'd been conducting hunts on outlying settlements, trying to move Nischaka to tears."

"Rain goddess," Sunny murmured.

"I got that much," I muttered back.

The Wendigo chuffed. "The white settlers went in a

delegation and they stirred up the people who had built their city on top of our burial lands. Chopin and his men came with torches and Winchester rifles, and when they were finished there was nothing left but ashes and a hot, hot wind."

"Jeremiah Chopin wasn't a werewolf," I said.

"No, but the packs drank with him, visited his big house, and when they demanded the city be rid of us, Chopin would have been dead himself had he not listened."

"Go on," I said, thinking of the screams that must have echoed off Cedar Hill as the Wendigo village burned in a tinder-dry night.

"After the survivors were rounded up, we were given a choice . . . leave the city limits and never return, or every last man would be slaughtered and every last woman bitten and mated with a wolf man so our clan line would never be passed on."

"And they left you?" I whispered.

"I was no friend to any other Wendigo. I voted that we stand against Chopin instead of running into the night like whipped animals. They left me to be killed by the weres, and when I slipped the wolves I thought it best that I go underground."

"So why did you help Laurel Hicks?" I said. "She was sleeping with a were, and she hated your kind after they killed him."

"Because I've been alive a long time," said the Wendigo. "And I'm not the young buck I once was. Your shaman is dealing with forces that no one alive today understands, and primal creatures don't care what they hunt."

"Can Wiskachee be sent back like a daemon?" I said. If only it were that simple—daemons were downright familiar compared with this blood-soaked new world.

The Wendigo laughed, short and ending in another series of phlegmy hacks. "He's no daemon, Insoli. Wiskachee comes to the Wendigo when they offer him their own blood as payment, and he consumes whatever is in his path. You see Wiskachee coming, you go the other way, fast as you can. He's a storm, and he will rip the ground open and surge into the world, and everything in his path goes to ashes and dust. If you wanna get poetic about it, that is."

"Thanks," I said. "Thanks a lot. That was absolutely no help, in any practical sense of the word."

"Luna . . . ," Sunny rebuked, but I spun and stormed away. No closer to finding the shaman. No closer to discerning a motive.

Nothing I did would close this damn case.

So involved in my snit was I that I smacked into somebody, somebody who grunted. Somebody who smelled very, very familiar.

"You're a long way from home, Luna," said Lucas. I stared at him for a full five seconds in flap-jawed shock.

"Why are *you* down here?"

Lucas lifted one shoulder—healed from the bullet wound, I saw. He still stank of iron. "I followed you."

"Okay, look," I said. "I appreciate that you're taken with me, but it's never gonna work out. You're a Wendigo, I'm a were, you're family-oriented, I'm a workaholic . . ."

"I wanted to apologize," said Lucas shortly. Like most men, he seemed to have trouble with the phrase.

"Oh," I said, flushing. At the corner, I smelled and

heard Sunny come to a stop. She wasn't stupid, my cousin, but if I could sense her then Lucas could, too. "Look," I said. "I know you're under a lot of stress . . ."

"No," he said, meeting my eyes. His were silver. "Not for that."

My hand dropped to my gun. "Then for what?"

Lucas flowed forward, and I felt a cold, deadened feeling in my side, just below my last rib. I looked down and saw his bone-handled knife sticking out of my skin, just the hilt.

"For that," Lucas said.

"You son of a . . . ," I started as my legs went out and I dropped to my knees.

"If you don't want your tasty little cousin to die," he hissed. "Then don't scream."

I looked back at Sunny's shadow at the mouth of the alley. "I swear if you hurt her . . ."

"Shh," Lucas said, stroking my neck. "You were very good to me." He changed his hand and gripped my neck so tightly involuntary tears sprang to my eyes. "I mean that. As a surgeon, you weren't half bad. I healed fast. As a kisser, you could do with some practice."

My wound went ice cold, and I felt my heart flutter. The bullet-wound scar on my arm responded, flaring with chill fire. *Shit.*

"Silver blade," said Lucas. "Just to be on the safe side. You're pretty tough for a mutt."

The pain wasn't as bad as the phase, but it was close, and I groaned limply, trying to swat Lucas away from me. "Kill . . . you . . ."

"Those things you said. So impolite. My half-wit brother would never have the brains to plan four murders."

Mind screaming, the were chewing at my human thoughts, I tried to gather myself. The silver was poisoning me every second it stayed in my gut, and soon I'd pass out and go into cardiac arrest.

"But you seem to be the only one who knows, in that grand solitary werewolf tradition," Lucas said. "So unless your cousin gets curious, you're the only person I have to kill today. Thank you, Luna."

"*Fuck* you," I responded, and slammed my forehead into Lucas's nose. He hissed and loosened his grip on me enough to enable me to flop oh-so-gracefully onto the dock. I imitated a beached flounder for a few seconds more before I pulled the knife free. The pain got worse, but I could breathe again.

I rolled away as Lucas grabbed up the blade and drove the knife down again, spraying wood chips from where my heart had been.

"Oh, Luna," he muttered, cracking his nose back into place. My vision was going hazy, like I was on the bottom of a swimming pool staring up through clear blue water. "You are so lucky that I'm tired and low on blood."

I tried to scramble up and get to the mouth of the alley, the car, Sunny, but Lucas wrenched me backward by the shoulder and sent me flying into a wall.

Wood and glass and plaster crashed around me as I bounced off the surface and landed on the dock in a heap, my wound sending a hot jet of blood over my hip and thigh. I pointed a shaking finger at Lucas. "Stay away from me," I rasped.

He sighed. "Now, Luna. Nobody is going to be unduly shocked when you turn up dead, I think. Involved in an investigation that you were told to stay out of, hanging around with all kinds of scary critters . . ." He smiled, revealing a silver crop of fangs. "Couldn't have asked for a better cover. But you're not a bad person—in fact, I think you try a little too hard for sainthood. If things had worked out differently, I'd tell you to lighten up. My point is, it'll be quick and I will honor you, after death. I think you'll taste divine."

Lucas turned the knife in his hands and started toward me, reaching for my hair to expose my throat.

"Not again . . . ," I muttered, my thoughts slow and dull as fat rain droplets in a muddy pool.

"I promise you won't even feel it," Lucas whispered. "I'm a good hunter. I know how to finish and dress a kill. Your Sunny will get a shock, though. Might need therapy." And he laughed. It was a small laugh, and if Lucas were less intimidating I'd almost call it a giggle, but it flicked a spark of anger in me.

The son of a bitch was enjoying this.

I scrabbled down by my useless, blood-soaked legs and found a piece of glass from the broken window on the wall Lucas had thrown me into. I waited until he was close enough, spinning his knife between his palm and the tip of his opposite index finger. Before he could put it to work on me, I lunged, jamming the glass into the center of his stomach and making a mirror of my own wound.

Lucas screeched, that sound halfway between human and Other that the Wendigo made, and stumbled backward from me. He clapped his free hand down over the chip of glass in his gut as deep red-black blood dribbled down to pool in his belly button and the hollows of his slim hips. "Unbelievable! Don't you goddamn dogs know when to give up?"

"Not this one," I snarled. Blearily, some still-rational corner of my mind let me know that the panicky euphoria coursing through me was my body tipping over into shock, but I rode it and let it keep my eyelids peeled back and what was left of my wits about me.

"I take back what I said," Lucas snapped, coming at me with the knife again. "You're not worthy of being eaten."

"Color me disappointed," I snarled, then something slammed into the back of Lucas's head. There was a distinct *crunch,* and he actually staggered, the first light of the change rippling over his features.

"Get off her, you misty freak!" Sunny yelled.

Lucas turned, tossing his knife from hand to hand. "Mmm. Human. Magick. You're tempting me, witch."

Sunny brandished the tire iron from her car. "Stay back!"

"You hurt her," I told Lucas, scrabbling at the wall with my fingernails to pull myself upright, "and there won't be a place in this world that you can hide from me, you slimy, hairless piece of crap."

"Luna, you're not strong enough to brush a trail of ants off you," he told me, pointing with the knife. "Stay put." His nostrils flared as Sunny crossed swiped at him with the tire iron. "She's not worth dying over, Sunshine."

"It's *Sunflower,*" she gritted. "And I won't be dying anytime soon, you . . . toadstool."

When he turned away from me, I saw a gaping black hole in his skull where Sunny had hit him. I pulled out my gun and drew down on the spot. "I know these hurt when you're human. You wanna test my aim again, you murderous little shit?"

He slipped the knife back into its holster at his waist and winked at me. "Always with the gun. That theme is tired." He flowed past Sunny, knocking her down, and re-formed at the entrance to the alley. "Be seeing you real soon, Luna. It's been fun."

Lucas vanished with slipstream speed. Sunny got up, brushing herself off.

"Took you goddamn long enough!" I said when she pressed her jacket over my stab wound.

"Oh, be quiet. I had to run all the way back to the car and then sneak up on that crazy while he was distracted."

I looked at the spot where Lucas had vanished. A small stain of blood was all that remained. "I don't think he's crazy," I said. The bums, including the old Wendigo man, had started to come out of hiding.

"No?" Sunny said skeptically. "Look, you're going to need stitches. There's no help for this."

"No," I whispered, still looking at the blood. "I think he's possessed."

CHAPTER 19

After I talked Sunny out of taking me to the hospital, I got her to help me hobble into the apothecary's and get a clean dishtowel from the owner to press over the wound in my side.

"Trouble," she murmured when she left Sunny and I alone in her tiny kitchen.

"I can't believe this . . . ," Sunny said tearfully. "Why does this always happen to us?"

"Us?" I said, chomping on my lip to keep from yelling as I applied pressure. "Fate isn't being cruel, Sunny. I walked right into this one." The wound Lucas had given me wasn't deep enough to be fatal, unless I stood up and started disco dancing, but it was deep enough and it bled steadily and constantly, sending feathers of pain through me every few seconds. The silver had turned the skin around the cut black.

"You'd better tell me everything," Sunny warned, pulling up a chair across from me.

I looked around and found a sewing kit inside a sawed-off coffee canister. "Sterilize this needle on a flame," I told Sunny. "Then we'll talk."

"What for?" She sniffed. I got out strong cotton thread and a pair of scissors.

"What do you think?"

"Oh, gods," she murmured, taking the needle and passing it through the bright propane flame.

"On the subject of Lucas . . . I was stupid. I should have seen it." I leaned my head back, allowing my sandy eyes to drift close. Blood loss made all the corners of the world fuzzy. "The Wendigo back there said that Wiskachee rides on the backs of the unwary—nonbelievers. Like Lucas. And like me."

"He'd have to touch the fetish," said Sunny. "For the spirit to jump into his body."

"He did," I said. "When he tossed Jason's apartment. He had at least twelve hours from the time I left to the time Bryson and I got over there." The towel was soaked and I lobbed it at the sink, missing. It landed on the floor with a *splat* and a spray of red drops. Sunny whimpered.

"It almost got me," I continued. "I felt it, trying to get into my mind. Cold. Cold and passionless and hungry. Fortunately that idiot Bryson was there." I pulled up my shirt and dabbed at the wound with a fresh towel. "See if she has anything to sterilize this with." Both of my palms and most of my exposed stomach were crimson, blood filling the kitchen with a pungent copper scent that made it hard to breathe.

"Jason must have been a carrier, too," I said. "And he realized it, and he got rid of Wiskachee the only way he knew how. Maybe the only way at all."

"I'd believe Stabby Boy is possessed," said Sunny. "In a heartbeat. But who would summon this thing? What purpose?"

We were back to that again. "I don't know for sure,"

I said. "But it has something to do with the treaty, the were packs who signed it, and fucking them up, I'm thinking. What better revenge than summoning Ye Olde Hunger God to feast on your enemies?"

"A working like that would take months, if not years," said Sunny. "Why not just get the weres in human form and shoot them with silver bullets?"

"I don't know," I murmured. "I don't understand the Wendigo well enough." I had a beast in me, but not a monster. I didn't know what it was to have their ceaseless hunger and their disregard for anything else.

Sunny ran the needle through the gas flame until it was red hot, and threaded the needle for me with a fine, tight knot. I took it from her but every time I moved to make the first stitch, the sides of my wound pulled apart and fresh blood flowed.

I slumped in the ladderback chair, gasping. "You're gonna have to do it."

All of the color drained from Sunny's face, like she was an old cartoon. "No. No. I'll get arrested for you, I'll drive you into bad neighborhoods, I'll put up with as many bitchy comments as you can throw, but I will *not* stick a needle into your living skin."

"Sunny . . ."

"Luna," she said crisply, making a slashing motion with her hand. "I'll faint."

"If you faint, I'll die," I countered. Her eyes gleamed, but she picked up the needle with shaking hands. I wouldn't die for a good two or three hours, but I was past the point where I felt bad for stretching the truth.

"What do I do?" Sunny asked in a small voice.

"Pull the skin around the wound together, put the needle and thread through the seam, and *yeowch!*"

Sunny jumped. "Did I do it wrong?"

"No . . . ," I squeaked. "No, that was good. Just try not to surprise me next time, 'kay?"

Sunny worked for a few minutes in silence, face set and body stiff as the ones on slabs in the morgue downtown.

"At least he didn't stick around," she said at last. "Maybe I scared him a little."

"Lucas?" I said. "Maybe. Although in the cottage—probably when he was going to try and kill me the first time, before the spirit made him try to eat my head—he was pretty smooth. Asking questions, seeming interested . . . he asked me about the Serpent Eye girl, Carla, and I told him about Bryson . . ."

I shot up in my seat, making Sunny shriek and drop her needle. "Hex me," I moaned. "Bryson." I dug Donal's cell phone out of my pocket and stabbed at the keypad.

"Huhello?" Bryson grumbled, sounding like he was talking from the wrong end of a megaphone.

"David!" I shouted. "Are you with Carla right now?"

"No," he said pointedly. "It's the middle of the night, Wilder."

"She has a protective detail?" I said, feeling my gut twist.

"I ain't stupid," said Bryson. "Of course she does. What is it, Luna?"

"Get to her," I said. "Don't let her out of your sight until I call you."

Bryson grunted and I heard shuffling on the other end of the line. When he spoke he sounded ten degrees more alert. "You pick up the trail?"

"It picked me," I said. "Picked me up, stabbed me, and ran off to finish its murder spree."

"Huh?"

"Never mind, David. Just call the detail, have them move Carla and get to her. I'll call you as soon as I can."

"Hey, hey," said Bryson. "Am I in some sort of personal jeopardy here?"

"Yes," I said. "Ow!" Sunny spread her hands and mouthed *Sorry.* I snapped "Be careful!" back before I spoke to Bryson.

"I didn't sign on for any of this . . . ," he was muttering.

"David, believe me, you do not want to explain to Morgan how you let a material witness get all her blood sucked out," I said. "She's touchy about stuff like that."

"Wilder . . . ," Bryson started, but I hung up.

"I can't believe this," I muttered. "How could I be so dumb?"

"Don't berate yourself," said Sunny. "It looks like if he wanted the information from you, he was going to get it. With or without the making out."

"Could we not go there right now?" I said, feeling my face turn hot. Lucas's mouth had been so cool, without all the implied dominance Dmitri brought to our kisses, our everything. *How could you be so stupid, Wilder?*

Come on, I said, mentally throwing up my hands, *did you* see *Lucas?*

"He was . . . very nice," I elaborated. "And . . . just nice."

"Yes, and so was Ted Bundy," Sunny said, tying off the thread and biting it. "Done. Thank the gods."

I examined my side. The wound was closed, the bleeding slowed to an ooze of dark red between Sunny's neat, tight stitches. "Good work."

She managed a small smile. "As if I'd give you anything but."

I wasn't on the verge of passing out, and now the facts started to line up again, unpleasant and glaring as key marks on the side of a fresh paint job. I had to get to Lucas before he killed Carla. It was my only chance to find the wild Wendigo who'd started all this.

"I'm going to call Bryson back and find out what safe house he's at," I said. "Then I'm going over there, to finish this one way or the other."

"Not to nitpick," said Sunny as she cleaned the needle in the sink. "But you could barely dent the guy as a human, and I don't think he's gonna be that when he's getting his murder on."

"That's where you come in," I said. "You're going to make me a magic bullet."

"I'm all on board with a plan," said Sunny, "but . . . what the Hex are you talking about?"

"One of Grandma's spellbooks has an anti-transformation working in it," I said. "You know—the tincture that's lethal to weres? I'm willing to bet it'll slow down a Wendigo, at least long enough for me to kick him really, really hard." I picked up keys, extra bandages, and a disposable syringe—anything I could think of to help me put Lucas down.

Sunny jerked her car keys out of my hands. "All right. That, I can do. But at the rate you're shaking I think I'd better drive."

CHAPTER 20

On the drive, I pushed down the dark thoughts unspooling, the ones that said I still didn't fully understand what was being wrought on my city.

I called Bryson back. "Where are you?"

"Greene Street safe house," he said. "*Now* are you gonna tell me what's going on?"

"In a minute," I said. "Greene Street," I told Sunny. "How soon can you work that tincture?"

"As soon as I get home, mix it up, and get back to you," she said. We rolled to a stop on the corner and I jumped out. "It's number fifty-one, up the block. Hurry, Sunny."

The Green Street safe house was an unassuming clapboard town house tucked between two identical counterparts. The safe house, unlike the other two, was painted pink with boxes full of sun-wilted violets under the front windows. Nobody ever suspects a pink house.

I pounded on the door, feeling my wound pinch. The humidity clamped down around me and I started to sweat. "First thing I'm gonna do when I find you, Lucas," I muttered, "is make you pay for all the shirts that you've ruined."

Bryson's caramel-brown eye appeared in the peephole, and then he opened the door. "Christ, Wilder. What are you doing?"

"Saving your and Carla's butts," I said. "Let me in."

"Why is it that every time I see you, you're bleeding and demanding something of me?" Bryson asked as he swung the door wide.

"We do need to work on a relationship dynamic," I said. "Did you have a domineering mother?"

"David? Who's that?" Carla came into the foyer, rubbing her skinny hands over her skinny arms even though the house was stuffy.

"It's just the crazy werewolf lady," he said. "Don't go near the windows, Carla." She slunk back into the sitting room.

"Hey," she said sharply. "The back door's open."

"Impossible," said Bryson as I glared at him. "Whole place is alarmed."

From all the corners of the room, giggling started. "Bryson," I said, running for the back door. "Get Carla."

The lock had been splintered neatly away from the door frame, just a few chips of wood missing, as if something had simply flicked the deadbolt out of the way. I drew my weapon out and pressed my back against the doorjamb. Peered outside. Nothing.

A *brakichak* hissed at me from the ceiling. Bryson came into the room, dragging Carla. "Wilder, what in seven hells is that thing?"

"A pest," I said. "They turned off the alarm." Nothing stirred in the dank, airless space. The safe house smelled like an iron foundry. No way for me to scent for Lucas.

A shadow flickered past the back windows, then another, and another. "Crap," I said. "Lucas brought friends."

The power went out, and nothing but the street lamps shone. In the split second it took me to adjust, the Wendigo struck. All three of them went for me, taking me to the ground and banging my head against the floor. I saw stars, and then I saw nothing at all.

A phone somewhere was off the hook, and the frantic pulse of the dial tone woke me. The safe house looked as if someone had taken a chain saw to a frat party. Blood sprayed one wall in a long arc, punctuated by bullet holes. The furniture in the foyer was tinder and the door to the room beyond was off its hinges.

Feet in wingtips stuck out from under the heavy mahogany. "Bryson?" I whispered, clambering up to lift the door off. It weighed close to a hundred pounds. "Gods, I never thought I'd be saying this but . . . I really hope you're not dead."

"Why, Wilder," Bryson coughed, spitting out a mouthful of plaster dust. "I never knew you cared."

I grabbed him by the torn shoulder of his pea-green suit and jerked him into a sitting position. "Where's Carla?"

Bryson's eyes roved, the pupils different sizes, and his breathing was labored. "They got in . . . damn it, Wilder, I let them get away."

"Where did they go?"

"I was doing okay, too, you know?" Bryson muttered. "Got one of the bastards right in the neck. Arterial spray every damn place. Was doing fine until they threw a door at me." His breath hitched, and pain paled his face to the color of old paper.

"Bryson," I said, shaking him hard. *"Where is Carla?"*

"They took her out the back," he muttered. "Gone. Just gone."

I looked through the broken door. Greene Street rested in a hollow, and I saw the swell of the foothills, peppered with lights and a faint line of sunrise behind it. Just a hint, not even a promise of day.

"I'm gonna get busted back to crowd control . . . ," Bryson moaned.

I grabbed him by the shoulders and gave him a little shake. "None of that matters now. How long ago did they leave?"

"Not long," he moaned. "A few minutes. Just put me outta my misery, Wilder. Might as well be you."

"I know where they took Carla," I said. Jason had been staring at it every day he lived in the city. Made sense his possessed brother would go to the same spot. I handed Bryson the squealing phone and depressed the disconnect button. "Call an ambulance before you pass out from that concussion and you get more brain damage than you've incurred already. And give me your Sig and the keys to the Taurus. I lost my weapon when those bastards hit me."

"Where do you think you're goin'?" Bryson demanded, punching 9-1-1 unevenly on the keypad.

I climbed over the wreckage to the front door. My answer came out without thinking, and I meant it more than I've meant anything in my life.

"To stop Lucas Kennuka."

As I sped through downtown and into the hills, I caught sight of fires along the roadside. An SUV was wrapped around a telephone pole on Winchester Drive, which wasn't terribly unusual on a Saturday night in the summer, but as my headlights flashed over the scene I saw a pair of naked, fish-white figures skitter away into the darkness, and tightened my hands on the steering wheel.

Somewhere, a siren echoed above the bay and emergency lights sped across the embankment on Highlands.

"Hex me," I muttered, spinning the wheel hard to make a turn onto Garden Hill Road. The cemetery was less than a mile away, but I ran into a road closure, an ambulance and a patrol car's occupants working over a pair of still figures on the pavement. A darker stain spread from underneath one of the bodies.

A uniform came over to wave me around and I flashed my badge. "I need to get through, Officer. It's a police emergency."

"Lady, look around," he said, sighing. "This whole damn precinct is a police emergency."

"Watch that body," I said, turning the wheel to go around the cordon. "If it gets back up, use fire."

I pressed down on the gas, praying harder than I had in a long time that I wouldn't be too late when I got to the graveyard. Sunny's cell phone went straight to voice mail.

"You'd better get this. Bring the tincture to Garden Hill Cemetery. And bring it fast." I swerved around a snarling, incorporeal body that shied away from my headlights like they were sunlight and it was Dracula. Pulling to the curb in front of a burnt-out survival shop, I dialed Mac.

"Luna Wilder," he said. "Why do I know that somehow, this is all your fault?"

"Mac, how fast can you get SWAT to Garden Hill?"

"Wilder, this is chaos. There's no way."

"Mac," I said. "I'm sorry. When this is over, I promise I will make it right. I need you to help me now, though, or there won't be anything left to cry over."

He sighed. "*Maybe* half an hour. Reports from all over of animal attacks, traffic accidents, people seeing ghosts. It's hairy out there."

"Trust me," I said, looking at the distant mound of the graves. "It's about to get a lot hairier."

"Wilder, whatever you're thinking about doing, if it requires SWAT backup, then you *wait for SWAT.* Is that clear?"

"Yeah," I said. "But I can't."

Mac exhaled. "Of course you can't. This is why my blood pressure is so damn high, Wilder."

Donal's phone buzzed with a waiting call and Sunny's number blinked at me. "Mac, I have to go."

"If you're running around Garden Hill in the dark, watch your step," Mac said. "You know that place is lousy with unmarked graves."

A Wendigo howled from somewhere hidden. "Yeah. I heard."

Sunny had rung off when I managed to manipulate Donal's BlackBerry into answering her call. I cursed at it and punched buttons to bring up the last incoming number. Underneath Sunny and Bryson, JASON KEN-NUKA stared at me.

"I'll be a Hexed human," I said, blinking at it. The calls went back months, before the killings and any of Jason's surveillance.

"Shit," I breathed, and gunned Bryson's car toward the cemetery.

Sunny was sitting in the Fairlane outside the gates, head rotating back and forth like it was on a stick. I parked crookedly behind her and rapped on her window. "What are you doing driving my car?"

She shrieked, arms coming up in a kung-fu posture. "Gods, Luna! Don't do that to a person!" Sunny rolled

down the window and handed me a stoppered glass bottle, warm to the touch. Inside, pewter-colored liquid
winked at me. "That's the best I could cast in thirty minutes. I called the working using a four-corner spread inside a circle and—"

"Will it hurt?" I interrupted.

Sunny smiled grimly. "Like a motherfucker."

"Okay, then. Take Bryson's car and get out of here.
It's not safe."

"Oh, no," said Sunny. She got out and crossed her
arms, staring up at me. "I'll wait in the car, but I won't
be sent away like some sidekick."

"I don't have time to argue with you," I warned. The
BlackBerry hung like a weight in my pocket.

"Then don't," Sunny said. "Get cracking. Kick ass."

"Yes, ma'am," I muttered, getting into the car. I took
the disposable syringe out of the car's first-aid kit and
flicked the cap off, drawing a full measure of the tincture into the barrel. I stuck it up my sleeve, letting the
hypo hold it in place, and put the rest of the tincture in
my jacket.

Then I drove through the cemetery gates.

CHAPTER 21

Garden Hill Cemetery isn't used to actually bury people anymore. It got filled up some time in the 1950s, and just before the Hex Riots there was a scandal involving gravediggers exhuming the bodies of Nocturne City's forefathers to resell plots. They dumped the bodies down in Waterfront, where I guessed they hoped to pass the desiccated remains off as Halloween props, or reanimated mummies.

The cemetery itself is poorly lit, with intermittent roads that go nowhere and plenty of sunken graves waiting to break your ankle. When I worked the area as a patrol officer, the most trouble I got was when I was assigned to the Bowers over Halloween and had to deal with a pack of wannabe blood witches attempting to sacrifice a cat. Our watch commander adopted the cat, and I let the nascent black magick workers get a flash of my were teeth, which settled them down pretty quickly.

If only it were that easy now.

The crooked sign pointing to the historical part of the grounds was obscured with a were pack's spray-can tag, but I knew the place well enough from rousting junkies and lover's lane couples to make the turns through the gathering fog without too much trouble. The Fairlane pulled under me as I took a corner too fast and clipped a headstone. "Sorry," I muttered to the displaced spirit.

My eyes swung back to the road and I screamed as a shape darted in front of my car, slamming on the brakes out of reflex. The Fairlane fishtailed sideways, laying up against a monument, and my head whipped forward, clipping the steering wheel. A trickle of blood leaked into my eyes.

From outside, just out of view in the fog, I heard laughter. "Poor little detective dog. Did you get a bruise?"

"Hurt a lot more than that little prick you gave me," I yelled back, fighting to disentangle myself from my seat belt. My door was dented in, and I kicked it open. " 'Little' being the operative word there. Where are you, Lucas?"

"Behind you," he hissed, and hands wrapped around my shoulders, talons sinking into my skin below the collarbone. I tried to duck him, but my feet were off the ground and I was flying before I could breathe.

The headstone I landed against wasn't particularly soft, but it broke under the impact and saved me from crushing my spine like fresh celery. My knife wound opened again and started to seep.

"Putting your blood in the air?" Lucas shouted at me. "Are you really that arrogant, Luna? You think you stand any sort of chance against me?"

I saw him appear against the lights from the street, on top of a small burial mound. He was just a hunched black shape, his pointed ears stabbing through the fog and his teeth shining out of his shadow-body.

"I have to say, you've lived this long," Lucas called.

"You *might* actually have some survival instincts. But *she* doesn't."

Two Wendigo, still human, dragged Carla up to meet him. She was struggling, but feebly, and I saw one of the Wendigo give her a shot in the neck of the stuff they'd gotten me with. That night in the Plaza seemed decades ago now.

"Leave her alone!" I screamed, standing up even though it hurt more than sticking my toe into a paper shredder. "You have a fight with me, not with her."

"Oh, I disagree," said Lucas. "My fight is with every last one of you sniveling bitches. But you had your chance, Luna. Her blood will spill just as red as yours."

Lucas walked over to Carla and without any ceremony or hesitation drove his talons into her chest, drinking her blood down. His face was calm, peaceful, as she twitched under his grip. It seemed impossibly slow, but it was less than ten seconds before she crumpled, dead, at Lucas's feet.

"Stupid mutt," Lucas hissed. He toed the body in disgust. "Get her away from me."

I had started moving when Lucas began to feed on Carla, but I was intercepted by Ponytail. He flowed into the space in front of me, seeming to take no time at all, and stuck out his arm. One moment I was bearing down on Lucas; the next I was on my back, vision totally black and a pain in my lungs as my throat closed from a blow.

The Wendigo shook out his arm, a bruise blossoming where he'd clotheslined me. "She's solid. Fast, too."

"Leave her with me," said Lucas. "Since you couldn't keep a leash on her before."

"Lucas, I told you . . ."

"At this late date, Charlie, do you really want me to

hear your excuse?" Lucas said. "I swear, you wild pieces of shit will be the death of me."

Charlie whimpered and then I heard the rasp of Carla's body being dragged away.

Lucas leaned down, brushing hair away from my face. "Breathe. Breathe, Luna. I prefer live meat." He chuckled. "That's five. And not a thing you did stopped me. Poor little puppy."

He stroked my cheek, and I batted him away, rolling to my feet. "Why don't you come on out and join this party, Donal?" I shouted to the graves. "I know you're watching. That's your game."

Lucas flowed forward and backward in alarm, snarling at me. "You don't know what you're saying!"

I looked him in the eye. "I'm not talking to you, Wiskachee. I'm talking to Donal Macleod."

He came walking, with only a slight limp from our last fight, from behind a mausoleum. Two of the alley goons hung back in the shadows. "Too clever by half, just like all Insoli. That gutter cleverness, which I despise."

"There is no shaman," I said. "You gave that fetish to Jason Kennuka and let Wiskachee possess him."

He spread his hands. "Guilty."

"You had the weres killed by Wendigo so it would look like a vendetta."

"I did." He stroked the scar that ran down from his mouth. "Your deductive reasoning is top-notch, missy. Aren't you a bit curious why I'm unconcerned?"

Actually, I was, but I'd been hoping he wouldn't notice. From behind me, Lucas started circling and I backed up against the mausoleum, trying to keep Donal and him both in sight.

Donal took a fetish from his pocket, much like the

one that I'd found in Jason's apartment, except I could *see* the magick around this one, black and curling with a merciless hunger. "This is the part where I tie up loose ends."

He raised the fetish so its mouth gaped at Lucas. *"Wiskachee, necht tagh."*

"What—" Lucas said, and the fetish stirred, opened its mouth and eyes, and groaned. The ground under me vibrated and I stared as Lucas's thin gray Wendigo skin stripped off, revealing smooth pink muscle and bones like liquid silver.

Lucas screamed, a very human scream, and fell to the ground. "I don't *believe* in it!" he shouted as Donal stood over him, wielding the fetish like a demonic vacuum.

"That's what made you useful, boy," said Donal. "I didn't buy your services away from those idiot Loup because you were a superstitious foul-up. But now you've done your job, all but the last bit."

The fetish ate, jaws twitching like it was alive, and Lucas writhed. His screams turned into whimpers, and finally he could barely breathe. As Donal watched with a smug expression, I grabbed him by the throat and bent him over a gravestone.

"Why? He did his job!" I tightened my grip. "You got him possessed by a fucking dead god! You made him take down all of the pack leaders—anyone who posed a fucking threat." I warmed, seeing all the pieces of what Donal had done fall together in my mind. "You made *yourself* god. Wasn't that *enough*?"

Donal's goons dragged me off, and I fought, kicking out at whatever I could hit. Macleod coughed and straightened his collar. "Except for you, and that's a real shame, missy." He walked up and slapped me, splitting

my bottom lip. "For the choking. You need manners."
On the ground, Lucas moaned softly, his eyes rolled
back in his head. He was human, blood streaming from
a hundred shallow bite marks all over his body.

"You can't just cut out the opposition," said Donal.
"You've got to solidify your position. And there's nothing like a little apocalypse to do that." He took Lucas's
silver knife away from him and drove it through Lucas's chest in an economical movement. Lucas twitched
and went still. Donal wiped off the knife and gave it to
the goon not holding me.

"That's the blood. Get me the sage and that printout
I have to read from." He checked his watch. "Our mutual friend will hold up his end. Before tonight is out,
I'll be the only pack were in Nocturne City worth considering."

Before I could articulate my thoughts, which right at
that moment ran to *Fuck,* the ground began to vibrate
ever-so-slightly, as if a train were about to pass us by.

"You think the packs will just welcome you in? Alpha of alphas? Some kind of gods-damn kingdom?" I
shouted at Donal. He lit the sage stick and began to
smudge the air.

"Yes, when I stop the Wiskachee from feeding on
their spineless hides."

He held up his bloody hand, letting it drip over the
patchy earth of the cemetery. *"Wiskachee gen kah,
muscun ne kah. Nis kee."* Translating ostensibly for my
benefit, Donal said. "Wiskachee, I come to you now
with the blood of the unwary. I kneel."

Donal knelt down and pressed his hands into the
earth. "I come to you now with anger in my heart, and
I kneel."

The shaking increased exponentially, rising and

falling like something were breathing below us in a great chamber.

Donal raised his palms upward and I felt something unpleasant wrap around us, heavier and hotter than the wet air from the bay. "I come to you now with hunger in my soul, Wiskachee, and I kneel," Donal whispered. "Come to me, devourer."

As Donal touched his bloody palms to the earth once more, the third earthquake hit.

The two weres looked alarmed, but Donal only laughed. "Good man, Danny. Right on time!"

I thought of the three working circles behind the cabins, the ones that had absorbed my unwary blood. It wasn't blood magick or caster magick, but they worked something all the same, and it was here.

There was a roar like I was in the path of a semi truck and the ground rippled underneath me, throwing me onto my side and smacking me against a headstone. Donal grabbed on to a stone angel. The two thugs fell on their asses. I was free, if a bit concussed.

All around the cemetery, graves began to uproot, stones flung into the air as the ground shook. Coffins rose through the shuddering, cracking ground, spilling their contents free. I clung to the headstone I'd hit, feeling a few fingernails snap off as the force of the quake yanked me back and forth.

At the center of it all Donal watched calmly as a chasm opened at his feet and disgorged a host of old-style pine boxes, their nails shrieking as the dry wood shattered on impact.

"Wiskachee!" his voice carried over the roaring and shaking, the sound of car alarms and falling brick from the street. "Wiskachee! Come!"

Just as it had risen to a crescendo faster than I could

react, the shaking stopped. A crack in the earth had opened in front of Donal and the still body of Lucas, mummified and embalmed bodies littered everywhere as if an enormous dog had dug them up. From the city beyond, I could see fire and imagined I could hear the screams that went with it.

"Disappointed?" I called to Donal, forcing my vibrating hands to let go of the headstone. My speech was thick and I wiggled my jaw, feeling a fresh bruise from where I'd hit rock.

"No," said Donal, his eyes bright with reflected flames. "It worked out exactly."

From the turned earth near his foot, a hand emerged. It was gnarled and nut-brown, with long gray nails that looked sharp as butcher knives. Another hand followed it, arms, a head full of wild iron gray hair. The thing pulled itself out of the grave chasm hand-over-hand, sliding along until, grunting, it came upright.

"Wiskachee," Donal murmured. The thing scented the wind with thin, snake-like nostrils and then grinned, displaying teeth that would make any Wendigo weep in envy. They shouldn't *fit,* teeth that big, I thought desperately, but Wiskachee's fangs were blacker than an ink bottle spilled in the night, and razored at the tips like steak knives.

Around his feet, a host of *brakichaks* spilled up from the chasam, giggling and chittering as they scrambled away into the night.

"That's it?" I said, trying to keep my mouth moving so my mind wouldn't be able to fully process what was happening. If I let myself stop and think, I'd panic. "That's your hunger god? He looks like a damn piece of lawn statuary. I could take him home and stick him in the rosebushes."

Donal laughed silently, his shoulders shaking. "Her," he told Wiskachee. "You can have her."

Wiskachee, at his full height, came to maybe my collarbone, with his dirty gray hair making it to my nose. He was long-armed and potbellied and had bright pure black eyes, like the daemons I'd encountered. Wiskachee was no daemon, though. His little stooped shoulders and his skin like a wrinkled, rotted fruit contained power I could taste. When Donal told him to have at me, he smiled, child-like, and hissed something in the Wendigo language too fast for me to hear.

"Take as much as you want," Donal answered. "You have until I call you back to earth."

Wiskachee looked at me, smiled, and winked. Then his long arm lanced out and embedded claws in Donal's chest. I realized the gray around him was spectral, and that he hadn't sunk his claws into flesh but into the magick that made Donal a were. Black flowed in to cover the bright, misty green that hung around Donal's spirit. I felt a sharp pull as he began to suck it all away, and I started to scream in concert with Macleod.

Donal began to change, losing his skin and hair and becoming the construct of Wiskachee, like his niece. Wiskachee gloried in his death, and I buried my head on my knees, trying to keep the feedback of ambient magick away from me, because Pathing in such an atmosphere would probably kill me.

As suddenly as they'd started, the sounds stopped. I opened my eyes and saw something wholly different than when I'd closed them. Wiskachee was no longer stooped and ancient, clothed in gray scraps of power. His corporeal figure remained, but behind it was a vast shadow that rose into the sky and expanded outward as the volume in my head increased. *This* was Wiskachee, this great towering hunger that blotted out everything else. His corporeal construct couldn't hold the ancient, bottomless nothing that was at the center of his power.

"Stop it," I tried to say, but screaming seemed to be the only sound left to me. Wiskachee laughed, his shadow-face opening a mouth the size of my car to display serrated teeth.

"He'll taste them all," Donal hissed from his new mouth. "Every last person in this city sucked dry."

I rose and ran at Donal. He turned and extended his taloned hands toward me, and I felt the pain from five yards away as he sank his claws into my aura.

"Bad girl," he rumbled thickly. "Trying that same old trick. I can drink your soul down now, little wolf. Any other brilliant plans?"

The mocking tone in his voice did it. Even when I'm nearly dead and being psychically drained, being patronized by crazy people is not something that I'll take smiling. Around my growing fangs, I snarled.

"Just one."

"Fighting back." Donal sighed. "How I'd hoped you wouldn't. Cheapens the moment." He closed the space between our physical bodies, drawing back his talons to sink into my heart. I stayed still.

"Terror-stricken," Donal said. "Delicious."

"Waiting for you to get close," I corrected, and jammed the needle holding the tincture into his neck.

Donal howled and windmilled away from me, the spell lighting up his veins as the magick of Wiskachee fought with Sunny's working. He flickered back and forth, limbs and organs shifting and re-forming as blood sprayed from his mouth, leaked from his eyes, and he fell over, convulsing.

With a great effort, I blocked out the screams and

stared into Donal's face, into those black, amused eyes that were like the button eyes on a particularly creepy child's doll.

"He's a killer," I told Wiskachee, pointing at Donal's lashing body. I was very weak, held up largely by Donal's claws, and my voice was too weary to come out anything but a whisper. "He killed your sacrifice. There was no willing blood spilled here today."

Wiskachee held my gaze for a moment. *"Tauthka du dan?"* he breathed.

"No!" Donal moaned. "Why would you listen to a wolf instead of *me*? I brought you back. I *believed*."

"Try telling the truth a little more often, Donal," I said. "You might die less."

Wiskachee hissed, his lips curling back over his teeth until all that showed in his face were razor edges.

"No," Donal bubbled, his lungs sucking with fluid. "No, nonono . . ."

"I am free," Wiskachee purred. "And *hungry*." He made a move toward us, and Donal clawed at me, trying to shove me toward the hunger god.

"Take her! Not me! I don't deserve this!"

Wiskachee swiped at us. I got the feeling he wasn't very choosy. "Fuck off!" I screamed, kicking at him. The pain as our magicks brushed was extraordinary. I may have been outgunned, but I wasn't going to let him feed on me, not without a fight . . .

Something hit me from behind, shoving me out of Wiskachee's reach. "You don't touch her," Lucas gasped.

He was bleeding freely from his chest, staggering and blue around his lips and eyes from shock.

Donal goggled at him from his prone position. "How . . ."

"Hard to con," said Lucas. "Even harder to mother-fucking kill."

Donal swiped at Lucas and I intercepted the swing, bending his wrist backward and snapping it in an easy motion. Lucas swayed on his feet, coughing, spitting black-red arterial blood from his lungs. "You think I didn't know?" he snarled. "You think I hadn't seen a fetish before? I *wanted* to kill them, all of them, and you let me."

I felt like I was going to be sick. "You *let* yourself be possessed?"

"For the chance to kill those weres?" Lucas said, softly, fading out like a bad radio signal. "Absolutely."

"Lucas." I started to shake. My own shock was catching up with me. "Lucas. Look at what you've done."

"I'm sorry, Luna," he said. "But you wouldn't understand."

Oh, *Hex* that. "I wouldn't understand?" I screamed. "How dare you! How fucking dare you, Lucas? You put my city on the line and that's all you have to say for yourself?"

"My whole life was that treaty, poverty, and a father who beat me because of the rage inside him over what was done. The weres and the Wendigo ground under their heel. It's not *right* and I'm going to burn it to the ground so that no one else goes through a life like mine. It's a poison that needs to be expunged."

"The world is not black and white," I whispered. "Weres and Wendigo . . . it doesn't *matter*. You *change* it, you don't burn it and start over. What was done to you was horrible, and wrong, but we get a life and we have to *live* it, Lucas."

Lucas went to his knees, tears streaming down his

face. "I just wanted to make it better. Mend it, by smashing it. I had to try. I did what I had to do."

I looked back at Wiskachee, at that great shadow waiting to consume my city. "I am, too," I told Lucas. Then I grabbed Donal and shoved him toward Wiskachee's waiting arms.

The claws went in, and Donal gave a scream. This time, it was entirely human and borne on pain. The blood drained from his face and the life light from his eyes, and I watched, transfixed for a moment as Wiskachee suspended Donal in his black shadow, draining him until he looked as if he'd been dead for a week.

Wiskachee sighed, and again I felt the dead sensation in my head as he surveyed the city around him, head tilting as he listened to the screams. "So many to feed me. Your offering pleases me, wolf. I will be engorged."

"Hex that," I said. "I was just distracting you with Macleod so I could get away."

I got to my feet and ran for all I was worth, flat-out toward the road. Behind me Wiskachee let out a howl and began to chase me, the ground shaking under his immense power.

CHAPTER 22

I looked back only once while I ran, and saw Donal and Lucas still on the ground, Donal spent and Lucas corpse-still.

Years later, it seemed, I fetched up against the Fairlane. Wiskachee's magick made it hard to move, to think. Dimly, I knew he'd begun to feed on me, on everyone within reach. I was dizzy and my fingers shook so hard that for a long time I couldn't turn the key in the ignition. I could hear whispers, screams, the sounds of a thousand souls that Wiskachee had already consumed.

The Fairlane rumbled to life and I turned it up the hill, zigzagging between graves and heaves in the earth, accelerating until the cylinders screamed.

Wiskachee was standing on the hill, and his shadow was visible now, growing with every mind that he touched and fed on. I aimed my grille for his physical body, the tiny potbellied target almost comical under the nightmare shadow form.

I gunned it straight into him, and he hissed at me on the other side of my windshield, his mouth opening impossibly wide. His fingernails screeched along the hood as I put my foot to the floorboards, the Fairlane's tachometer springing into the red zone.

Carrying him forward, the car roared toward the lip of the chasm Wiskachee had crawled from, his screams reaching above the sound of the engine and his fists making hairline cracks across the windshield.

I let go of the Fairlane's wheel. "I'm sorry," I told my car, and then I opened the door and dropped out, shoulder-first like the police academy taught us, tucking my legs up and tumbling and tumbling until I rolled to a stop against a grave.

The Fairlane crested the edge of the chasm, suspended for a second, and then fell. The crash shook my teeth, and an orange fireball blossomed out of the crevasse with a *whoosh* as the gas tank caught.

I got myself up and tottered over to the edge to look down, to be a witness so I could be sure, later, that Wiskachee was gone.

He was still screaming, pinned under the burning wreck of the Fairlane, and I watched as bits and pieces of his shadow form began to ash and drift upward on the hot wind of the fire. The flames licked his skin, blackened it, turned it to fine powder and then to nothing at all.

When Wiskachee stopped screaming, I turned and limped toward the cemetery entrance, weaving and dipping as if I were seventeen again and drunk on cheap wine coolers, trying to act natural on my way home so the cops wouldn't pull me over.

I screeched when something grabbed my ankle. "Wolf . . . die . . . ," Donal Macleod moaned. He was desiccated, his eyes bulging from their taut sockets, but his grip was death.

"Pack it in, you sorry son of a bitch," I said, and shook him off. "Alpha of alphas, my ass."

"At least I strove for greatness!" he cried. "You'll always be a gutterwolf!"

"Mr. Macleod?" One of the thugs emerged from behind a hillock, looking around at the wreckage. "Sir?"

I pointed at the goon. "Go back to your pack house. Tell your leader what he's been up to."

The two weres looked at each other, and then hauled ass out of the graveyard. I took my handcuffs off my belt with numb fingers and clapped one end around Donal's wrist, the other to the handle of the mausoleum door. "They'll kill me!" Donal cried. "The pack's justice . . ."

"Is nothing compared with mine," I told him. "I'll see you when I testify against you at your trial, you piece of shit."

Lucas had no pulse when I knelt next to him. After a few seconds his chest jerked and heaved, and then he went still again.

I should hate the guy, but I couldn't. I put my hand over his wounds instead, cold blood coating my palm. "Now we both know what it feels like," I murmured. "If you die on me, I'm gonna be pretty fucking pissed off."

Lucas made no response, his face drawn and bloodspattered. I sat next to him, touching him, until I saw flashing lights and a SWAT van bumping over the road toward me.

McAllister jumped out of the lead car and wrapped his arms around me.

"Mac?" I goggled at him.

"You were maybe expecting Lon Chaney?" he asked, holding me at arm's length.

"After the night I've had," I told him, "don't even

joke about that." I put a hand to my head, still finding fresh blood. "Oh, gods. Where's Sunny?"

Mac jerked his thumb at the passenger's door, which erupted to reveal my cousin. "Riding shotgun. Flagged us down when we got here. She can be as stubborn and insistent as you, Wilder. Must be a genetic thing."

Sunny ran over and threw her arms around me, so hard that I stumbled and fell against the hood of Mac's car. "You stopped it," she whispered.

"Stopped what?" Mac demanded. "What the Hex is going on here, Wilder? Is that *fire* I see up on the cemetery hill? And who the hell is the stiff?"

I sighed. "Lucas Kennuka. Five homicides, assault on a police officer, and . . ." My legs wobbled as the night caught up with me like a tidal wave catches a beach bungalow. "Look, just go easy on him, all right, Mac?" I tilted my head toward the flames that were just visible over the ridge. "That fire . . . that, you wouldn't believe, even if I had the energy to explain it."

Mac looked at the fire, back at me. "There will be questions, either way."

Sunny supported me as I woozily rolled my eyes. "I think that's the least of our worries right now, Lieutenant," she said. "Could we maybe talk about getting an ambulance for my cousin before she bleeds to death in the street?"

"Yeah, yeah," said Mac, still gazing at the fire. "I called a bus."

We watched in silence as an ambulance worked its way among cars that the earthquake had flipped on their sides and wreckage thrown by the tenements that lined Garden Crest.

The EMTs came running, flashing lights in my eyes and speaking their staccato code to one another. They tried to pull me away from Sunny but she wouldn't let go of my undamaged hand, and finally they let her sit next to me in the back of the ambulance while one EMT took my blood pressure and gave me painkillers and the other stitched up my forehead.

"Ow! Damn it!" I growled at the EMT, who backed away with his hands raised.

Sunny coughed and brushed her lips with a finger. I clapped my free hand over my mouth and felt fangs still there. "Sorry," I told the EMT. "Just been a stressful night."

More police cars arrived while they worked on me, a cluster of officers around Mac, and eventually Captain Morgan pulled up, wearing sweats, her hair in a ponytail. She looked toward me and gave a great, long-suffering sigh.

"Officer Wilder?" she demanded, putting one foot on the bumper of the ambulance.

"I know, I know," I said. "I'm off the force, effective immediately. Can you at least tell me it's without pay while the painkillers are still working? Takes the edge off."

"If that's what you really want to hear," said Morgan. "I was going to tell you that Detective Bryson is in stable condition at Sharpshin, and I hope you follow suit. But really, I'll say the rest as well."

"That's fine," Sunny assured her when I started to open my mouth. Morgan gave us both a severe glance.

"Do not think for one second that we will not be talking about all of this later, Officer Wilder." She nodded curtly and stepped down as the EMT shut one of the ambulance doors.

"Captain?" I called. She turned her head back, a long-suffering look in place.

"Yes, Officer?"

"I'm sorry. About my insubordination. It won't happen again." Saying that out loud was, by my reckoning, by far the most painful thing I'd done tonight.

Morgan's lips twitched. "Apology accepted, Officer."

I looked at Sunny. "See? I can not antagonize people. Sort of."

"I'm so very proud of you," she said.

The EMT put a gauze patch over my cut. "You riding with her to the hospital?" he asked Sunny.

"As long as I can," Sunny said.

Mac came jogging over before the other door shut. "I'll be there as soon as I can. You gonna be okay?"

I nodded, even though the movement caused lights to twinkle at the corners of my vision. "Yeah, I think so, Mac."

"Good." He started to walk back to the cluster of uniforms and SWAT, then turned around. "Hey, Wilder. Where's your car?"

The hospital emergency room was a riot of blood and crying and nurses running back and forth while constant codes blared over the PA, but Sunny got me to a quiet curtain and after a few hours an intern looked at my head and my side wound, restitched Sunny's work, and declared me fit to go home.

"Normally I'd tell you to stay overnight, but it's the ninth circle of hell here and I'm up to my ass in major injuries. Go home, Officer." He scribbled a prescription, gave it to Sunny, and rushed out of the curtain as a gurney rolled by surrounded by nurses shouting vitals.

"Male, approximately age thirty, unconscious and unresponsive, blood pressure one forty over sixty and falling, stab wound to the upper left chest . . ."

I watched Lucas's face, half hidden under an oxygen mask, roll by toward the trauma unit, his shirt cut open to reveal the thin deep wound over his heart.

"I'll be damned," I muttered as he passed me by. Sunny came out of the curtain.

"What?"

I looked back toward a pair of uniforms in the waiting area. Looked toward the doctors working over Lucas. One of them caught my eye. "Hey, you know this guy? He your John Doe? He has a custody tag on his chart."

Lucas choked, then, spitting a mouthful of blood against his mask, and a nurse shouted, "I've got a rhythm!"

The two uniforms got up and went down the hall toward the cafeteria.

"Nope," I said to the doctor. "I've never seen him before in my life."

"Hex me," the doctor cursed, and ripped the red tag off Lucas's gurney. "Get him prepped for surgery and call the ICU."

Sunny, standing a few feet behind me as Lucas rolled away, gave me a disapproving look. "We all have our reasons," I told her, and didn't elaborate. Lucas had done a terrible thing, but he'd saved my life. We were even, and if he was smart, he'd never show his face to me again.

Sunny rolled her eyes but didn't say anything more.

As we exited the hospital and its sounds, I heard the distinctive chug of a bike over the ambulances and traffic diverted from the quake-ridden freeways for the morning commute.

Dmitri was waiting for me as the traffic parted, and I nudged Sunny hard. "Did you call him?"

"No," she said, drawing the word out. "No, this one

was all on his own." She moved away from us as Dmitri and I regarded each other. "I'll go get the car."

"You didn't come for me," Dmitri said when I was close enough to touch. He didn't try it. "When you figured out what the Wendigo had done, you didn't ask for my help."

"This was mine to deal with," I said. "And you made your feelings pretty clear."

He sighed and rubbed his chin. "Luna, you of all people should know I don't always mean what I say."

"I do," I said. "But this was mine to do, and I didn't want to put you in that position . . . that night." I pushed a hand through my hair. "You scared me. I had to go deal with this on my own, and I'm always going to deal with my problems on my own, as long as this daemon blood is in you, because I never want to see you like that again."

Dmitri finally reached out and took my hand. "Okay."

I blinked at him. "Okay what?"

"Okay. I won't try to force you anymore. You're Insoli. You and I, we've got our problems. But you're mine." He looked at me, and all I could think about was Lucas, back there in the hospital. How cool his skin was to my touch. How he'd made me feel safe before.

I felt something like a stone in my chest, made of my feelings for Dmitri.

"I know this won't be easy," Dmitri said. "But I want to give it another shot. I think it could work out, Luna. We can *make* it work."

I smiled at Dmitri, sadly, before I dropped his hand. "I think you're right. It could work out. I could learn to let you in and you could learn to stop being an alpha and maybe we'd have a few good years before the daemon blood made you forget." I inhaled, breathed out, and felt the next words crawl out of me like little pieces of flesh. He'd come back to me, even with everything that had happened. I couldn't let him do it again.

I grasped responsibility like a handful of broken glass. "But I won't do it, Dmitri. We'll never be able to sit still with each other. I know I take too many chances and I have a horrible temper and those are my poisons to purge."

I swallowed and took a step back, onto the curb. "This isn't about me, Dmitri. You're changing. One day, this thing inside is going to take you over and as long as you're with me, you won't try to help yourself. You'll just try to protect me."

Feeling like my bones weighed a thousand pounds each, I met Dmitri's eyes. "When those days come, the daemon bite will finally take you over and I won't have Dmitri, anymore. You'll get hurt, or killed, trying to be the person you were. And that will be the saddest day of my life and I just . . . I can't. I can't and won't be responsible for you dying. I'm sorry."

Dmitri sagged in the seat of his bike, his eyes flickering from green to black in the space of half a heartbeat. For the first time, I wasn't afraid to see the daemon in him.

"Are you telling me this is it?" he demanded roughly.

I kept smiling, because it was either that or cry. "No, Dmitri. I'm telling you good-bye."

EPILOGUE

It was a month before all of my investigations and inquiries were through. By the time I went to the Seaview Gardens, the new cemetery by the cliffs on Highway 21, the scar from Lucas's knife wound had faded away to nothing but a pale white starburst.

I put the charm, devoid of magick now, on the flat stone that was carved LAUREL LYNN HICKS, BELOVED DAUGHTER.

"Not doing this for forgiveness," I told her. "Just putting things back where they belong." I doubted I'd ever be able to forget seeing Laurel on her floor, and the twist inside of knowing it was my fault. But I could make it right, for her spirit at least.

"Be seeing you," I said, noticing that someone had left daisies in the flower holder next to the stone. Laurel, at least, wasn't alone.

I drove my rental car downtown, and didn't hesitate on the steps of the Twenty-fourth before going in. I nodded to Rick at the front desk, and slipped past Morgan's office to knock on Mac's door.

"C'min," he muttered around a mouthful of something. I smelled turkey and rye bread, and even though my stomach was fluttering my mouth watered.

"Spare a minute for the prodigal daughter?" I asked, sticking my head around the frame. Mac set his sandwich down in the deli wrapper and brushed his hands off, motioning me in.

"You look good for someone who's been through hell, Wilder. Pale, though. You eating?" He offered me the unchewed half of his sandwich.

"Not overmuch," I said, thinking of my silent, still cottage and my bed, which was just plain empty. I waved the sandwich away.

"What's on your mind?" Mac said. "You've got to be close to going back on active duty with SWAT, yeah?"

I let out a little laugh, dry. "Yeah. You would get right to the point, Mac."

He stared hard at me. "Wilder, what is it?"

There is no easy way to say the hard things in life. You just have to get it out fast, like tearing off surgical tape.

"I'm quitting, Mac."

McAllister didn't choke on his sandwich, but only because he'd stopped chewing. He swallowed fast. "What? The Hex are you going on about, Wilder?"

I looked at my feet. "The Kennuka case proved that I can't do this anymore, Mac. I lost my edge. I went *over* the edge and it's been real damn hard to come back."

The time alone, especially at night, had at least given me the space to see that I'd let Lucas wrap himself around my heart and brain like thorns strangle a tree. I was no kind of cop, and not even that great of a person.

"I can't do this again," I told Mac. "I'm going to quit."

Mac started to laugh, a hand over his mouth and his eyes crinkling up. "Oh, Luna. You truly are the queen of dramatic bad timing."

I'd expected Mac to shout at me, maybe swear or even fling some furniture, but the quiet chuckles were downright creepy.

"What exactly is that supposed to mean, Mac?"

Mac reached into his desk drawer, underneath his pack of cigarettes, and pulled out a black leather case. He tossed it across the desk and I caught it reflexively. "This came through today. I was going to call you in the morning when I got off shift and offer it to you, but hell, in person is much more theatrical."

I flipped open the case, a little larger than a deck of cards. A silver-and-bronze badge gleamed there, with my number and my name underneath the crescent moon rising that was the seal of the city. Beneath my name, the rank spelled out LIEUTENANT.

"Things change, Wilder," Mac said, rolling his wrapper into a ball and launching it at the wastebasket in the corner. A dozen crumples of paper attested to previous attempts. "Nobody can ignore people like you and Kennuka any longer. The commissioner handed down the directive right after you transferred to SWAT. It's a new task force, with a new lieutenant. You were the only one I recommended."

I smiled at Mac, and handed the badge back. "I'm not the woman for the job, Mac."

"You're the only were on the force that I know of, and even if there were ten of you, you're the only one I'd want. I'm the departmental liaison for this thing. It'll look good when my pension rolls around. Help me out here, huh?"

Standing up, I touched my stab scar. "This won't end

the way you and the commissioner think it will, Mac," I said. "People hate us, and the weres in this city hate me even more, especially now that the six most powerful are dead and everyone else is chewing on throats to fill their shoes. You'd have a bloodbath on your hands."

"As opposed to when you run off half-cocked and light stuff on fire?" Mac said.

"I won't do it," I said. "I can't look out for every were and caster witch in the city." I put my hand on the doorknob. "I can't even look out for myself."

"Luna," said Mac. "You can walk out that door, and for a while you'll be okay with whatever you chose to do after this. But eventually you'll come back. You have it in your blood, just like the were. This city will eventually rip itself apart, unless we have some people like you out there. So go ahead." He put the badge away and pulled a stack of files close to him. "You'll be back."

I walked out of Mac's office, thinking about how I always managed to be in the thick of trouble even when I tried to live a life that took me nowhere near it. I let Lucas get to me because I was angry and restless and didn't trust my instincts. I was ruled by the were now, with a grasp more subtle and fine than when it had taken my body and killed, but I was ruled all the same.

There was no way I could be the head of a unit that saw people like Lucas and things like Wiskachee every day. No way in any of the seven hells.

A minute later, I walked back into Mac's office. He didn't even look up from his paper when I took the badge from his desk.

At least he didn't say *I told you so*.

The press conference didn't get much coverage in the wider media, although Janet Bledsoe showed up, no doubt hoping I'd start another riot and burn the city down so she could be the headliner on the evening news.

Even though it was after Labor Day, I fidgeted inside the pantsuit and wine-red silk shirt Sunny had insisted I wear. The heat was abating, slowly, like it always did at the end of a long summer, crawling away from the pavement and my skin, leaving sweat in its wake.

"Will you stop twiddling at your buttons!" she demanded. "You look fine."

"I look like I belong in the Hexed circus," I muttered. "How does Mac do this?"

"This? I leave crap like this to Captain Morgan," Mac said. "You'd better get out there before they eat all the free pastries and start turning on each other, Wilder."

"Words of support just when I need them most," I said. I was hiding everything behind a sharp remark these days. When Dmitri had come to get his things, I had suggested flippantly we hold a garage sale with the proceeds going to my retail therapy.

Dmitri had been gone for a month. My wit was doing a piss-poor job of keeping me company.

The blue curtain smelled like dust and cigarettes, and the podium in the Nocturne City PD press room was supported on one side by a stack of bricks. The microphone squealed when I got too close, and the chatter in the room lulled.

I looked out into the sea of lights and faces, ranging from disinterested to hostile.

"Good morning," I said, my voice reverberating through the tiny room in the basement of the Justice Plaza. None of the reporters reacted, even to raise a pen. Their eyes were as unblinking as Lucas's eyes, just before Wiskachee consumed him.

I inhaled, closed my eyes, and then looked back at Sunny, and Mac. Sunny smiled at me and Mac made a *move along* gesture.

They were behind me. I turned back to the reporters and their cameras. "Good morning," I said. "I'm the lieutenant heading up Nocturne City's newest police task force, officially designated the Supernatural Crimes Squadron."

A few cameras snapped and I let my words sink in, meeting each pair of human eyes with mine. I blinked slowly, and let them blaze gold. "My name is Luna Wilder, and I'm a werewolf."

Read on for an excerpt
from Caitlin Kittredge's next book

WITCH CRAFT

Coming soon from St. Martin's Paperbacks

Chaos crept up on me like someone had tossed a stone into a pond. I was sitting in a window booth at the Devere Diner, shoving a double bacon cheeseburger into my mouth while across the expanse of red formica table, Detective David Bryson did the same with a grilled chicken club.

"Cholesterol," he explained around a mouthful of lettuce and dead bird. "Doc said I'm going to keel over if I don't cut back on the carbs or calories or what have you. Put me on one that whatchacallit—Long Beach Diet."

"South Beach," I corrected him, taking a pull at my diet soda. Just because I have a werewolf metabolism doesn't mean I need to abuse it.

"However you call it," Bryson said. "All I know is that in a week, I get to maybe eat a burger once in a while." He regarded his sandwich the way most people regard a dead pigeon on the sidewalk.

"My sympathies," I said, and signaled the waitress for a slice of pie. Bryson glared at me. The waitress finished writing an order for two uniformed cops at the counter and sashayed over. Bryson checked her out. She checked him out.

I cleared my throat. "I'd like a slice of key lime, when you two are done."

"Krystal," said Bryson, reading the nametag. "You ever get down to my part of the city, cutie?"

"Depends what part we're talking about, honey," she said, batting her heavy fake eyelashes at him.

I kicked Bryson on the ankle. "Pie. Key lime. Essential to my continued good health and temperament."

A fire engine roared down Devere, sirens going full blast, and drowned me out. The waitress cupped her hear. "Huh?"

"Key lime!"

A pair of patrol cars followed, their lights revolving heartbeat-quick, tires laying black rubber streaks as they took the turn onto Hillside Avenue at top speed.

"Say that one more time, honey." The waitress was still smiling at Bryson. She was brassy-skinned from a spray-on tan and had a red bouffant piled on top of her head. She and Bryson, who was a bull-necked man with powerful arms, a greasy pompadour, and small bright blue eyes, would make a cute couple. You know, if you were into that sort of thing.

"Key lime," I said, rubbing the back of my neck. I could still hear the sirens, even though they were long gone into the crisp October air. Were hearing is sensitive. I could hear Bryson's heartbeat too, how it quickened when Krystal looked at him.

It was five days before Halloween. The leaves were falling, and paper pumpkins and ghosts were everywhere. Halloween made everything seem benign. You could almost forget that the real monsters might be sharing a subway car or a cubicle with you.

The patrolmen at the counter jumped as their radios crackled. The dispatcher burbled their call numbers and then squawked out "eleven-seventy-one in progress at one-oh-seven Hillside Avenue. Fire and rescue en route. All units respond."

To give the cops credit, they were a well-oiled machine. One dug out a twenty and threw it on the counter while the other grabbed his car keys off the counter and ran out the door to start their prowl car. "Dispatch, Ten-ninety-seven is en route," the second cop bit off into his clip mic, before he followed his partner.

The ripples spread out from the stone fall, and a beat after the door slammed shut behind the two uniformed cops, my BlackBerry went off. Bryson's pager followed it a moment later.

I tore it off my belt and looked at the text message. *107 Hillside. ASAP.* That had to be Annemarie. Only she would dare *ASAP* the boss. Bryson looked at me, blinked once. "One-oh-seven Hillside?" he asked. I nodded.

Bryson snapped his fingers at the waitress. "Krystal, doll? We're gonna need that pie to go."

I smelled the smoke before I saw it—my nose is my best feature, and I'm not just talking about it complementing my pretty face. Weres can smell a lot, which normally is a mixed blessing. Do you have any idea how a hobo smells to a werewolf? You're better off not knowing.

A black cloud stained the faded-denim blue of the sky, boiling up from the crest of the hill. I pushed my foot down on the accelerator of the Ford LTD that I'd gotten from the motor pool a few months previously, and was rewarded with a groan from the transmission and no discernable increase in speed.

I hit the steering wheel. "Piece of crap car." My previous ride, a 1969 Ford Fairlane, had blown up when I drove it into an open chasm with a pissed-off Wendigo spirit clinging to the hood. Both the spirit and the car were crispy now, and I was back to driving the Cop Standard model, stale upholstery, dubious brakes, and all.

"Jesus Christ, that's a big fire," said Bryson. "Somebody's McMansion is McToasted, for sure."

We were in the exclusive section of the Cedar Hill neighborhood now, Victorian stately homes sitting shoulder to shoulder with large modern monstrosities shoved wherever the developers could find a spare greenbelt. They were uniformly hideous. "How much you wanna bet me it's the fucking ELF or PETA or one of those fucking hippie groups that sets their armpit hair on fire to save the whales?" Bryson said.

"I think we wouldn't have gotten paged," I murmured as I rolled up on the scene. Three ladder trucks were hosing down a blaze that was giving off enough heat to break a sweat down my spine and curl my hair, even from twenty yards away. A token ambulance and a phalanx of patrol cars had the street blocked off, and neighbors were staring.

We crossed the street to the cordon and I found the fire chief on scene, a barrel-chested man named Egan. "I'm Lieutenant Wilder," I said, flashing my badge. It was still new enough that the shine hadn't come off the bronze crescent-moon seal.

Egan grunted. "So?"

"With the Supernatural Crimes Squad," I elaborated, and waited for the inevitable wisecrack, sigh, or meltdown that followed with most city personnel.

The big fire chief just grunted again. "We don't need you."

That tone carried so much more than the words

would imply. *We don't need the freak squad reminding the plain humans that there are things in Nocturne City that will bite their faces off.*

"Someone paged us," I said. "You mind filling me in, since I left a perfectly good lunch for you?"

"No," Egan said. "In case you hadn't noticed, we got a situation here."

A month or two ago I probably would have grabbed him by his polyester tie and made him do what I wanted, but instead I shielded my eyes from the smoke and stepped back. Letting Egan know he was in control, that his manly manliness was secure. "When you've got the fire under control, Chief, you and I will talk again." *And when we do, it will be for a royal dressing-down on your part, Mister.*

He didn't pick up on my nuances. Men are like that.

I recrossed the street to find Bryson scooping the last of my key lime pie out of the box with his fingers. "Dammit, David!" I yelled. "What happened to your diet?"

"Hey, I got job stress," he shrugged. "My nutritionist said I'm a emotional eater."

I turned my back on him and leaned on the hood of the car, watching the blaze. The house wasn't a McMansion—it was one of the old ones, an old timber-frame place with too much scrollwork, now a nightmare of gingerbread and burning shingles that made me cough.

Egan strode around looking important until he realized he wasn't doing any more good than Bryson and I, and stomped over to us. "Guy that lives here is named Howard Corley," he snapped, like he was giving me an order. "Deals in antiques. Works from home."

He paused to let that sink it. I winced as I looked at the smoke and the flames, which had started to recede, barely. "You think he was in there."

"Car's in the garage," said Egan. "Gas tank blew, almost took the scalps off a couple of my men. No reason to think he's not."

I wasn't any closer to understanding why Annemarie had paged me, but I smiled at Egan anyway. "I appreciate it, Chief."

"Yeah, well. Keep your spook squad out of the way if it comes to that."

Then again . . . I sighed and kicked at the concrete, forgetting for a moment I was wearing classy Prada flats instead of my usual combat boots. "Shit," I sighed. The wardrobe that went with being lieutenant of the most-hated task force in the Nocturne PD was massively expensive, the headaches even larger.

"I have better things to do than stand around a crime scene that isn't even ours. Or a crime scene, yet," I complained loudly to Bryson, hoping Egan heard me.

"Well, here comes Hotlanta. Why don't you ask her?"

Hotlanta was Bryson's personal nickname for Annemarie Marceaux, a firecracker-redhead who hailed from Louisiana . . . one of the northern parts, with some tongue-twister French name. She was tiny and slender and efficient, a near-constant *Bless her heart* smile in place. A new hire in the department, she'd been shunted to the SCS and taken the news pretty well, at least outwardly.

"Sorry I'm late, ma'am," she hollered at me. "Damn traffic cops wouldn't let me through!"

She was also profane, funny, and a hell of a lot nicer than an ex-special victims detective had a right to be. I liked Annemarie. Bryson snorted, low. "Here she is, Scarlett O'Hara."

"Hello there, David," she said brightly. "You're looking slender today."

Bryson turned about eight shades of red, and wiped the sweat away from his forehead. "Hiya, Annie."

"Lieutenant," she said breathlessly. "I'm sorry for the cryptic message, but I was in the area and I saw the blaze start. There's something here for us, believe me."

"Okay," I said. "Spill it." The firefighters had finally gotten the flames under control, and new smells were creeping in—char. Cooked electrical circuits. Burnt meat.

Egan had been right about someone being at home.

"I saw the fire start, ma'am," Annemarie said. I focused on her, and tried to block out the smell.

"You don't say."

"Yes," said Annemarie, stepping out into the street and gesturing at the traffic cameras at the intersection. "I think those picked it up, too. It wasn't like anything I've ever seen, Lieutenant. It caught all at once, from all points. An inferno."

"And you just happened to be driving by?" I cocked my hip and glared at Annemarie. Her cheeks were flushed from the fire, and she seemed almost happy. I don't know too many people who get happy about fire and death, except weirdos, and I had enough of those in my life already.

"Oh, I was visiting a friend who lives on the other side of the hill," she said. "Going to clock in when I saw the fire. I called it in and paged you, ma'am."

"Detective Marceaux, if you don't stop calling me 'ma'am' I'm going to slap you right in the head, got it?"

She nodded, going even redder. "Sorry ma' . . . Lieutenant."

" 'Luna' would be just fine, Annemarie. Go find out when we can walk the scene, and call the rest of the squad."

After she walked back to her own car, Bryson snorted. "Time was, I only had to put up with you. Now there's another one running around, like some kind of tiny, evil doppelganger."

"David, did you actually just use the word *doppelganger*?"

He spread his hands. "I watch a lot of horror movies. So what?"

I shook my head, hiding a smile. "Never mind."